RIGHTEOUS JUDGMENT

JACOB GRAYSOL

This book is a work of fiction. Names, characters and incidents are the product of the author's imagination or are used fictitiously. Any resemblance to actual persons, living or dead, or events is entirely coincidental. Places are either the product of the author's imagination or are used as fictitious settings for imaginary events.

First published 2019, Edison, NJ

ISBN: 978-1-7329167-0-8 (paperback)
978-1-7329167-1-5 (e-book)
978-1-7329167-2-2 (hardcover)

Library of Congress Control Number: 2019932259

www.jacobgraysolnovelist.com

For Luann, for everything

This novel is a work of fiction. The identifying characteristics of three unregistered chemicals have been changed in the interest of public safety; their laboratory names and formulations are protected by the attorney-client privilege laws of the State of Massachusetts, SJC Rule 3:07, RPC Rule 1.6(a) et. seq.

- 1 -

Phil Bolton only heard the doorbell, ringing incessantly—*asshole!*—until he made it down the Cape Cod's narrow stairs and grabbed the doorknob; then it stopped, like a cue for footsteps behind him, sneakers on tile. He turned toward the kitchen, then froze at the sight of three guns pointed at his face, held at eye level by intruders wearing repairman's uniforms, ski masks, and leather gloves.

"Don't panic, Mr. Bolton," the tallest of the trio said in a high-pitched voice. "I am Alpha. We won't hurt you or your wife if you obey us. We just need to borrow your lives, for a few days."

Phil's thinking was muddled, and he started trembling. *What do they want? He said something ... "a few days." I can't let them stay a few days! But also ... something about my wife. They know about Jen!*

"Leave my wife out of this," Phil said at last. "She'll be at the law school for a while." He wasn't as good a liar as he was an engineer, but he knew from Jen's short stint in litigation that a half-truth was easier to pass off than a complete fabrication.

"You don't need to lie to protect your wife," Alpha said. "We know she teaches Search & Seizure on Thursdays, until 3:30. Just cooperate, and we'll leave both of you unharmed. Understood?"

Phil forced a slight nod.

"Good," Alpha said, lowering his gun to waist level but keeping it pointed at Phil. "Now, kindly let my colleague inside."

Phil turned to open the front door. Grabbing the knob stopped his right hand from quivering, but it started shaking again when he let go. The unmasked broad-shouldered young man slid in and closed the door, then stepped back to stand arm's length from the line of fire.

"That's it," Alpha said to Phil. "Next, come take a seat in the kitchen."

Phil stood in place, shaking harder, eyes wide and darting between the raised guns Alpha wanted him to approach.

Alpha stared at him, then used his left hand to guide his cohorts' pistols lower. "Come on," he ordered, "I'll back in ahead of you."

Phil plodded across the living room as Alpha and a man in a blue ski mask stepped back; the unmasked man and a green-masked thug maneuvered behind him. Phil started to feel that he was thinking like himself again after a few steps, though scared, and tried to take stock of the ringleader. A black ski mask covered his hair and most of his face, but Phil made out a pair of distant, brown eyes. The gunman was an inch, maybe two, taller than him, probably 5'11", and neither fat nor thin. He sounded pretentious, with no accent and that unnerving, high-pitched voice.

Alpha dragged a wooden chair into the middle of the room with his free hand, turning it to face away from the table. "For you," he directed.

Phil approached the chair, sidestepping two large gym bags, sat on the thin red cushion, and stared once more at his tormentor. One of the men behind him slipped a contoured black sleep mask over his eyes. Then they pulled his wrists back, rubbing his arms against the wood, and stretched him to his limit. He heard rattling, then felt the cold metal of handcuffs being secured, first on each wrist, then individually to the back of the chair. While he was being gagged, he twisted and pulled each wrist against the restraints, then settled back to stillness, defeated.

"Shroud the living room windows and find the professor's desk; she should be here within the hour," Phil heard Alpha command.

He perked up—his captors' careless conversations might provide clues to their identities later. His hope was dashed when a distant whir amplified to the *Star Wars* soundtrack blaring through headphones they secured over his ears. Now he had nothing to do but wait, and try to think.

* * * * *

Home few minutes late, honey, Jennifer Bolton texted from the crowded elevator. *Two new student volunteers :) for domestic violence clinic. And Sandy Yu, who got us to adopt the hippo, wants me as faculty advisor. I'm up to four :o Is it really only the 21st?*

She reached Interstate 280 at 4:00, beating the daily Manhattan commuter crush through Essex County, relaxing to the Eagles on satellite radio all the way to South Orange. At 4:20 she tapped the blue button that started the left garage door opening. After she parked, she grabbed her satchel from the passenger seat, pulling the strap onto her shoulder to bear the weight of her textbooks, and poked the other blue button, six feet up on the wall, to lower the door closed. While the motor was groaning, she opened the door and was engulfed in the fragrance of strawberries and vanilla.

Kicking off her shoes and stepping onto the shag carpet, Jen found the den window shades down and saw one of their scented candles burning on the nearest end table, a printed note beneath. Her lips curled in a sly grin. "Phil?" she called. She took two steps toward the note, and the grin vanished—*SILENCE IS AN IMPERATIVE*. "Phil?" she shouted across the den, toward the kitchen and the rest of the house.

A young intruder bounded into the doorway from the kitchen, his left index finger against his lips, his right hand aiming a pistol at her eyes. He took three more strides into the den, and was followed by another gunman, this one wearing a black ski mask.

Adrenaline sent Jen's heart racing; but, surprisingly, her reflex wasn't to scream. "What do you want?" she begged, hands raised and trembling.

"All in good time," the masked man said. "I am Alpha. Your husband is safe, and if you obey us, you will be, too. We simply need to borrow your lives for a few days, for a greater good."

Alpha paused. Jen continued to shake. She'd represented wrongful arrest victims *pro bono* and had empathized with their fearful narratives of facing guns, but had never herself experienced pistols looming so large.

The silence was brief. "Now, get down on the ground."

Jen knelt upright, unsure if that would satisfy her captor, but fearing that lying prostate would leave her more helpless.

It seemed to work—the unmasked accomplice circled behind her.

Then Alpha approached, his handgun growing to a cannon. Jen grimaced and turned her head away.

"No, no … stay with me," he said, lowering the muzzle toward her chest, then falling silent again.

She glimpsed his gesture from the corner of her eye, and her panic abated. *They've overpowered Phil … and I'm defenseless against the guns … but I can still watch, and think.* She turned back to face the gunman.

"Relax your arms," Alpha directed.

She was too scared to relax anything, but managed to drop her arms. *Shit, he said "a few days!" Maybe that rules out murder, but rape? Or torture? I never thought I'd wish for someone to just rob my house.*

"I'm moving your bag," he said, grabbing the strap.

She lifted her not-relaxed-enough arm so he could slide the satchel free in one motion, then watched him toss it onto her leather armchair. She'd remember where to find her cell phone.

"Now, hands behind your back. And don't fight Tripp."

She put her arms straight back. The duo acted unfazed by her token resistance, with Tripp clicking her left wrist into a handcuff then chafing her skin as he pulled it past the center of her back. She winced, then felt him use his right hand to position and secure her free wrist.

She decided to break her silence. "My husband, is he—"

"He's fine, as promised," Alpha said. "There's an exercise coming up, for you alone. I'll let you speak to him first, provided you only say what I want you to."

"Yes. Whatever you want."

Alpha holstered his gun, and Jen sighed. He gave her directions, and she recommitted to following them after he finished. Then she stood, with Tripp's help, and the threesome proceeded across the room and into the kitchen.

When she saw Phil restrained, Jen ran—as best she could with her hands cuffed—and knelt on her right knee, touching her shoulder to his left arm. A blue-masked intruder removed the deafening headphones. "Honey, it's me," she whimpered. "I'm OK. Did they hurt you?"

Phil shook his head.

"You're the most important thing to me. They said if we cooperate, we'll be fine." She heard Phil groan through the tape and cloth, then stop. "I'm going to do whatever they say, so we can have our normal lives together after this—"

Alpha thrust out his palm. "That's enough! Downstairs with her, headphones for him!"

As Blue Mask worked the headphones back on, Phil bobbed and shook his head defiantly, which signaled to Jen that his spirit was intact. Like her, he'd be thinking of resistance, and rescue.

While Blue Mask minded Phil, the others forced Jen through the kitchen, then down the basement stairs, which she conquered with baby steps. She saw Alpha dart his eyes over the secondhand filing cabinets, hanging pictures, and wall bricked with oversized maroon and navy legal textbooks. Then he scanned the laminated desks, took three strides, and pulled out her black swivel chair, readily distinguishing her treatise-heavy desktop from Phil's, with his state of the art micro speakers, external hard drive, and red-handled metal nutcracker with a dozen exposed gears.

Alpha flipped his palm toward the chair. Jen walked over and hunched slowly, stretching her fingers for the back of the seat, and landed in place.

"We'll be executing a plan over the next few days," Alpha droned, shifting back into view on her left side while Tripp moved to her right. "That's our priority. Limiting collateral damage is secondary. So if we need to hurt either of you, we will…. But if you cooperate, we'll leave you safe."

Jen bit her lip, then turned her head to look at Tripp.

"I know you can identify Tripp," Alpha said, "but we don't fear you as a witness. He's upset some very … *unforgiving* men, and I'm financing a life for him far away from them and the so-called rule of law. He'll be gone long before the police begin their pursuit." Tripp's head bobbed as he smiled at the leader, and Jen nodded twice as well.

"Perversely," Alpha added, "if I were inclined to share our plan, I'm certain I could convince you to participate voluntarily."

"Try me," she replied.

If Alpha reacted at all to her provocation, it was imperceptible through the mask. "We've kept your performance simple. You're known for organizing protests against injustice. We've prepared an editorial under your name calling for another one, a march on Newark

City Hall, to run in tomorrow's *Star-Ledger*. I'm sure you can convince Mr. Reich to make space for it; he seems to like your work."

"I'll try," she said, downplaying her good working relationship with the editor-in-chief and concealing their friendship.

"Tomorrow morning," Alpha said, "you'll cancel your classes for the day and Saturday's *Law Review* board meeting, under the pretext of leading the march, which you'll encourage your students to join."

He's overlooked the firewall! she thought. Law professors couldn't send bulk messages to students or access the grading system without being logged in from their secure terminals in the law school building, a precaution against hackers disrupting classes or tampering with records. Trying to do so from her laptop would prompt an inquiry from concerned officials, maybe even a visit.

Her hopes were short-lived.

"Tripp's been pretending to be a Seton Hall law student for the past few weeks, since classes started. He's learned that message must come from your office. I've planned for you and him to finish that by 7:15, so you shouldn't run into anyone and need to lie about meeting with your student before breakfast." Alpha paused. "And don't get any heroic ideas. If he loses track of a single action you take, your husband will suffer the most dire of consequences."

Jen nodded, wanting to appear cooperative. And the creep wasn't asking her to kill anyone.

* * * * *

Jen looked up from her desk at Alpha, who was still towering to her left; she'd read his script into the phone but had been thinking about how to signal her friend.

"Not so flat," Alpha said. "And during the actual call, you'll be reading just the remarks I point to. Verbatim."

She gave a lackluster nod and turned back to the script. *Marc DeLoren is their top crime reporter*, she thought. *How can I sneak in "Marc"?*

"Tripp will be your computer surrogate, if necessary."

She glanced at Tripp, feigning attention. *Say "Marc" instead of "march"?*

"And if you make any effort to draw help, our plan still moves forward, in a world short one law professor and one engineer!"

Jen registered her cue and gave two perfunctory nods.

"Listen!" the leader demanded, grabbing her left shoulder.

She turned back to him with a start. His eyes were so angry. He let go and faced Green Mask at the bottom of the stairs. "Go up to the kitchen." Alpha locked eyes with her before continuing. "Strike Mr. Bolton in the head, hard enough to knock his chair over!"

"No!" she screamed, surging forward, tugging the handcuffs. "I've done everything you asked!"

Alpha raised his right hand, halting his colleague, but kept silent.

"Please don't hurt him," she sobbed. "I just want us to get out of this. I was ... being stupid. But I'll stop. I'm all yours. Please!"

"I suppose you could show me that violence isn't necessary," the leader offered.

"I will! I promise!"

He put his left hand on her right shoulder and stared into her eyes. "*How* will this call go?"

"Just like you said.... *Exactly* the way you told me."

Alpha looked at his cohort and said, "Sounds good enough." Then he returned both hands to his sides.

Jen leaned back and looked down, trying to calm herself. *Subversion takes a back seat. Never forget he's watching.* After a fifth deep breath, she looked up and nodded, and Alpha pressed the "Speakerphone" button and dialed Reich's number.

The newsman answered on the second ring. "Jen, wonderful to hear from you! Is this friend-to-friend, or professional again?"

Alpha pointed to one of the paragraphs. "Ed, this call is strictly business. The legislature is keeping me so busy, I barely have time for teaching."

She hoped her acquaintance might sense the rude tone and dull humor of the message, but kept her poker face when he replied empathetically, "We all get stuck *there*, Jen. How can the *Star-Ledger* help?"

Alpha poked the middle of the page. She considered reciting the long reply with a scripted cadence but feared provoking her captor. "The agencies are reshuffling their program priorities. I don't think Trenton's planning to fund the Forensic Review Unit adequately, so we have to beat the drum here in Newark. Do you know how many wrongful convictions we've had overturned from DNA back-testing?"

"Great topic for a magazine, Jen, but doesn't sound like news. The budget process drags on for months. Maybe over the next week we build a human interest story on the prisoners set free, and you get quoted plugging for more money for the Review Unit?"

Alpha shook his head.

Jen had advocated off-script for two dozen years—debate team, law student, professor. "No," she replied. "We're marching on City Hall on Saturday, which *is* news, and my editorial is a prelude to that. You have to print it tomorrow, Ed, or miss the party entirely. I could owe you one ..."

"Well, I'd never want to miss one of your parties, Jen. Consider it done, if it's not too long."

Alpha nodded, and pointed to the last remarks on his page. "I'll send it in a minute," she read. "I think it's publication-ready, but I'll leave any editing to your capable hands. Could I be rude and jump to a call on my cell?"

"Well, I'll be sending Sarah or Dylan to cover your march. I'll forgive the rudeness if we get an interview."

Alpha was alternately nodding and signaling "cut."

"Sure, Ed. Say hi to Mags."

Alpha disconnected the call, too quickly to tell if the editor had a reply, then turned back to her. She was expecting an approving nod for a moment—the shortest moment of her life. Alpha wrapped his left hand across her neck and forced her against the seat, jabbing the handcuffs into her back and rolling the chair several inches. His right hand pressed his gun into her cheek, scary yet redundant—she was powerless against his chokehold, her writhing securing only tiny gasps of air.

"Who is Mags?" Alpha barked. "Who is Mags?"

Jen could only mouth the answer. And mouth it again. Then Alpha loosened his grip, allowing a stifled breath and a murmur. "Ed's wife."

"Prove it!" he demanded.

Tripp chimed in while facing the computer screen. "We're fine. *Find Them* says Margaret Reich is his wife."

"Idiot! If everyone calls her 'Maggie' or 'Peg,' the police are on their way." Then, leaning so close she could smell coffee on his breath, "Proof!"

Margaret Shelby Reich was always simply "Mags"; it wasn't something she expected to need to prove. She could picture "Mags" written plenty of times, but nothing to show Alpha. *All those thank-*

you cards—they'd be with her. Birthday cakes? Invitations? And the gun, the stranglehold ... so hard to think.

Then it dawned on her. "Ask Phil," she gasped.

Alpha took his hand off her neck and covered her mouth. She filled her chest with invigorating breaths. He also eased off the gun, but kept it touching her cheek. "Everyone calls her that, not just you?" he asked.

Jen nodded under the leather glove, continuing her hearty gulps.

Keeping his eyes on her, Alpha called to the third henchman. "Gamma, make sure the music was running through Mr. Bolton's headphones this whole time, and that even Beta couldn't hear the professor's sign-off. Then free him to utter a single word, what he calls Ed Reich's wife."

The accomplice clumped up the stairs, leaving her pinned, silenced, and at the mercy of a single-minded gunman. *What if Phil reflexively says "Margaret?" Or he's asked her first name? What if they think he'd overheard me say "Mags?"*

Her entire body relaxed when Gamma returned, nodding. He whispered in Alpha's ear, and the leader holstered his gun.

"All right, Professor. If we get our march, you'll get your lives."

* * * * *

To Jen's relief, the brutish leader was now turned away from her, facing the computer screen, between Gamma and Tripp. "Get it now," he directed, sending Gamma clumping up the stairs again, opening a clear view of the photographs on her desk. Jen smiled, as she always did, at the graduation picture, wearing the black gown with Harvard Law School's purple crows-foot emblems, Mom beaming in her favorite Laura Ashley print dress, and Dad blue-suited in his wheelchair, their last picture together before his pancreatic cancer ... it was wonderful he'd been there. Phil was in the silver frame, grinning, not tied up wearing the *Lovable Nerd* sweatshirt she'd gifted him that he only pretended to like, but ecstatic that his birthday tickets to *Macbeth* included a backstage meet-and-greet with Patrick Stewart. That was just before she'd turned thirty, almost ten years ago, when they were newlyweds and safe and free.

She stayed fixed on young Phil, undistracted by Gamma returning and plopping down a gym bag. Alpha's high-pitched remark, though, forced the present back upon her: "Necessary precautions."

Gamma approached with a sleep mask, and Jen decided not to resist. The blaring headphones were different—she shook her head and twice protested "Too loud!" Then she felt a gloved hand under her chin, tilting her throbbing head, and a piece of tape pressed over her mouth; she groaned but it held in place.

The isolation probably freed her from demands—and threats—but made her focus on her pain and dread. She tried to ignore the blasting in her ears and shifted the handcuffs off the sore spots on her back. *Shit, they're going to keep me like this until I go to Newark tomorrow.... Shit, what happens after that? My career ... all that work ... and Phil—it can't come to naught because of some lunatic! It can't!*

After another apprehensive minute, she resolved to stop dwelling on her fears and get pragmatic: would cooperating save them from the monster? As best she could with her head pounding, she mulled over everything Alpha had done and said. His aggression seemed, oddly, rational; he'd only resorted to violence when he hadn't gotten what he'd expected from her. She would obey, make him believe she was cooperating, and seek rescue only stealthily. And, given the chance, be a keen observer, to help the police when this was over.

* * * * *

Ten minutes after gagging the professor, Alpha saw Ed Reich's e-mail approving the forged submission. "Don't ever question my wording again," he scolded Tripp. Then he pulled a syringe from a leather case in the gym bag and jabbed Jen in her left thigh.

She jerked away, shaking her head and forcing out a nasal moan, then sat still again. Soon the diazepam left her head bobbing, then brought on a full slump.

Rather than give her twelve hours to concoct a plan of resistance or suffer a break from reality, Alpha had forced a thoughtless slumber. It would also give him a chance to rest, and he wanted to make a good impression on Judge Frenzel the next day.

- 3 -

Alpha, Beta, and Tripp returned to the Boltons' house before dawn in an *A&R Windows* van. After moving Phil from the bedroom to the basement, Alpha and Beta went back upstairs. "She wasn't any trouble overnight?" Alpha asked Gamma. "And no signs of allergic reaction?"

"Nope. It *was* easier having them both in the bedroom."

"I told you it would be worth untying them and dragging them around," Alpha said. "Easier for you, and no marks on her wrists or mouth." He stepped to the near side of the bed with Gamma, while Beta circled to her right. Then he pulled down his ski mask, and the others followed suit. "She can stay under the blanket, just grab her arms, while I take care of this." He peeled the backing from a strip of tape and resealed Jen's mouth, then pulled a hypodermic needle from a leather pouch he'd left on the dresser. "You re-administered the Valium six hours ago?" he asked Gamma.

"Yep. Right at midnight."

"Then a half-dose of flumazenil should do the trick."

* * * * *

Jen stirred, cracking her eyelids and twisting to roll to her right, then sensed her immobility. She popped her eyes open and thrashed under the blanket, screams muted by tape, outstretched arms pinned by masked attackers squeezing her wrists. She soon reached full consciousness and flopped her head back, staring at the ceiling; this nightmare was, in fact, her reality.

"Remember, your husband's well-being depends on your cooperation," came the high-pitched wake-up announcement from her left.

Jen rolled her head right.

"You're awake enough to recall your predicament?" Alpha asked.

She lifted her head to the left, facing Alpha, and nodded.

"You *shouldn't* run into any of your colleagues this early, yet I insist on some precautions. Dress as you would for a normal workday—same hairstyle and makeup as yesterday. Nothing to leave behind, no jewelry … except keep these on," Alpha said, tapping her wedding and engagement rings. "And nothing comes back with you, not even a paper clip." He paused, and she nodded again.

"We've laid out a sheer outfit for you, with no pockets, and we'll be invading your privacy, keeping watch while you get ready."

"Mmph mmph," Jen forced while shaking her head.

"That wasn't a question! Have you forgotten yesterday?"

She glanced at each of the men, lowered her eyes, and shook her head.

"That's better." He rubbed at a corner of the tape, then pinched the edge and pulled it off her mouth.

"Ouch, goddammit!" She licked her lips, tasting for blood.

Alpha stepped back and nodded to his accomplices, who released her arms.

Jen rubbed her wrists for a few seconds and started to stretch, then jerked her arms down to grab the retreating blanket. "My robe," she demanded, scowling.

Alpha shook his head. "Not negotiable."

She still swam in bikinis; yesterday's bra and panties wouldn't reveal much more than that. And these would be the men who'd stripped her down in the first place. Plus her bladder was about to burst. Besides, she really had no choice.

Jen huffed, and blushed as she got up from under the blanket. She glimpsed the intruders' leering eyes and knew at once that all three were straight, although Alpha was more discreet. She trod into the oblong bathroom, and shuddered on hearing Alpha's footsteps on the beige tiles behind her, keeping the door wide open, with Beta and Gamma staying in the hallway. She reached the toilet, turned around, and grabbed her panties. "Well?"

Alpha looked back and circled his finger to get the other two to turn around, then faced her. He seemed conflicted, pausing before uttering, "Too much at stake."

"You're a sadist who won't even admit it to himself," Jen said before pulling down her underwear and answering nature's call. However much violence this thug considered justified for his grandiose scheme, she hoped her accusation would temper his extremes.

She finished, looked around, and shrugged at Alpha. Their bathroom had been stripped—everything usually on the counter or in the shower, even the basket of magazines on the floor, was missing. And there was a blue plastic bin by the sink, near Alpha.

"Three squares of toilet paper," he called out as he handed her sheets from a roll they'd packed in the container.

"Three squares," Gamma answered back.

"Don't flush," he instructed.

Jen pulled her underwear back on in one motion as she stood up.

"You two can turn back around," Alpha said. He switched positions with her, looked in the toilet, and announced, "Three sheets, accounted for."

Alpha was again a step ahead of her. She hadn't thought to drop a razor in the school's elevator or leave a Q-tip behind at the security desk, but perhaps would have during the course of the morning. Every item she used, from toothbrush to soap, was retrieved from the blue bin, announced, and returned. They'd also taped a photograph of her to the mirror, obviously taken after they'd drugged her the previous day. She'd repeat parting her light brown hair on the left and going light on blush but somewhat heavy on mascara—not that anyone would be around at 7 AM to notice. After sneaking glances, in vain, for any mark where Alpha had clasped her neck, she continued on autopilot, using the lull for contemplation. When she thought of a signal to leave at work, she could barely contain her smile.

* * * * *

Jen shrugged at the dressing mirror—she wouldn't ordinarily wear a white silk blouse with a tan bra, nor without a jacket, but didn't expect to garner attention from it, either. The blue skirt might offer a better hiding place if she could think of anything worth smuggling back.

She turned, looked at Alpha's holstered gun, and swallowed hard. "Show me that Phil is OK, if you want anything more," she said. "Not negotiable."

"Fine," he said. "He's sedated, like you were; don't expect much."

She followed Alpha to the basement, Beta and Gamma trailing behind, and stifled a cry when she saw Phil. Other than the rhythmic chest movements, he sat limp and helpless, wrists and elbows taped to the arms of his chair and feet bound together.

"This doesn't have to be his end. Look there, on your desk," Alpha said, pointing past Tripp, who was reading her e-mails again, to a split-screen display. "We will monitor *everything*. If Tripp doesn't make the assigned detours, or gets stopped *anywhere*, we'll know, and your car becomes a target and your husband's will goes to probate."

Alpha led her upstairs and through the kitchen, and Tripp followed. She glanced about the den, and noticed that, as in the bedroom, the shades were pushed inward by opaque sheeting that covered the windows. Tripp put his holster and gun into a black gym bag on the armchair, where her satchel had been. Then they walked into the garage, and Alpha brought her to the driver's door of the Lexus. "Tripp has your instructions, and a cover story for you to memorize."

Jen sat behind the wheel, while Tripp went around to the passenger seat, his feet straddling what looked like a cookie tin.

"Don't try turning him," Alpha warned. "He knows his life becomes worthless on my say-so." He closed her door, walked over to press the blue button, and disappeared into the house.

"Better obey General Pompous there," Tripp remarked as she backed past the van in the driveway. It seemed he was making a joke, but she dipped her head in an ambiguous nod as cover. "Head for South Orange Avenue. We're going that way to the law school. And I like it cold," he added, dropping the thermostat to sixty-six.

After she shifted into drive, he spoke again. "Our success determines whether your husband lives, but I can make you suffer if I don't like *how* you follow along. To start, I only want you talking when it's necessary."

Jen didn't want to anger him, but she had a plan, and needed to know if he was distractible, and what he'd do if stressed. "OK … Silent unless I need instructions or the bathroom."

"No!" he yelled, pounding the dashboard. "You nod when I give orders, and you'll get directions when I give them. Unless we run into a nosy jerk at Seton Hall, I'll punish you for speaking without my prompt! Starting now. Understood?" he asked, lightly pushing up and down on her chin to force a nod.

As they approached the first turn, Jen shivered, and closed off the chilly air from the vent near her window, holding her tongue. After the turn, Tripp gave instructions—some vague, others detailed, choreographed. He also droned on about a fictitious research project, when they would've met to discuss his drafts, and mundane personal details—enough to assure their stories would match if they were confronted. Occasionally he'd have her turn off the direct route and then regain course, presumably creating a GPS trail to signal his colleagues. She contemplated trying to memorize the new route, but decided that wouldn't be much of a clue when this was over, and focused on his directions.

They reached LAZ Parking three minutes before seven. She was about to regain the home field advantage, this time against a far lesser adversary.

4

Jen circled the parking deck to reach an empty row, then slowed to pull into a space. "Not here," Tripp said. "Level E. We want to be alone on the way out, too."

When she'd parked and turned off the engine, he extended his left hand. "Keys. And pop the trunk."

Jen pressed the "Trunk" button on the key fob and exaggerated her confused expression. "You'll see," he said. "It's the first surprise."

They walked back, and he lifted the lid, revealing two cardboard file crates. "Idle hands … blah, blah," he said, pointing to the one on the left. Jen reached her hands into the cut-out handles and pulled back effortlessly, then Tripp balanced the other box on his knee and closed the trunk. They walked side by side: her on the left, as scripted, him watching her, feigning conversation.

As she traversed the garage, Jen rethought her plan—the box was a bad omen. Scribbling a note to drop in the hallway or near the trash for the cleaning crew had seemed unworkable and perilous, so she'd settled on an ambiguous signal, something more difficult than risky. Now add in *surprises*—another obstacle, as if self-maiming wouldn't be hard enough.

Once outside, she glimpsed the law school's curved glass exterior wall, then stared ahead and remained beside Tripp as he followed the familiar bend toward the entrance, not a helpful soul in sight.

"You start when we get in," he reiterated as they approached the revolving door. "Eyes on me, every odd-numbered amendment in the Bill of Rights, animated so the guard doesn't want to interrupt you. Left hand in the box handle the whole time, right comes out just for your signature … your *real* signature."

Jen followed him through and began her recitation as they proceeded to the security desk. Tripp rested his box on the counter and pulled his ID and hers from his pocket, confirming that the miscreants had been shopping in her satchel overnight. Stan Keyes, the familiar overnight-shift guard, barely glanced at Tripp's convincing fake, then nodded at both of them after they'd signed in, without interrupting her recital or checking the file boxes.

In the elevator, Tripp pressed "4" with a corner of his box, then said, "Stop now, we're alone."

She ended the monologue and took stock of two flaws in Alpha's plan on their way up. Tripp's portrait would now be stored in the Cloud, from the elevator's security camera, and she could free the brain cells that had catalogued his straight black hair, thin face, and discolored third tooth on the right side of his upper jaw. Also, they'd sent her to work without a handbag. *Alpha's team seems strictly a boys' club; maybe I'll get a chance to exploit that.*

Forty steps, she'd once estimated, brought them to her office. She shot desperate glances down the hallway when Tripp shifted his focus to the doorknob, but found no eyes to contact. She followed him in, and he directed, "Close the door with your elbow, then turn and face it."

Jen faked clumsiness in nudging the door, stalling to survey her office before pivoting toward the opaque glass. Unlike her bathroom, the office seemed undisturbed. The midsized desk she swapped up to upon earning tenure had empty workspace in the center, with her computer, phone, and a photo of Phil with a lemur on the right, and a wooden desk organizer and two stacks of folders on the left. There were two drab metal-framed visitor's chairs, and her own low-backed blue chair, which she could hear rolling over the noise of Tripp rummaging through her drawers. "Scissors? Knife?" he asked.

"I think scissors in the middle drawer."

"Honest Abe!" he said. "That *is* where you left them, and now they're somewhere else. Time for surprise number two."

Jen sucked in her lips and felt herself sweat. She only had the one plan, and needed some freedom to pull it off. She'd hoped for a moment when her captor would have to concentrate on the class cancellation protocol, so she could sneak a small Post-it note from a folder or the pad. Then create a distraction to slip it into her mouth, and bite her cheek hard enough to stain the paper with blood, swallowing to conceal her wound until it clotted. Then, finally, another diversion to spit it out outside her door and kick it against the jamb—hopefully, hopefully, suspicion-raising to anyone going to her office. Tripp's lingering silence—chair remaining still, drawers staying shut—left her in an anxious limbo.

"Turn around, Professor," he said eventually. She did, and saw Tripp's box on the right visitor's chair and a flat yellow folder on the other. "Your husband needs you to sit. Box on top of my box first, then hold the folder with two hands until I ask for it."

She started to drop her head but stopped herself to hide her discouragement. She walked forward, glancing about fruitlessly for any accessible paper, and set her box down. Under Tripp's stare, she used both hands to grab the folder, and thrust it toward him when she sat down before holding it on her lap. She couldn't fathom reaching her supplies without a conspicuous release of the prop, and ruled out tearing off a corner as suicidal.

"Password?" he demanded, fingers on the keyboard.

"Same as both times you asked me in the car. Lowercase 'i-o-t-f-a-m-p-u-e-j-e-j,' 'in order to form a more perfect union, establish justice … establish justice.'"

Tripp proceeded to ask for her course schedule, which she knew he already knew, and continued with questions and glancing up every few seconds while he clicked through the protocol. At best she could pull a thread from her skirt or break off a fingernail—signals drawing attention from nobody. Her only remaining hope was getting interrupted by a curious colleague, which never happened.

Soon, Tripp turned the screen toward her. "You're done once you get these confirmations?"

Jen nodded.

"If the students don't get cancellation notices, we'll find out soon enough."

"Honest Abe, remember?"

She watched him log off the network and turn off the computer. "Heading home!" he exclaimed. He had her lay the folder on the desk and hand him her box, then pick up the bottom one, which also felt empty. He freed a hand to inspect the folder, and checked around the chair she'd used.

They retraced their steps to the garage; her scheming had come to naught. When both were seated in the car, he returned the keys. "I guess we *could've* kept you at home," he said. With nobody around to challenge his presence in her office, and armed with her password, his fake ID, and the key, Tripp could indeed have sent the messages alone. "Start the car and wait fifteen seconds," he instructed. "We still have a signaling protocol to follow. And I have some planes to catch."

* * * * *

After being diverted toward the train station, Jen was permitted a long drive on South Orange Avenue. A lull. Time with her thoughts. Something she looked forward to ...

Except now.

She'd done everything the kidnappers wanted ... *everything*. Alpha had promised that would keep her safe. And he'd sounded convincing. But a madman would've said that, too; said it convincingly. She didn't really know....

Tripp remained silent—a reward for her cooperation? Or solace for her last moments alive?

She stopped at a traffic light. Rules, and expectations. *We stop for them, they stop for us.* Reciprocity ... good faith. They got what they wanted, and that was supposed to be enough.

Or am I being naïve?

Her tasks were completed: they didn't need her alive, didn't need Phil as currency. She was expendable, vulnerable, even more than when Alpha was cutting off her air. He could be brutal—ruthless, too? Two gunshots would be so easy for them, and quick. Her hands started shaking; she clutched the steering wheel but couldn't keep them steady.

Jen reached the last traffic light before her house. If Phil was already dead, if she was driving to her own murder, this would be her last chance to run.

But what if she was wrong?

She'd be killing Phil.

Never. That was the last thing she'd risk.

Calming breaths and obedience—it was her only choice. Ignore their van in the driveway. Disregard Alpha peeking into the garage, and his holster. Acquiesce to being manhandled into the den, then backed against the door. Give Tripp time to step back to the left of his leader, now four feet in front of her.

"Phil?" she asked Alpha. "You ... you promised—"

"Inspection next!" Alpha said, shaking his head. "Shoes, skirt, shirt."

"Wait!" Tripp said to him. "I watched her the whole time, hands always full."

Yes! she thought. *I was faithful—tell him! He doesn't need to kill us!*

"You know the plan," Alpha replied, while keeping his eyes on her.

Jen looked at Tripp, then back at Alpha. Shuddering, she kicked off her flats and undressed.

Alpha tossed aside each shoe after looking inside, and shook out the clothes before dropping them at her feet. "You can be quick about the rest, but I have to be sure."

Just kill me if you're going to! She didn't know what to do.

Alpha pulled out his gun with his right hand and pointed it at her.

She winced and trembled; Tripp's eyes widened. "Stop!" he exclaimed, grabbing Alpha's arm. "Did you invoke *Titanic*? I'd signaled *Lifeboat*. She did everything I asked—"

"And now she has to do what *I* asked," Alpha retorted, pushing Tripp's hand away. "Right now!" he demanded, glaring at Jen.

"OK!" she replied, raising her unsteady hands. She slid her right strap down with her left hand, covering her breasts with her left forearm, and lowered the left strap with her right hand. After a deep breath, she pulled the B-cups down and quickly re-covered. She took two steps for the panties, a short reveal then re-cover facing forward, and a brief one facing away.

When she turned back, the demon dropped his right arm to his side, and she sighed.

"You'll be tied down in bed for about a day," Alpha said. "You'll get uncomfortable, and probably messy. Choose if you want to put that outfit back on."

Jen nodded and started to dress. The notion of being tied up for so long perversely offered the relief that Alpha would let them live.

5

Todd Sapphire repeated aliases in his head as he drove the box truck down Irvington's Millhead Street. For two hundred yards, he followed the fenced grassy perimeter that ringed an imposing spike-crowned stone wall, then turned left down the driveway to Essex State Prison. He stopped at the entrance gate at 8 AM, coinciding with the hacked requisition order for Saturday, and handed over John Commoner's photo ID, showing him in his light brown wig and fake chevron mustache, but with sunglasses off.

Two guards studied his face, his ID, his passenger, and the truck. "Woodman's Paper Supply … This thing'll be empty when you leave, John?" the sergeant asked over the clunking engine.

"We're not hauling much today, and you get the whole load."

"Then we'll only be inspecting you on your way out," the sergeant said, handing back the ID while his colleague scribbled in the logbook and opened the gate.

Todd nodded and turned toward Jaguar in the passenger seat. "No inspection," he repeated for the microphone.

* * * * *

Righteous took out his earbud, turned the light back on in the cargo cube, and held a finger to his lips, reminding his cohorts to remain silent until the truck cleared the gate. He'd been on one of the prodding narrow benches they'd welded along the sidewalls, seated farthest to the back, for what felt like an hour, and stood for relief, grabbing the netting on the cargo cube's ceiling. The four Panthera to his right and five across from him followed suit. The dim light sufficed to show that their makeup jobs could have earned Oscar nominations: lips, eyes, and complexions distorted enough, together with the wigs, to render masks unnecessary and surveillance photos useless.

Righteous turned toward the front of the truck, facing the sheet metal partition they'd installed nine feet in to divide the cargo cube into two compartments. The metalwork had inspired nicknaming the rear section "the Can," despite its corners. A pallet with three identical large cartons took up much of the center of the Can between the benches; they'd also managed room for their electronics and guns. Directly behind him, inches from the roll-up door, were two dozen boxes they'd stacked from inside to conceal themselves from the gate guards—drawing guns that early would've been a last resort.

The truck drove forward for a minute, then turned and stopped. "Lion's backing up! Move these in!" Righteous said, patting the box wall. "Bench-to-bench, so we'll be hidden but the sides will be clear!"

While eight Panthera restacked the cases, Righteous stepped to the front of the Can to watch the approaching loading dock on-screen with Lynx. "Let's see if Head Smasher's right—he said there'd be six guards and six prisoners."

"You're worried about that?" Lynx asked.

"Not really. You spend twenty years in maximum security, you get connected and know where everyone is, and when. Just like I trust Gas Can's maps. Parolees know it all. And they're cheap informants. How about your bit? One guard with a radio can stop a hundred convicts—they've always got a response team at the ready."

"I just need the door open, to be certain," Lynx answered.

The truck stopped again, and Righteous looked at the monitor. "It's twelve," he announced. He shut it off, then surveyed the boxes and nodded. "Positions, everyone." The Panthera squeezed to the center of the Can along both sides of the pallet, facing back. Tiger turned off the lights.

When Lion rolled up the cargo door, Lynx launched the first salvo of the attack, activating two sets of midrange frequency jammers. Then the inmates moved into the truck, out of view of the security cameras, for the fake delivery, while Lion and Jaguar were to edge toward the prison's receiving room door along the dock, backs toward the gate guards.

Righteous rapped the sidewall twice, and six armed Panthera in khaki prison uniforms stepped onto the benches to get past the cartons, then ran out of the truck. He and two other Panthera, dressed as guards, followed to the back of the truck on the right side, pointing handguns and shouting, "Move! Move!" to force the real inmates to the left. Bobcat, also wearing a guard uniform, turned on the lights and stayed in the center of the Can, shuffling boxes and clearing a path along the left side.

Then Righteous peered out, and grinned at the scene. All six guards stood rigid, staring from gun to gun; two had grown white-knuckled, still pressing their radio panic buttons. "Move them around!" he yelled. His informants had revealed that video evidence was rarely presented at disciplinary hearings, and consisted of grainy, indistinct images when it was. He'd deduced that the feeds from the dock cameras would show broad motions from six guards, six apparent inmates, and both deliverymen, but would lack the clarity for discerning that his impostors were armed and directing the guards' movements.

Righteous turned back to the convicts. "You'll be taking orders from us today, if you want to live. Now, get on that bench, and scoot all the way in!"

Five of the prisoners looked to a scowling six-foot-tall Latino with an open-mouthed rattlesnake tattooed down his right forearm; he alone displayed more rage than quiver. Then he seemed to count the guns with his eyes, muttered, "*Pendejos*," and sat down and slid to the front. The others followed his lead.

Righteous said, "There are restraints hanging under each of your seats. I don't want any trouble while I'm gone. Quickly!"

Again following the Viper, each of the convicts handcuffed himself to the bench.

"Switch the guards!" Righteous called out of the truck.

His order drew small teams of fake prisoners and real guards into the Can, to load boxes onto three pallets and roll them out with pallet jacks, staged so the camera operator and gate guards wouldn't realize that Sergeant Brinnell and three of his men were being handcuffed on the truck and replaced by Righteous and his uniformed colleagues, now equipped with prison-issued key cards and radios. Righteous interrupted the activity once, grabbing Cougar's shoulder to admire his convincing makeup transformation into Officer Graceman's doppelgänger, from social media images.

The two guards who remained on the dock, Sergeants Reiley and Scolaro, were first compelled to hold clipboards and feign supervising unloading the truck, then forced along as the pallets were rolled into the penitentiary. Lion went to the driver's seat and flipped through papers, while Jaguar went into the Can and closed the door, doubling as guard over the chained captives and auxiliary technology supervisor.

* * * * *

Once inside the pale blue receiving room, the Panthera who were dressed as inmates positioned the pallets and restacked the lighter boxes to create a modest camera blind spot. Then they took turns crouching behind the cargo and changing into guard uniforms. The shortest of them, Tiger, next cut open the three oversized cartons, exposing the team's rolling storerooms, draped with printed linen sheets to pass as library carts when viewed down a hallway or through security glass. Then he sliced into two more boxes and distributed counterfeit riot gear and six orange vests stenciled "DRILL."

Righteous addressed Reiley and Scolaro. "We can't be stopped now," he lied. "It's just a question of whether we have to shoot any guards along the way. Keep your hands on a cart and sound convincing if we're confronted, and we won't have to kill anyone." Then he and three of his men walked the captives and the cloaked carts out and down the labyrinthine gray corridors, with the fake riot response training team trailing fifteen feet behind. Cougar used a seized access key to open three doors along the way. Shortly past the last one, they turned left into the hallway leading to cellblock D, and Righteous grinned.

He had obsessed over cellblock D for years. For convictions for murder, torture, or aggravated rape, judges could subject eighty-eight of the nightmares of society to long hours of limited light and scant human contact. They ate in their cells, and prison officials frequently cited "behavioral concerns" to deny mandated exercise time. The small windows were opaque, and cons could only leave their cells if shackled; any hesitation in offering their wrists out the tiny slots that the guards clunked open would leave them confined for the day. They were rotated to new cells every four weeks and were subjected to frequent body searches. Warden Minero boasted there had been no guard injuries in D block, and every liberal lawyer in New Jersey called for it to be razed.

Soon the frontrunners converged at the cellblock door. "Sergeant Scolaro," Righteous said, "Sergeant Jackson should be in charge of the block now. You'll scan your key, and his monitor will show you up close, Sergeant Reiley and us four right behind, and the geared-up team there in the distance. We know that unannounced response drills are conducted in every cellblock. For your sake and his, you better convince him that *this* is a drill, simulating contraband delivered in the library carts." He paused until Scolaro nodded. "And of course," he bluffed, "using any of the current code words would be fatal." Scolaro nodded again.

Righteous knew the four-guard teams in cellblock D spent most of their time in the control room, monitoring the two floors of cells from padded chairs at a large console behind two large thick-glassed windows. Jackson would reply from there. "You bringing us a whole party, Scol-man? There might not be enough prisoners to go around."

"Just some wannabe heroes thinking they need practice to beat up our librarians," Scolaro answered.

"I'll buzz you in, but keep me out of that skit; I'll never hear the end of it if I have a black eye in my wedding photos," Jackson said.

The clank brought the deception to its end. Righteous ran toward the control room with his Beretta drawn, leading the Panthera into the dreary cellblock, supplies and captives in tow.

Sergeant Jackson lunged right; his frenetic button pushing set off the lockdown alarm and, Righteous presumed, time-locked the prisoners' cells and disabled key card entry to the control room. When Righteous reached the window, he could make out Jackson's red-faced entreaties into the phone: "They've got guns! They've got guns!"

The Panthera continued their coordinated attack. Three of them shoved Reiley against the cellblock door, face against the window, and taped his hands behind his back. Three others bound Scolaro and forced him to the control room door. Righteous and Cougar held messages against the control room's left window—*LET US IN AND YOU WILL SURVIVE* and *ONE MINUTE BEFORE YOU DIE.*

When Lynx and Bobcat attached a detonator and an explosive brick labeled "C4" to the right window, all four guards crouched down behind the console. "That shit is real!" one yelled. "Let's give up the room, and we stay alive, like Scolaro."

"We can't just surrender!" Jackson objected. "This is crazy—the most conspicuous prison break ever! Who knows what they'll do next!"

"No, Pittman's right!" another insisted. "The glass won't protect us from C4! Come on, Sarge! I got a baby girl!"

After a silent moment, Sergeant Jackson raised his hands above his head and rose slowly. His cohorts followed suit, Officer Breslin waving his arms as he stood.

Righteous and Cougar dropped their notes. While Righteous walked to the door, Cougar stared in, then yelled "Pittman!" as he turned an imaginary key. Pittman crossed behind Winzer and nudged Jackson to the left to access the button to unlock the door, then nodded to Cougar.

Righteous entered with his gun raised, encountering four wide-eyed captives—*frightened is good, desperate is not.* "I'm a simple man," he said. "If you cooperate, you'll be free before dinner. If you interfere, in the slightest, I'll spend a bullet. Anyone want to test me?" He pointed his gun from guard to guard, causing each to shake his head in turn. "Good." He sent them out one at a time, and the waiting Panthera taped their wrists and mouths. Bobcat and Cheetah broke off and started around the cellblock with paintball guns, first rendering the cameras useless, then shooting at the four apertures evenly spaced across the tall ceiling.

When Righteous was alone in the control room, he grabbed the dangling phone and replied to the authority figure insisting on an update. "Jackson isn't here," he announced in his deep voice. "I am Righteous, leader of the Panthera. We control D block, and hold sixteen hostages. Guards will die if you approach the cellblock! Guards will die if you approach my truck! Guards will die if you cut the power! You are to stand ready for my additional demands!" Then he hung up.

6

The lockdown alarm sent Warden Rolando Minero—all 250 pounds of him— rushing across the prison to the command center. He stopped inside to catch his breath, shook his head at the dark video screens mounted on the front wall, then skirted past two rows of computer jockeys to reach Captain Adam Revano as Righteous's rant played over the speakerphone. "Damn, Adam! What have I missed? And what the hell's going on with the cameras?"

"There seem to be twelve of them, disguised as guards," Revano replied. "They breached in a delivery truck, reached cellblock D, and were in the control room within a minute or two. I didn't see anyone hurt, but then they took out the cameras, so we can't be sure. He's basically asked to maintain the status quo, and protocol is to start with containment anyway. All I've done so far is escalate the lockdown from 'count in place' to 'return to cells.'"

"I'm leaning toward going by the book as well," Minero said, "but redirect any guards who'd assist D block during lockdown to report here instead."

Then he turned and raised his voice. "I want a full report from the gate guards about that delivery truck—when it arrived, who was in it before, and who's in it now. Make sure we have the firepower to stop it if it moves—but do *not* approach it without my order. Also, I want a full review of the security tapes, tracing how many people entered the cellblock and tracking them backward until we know how they got there from the loading dock. Tech team: I want a plan on how to get an eye in there. Broderick: see if 'Righteous' is a known alias in the system, especially if there's a link to any of the D block inmates. I want the governor on standby, and redphone Director Arden—it's time to bring in the Newark Police Department. And don't forget about the rest of the prison; I want to know that all of the cons are in their cells."

That damn training finally paid off, he thought.

* * * * *

After conveying his threats, Righteous opened the door and called "Ready!" His team herded the six bound guards into the control room, forced them onto chairs, and blindfolded them with sportswear headbands. Then he led eight Panthera back out, setting them to work in the cellblock's common area, while Cheetah stayed behind and turned on a recorded loop of a grating jackhammer. Most had mundane tasks, like taping over the window on the cellblock door; Tiger's work, though, was exacting, requiring him to handle sealed tubs with the care given to organs being delivered for transplant.

Righteous remained the only one who spoke at length, next rallying the inmates, twenty at a time. "We're here to rescue three of you; but all of you are free from the screws for the rest of the morning!"

The convicts started shouting at each other, mostly pent-up threats, and one plea: "Jesse, if these yo' boys, don't fo'get your homie."

* * * * *

Bobcat's electric winch was the heaviest piece of equipment smuggled in by the Panthera. Designed for mounting on a garage or factory floor with 3-inch concrete screws, it could pull a disabled pickup truck, or de-hinge a cell door. After donning goggles and a dust mask and sticking in earplugs, he set the depth of the concrete-boring shank and worked his drill.

* * * * *

Righteous had always worn a dark brown wig and makeup around the Panthera—when they were planning, when they were rehearsing, and, with a fake beard and sunglasses, when he was interviewing as "Tom Jefferson," lobbyist for The Victims' Surrogacy. He trusted his vetting, but felt most vulnerable at the recruiting meetings and didn't want to take any chances. Nick Lorelz was his sixth and had just said "rape." Righteous gasped. "I'd just heard robbery and strangulation."

Lorelz shook his head. "The coroner said they pistol-whipped her, then pinned her down, and ..." He stared at his ring finger. "Three years ... those evidence photos ... the bruises on her arms ... what they did to her face ..."

"At least the police did *their* jobs well, arresting Len Maples and Tony Colefire at the scene."

Lorelz took several deep breaths then looked back up. "Yeah, probably just a few minutes after they killed her. Maples and Colefire had lured the deliveryman with a pizza order. They bludgeoned him to death and got his car and the addresses. They killed Sonny Harding next, and took armfuls of electronics … but nobody called the police. It was the pizzeria getting worried that started the search for the car."

"You got my attention by going after them yourself. I read the court transcripts."

"My testimony at sentencing? Didn't change a thing."

"Actually, the records from *your* arrest. Hacking Cablevision's computer system and blacking out the prison televisions."

"Didn't realize there wasn't TV in the high-security cellblock."

"But you had virtuous intentions," Righteous said, "and it was smart to weaponize your computer wizardry. You just needed a better plan … maybe some research."

"*You* see my side of it. But, jeez … they almost put *me* in jail."

"Good thing you had a sympathetic judge."

Lorelz shook his head again. "No. I wish there were no such emotion; I'd still have Vickie. Did you know that ten years before her, those animals killed the security guard at a jewelers? *Sympathy* put them back on the streets."

"Let me guess: reduced sentence for testifying against the triggerman?"

"Exactly.… How did you—"

"Because it's not just you, Nick. It's the system," Righteous said. "You're not the only person who thinks those monsters shouldn't be getting out in twenty years. I promise."

* * * * *

Tiger, like "Lynx" Lorelz, brought a technical skillset to the Panthera. Righteous met with him, one-on-one, on New Year's Day, and handed him a thin folder. "Shred and burn this when you're done."

"Shred and burn," Tiger replied, pulling out the handwritten notes.

"Have you ever heard pesticide chemists refer to an uncontained kill event?"

Tiger shook his head while scanning the pages.

"They try to engineer lethal compounds safe enough for human handlers and consumers who might ingest traces, and wildlife. Sometimes the failures are striking … with biphostrolene, *all* the lab mice died, and the samples and files were turned over to the Army. Those notes you're reading would be considered Top Secret."

"They basically combined two conventional toxins," Tiger said.

"That's why the theorists were so hopeful. They expected it to deteriorate rapidly, which it actually does, and knew atropine would be an antidote, which you need if you're going to manufacture it here. But aside from being so lethal to mammals—"

"Pure BPT gasifies at room temperature!" Tiger read.

"I never said it would be easy …"

* * * * *

Tiger knelt outside the control room and repressurized the paintball guns. Then he put on thermal gloves and gingerly replaced three ammunition hoppers with tubs of his custom-made orbs from the dry ice cooler.

Six of the Panthera paired off to make rounds of the cells, shouting over the noise of the drill, "We're going to shoot acid in there to soften the concrete—make sure you don't touch it!"

Inmates who believed the escape ruse would experience a moment of false contentment when the slots in their doors were opened; skeptics jamming a bible against the opening or grabbing for the weapon were outmatched by a spotter using a hammer and pipe to force in the gun muzzle. Each would hear three pellets shattering on his floor, then the slot clanging shut after the gun was pulled back; within a minute, he'd be gasping from the biphostrolene, and then unable to breathe at all.

I've cured a plague, Righteous thought.

7

After issuing his orders, Warden Minero sat at the central console and watched the lockdown on-screen. Every guard not stationed in a cellblock, whether on shop duty or supervising the kitchen, brought his inmates to their cells and then reported to assist a designated block. Response officers lined the hallway outside D block and took positions around the loading dock and at the gate to cover the truck. When the movement stopped, Minero took to the speakerphone. "Head count, A block!"

"All prisoners secured in cells, 356 out of 356 accounted for," Sergeant Bookman replied. "Twelve of twelve assigned guards present, twenty of twenty supplemental guards present. Phase one complete, A block."

"Head count, B block!" he barked next.

"Four empty cells. Two hundred two out of two-oh-six accounted for and secured. Four missing, last assignment loading dock. Six of six assigned guards present, seven of ten supplemental guards present. Three missing guards, last assignment loading dock."

"Loading dock! Shit!" Minero exclaimed. "Gate leader! Full report on that truck!"

"Sergeant Moore, sir. Entered eight o'clock exactly, scheduled delivery from Woodman's Paper. One driver, one passenger. Guards and prisoners met them at the dock. After unloading, driver returned to the cab, the other guy went to the back, out of view. I guess I'd figured he was cleaning the cargo cube, or taking a drag, or—"

"This is a prison, Moore! People can't just stroll around for a smoke!"

"He's a civilian, and all the inmates were inside! Normally, I ... Well, sure, now I know I screwed up. Anyway, just before lockdown, the driver also went to the back. No movement since. And now we know the cargo door is closed."

"And the missing men from the loading detail?" Minero snarled.

"Negative, sir. The loading detail wheeled the cargo into receiving."

"Warden!" Officer Canfield interjected, drawing Minero's glare and stunned gazes from everyone else in the command center. "Video clarification," he added, pointing to the central monitors. "From the dock camera recordings."

Minero turned to the front of the room. "Are the images always this grainy? Or did they fuck with our video feeds?"

Canfield stayed silent for a moment, then narrated the on-screen progression. "Here's where the loading detail is entering the building. But the guards are acting … off. That one who looks up a couple of times—I thought it was Graceman—he lets the inmate get behind him. Then nobody checks his watch when they enter. And the other ones fixate on the boxes and those clipboards, like they're avoiding the cameras. So six maybe guards and six apparent prisoners enter with the delivery, then here, later … poof! Nobody dressed as prisoners—just twelve intruders outfitted as guards for a heavy response drill. That means the real loading dock guards and cons must be on that truck."

"Good work, Canfield," Minero said, nodding. "Line up the videos for what they did next." He then leaned back in to the console. "C Block, report!"

"One empty cell. Two hundred twenty-two out of two hundred twenty-four accounted for and secured. Two missing, last assignment loading dock. Six of six assigned guards present, nine of ten supplemental guards present. Missing guard's from the loading dock, too."

"That's *ten* from the loading dock," Minero said. Then he looked at the contingent standing at the command center doorway. "Who's working with you, Wolfson?"

"Response teams in position, plus supplemental D block guards, redirected here."

"How many should you be?"

"Ten covering D block egress routes, ten positioned around the truck, and should be eight here, sir. Scolaro and Reiley not reporting."

"Scolaro?" Captain Revano cut in. "The last thing Jackson yelled was, 'They've got Scolaro!'"

"So some of the loading dock hostages *aren't* on the truck!" Minero boomed. "Canfield! You and Silva scrutinize those crappy videos. Figure out how many outsiders there are and which guards or inmates were forced along from the dock." Then he turned to Revano. "What do these nuts want, again?"

"It doesn't add up," Revano said. "Breakout is the only thing they *could* want from a prison, but escape depends on stealth, not force. They also insisted we keep the lights on," he added with a shrug.

"Force, huh?" Minero mumbled. He turned to Sergeant Wolfson again. "With the prisoners locked in, we can spare half the guards in each cellblock. Reinforce the siege of D block—I want to negotiate with this Righteous from a position of strength."

Wolfson nodded and left the command center, while Minero strode toward Sergeant Broderick, with Revano following. "Any manifestos attributed to Righteous?"

"No, nothing. He's not in the law enforcement databases, and nothing on the internet, either."

Minero shook his head. "He must just want someone from D block. Make sure all those prisoner files are up-to-date; the answers have to be there." He turned to Revano. "Did you track down Director Arden?"

"He's expecting our call."

"My office," he directed, leading Revano out, then behind closed doors. "You agree about calling in Newark PD?"

Revano nodded. "Absolutely. We can handle anything that starts here—inmate-on-inmate, inmate-on-guard. But outsiders with guns and explosives? You've got to call them in."

"I'm going to lead off reminding Arden that prisoner retention is non-negotiable. If we ever capitulate to one inmate breaching the perimeter, every convict in the system starts hatching a hostage-taking plot."

"Good idea. I've been thinking ... before the call ... we make some show of force, like turning up the heat. They wouldn't kill over that, right? I just won't be happy until I make Righteous *un*happy."

"In due time, Adam. He'll come to regret staging this while you were on duty—if he lives long enough for regrets."

They called the director, and Minero explained the situation.

"Seems squarely within Essex County Emergency Protocol," Arden responded. "But you can't have my very top guy—Lieutenant Oppenheimer's babysitting City Hall during some pro-criminal demonstration, and the mayor likes him. Let's see … Ted Carson is the next guy down on Saturdays. I've dealt with him a few times, he gets the job done. He's less experienced than Oppenheimer, but makes up for it in smarts. Don't expect to make any personal connections, though."

Minero looked at Revano and shrugged.

* * * * *

Forty minutes after lockdown, the heaviest bedroom doors in Irvington were sequestering corpses in their cells. When Bobcat stopped drilling—ending the whirs and dust—Righteous called out, "Tiger, air test!"

The scientist tipped a small bottle to wet a cotton ball, then smeared a clear liquid onto a glass slide. He waved the slide back and forth for ten seconds, inspected it, and raised his left thumb.

"Cleared for Cover Phase!" Righteous yelled to his men.

Tiger walked toward cell D23, and Leopard lugged a large metal cask over to him. Lynx started rigging electronics and explosives. The other Panthera led the blindfolded guards into the common area, accompanied by the annoying jackhammer recording. When the control room was empty, Righteous went to the phone console and pressed "Command Center."

"I'm calling for the warden. I know he works Saturday mornings."

"This is Warden Minero. I'm sure we can work this out, Righteous, without you or your men getting hurt."

"You're *sure* of nothing! *I* am sure that you'll act to protect your officers, and that I'll be driving away from here soon."

"I suppose one hand could wash the other. As a start, if you free a couple of guards, I'll commit to keeping those lights on for you."

"I don't make concessions for lights," he scoffed. "There are six doors between here and the loading dock if we retrace our steps. Within ten minutes, I want the cellblock and outside doors unlocked, and the other four wedged open. Also, twenty-four men will be leaving for the truck in twenty minutes. If you impede us in any way, we kill the hostages. Any attempt to sabotage the truck, and they all die."

"Hold on! That's way beyond protocol!" Minero paused. "How about you release a couple of guards first, and then I'd have justification to bypass the rule book."

"*First?* This isn't a negotiation of equals!" he rumbled. "I suppose, if you do it *exactly* as I want, I won't need all of them. I could free Sergeant Jackson when we get to the loading dock."

"That's a start … a good start. It'll take more than ten minutes to get the route cleared, though, but I can get approval within ten."

"You've had plenty of time to line up your team! If your superior isn't on board in *five* minutes, I'll start throwing fingers out the cellblock door!"

"OK … relax. I can probably do five."

"That's better. And from now on, I want to speak directly to the decision maker. Who's in charge?"

Minero paused again, for only a second. "Lieutenant Ted Carson, from Newark Police Headquarters. He should be on the grounds in fifteen minutes."

Righteous smiled. The Panthera had put Jennifer Bolton through so much to get Carson to the top of the leadership assignment list.

✳ ✳ ✳ ✳ ✳

"I've downloaded the prison floorplans and roadmaps of Irvington," Carson said to Detective Youngman, shoving open the back door of police headquarters without breaking his stride. "The rest we're supposed to learn from Captain Revano."

"I guess I'm driving, then," Youngman said.

Carson tossed Youngman the keys before getting into his Malibu, then propped his laptop against the dashboard and debriefed Revano on speakerphone. After hanging up, he studied the prison layout and radioed the SWAT commander. "It's worse than I'd figured. Add another tactical team, and get a helicopter on standby."

Revano called back and introduced Minero, whose baritone boomed over the phone. "Those gunmen barricaded behind a cellblock door … would you mind if we pack them into a box truck for you, with one fewer hostage?"

"They're ready to leave so soon?" Carson replied.

"They—actually the leader, Righteous—demanded safe passage for eight inmates, his team, and the captive guards. I'd been worried that if we got a chance to take out the guys in D block, we'd lose the hostages in the truck, or if we moved against the truck, we'd get a bloodbath in the cellblock. Getting them together seems a win for *us*."

"Revano didn't portray Righteous as generous, or foolish," Carson challenged. "How do you feel about eight prisoners leaving the cellblock?"

"Well, however clever his plan, he miscalculated on that," the warden said. "The sergeant set the time locks, so those cell doors can't come unlocked until an hour after Righteous says he's leaving. I know they hauled some equipment in, but they'd sure need a big can opener. *I* don't think he can get them out."

"He succeeds at everything else but bungles opening the cell doors? Let's assume he gets them out."

"Fine. If he could, moving them to the truck wouldn't bother me. It's still within the prison grounds, so it wouldn't violate prisoner retention, and *we* have the firepower to stop a truck, so I assume Newark PD could obliterate the thing. And he's more likely to release hostages if he's vulnerable."

"Back to presuming him a fool," Carson said. "I'm still worried it's *us* missing something. Is there a good alternative? A hostage rescue you've practiced where the guards survive?"

"If the guards are safe in the control room, we can gas and storm the cellblock. If rioters take hostages with makeshift weapons, we try psych tactics. But intruders with guns, in the control room? Our guys are dead if they're out to kill."

"Thanks, Warden. Give him his transit if we get the officer back. Try for more time, but don't provoke him. And make sure I can communicate from the guard tower—that's where I want to set up base. Then call back when you're done. I want whoever's been studying the videos on the next call, too."

"Sure, Lieutenant."

* * * * *

"I'm missing something if the warden's right, and missing something if he's wrong," Carson muttered before concentrating in silence, oblivious to the passing urban landscape. His ringing cell phone broke his trance.

"All set," Minero announced, "but I couldn't get more time. So we have five minutes to clear the path, and then ten minutes after that before they leave."

"That's still enough. The primary SWAT team is almost there, and we'll have uniforms at the gate before they're out, too."

"Good. We've already opened the hallway doors, and my guards are securing the approaches to the cellblock. We thought it would make a strong showing to put police inside where he can see them, down intersecting hallways along his route."

Carson huffed. "No, that might spook him too early. We want him on the truck, like you said, remember?"

"Got it."

"Got it? Missing it!" Carson stopped himself. He'd promised Captain Burgess he'd work on his tact—but there wasn't time for that now. "There's so much more to do! I bet they're wearing gloves ... transparent ones; but they must've handled the boxes before today. Have a fingerprint team dust that room where they changed into guard clothes—just clear them out when the Panthera leave the cellblock. Also, check for prints at the gate, when the driver signed in, and send me the alias he used. On the way in, they kept the cameras intact and avoided looking at them; on the way back, they might shoot them out. You wanted to use the intersecting hallways? Tell your tech guys to refocus any cameras that are off the route so they can get a view of crossing traffic. I saw five or six good places on the map. Have all your guards put on caps, so we can tell the gun-wielding good guys from the gun-wielding impostors—but of course, have your video team confirm that the frauds are bareheaded when they come out. You find anything that IDs any of those guys, you tell me, pronto. Got it now?"

The line grew silent, his blunt directives no doubt extra humbling for being obvious in hindsight. "Executing your orders right away, Lieutenant," Minero muttered.

8

Righteous perused Lynx's work, one two-foot closed metal box on top of another, and two open cubicles stacked on their right. The bottom cubicle held five putty bricks, including the explosive that had scared the guards out of the control room, with a dozen wires poking into the column. There was a circuit board in the top cubicle, along with a few antennae, two elongated lamps, and three palm-sized components resembling satellite dishes. "Just what we need to keep control of the cellblock after we leave," he said.

Turning toward cell D23, Righteous saw Tiger, wearing heavy gloves and an upturned face shield, and they exchanged nods. Then he walked with Lynx to the line of bound guards and stopped before the youngest-looking one, Officer Breslin. He waved Bobcat over, and motioned "cut" with his finger to get Cheetah to silence the jackhammer loop. Then he grabbed Breslin's shirt with both hands and yanked him forward. "You can be an extra gift to Warden Minero, if you're as smart as a parrot," he snarled. "Are you?"

The captive nodded, and grunted.

"I'm going to free you to speak. But you can only say what I tell you, nothing else, and only whisper. Understood?"

Breslin nodded again.

"Here's your script. It's longer than a sentence, but easy to remember:

> I saw a fancy bomb, danger all around!
> If you go in without instruction—danger all around!
> Edward Carson will get instruction soon, wait your ground."

Righteous repeated the rhyme four times, released his grip, and peeled the tape from the guard's mouth. "Your turn."

Breslin whispered the lines verbatim, but with two fearful pauses. Righteous forced him to repeat it three times, and the hostage hesitated less with each accurate rendition.

"Now, say something else," Righteous directed.

"Why—"

As Breslin uttered his first syllable, Righteous punched him in the gut, doubling him over. Lynx and Bobcat returned him to his feet, and Righteous asked him to repeat the poem. The guard wheezed and gasped, but performed without error. Righteous then instructed, "Now, speak your mind."

"I saw a fancy bomb—"

"Tell me if you're OK."

"—danger all around—"

"Say something else!"

"—If you go in without instruction—"

"Stop! That's enough, you're my parrot. Now, you're coming with me."

The guard turned his head from side to side until Lynx grabbed his arm and pulled him to the right, then pushed him to kneel, ten feet from the bomb. Righteous spoke from behind him while pulling up the blindfold. "You get a peek. I want your warnings to be sincere." Five seconds later, Righteous signaled Tiger, who was in their line of sight left of the bomb. Tiger sprayed chlorine trifluoride on the window of cell door D23, burning the glass and drawing Breslin's focus with the fireball and crackle before Righteous put his blindfold back on.

"Count to yourself," Righteous told the guard. "Every time you hit a hundred, repeat the poem. Once you leave the cellblock, repeat it every count of ten. Clear?"

Breslin nodded.

Righteous turned to Lynx. "He's ready." Then he called "Done!" to Cheetah. Soon Breslin was back in line with his cohorts, all suffering the jackhammer recording. A minute later, Cheetah stuck cotton plugs in Breslin's ears, and did likewise to Jackson. Righteous wanted full control over what those two would report.

* * * * *

Righteous called the command center back. After the first ring, he heard four harmonic tones.

"This is Minero. I've auto-conferenced Lieutenant Carson."

"I'll only need to speak to *you* this time, and won't have to shoot anyone if you've kept your word about the doors."

"The outside one is unlocked, the rest are open, and you have local control for the cellblock door," Minero replied.

"Very well. Our next conversation will be when we leave the cellblock." Righteous hung up and took a deep breath. Though fear, true fear, was difficult to fake, if any group was susceptible to deception, it would be the scared blindfolded guards in the noisy common room. He waved both hands over his head to signal Tiger.

"Get out of here! Get out!" Tiger yelled, starting shouts from the other Panthera louder than the jackhammer sounds, turning the heads of the four hearing captives. The captors' actions matched their cries; they rushed the guards out of the common area. Within a minute, everyone was crammed back into the control room.

Righteous also tried to sound worried. "Shit! We can't go out there *now*! Seal the door!" He surveyed the breathless guards and phoned the warden.

"Minero here, on speakerphone, with Lieutenant Carson patched in as well."

Righteous shifted to outrage, certain the disoriented captives would perceive it as disingenuous. "What's going on! The hallway is lit like the Vegas strip! I want all the utilities along the route shut down immediately! Ten minutes, tops! No electricity, no gas, no water. I don't want to see a light in any hall, smell cooking from the kitchen, or hear a toilet flush."

There was a long silence, which confirmed that his belated, nonsensical request had confounded the officials. He grinned, and waited to seize on any pushback as a provocation. Revano eventually took the bait. "Your route is safe. We can get the lights out over a few minutes, but we'll need more time to get to the plumbing valves."

Minero and Carson both tried to intervene over the line, to no avail. Righteous laid the handset turned up on the console, letting the phone pick up the sound of Cougar taping the seams around the door, and then his gunshot.

"Great plans have great costs," he'd told his team. His true timeline included shooting one of the guards to prove his resolve, angling the gun to minimize the risk of a ricochet. He returned to the phone. "The groom-to-be, Sergeant Jackson, has been shot … through the arm. I can stabilize him for thirty minutes. If you meet my demands without delay, his prognosis will be good. Are any more gunshots necessary?"

"This is Carson. The warden is sending his best men to shut everything down. I'm sure it's just a few main junctions and you'll be good to go."

"Confirming that," Minero added. "Striving for five minutes, but definitely within ten."

"Righteous," Carson said, "we'll owe you one if you send Jackson out now. Whatever risk you're taking with his life isn't worth it. You're getting what you want."

"You now seem to have nine minutes left to comply with my demands," Righteous said. "Our conversation is over until then."

* * * * *

Carson received the incoming call as soon as he disconnected from Righteous. "Private line, Lieutenant," Minero announced.

"I'll skip the obvious, Warden." There wasn't time to rant about Jackson getting shot. "You were sincere about the five minutes?"

"Very. I can cut the electricity by zones from here; that's standard riot control. Gas is easy to shut off, too, by design. If there's a leak, we can't exactly have the inmates evacuate the facility. And Revano is signaling that maintenance is working on the water."

"I can understand wanting the lights out, so his team can't be targeted. Any idea about the gas and water?"

"Just some stupid things. If they hope to blast their way into another cellblock on their way out, they might be worried about igniting a gas line? If they're going to start a fire, we'd be incapacitated without water?"

"Yeah, it doesn't make sense." Carson paused to think. "He didn't ask for this earlier, right?"

"Right. He yelled as if we'd deceived him on that, but he hadn't asked about gas or water until a minute ago, and lights he'd wanted *on*."

"Righteous is too careful to forget asking for that. This can't be about the utilities." Carson paused again, then his eyes widened. "I'll call you back," he said before hanging up. Then he turned to Youngman. "Any guess why the Panthera would want to delay their own escape?"

9

Ted Carson plodded up three flights of stairs to the top of the guard tower, now his command center. The room had seats and electronics for four, and a 360-degree view. He envisioned it usually being a boring hellhole, guards watching the side of a building to make sure nothing was happening. But soon, it would become the grandstand of his standoff with the Panthera, the truck merely seventy yards away. With numbers and time on his side, he should only need restraint and patience to get the hostages free.

Unless …

He called Minero. "Do you think Righteous wants to die?"

He'd seen the distraught and the disturbed, primed to take out victims at the slightest provocation, leaving no choice but a rapid, deadly confrontation.

The warden hesitated before answering. "I think 'no.' But breaking in here, with guns … he's certainly *willing* to die…. I guess I can't *guarantee* we're not dealing with a reckless lunatic."

"I can't either…. Let's keep trying to win back a few guys at a time. Can you get here before I have to call him back?"

"With two minutes to spare."

* * * * *

"Let me guess … defensive tackle?" Carson greeted the hefty, six-foot-two warden.

"Linebacker, actually. These thirty extra pounds," Minero said, patting his belly, "I blame on my mother-in-law, for teaching my wife to cook pastelón."

"Afraid I can't relate," Carson said, raising and turning his left hand to display a bare ring finger.

"Well, I can't place your sport," Minero remarked, scanning him up and down. "Too top-heavy for cross-country … five ten's usually too short for varsity hoops … not beat-up enough for wrestling. Tennis?"

"Closer the first time—track. Ran the 440." He looked at his watch. "Shall we?"

Minero nodded, and connected them to D block.

"You've met my demands?" Righteous answered, his bass resonating from the console.

"The utilities are off," Carson said, "and the doors are still open. But now, you have to reconsider sending Sergeant Jackson out early."

"We'll be heading out with him soon enough!"

"We have EMTs standing by. The stress could be making him more vulnerable than you think—"

"Not my concern! This plays out my way, not yours! And to make sure of that, *I'm* keeping control of the cellblock after we leave. We've armed a powerful explosive, which we're controlling electronically. If we're assaulted, I'll set it off, and you'll need more undertakers than EMTs. If you open the cellblock door before you're told, the bomb goes off. I'll leave an extra witness for you in the hallway, as proof."

Carson muted the phone and turned to Minero. "I don't like him leaving the cellblock rigged to blow, but I can't push back while he's threatening the guards. Our bomb squad *is* good at overriding signaling devices."

The warden shook his head. "Through a sixteen-inch double-cinder-block wall?"

"I don't know." Carson paused. "Think about evacuating the adjoining areas. And it sounds like he's grabbed an extra prisoner to vouch for the danger; keep some guards ready for that handoff."

Minero nodded, and Carson reactivated the phone. "Understood. We enter the block only after you say."

"Once we leave the cellblock," Righteous said, "I'll use Sergeant Reiley's radio to contact you, channel C. The signal interference at the dock was temporary."

"Righteous, I want to keep working together on getting what you want, but you'll have to show some flexibility if you keep throwing in these twists."

"Hope as you choose."

* * * * *

Righteous stood at the cellblock door, growing nervous for the first time that day. *He* was now the outlaw. The killer. The *target*. He'd be exposed in the corridors, exposed on the loading dock. Exposed and outgunned. He looked down to make sure his hands weren't shaking, then waved his men out.

The first eight left in pairs, each accompanied by a blindfolded guard. Illumination came from small shoe-mounted LEDs to avoid presenting a lethal target.

Righteous left last with Tiger, pushing Breslin and Jackson. Tiger walked Jackson four steps down the hall, then stopped and held a gun to his nose. Righteous shoved Breslin backward and removed his earplugs. "You're in front of the cellblock door; this is where you'll stay." Then he dropped a small metallic cylinder down the guard's shirt. "That's a microphone. Don't deviate from the script, not one word. You get ten seconds between repetitions—don't take longer. Even out here, the bomb would shred your flesh if you test me or if that door opens. Understood?" Breslin bobbed his head five times. Righteous joined Tiger to share Jackson as a shield for the walk to the truck, glancing back once to see his parrot remaining propped against the door, lips moving.

* * * * *

Carson watched videos of the intruders' egress on a monitor in the tower. "Overkill, hiding behind the guards," he said to Minero. "The bomb sets them off-limits. They're cavalier about the cameras, though … maybe they're disguised?"

"Maybe … probably."

Carson turned to the speakerphone. "Officer Canfield, keep following these sixteen, but also toggle in shots of the eight others, the prisoners going with them."

"Sir … this is everyone," Canfield said. "The door's closed, and only sixteen people left, all dressed as guards, without hats. And six of them seem to be real guards."

Carson exchanged quizzical looks with Minero, then stared out the window. *More tricks! But I can't get outsmarted now … not now!* "Are you sure?"

"Certain about the head count, Lieutenant," Canfield replied. "And the ten without blindfolds, as best we can tell, match ten who came in from the truck. No one here thinks they're inmates, and the one who most resembles a guard … we don't think he's Chet Graceman. I have Breslin in full view now … even with the blindfold I'm sure it's him. And Jackson faced the first hallway camera, and four of us agree it's him. From what we can make out, it's Reiley, Scolaro, Winzer,

Pittman, then Jackson. I mean, Warden, just check that thicket on Winzer's head. Who else could that be?"

Carson disconnected the call and faced the screen as he spoke. "The escape that wasn't?"

"Most escapes fail," the warden said. "The time locks—"

"Yeah, they didn't bring the right can opener. So they hacked your requisition system, outfitted their truck with radio jammers, and brought light-up shoes ... but didn't count on the cells being locked?"

"Of course they *realized* it; they underestimated the challenge."

"They're not acting like they've been stumped: Righteous sounds confident, and they're moving smoothly in tandem. I don't think they've been forced to deviate from their plan." He turned to Minero. "I think they got what they came for ... and it wasn't to break out eight prisoners."

"There's *nothing ... else ... here*. I trust my team, and I trust the locks. How about we agree that that truck isn't going anywhere, and we nail down the rest later?"

Carson huffed, and picked up his radio. "Team one: Approach Officer Breslin, but do not open the cellblock door under any circumstances. SWAT team: They're continuing toward the receiving room. Acquire shooting lines when they emerge, then await my orders. All other teams: Continue standing down."

He turned back to the video, cringing each time Jackson stumbled. Eventually, the wounded guard and his minders reached the receiving room. The coffee-haired one who'd shoved Breslin guided Jackson to lean against a wall, then continued across the room to the loading dock door and checked his watch.

"They're coming out!" Carson radioed, striding to the window with Minero. "No shooting without my order!" A minute later, the timekeeper emerged, scouting the police snipers aiming at him from the roof, and the guard tower. After a moment, he seemed to smirk, then spoke into a radio, or perhaps a phone, and an accomplice emerged from the back of the truck. Then he waved, and the Panthera shuffled in a tight mass across the dock with the hostages. A blond captor removed Reiley's blindfold and held him, squinting toward the tower, for five seconds, then forced him onto the truck. The Panthera continued posing and stowing the guards, until only the shortest gunman and Jackson remained on the dock.

Righteous radioed from the cargo cube. "Lieutenant! Nobody is to get any closer to the truck or the loading dock. We'll free Sergeant Jackson momentarily, as agreed."

Carson nodded to Minero, and the warden stepped back to a phone. "Medical team to receiving!" he ordered.

Jackson kneeled on the dock. His captor cut the tape around his wrists, then scurried into the truck and clunked the door down. The sergeant bobbed his head as if counting, then used his right hand to peel the tape from his mouth and throw off his blindfold. He rose, trudged across the dock, and was helped into the receiving room by two women wearing medical scrubs.

"If they … no, *when* they stabilize Jackson," Carson radioed, "bring him here. Send Breslin here as well. Everyone deployed inside the prison except team one, reinforce the perimeter around the truck."

"Lieutenant, this is Officer Lee. Breslin is acting strange. He's not answering our questions and won't move away from the cellblock door. And he keeps saying your name and repeating some warning about a bomb."

"Ease off!" Carson ordered. "Bomb squad, get to that guard! See if he's booby-trapped, and bring him to me in one piece."

"Lieutenant! Breslin's reaching for the radio," Lee said. "I'm putting him on."

Breslin's desperate, dry voice came over the radio. "I saw a fancy bomb, danger all around. If you go in without instruction—danger all around. Edward Carson will get instruction soon, wait your ground."

Lee soon added, "That's what he's been saying since we got here."

"Tell him I won't enter the cellblock until I have instructions."

A few seconds later, Lee reported, "He nodded back, Lieutenant!"

"Ask if he thinks his captors are listening in on him."

"He nodded again."

"Bomb squad, sweep for transmitters as well—the kid thinks he's on the verge of being blown up. They want to make sure that door stays—"

"Lieutenant Carson," Righteous called over the prison radio, "time to discuss our future."

Carson switched hands. "I'm here, still awaiting word on Sergeant Jackson."

"You should also listen to Officer Breslin, if you haven't already. He'll be useful for persuading your superiors to accommodate my next request."

"Not so fast on the requests! Not after the gunshot and lying about the small crew leaving the cellblock! I want to keep working with you, Righteous, but your plan has to include some concessions to me now."

"Don't presume to fathom the nature of my plan! There's reason for all I've done and all that's happened!" Righteous paused, then returned to his subdued deep monotone. "We're leaving soon, flying out of the country. That means another law enforcement branch will take charge of pursuit, and you'll be staying here, investigating the crime."

"You're still jumping ahead. Driving away with six prisoners and eight guards isn't a request we'd take lightly."

"Yes, I was jumping ahead. You have an important role to play, and I wanted to prepare you early. We went to a lot of trouble to make sure you'd be here today."

Minero shot Carson an accusatory look, and he blushed and shook his head. He didn't have time to defend himself, or ponder whether Righteous had actually chosen him, how he might have done it, and why. "It must be uncomfortable in there. Send out a couple more guards, and I can send in cold drinks."

"Our truck is leaving for Pennsylvania in twenty minutes," Righteous said. "We'll deal with the local traffic and the short stint on the Parkway, but don't create any surprises. Once we reach Interstate 78, you'll set up a rolling blockade so it's clear for one mile behind us, and you'll block the on-ramps as we approach to keep space ahead of us. And no helicopters, either. When we're ten miles from the border, you'll divert any traffic off at the Route 22 exit, giving us an empty bridge over the river. Clear all police from Lehigh Valley International Airport, Allentown Queen City Airport, and Braden Airpark, and don't sabotage any planes or equipment there. In return, we'll make a stop in New Jersey to release one guard, unharmed, and you'll get another two at the airfield. The alternative—if you'd call it that—is visiting guards in the morgue."

Carson turned to Minero, off-radio. "Three more guards for us …"

Minero shook his head. "Sacrosanct."

"Prisoner retention should be an ideal, not a stricture. How hard is it to track a truck in daylight? You bus them out to court and the hospital sometimes, right?"

"Shackled and supervised … completely different. And you know that."

Carson pressed the "Transmit" button. "I'll try with the higher-ups, Righteous, but asking to fly around with those convicts will make it tough."

"I'm sure that would've made it hard. But we're not bringing any inmates along."

Carson smiled at the nodding warden. "You'll prove that?" he radioed.

"When the time comes."

"*That* simplifies things. But I'll still need clearance—your demands cover a lot of geography."

"I haven't left you a choice," Righteous said. "But I have left you twenty minutes."

10

Carson briefed the governor and Police Director Arden on a conference call with Minero, then presented his analysis. "The long drive helps *us*. Time wears more heavily on the criminals, and he's promised to release more captives along the way—we've already got two back of the four they took from the cellblock. We just need to make sure we don't lose the truck or let them sneak off it—which should be child's play with the right airplane." He nodded at the warden.

"Minero speaking. They aren't taking any inmates out, so we're not waiving prisoner retention. We can focus on what's best for my men. I don't see anything good coming from the guards being confined with a dozen armed thugs in my loading bay."

"This is Arden. If we coordinate this, the bastards won't stand a better chance on the road than at the pen. We shift truck pursuit to the State Police, and maybe add aerial from the National Guard, like Carson said. The headline will be, 'Locals save two guards, Staties rescue the rest.'"

"No disrespect, Lieutenant plus two," the governor challenged, "but if you're underestimating them, will letting them go make it worse, or much worse?"

Carson bit his lip, and took a deep breath. "No disrespect back, Governor," he forced out flatly, "but even if I'm wrong about the Panthera, in a close quarters hostage situation, making the captors feel less desperate is paramount. And the best of law enforcement can track a truck, and everyone on it, ninety-nine times out of a hundred. Even if they somehow slip away, we'd just need to catch one, and we milk enough information from him to bring in the whole gang within a month."

"So we're taking terrorists with no chance of escape and giving them a small chance, speculating that'll make them less volatile around the guards?"

Carson clenched his fists, but before he could strike back and hang himself, Arden interjected. "Will, there's always some chance, but the lieutenant was citing worst-case scenario. We get State Police resources, that truck isn't leaving our sight, and neither would any planes at those airports. Just maybe they thought of something new, some Hail Mary where a few evade the sensors and we catch them in the woods the next day, that's what I'm hearing. Versus a bloodbath as the alternative."

"Just looking at all sides, Zach," the governor replied, remaining silent for a moment afterward. "I'm sure someone at State Police can track a getaway truck; I'll get the ball rolling with TEAMS."

Carson gave a reassuring nod to Minero and whispered, "Technical Emergency and Mission Specialists—rescue experts."

"Lieutenant Carson," the governor continued, "that leaves you and the warden to deal with the mess at the prison. If you discover anything useful, pass it on—you still know this guy better than anyone else."

I know the scheming bastard knew I wouldn't be leading the pursuit, he mused.

After Carson hung up, Officer Lee reported that Officer Breslin was microphone-free and warning about motion sensors and antennae on the bomb, and Director Arden forwarded the contact number for State Police Captain Dee Wilcox, who would take charge of pursuing the Panthera after they left the compound.

Then Carson radioed Righteous. "We're clearing the final hurdles here. Please advise on releasing the prisoners."

"Six convicts will leave here shortly—alive, if they obey us, or shot and tossed out if they don't. After they've cleared the dock, three more men will exit, two going to the cab, and the third, Officer Pittman, to the guard tower. Logic dictates that's where you and the warden are now, right?"

"That's right."

"Pittman's seen that the men remaining on the truck aren't prisoners. The warden will have three minutes to question him and clear us to leave—the warden alone. You and I have another important matter to discuss."

Carson turned to Minero. "Another guard!"

"Another guard."

"And that disdain for the inmates … an exaggeration to scare them off the truck?"

"I suppose."

Carson returned to the prison radio. "Give me a minute to alert my team about the movements, then go ahead."

He radioed his units to hold their fire, then spoke to Minero. "They probably didn't put Pittman's blindfold back on when they forced him into the truck, and a disguise will only go so far."

Minero nodded. "You get to really know the cons doing this job—how they look from any angle, the faces they make, how they talk. He'll know if they're trying to sneak one out."

* * * * *

Righteous sighted the convicts on the cramped truck, one after the other, with his Beretta. *Temptation, temptation!* he thought. Then he rolled up the door. "Anyone who doesn't march straight into the building gets a bull's-eye to the *cajones*," he said.

His colleagues uncuffed one inmate at a time. The first five left silently, some casting angry stares; the Viper was bold enough to speak. "Hey, if you're gonna off Screw Winzer there, let me save you a bullet." Righteous shook his head and lowered his aim. "Alright, alright!" the tattooed prisoner responded, scuttling off the truck.

Righteous leaned out and watched the convicts reach the receiving room. Then he donned a headset and forced Pittman, hands still taped behind his back, and Reiley, hands cuffed in front of him, in the opposite direction along the dock. The guards stopped and turned when the cargo door rattled closed behind them, then continued until they reached the far wall. Righteous pointed down the stairs with his gun, and Pittman leaned backward against the handrail and eased down sideways. Reiley and Righteous followed, and the three of them walked to the passenger door.

"The warden is waiting to speak with you in the guard tower," Righteous told Pittman, nodding toward the structure. The guard wasted no time starting away from his captor, his torso bobbing side to side as he reached a jogging pace.

"I know you work in the Prisoner Transport Unit on Thursdays," Righteous said to Reiley, "and I'd rather keep our driver in back. Go in ahead of me, then climb over the console to the driver's seat."

Reiley maneuvered as instructed, grabbing the steering wheel with both hands for support, then straightened up and looked at the dashboard. "I'm licensed for buses and trucks, but mostly I drive vans," he protested.

Righteous took the passenger seat and closed the door. "Just concentrate on the driving, and don't try to be a hero, and you'll be fine. There is one precaution," he said, pointing to a handcuff dangling from the steering wheel. "Cuff your left hand to the wheel. I'll free your right hand when you need it. We've had some dry runs; you'll be able to turn safely if you take it slow."

Reiley compressed the shackle, producing five clicks.

Righteous nodded, then pressed his microphone before speaking through the headset. "Cab secure," he advised Lynx. Then he picked up the prison radio and stared at the figure in the guard tower window. "Lieutenant, you seem to be alone."

"The warden's with Pittman," Carson replied.

"But the sergeant's here next to me, so I won't be as direct as if we were speaking privately."

"Whatever you see fit."

"I've been honest in delivering everything I've promised you, and will continue to be. But I've been misleading in other ways, for the greater good. I think you care about the world, and understand that actions have consequences. I believe sometimes a noble individual would do the right thing, make a difficult choice, where a group might not."

"Releasing the guards would be the right thing."

"That's not what I'm driving at! I have a different agenda. It includes you, and requires you to understand that I don't hold any animus toward you. So I'll share that you left the office alone on Monday at six, went home to 152 Grand Elm Street, then left forty minutes later to pick up takeout at Ancient Wok."

"Listen, jerk!" Carson said. "Instead of following me around then hiding behind those hostages, let's meet face-to-face."

"Easy, Lieutenant. Read between the lines: you were vulnerable to me, but I had no interest in hurting you. And I still don't. If you follow *all* of my instructions, you'll live through the day."

"Free the guards if you want to make a peace offering, Righteous."

"The greater good, Lieutenant. Here are your instructions: You'll open the gate in five minutes. Wherever you go afterward, make sure you have reception on your police cell phone. You'll open the door to cellblock D only after hearing the phrase 'restless and waiting.' Only *you* are to enter the cellblock, not a bomb squad expert—we've configured a challenge to the disarming sequence that you alone can meet. And don't try sending in some remote-controlled stand-in— we've employed a tactile lock to prevent that. If you bring in a second person before you've disarmed the device, it goes off. No one will be harmed if you comply, but there'll be devastation if you don't." He turned off the seized radio, then decided to sling it onto the dashboard to impress that these demands as well were nonnegotiable.

* * * * *

Carson struggled with the latest communication. *I'm helpful to this madman? What "greater good" comes from guns and explosives? He's delusional, on top of everything else.*

Minero and Pittman entered the room. "My man did a fine job," the warden bragged. "The hostages on the truck are healthy, and they're all certainly guards. All of the captors are made-up, but none of them are D block prisoners."

Carson nodded. "Do you feel they'd get violent if provoked?" he asked the guard.

Pittman lowered his eyes. "The gunshot in the control room ... so close by. It could've been any of us ... and it could've been worse."

"Officer Jackson is going to make a full recovery. Any idea who they were after?"

"They kept us from seeing and hearing much. There was almost always this jackhammer sound ... and sometimes a drill. But it felt organized for the longest time ... like when we moved, we moved together. Then all of a sudden, chaos ... scrambling into the control room, and it sounded like they were taping the door shut. Something went terribly wrong ... no way they got what they were after." Pittman paused. "It felt like we all could've died."

Carson nodded at Minero, who led Pittman out.

"Did I miss anything?" Minero asked when he returned.

"*I'm* going to disarm the bomb."

"And the bomb squad will handle the detective work?"

Carson shrugged. "He's rigged it that way. Apparently, I've made an impression."

"Hopefully the *right* impression. Seriously, he could—"

"I know ... I know." Carson swallowed hard. "There'll be time for worrying about myself later."

Carson walked to the speakerphone and called Captain Wilcox. "I might've overpromised—I made it sound easy to catch them if they scuttle off the truck."

"'Easy' isn't too far off," she said. "With the plane we're borrowing and the infrared sensors, they'd stand out like flamingos on a ski slope. And we'll have a battalion on the interstate behind them, and dozens of troopers along the route. Plus a bomb squad, just in case, thanks to your heads-up."

Carson pressed "Mute," and turned to the warden, nodding. "She's got this. Open the gate." Then he picked up the prison radio to introduce Righteous to the woman he was sure would oversee the Panthera's capture.

11

After repeating his travel demands to Wilcox, Righteous instructed Reiley. "Drive five miles over the speed limit, when you can. No needless swerving or jerky stops, and no accidents."

Reiley nodded. "OK."

"I'm going to free your right hand," Righteous narrated as he released the cuff, keeping his gun pointed at the guard with his right hand.

Reiley shook his freed wrist a few times. "What if that open loop catches the steering wheel?"

Righteous looked at the dangling end. "Lock it to your left arm, higher up than the other two." Reiley complied, two clicks securing the chain away from the wheel. Righteous leaned back diagonally against the cab door and his seat. "Drive to Interstate 78, westbound— the route home, if I'm not mistaken." The guard scowled at the privacy intrusion; Righteous raised his gun a few inches. "Go now!"

Reiley started the truck and drove past the thick stone walls and down the exterior driveway, then turned right onto Millhead Street. Righteous called Lynx through his headset. "Precisely 10:20—God couldn't have planned it better."

As they proceeded, Righteous searched ahead and in the mirror from time to time, but always returned his gaze to Reiley, reading the guard's body language: nervous eyes darting between road and handcuff at every turn, making sure he wouldn't twist the links; shoulders relaxing when he reached I-78; and blinking as he passed Exit 40. "Hands on the wheel, and you'll be with Justine for dinner," Righteous assured him.

Sixty miles from the prison, Righteous pulled a cell phone from the center console. Lynx's wizardry would render Wilcox's interception of the call useless: the phone would register as being the

Attorney General's, and records would show the number reached to be unassigned. "Chief, it's 11:26. Escape is a platinum medal. Advise you signal Carson." He knew it was odd to refer to the time as "11:26" rather than "11:30" or "almost 11:30." Odd was memorable. Memorable was good.

Then he called Wilcox. "The road's been clear; I'll hold up my end. Have the troopers stop traffic after the Pittstown exit, and we'll stop to release Sergeant Scolaro."

Righteous pocketed the phone, then pulled a metallic-and-glass egg from the console and mounted it onto the dashboard. "Cab camera visual and audio check."

A reply crackled from the device: "Clear picture of road and driver. Audio OK."

He spoke to Reiley. "Our first stop is on the shoulder half a mile past the Route 173 Service Road exit. I'm going to the cargo area; we'll watch you through that and give you directions. Follow them, and don't roll down your window or try to signal with the wipers or lights … I'd hate to have to stop the truck from back there and shoot you."

"Water," the guard uttered. "Bathroom. Please."

"You'll manage awhile," Righteous said. "Here, on the right. Stop at that mile marker." Reiley pulled over, and Righteous holstered his gun and disembarked, swatting the roof before climbing down, and headed back. He pulled out the phone, and after a minute, Leopard rolled the door open.

Leopard, Jaguar, and Righteous all had to help the bound guard to a standing position on the ground. "Stay upright, here on the shoulder, and you'll be safe for your rescuers," Righteous said. Then the Panthera climbed into the Can. "Regain course," Righteous called to Reiley through the dashboard egg. He looked back over to Leopard— *it couldn't be*; for the first time in the year they'd been working together, he saw Leopard's teeth when he smiled, and a dimple.

* * * * *

Leopard had seemed, to Righteous, even more deeply afflicted by grief than the other recruits, beyond his persistent aura of despair. It took three meetings as Tom Jefferson before he decided that Leopard would be up to the job. "You were really close to your brother," he'd prompted at their second dinner.

"We were tight growing up. I only made a few good friends at Princeton, through what became the Black Student Union, but nothing measured up to what Floyd and I had."

"The professionals say you end up reaching acceptance, if you address it right—"

"—and that hate consumes the hater … I know. But I'm dealing with loss *and* a lack of justice. That's why I'm talking to your group."

"The Victims' Surrogacy is certainly looking to change things."

"The whole system needs fixing. The prosecutor wasn't even allowed to mention Gary Ronmeade's nine—*nine*—prior assaults. The witnesses said that deaf kid was just crushed into him by the crowd, and signaled an apology with his hands. But Ronmeade just went batshit and yelled, 'No one disrespects Tall G!' and shot him.… Then Floyd didn't do anything, he'd just come out of the Movieplex and turned toward the gunshot. 'What're you lookin' at?' … that's the last thing Floyd heard."

"Society says the life sentence is appropriate punishment."

"Sentencing … That asshole fired his lawyer when he was convicted, and at sentencing, he just turns from the judge, looks at my mom and me … and says …" Leopard turned away and rubbed his eyes, then looked back at Righteous. "I'd thought, when I'd heard 'guilty,' that Ronmeade was done being able to hurt me.… But he just says, 'If they'd left me alone, I'd've left them alone.' Like he blamed Floyd, like he's living his life thinking *he's* the just one. I can't bear that … I can't. Most days …" Leopard turned away again. "I'm sorry. You said getting personal helps with your lobbying, but I'm sure you didn't mean this."

"You don't need to apologize. The apology is owed to you."

* * * * *

Righteous had attributed Leopard losing his engineering fellowship at GE and treading water as an entry-level technician at the Salem Nuclear Generating Station to the stress and possibly depression over losing his brother. His sensitive job gave Righteous an ideal opportunity to test Lynx's skills; Leopard reported back three months before the prison break-in.

"You're amazing!" Leopard said to Lynx. "Those network firewalls are supposed to be impermeable." Then he turned to Righteous. "It seems when you get a warning at work, they put it in writing." He held up a report and read: "You waited until the containment door was shut before you entered the next control sequence, but you failed to await confirmation that it shut properly."

"You're *certain* that was him?" Righteous asked, tipping his head toward Lynx.

"I *never* sequence without a confirmation. Slow is how everything works there."

Righteous turned to Lynx and smiled. "All right. If you're sure they won't catch you, lay the groundwork to hack back in, and for the police schedules."

"I learned my lesson with Cablevision," Lynx replied. "If they suspect anyone, it won't be me."

* * * * *

As the truck cruised toward Pennsylvania, Leopard directed activity in the Can. First came re-blindfolding the guards; he didn't want them to see his masterpiece, not yet. Then he and Bobcat unfastened the sheet metal divider and rolled it up to open the front of the cargo area, exposing three tight rows of high-backed plastic seats on a wheeled platform facing the right side of the truck. The carrier's design was inspired by the Mountain Rocket, his favorite roller coaster; but he took care to keep its weight down, excepting the pressurized tanks filled with salt water under the rear seats. A web of tubes rose up from the base, connecting centrally overhead within a sturdy two-foot cube constituting a partial roof. He directed ten of the Panthera into their seats, then took one in the back row for himself.

Leopard checked his watch. "Five minutes!" he called out. "Secure harnesses!" While Leopard strapped himself in, the last standing Panthera moved about the front of the cargo bay, removing retaining pins from the truck's roof and sidewalls. Satisfied, Leopard raised his thumb, then leaned back, closed his eyes, and cracked a dimpled smile, reliving Gary Ronmeade's execution that morning.

* * * * *

Righteous contacted Reiley: "Expect detour signs as you approach the Delaware River—those are to keep traffic from *us*. You'll drive through, slowing to forty for the bridge."

Then he called Wilcox. "Sergeant Brinnell has taken ill. Keep all traffic off the bridge—both directions—and we'll stop to release him there, instead of at the airport. You'll still be my contact in Pennsylvania?"

"Still me," she responded, "loaned under governor's orders this morning."

Righteous ended the call, and felt Reiley brake the truck. The camera showed them approaching the crossing. "Sergeant Reiley, keep slowing down and get in the right lane. You'll see that some boisterous fans painted a large Nittany Lion on the Pennsylvania side of the bridge. Stop about twenty feet before the mascot, close enough to the side that only a bicyclist would try passing, and idle the engine."

When the truck stopped, Righteous returned to the intercom. "The key for your handcuffs has been taped to the roof, over the passenger seat, for the past twenty miles. You can't reach it, but your rescuers will arrive soon. Just remember this sequence: You'll hear a racket for about thirty seconds, then there'll be an obvious finale. Remain seated until then, for your safety. Then you'll have seven minutes before the truck explodes. If you wave the police over, they'll have time to free you and move everyone a safe distance from the vehicle."

The video showed Reiley struggling against the links. Righteous grinned, then moved his hand to a switch. "To Leopard, our own da Vinci!" he called as he started the machinery. Two winches drew a series of cables overhead, opening the accordion roof section that had covered the front of the cargo bay. The front halves of the sidewalls fell outward, but were hinged to the floor; the right half landed flat on the side of the bridge, while the left one crashed onto the road. Simultaneously, the modified hydraulic system for the truck's liftgate lowered the ends of three steel beam sections that were pivot-mounted under the truck, forming a tripod to blunt the vehicle against lateral movement. Four sharp beeps signaled that preparation was complete, and each of the villains crossed his arms to clutch his harness.

* * * * *

Captain Wilcox stood in the middle of the communications center, surrounded by eight TEAMS support officers at desks configured in a horseshoe, fixated on the mounted screen at the front of the room and the red thermal images from the newly exposed cargo hold. "That's at least ten people, under that spider-looking thing ... probably their whole gang," she said. "I don't know why they aren't—" Suddenly the screen flashed bursts of color. Four short-lived parallel yellow lines showed fluid spouting leftward, shooting across the road, thrusting the human heat trails rightward and off the bridge. Their images were quickly subsumed by a large crimson glow appearing as a perfect circle, like a hot air balloon over their heads. An instant later came a single heat track, cross-angled against the device's path. Then flares sputtered off the contraption, distorting the heat map for a few seconds; but it became clear that the circle was collapsing. Within moments, she could make out human heat images again, swirling downstream as a mass. "They're in the river!"

"They couldn't have survived *that* plunge," Officer McMurphy said.

Wilcox called Righteous. "No answer, of course." The bodies soon stopped moving, amassed against a pillar and making one large heat signature, indistinct in its center but with recognizable body shapes along the periphery. Reiley's right arm emerging from the truck made its own distinctive red trail.

"Move in!" Wilcox radioed. "All units move in! Get those hostages off the truck! Pursuit 1 and 2, work your way to the riverbank, home state side, north of the bridge." Then she turned to her next-in-command, Sergeant Detmueller. "Find out what boats we have, ours and any local PDs, Jersey and Penn sides both. Maybe Park Service, too. I want verification there are twelve dead criminals in that water, ASAP."

"Computer confirms accelerated heat loss since they hit the water," McMurphy reported. "Those are definitely bodies."

"That bright circle before—they thought they could drift away?"

"That could be a canvas covering some of them."

"Another escape plan foiled by physics," Wilcox said. "I still want confirmation there are a dozen."

"Captain Wilcox!" came a voice over the radio. "Sergeant Price, on the bridge. Hostage indicates explosion in five minutes!"

Evidence burn! she thought. "Get everyone off the truck, then get out of there! Rescue, then abandon!" She met the worried eyes of her team members and put the radio down. "Five minutes is plenty of time to get everyone to safety." She waited for a few nods. "So much for recon from the bridge, though."

- 12 -

"SWAT team released!" Lieutenant Carson radioed as the box truck rumbled past the gate. "Bomb squad and team one, remain at D block! Arriving fifteen minutes." He hustled down the guard tower stairs, then barked orders as he walked to the loading dock with a winded Warden Minero. "Youngman, boost that area so my cell phones work, and set up tracing and recording on my police line. Rogers, keep in touch with Wilcox's team—when they release that next guard, I want to know what he saw in the cellblock."

Having studied the prison layout, Carson retraced the Panthera's path to D block without having to ask for directions. When he got there, he put his fingers on the cold metal door. "Is Vertsen still in D?"

"*He's* one of yours?" Minero asked. "Yeah, he's in there ... and dozens almost as vile."

Carson shook his head. "First it was my job to put them in here, then I had to keep Righteous from busting them out, and now I have to stop his bomb from killing them." He shook his head again. "But somehow, that makes sense to me; it all seems right. You have to believe in the system, I guess."

"I'm sure Newark can survive with one Boy Scout on the force."

Carson shrugged, then waved over an auburn-haired man carrying a bomb suit, NPD lieutenant August Bell. "I think Righteous wants us to trust him, to keep us from rushing the truck. So I'm inclined to wait here for his signal."

"The alternative?" Minero asked.

Carson turned to Bell. "What's the best *you* could do, Marine?"

"*Semper fi*," he replied, "best ordnance disposal training in America. The guy had an hour to rig this up, so I'd need about ten minutes to check this prison-gauge door before I consider opening it. Then I have to worry about motion sensors, and whether he picked video readers or went microwave or infrared. I guess him being able to change from no one allowed in now, to exactly one person goes in later, rules out the basic systems. But even best case, it's slow—I mean snail slow, not just my-grandfather-in-a-walker slow—and still figure a one-in-five chance the sensor triggers anyway. That's why I'd wear this," he said, lifting his arms. "But I'd rather be behind a barricade."

"Sorry, Lieutenant. Sounds like we obey, and wait," Minero said.

"Get that guard Breslin over here," Carson called to Youngman. "I want to hear anything he might know about the bomb firsthand." Then he turned to Bell. "Give me a crash course, what I should know if they did everything right, and what I should know if the thing is held together with gum."

"Lesson one: let's move away from this door," Bell said, nodding down the hallway. "Lesson two," he said as they walked, "detonators." He began a lecture, and after every minute, he'd repeat, "But if they hadn't blocked the window, I'd have taught you everything you'd need to know by now." When Breslin approached, Bell muttered, "I bet he doesn't remember what I need to know—a picture would be worth a thousand words."

Considering he'd seen the device for only a few harried seconds, the guard proved apt at broad descriptions—"over it looked like two plastic tubes with frosted lighthouse beacons on top"—but he couldn't answer Bell's specific questions about the wires and the battery. Most baffling were the two closed metal boxes aside the explosives column. When Bell finished, Carson released Breslin.

"A picture would've been worth *ten* thousand of those words," Bell griped.

"Next break-in, I'll make sure they kidnap you instead," Carson said.

"Just leaves that many more permutations to teach you."

"Before that, Gus: could they have built it so if I meet some challenge—maybe typing the name of my kindergarten teacher into a keyboard—I'll be told an *easy* way to disarm the bomb?"

"With computers, easy is easy, if *that's* what they want. Typing the right name itself could disarm the thing, and we all make an early lunch. But most nutcase bomb makers don't want it to be easy—they want to turn you into red mist."

Carson let the lesson continue: despite Gus's endless complaining and delving into nuances that were impossible to keep straight, the talking took the edge off the wait. Then, at 11:30, his police cell phone rang.

The screen was filled with asterisks, artful camouflage from Righteous. He smirked, and brought the phone up for a few seconds.

"Did your phone lick your ear?" Minero asked.

"It … wasn't him. 'Restless and waiting,' but not deep at all … just an average-toned rasp." Carson huffed. "There's a new one to catch, a kingpin, besides the twelve on the truck."

"First things first, Ted," Bell said.

Carson nodded. "Twenty-five pounds' worth."

Bell started to loosen a strap on the bomb suit. "Gus," Carson said, "realistically … an amateur versus C4?"

"If he's after you, you probably won't see it coming … and this won't save you."

"I'd rather be mobile, then. And he said something about a tactile lock."

"You can change your mind about trusting him, though," Minero said.

"I can … but I haven't," Carson replied. "Mostly, I haven't."

"OK," Bell said, dropping the suit and pulling a pair of goggles from the helmet. "The microlens is here. It's wired to record everything on this chip, behind your ear—but nothing wireless, not around the bomb."

Carson nodded again, put the goggles on, and plodded down the hall. Alone. He felt his palms sweat. The key card panel flashed green—*Unlocked*. Only his doubts kept him from pulling the handle. *He could've attacked me Monday, and he didn't; he said to wait for the call, and I did; he warned me to enter alone, and I will.* He took a deep breath and inched the door open, shielding himself behind it. Then another deep breath before swinging his foot around to test breaching the threshold.

After five more seconds, he stepped into the common room, tuning out the door closing behind him, and gazed at the apparatus Breslin had struggled to describe. But he couldn't concentrate long. Something was, simply, wrong. He turned toward the cell door with the burn marks. Then he scanned the empty surroundings. Finally, his eyes widened—the silence! A cop getting recognized in prison triggers a clamor of curses and threats, and Adolf Vertsen was but one of his quarry in D block. Carson took three steps toward the charred cell, then stopped—*the nutcase might have the thing on a timer*. The eerie quiet would have to wait.

As Carson edged toward the bomb, his eyes were drawn to the hinged lid of the top metal box, and a message—*EDWARD CARSON: LIFT AND LOOK*. He turned, picturing Breslin knelt down. *He wouldn't have seen these words*.

This was too personal. Now was the time to back out and send in Bell. But he couldn't … and he knew it. With sweat building on his forehead, he scrutinized the device. Wires ran from a battery into a hole in the upper box—a power supply for something—and wires ran from that box to the detonator. But everything in between was concealed. He was in over his head … way over. His trembling hands confirmed it. But he had no choice. He steadied his left hand against the side of the box, and grabbed the lid with his quivering right. *I'm probably not wrong about Righteous. Most probably. It's more dangerous to disobey him*. Taking another deep breath, he raised the lid.

Clank!

Carson recoiled at the noise, but the cover stayed open several inches on its own. A double eyepiece, reminding him of a child's View-Master, had sprung to protrude from the opening, with black velvet concealing the rest of the gap.

He's not after me.

Carson pressed the bridge of his nose against the eyepiece, mashing the goggles into his eyebrows. It took a few seconds to grasp what was happening—he was staring at a dark purple screen and could discern images of letter sequences only with both eyes open, as if the characters were floating a micrometer above the screen, but still purple-on-purple. *Bastard wanted a private communication*, he deduced, pocketing the goggles rather than struggling merely to record an indigo blur.

"Mes-sage-to-beg-in-soon," repeated for a few seconds before the dispatch began. "No - dan - ger - to - you. - Ig - nore - your - sen - ses." *Bastard's smug when he writes, too*. "Pri-son-ers-have-suf-fer-ed-a-dire-fate-at-our-han-ds.-We-have-help-ed-the-in-no-cent-peop-le-of-New-Jer-sey-by-dis-pen-sing-jus-tice-more-com-men-sur-ate-with-the-cri-mes."

Shit … the silence! This wasn't *a breakout, it was vigilante mass murder! Wait! React later—the screen—*

"Whi-le-none-of-the-se-fel-ons-des-erve-a-tear-from-you,-many-wou-ld-dis-ag-ree.-Who-kno-ws-what-hav-oc-rei-gns-if-the-pub-lic-

lear-ns-what-you-per-mit-ted-here.-In-the-int-er-est-of-pe-ace-in-NJ,-we-have-laid-suf-fic-ient-fal-se-evid-ence-for-the-wit-nes-ses-and-for-en-sic-in-ves-ti-gat-ors-to-bla-me-the-dea-ths-on-an-at-temp-ted-pri-son-bre-ak-gone-wro-ng,-lead-ing-to-a-fat-al-chem-ical-leak.-FOUR-STE-PS-TO-SAVE-YOUR-WOR-LD-FROM-PAN-DE-MON-IUM:-Pre-tend-you-spe-nt-this-time-read-ing-thr-eats-aga-inst-your-fam-ily-if-you-pur-sue-us,-whi-ch-fal-se-ly-exp-lai-ns-my-ref-er-enc-es-to-pick-ing-you.-Re-veal-that-bomb-is-hoax-aid-ing-esc-ape,-only-top-bri-ck-is-real-C4-and-not-wir-ed.-Res-cue-two-cap-tiv-es-at-92-Brae-burn-Way-So-Oran-ge,-they-were-ess-en-tial-for-our-grea-ter-good.-Most-im-port-ant,-cho-ose-coro-ner-care-ful-ly,-must-lie-and-exp-lain-dea-ths-as-due-to-chlo-rine-tri-fluo-ride."

Carson's knees buckled. *It can't be ... singled out because of my influence with the medical examiner's office?*

He shook his head, then committed the message to memory, making nothing of the slight melting odor from the box. After that, he rechecked the stack of explosives. Only the bottommost brick was wired to the detonator; Gus had said only one needed to be. But if that one was fake as promised, the contraption was harmless, and he could move on.

He ran to the nearest cell, and through the small pane made out a figure sprawled on the ground. He scurried to the next cell and slid open the small slat ... another collapsed body. Then two more cells, two more bodies. He stepped back, panting, and lowered his head. When he raised it again, he turned to scan the other eighty cell doors. Pure agony.

Yet Righteous had left him no time for sorrow, just time to choose.

Playing along with the ruse could destroy his reputation and end his career. But the inmates *were* the state's responsibility, no less so because Righteous highlighted it. Every accident, every fight, every illness brought cries against the Department of Corrections—this massacre would generate chaos. How many violent cons would be released during the revamp to more prisoner-protected facilities? How many hardliners would add to the body count, killing and dying in copycat efforts? He'd put everything, his life, at risk for society before—but always within the letter of the law. Why was he feeling compelled to do it again?

And what if the cover-up was doomed to fail? His detectives would recreate a timeline and punch holes in any inconsistency, and

Forensics would analyze why chlorine trifluoride was brought in for a breakout and challenge how it turned fatal for the inmates alone. But the Panthera's plan had proven exceptional, Righteous hiding his true motive for hours, and Breslin and Pittman both attesting to the panicked scrambling. Then he realized he had an ace in the hole—he could go along with the lie now, and recant later if additional evidence revealed any gaps.

Still, he didn't want to put his career on the line without tapping his support system; though he considered himself the smartest detective in the county, he knew he wasn't the smartest member of law enforcement.

* * * * *

Rebecca Harwood shut off the water when her state-issued cell phone rang, and turned to her husband, brushing black hair from her eyes with the back of her hand. "Take out the cookies when the timer beeps?" she asked. "Please?"

"Why do you bake every time your Dartmouth friends come over?"

"I guess I'm nicer than you," she said, squeezing past him at the table.

"I thought you always left a junior doctor on call on Saturdays. So much for having *two* reasons to work as the Chief Medical Examiner."

"Well, the paycheck and uncovering the truth count for two." She raised her voice as she reached the den. "And the weekend interruptions happen, what … twice a year?" She picked up the phone and examined the screen. "Is this Lieutenant Edward Carson's official line?"

"Hi, Beck," Carson replied. "There's a big mess at Essex State. It's going to ruin your weekend and your week … probably everyone's at your office."

"We've taken five bodies from the prison before."

"This one's eighty, Beck."

"Oh, no."

"Yeah. Happened right under our noses." He paused for a second. "You have to be the first examiner here; our official call ends with me promising to update you on the failed breakout when you arrive. And we need to yellow submarine."

"It's been a while for that. All right, good-bye Lieutenant Carson," she said as she disconnected. She grabbed the handset for her landline, brought it into the bathroom, and shut the door. The phone rang, displaying Carson's personal cell number. "What's so secret?" she asked.

"I know what honesty means to you, Beck. I really do. And the truth is important to me, too. But there's a lie we need to tell. Some vigilantes broke into the prison to kill the lifers, and word getting out that it wasn't a bungled escape would wreak havoc. We'd get outrage from the left, copycats on the right, and felons released in the name of safety. People will die … more people."

Deceit—professional deceit—was unthinkable, asked by anyone else. But this was Ted. And he was probably right about the copycats … revealing the truth would lead to catastrophe. After a minute, she probed the cover story. "You have enough to send them away if I lie? They won't get out in twenty years because we convince everyone it was an accident?"

"I don't expect them to survive the day; Staties are tailing them with military hardware. But yes, if this goes to trial, they get life even without evidence of intent—still ten counts of kidnapping prison guards, at least one aggravated assault, weapons charges, and terroristic threats."

"I won't put my M.E. license at risk. If the lie blows up, I'm OK losing *this* job, but anything worse than that falls on you."

"Sure. I'm not trying to shirk this and dump it on you," Carson said.

"And you'll keep this from your team? I don't want to worry about anyone else spilling the beans."

"I have to."

"So if there are other conspirators, you'll be looking for vigilantes, while the rest of the Newark PD will be looking for sympathizers?"

"There *is* another one! They forced me to wait for a code phrase, outside the cellblock, and the caller was someone else." Carson paused. "But that doesn't change my mind. There's going to be a lot of physical evidence, so I can steer the investigation to the right suspects with that."

"Well, if you want medical analysis on the true cause of death, pick three guys nobody'll care about for me to examine personally."

"Does that mean you're in?"

Harwood looked at herself in the mirror. "I think I'm in. Only for you, though. And only because the alternative sucks worse. If I change my mind, I'll say something to you about hurting my wrist. You have about thirty minutes to think it through and decide the same. And of course the obvious thing."

"Which is?"

"Don't tell Mom or Dad … ever," Dr. Rebecca Carson Harwood told her brother.

- 13 -

Captain Wilcox was seated at the front desk at the right point of the horseshoe, tapping a pen, watching the infrared images with her team. As what seemed to be the last of the heat trails fled the truck, four others approached the riverbank from two cars.

"Truck evacuated," Sergeant Price radioed. "Six hostages rescued, all healthy. Bridge cleared of personnel."

"Good work," she replied. "Pursuit 1: What do you see down there?"

"There's a heap about thirty yards in, against the pier. I can make out some bodies and a bunch of blue plastic seats, but there's a gray canvas obscuring the view. Request permission to wade in and investigate."

"Any signs of life?"

"No. Just bobbing with the flow of the river. No footprints on shore, either."

Wilcox kept tapping. "It's going to rain truck parts soon … return to your vehicles." She looked across at McMurphy. "You can see how much colder the river bodies are than our officers'—two different reds."

"They're cooling, all right."

Wilcox's rhythmic rapping marked time. When five minutes had passed, she radioed the bridgehead, "I need to speak to Sergeant Reiley directly."

She filled the wait with thirty more taps. "Reiley here."

"How exactly did your captor threaten the explosion?"

"He said I'd hear commotion then a finale, then have seven minutes before the truck blew up. I twisted toward the door when the whirring started, and wasn't sure about the metal crashing onto the roadway, but then the jolting and fireworks—that was obviously the big finish. So I began counting and got my arm out the window to wave for you guys. I got over eighty when they reached me, so I said we had five minutes left."

Wilcox looked at McMurphy again. "Check when we timestamped the flares."

"Just shy of seven minutes ago!" she answered.

"Everyone stay down!" Wilcox radioed. She stared at the image of the truck, watching it survive another tapping refrain. She shook her head, then took to the radio again. "DelVecchio?"

"Bomb squad standing by."

"Pete, hate to do this, but they don't seem intent on killing lawmen, and we have to search and disarm eventually."

"Comes with the territory, Dee."

"Wait three more minutes, then approach the truck—carefully."

"We'll suit up and move in the robots."

The cooling bodies tossed for thirty more minutes while delVecchio's robots, then dogs, scoured the truck. Several more patrol cars had arrived at the banks, and a police boat from Allentown had anchored a safe distance from the mass, by the time he declared the scene safe. "It helped that the cargo section was mostly empty. Whatever didn't go over the rail, you can tow away as evidence."

Wilcox ordered the *Welcome* to approach the debris, and awaited the crew's assessment.

"Sergeant Conley, riverboat unit, reporting. Captain, most of them are obliterated. But it looks like eleven bodies to me."

"Keep looking! There's one more! Riverbank units: Search for a body downstream!" She put down the radio, mumbled "he made us wait," and turned to McMurphy. "If he'd blown up the truck after seven minutes, when would we have counted the bodies?"

"As soon as the boat arrived, at least fifteen minutes sooner."

"And if he'd threatened the bomb going off in thirty minutes instead of seven?"

"You would've sent delVecchio in right away … and he would've cleared us earlier!"

"We've been played!" Wilcox yelled to the room. "Give me every possibility for that twelfth man!"

"Heat sensor malfunction?" Sergeant Detmueller offered.

"No," McMurphy said. "It's working even now, we can see every officer. Maybe one of the heat trails that propelled off the truck was a fake—a heated fake—and the real guy blended in with the hostages and our rescue team?"

"Make sure scene commander didn't fall for that one," Wilcox said. "ID every officer who returned from the truck, and have the prison guards vouch for one another. And send units back to search under the truck, in case he tried that and thwarted the robots and dogs. What else?"

"Those flares blocked the heat images during their plunge, maybe the last guy had rigging to swing under the bridge somehow, and he's working his way across," Detmueller said.

"Perfectly timed to stay hidden from the infrared?" McMurphy challenged.

"Unlikely or not, I want the bridge architecture searched," Wilcox said. "Sandra, the flares mucked our view by being hotter than the men. Is there any way he could hide by reading as cool to the sensors, bags of ice perhaps?"

"He'd have to be covered completely," McMurphy answered, "otherwise we'd see a warm limb protruding from a cold …" Her eyes floated right for an instant before widening. "Shit! It *could* happen—if he stayed under running water!"

"Get more boats, and spread units up and down the banks, both sides!" Wilcox commanded. "He's coming out somewhere, if he hasn't already." Then she grabbed her radio. "Sergeant Conley, are you equipped for underwater search?"

"At normal depth, five feet, we could search down to the riverbed and across from our deck. But with these September rains, the river's at twelve feet here, so you'd want sonar. Except you won't find any north of Philly, not today. The governor ordered all underwater search equipment to the feds this morning."

Wilcox flung her pen against the wall, then grabbed a phone. She'd collaborated with the FBI dozens of times over the years, and needed only three calls to track down Special Agent Lehrer. "Constantine Albright ends shift at Salem nuclear plant at 1 AM today," he droned. "Post-shift computer review shows mishandling shortfall 500 grams fissionable material, flagged as potentially removed. Inadequate mass and purity for nuclear detonation, but grave contamination threat. Albright has seven-day vacation scheduled; his flight reservation to Cancun gets changed over the internet at 6 AM today, to Amman via Dubai, using a supervisor's override. He's taken into federal custody

8 AM, JFK Airport. NSA reports buzz of terroristic threat to Philadelphia water supply, starting Thursday night."

Wilcox shook her head. "You think Albright stole uranium to contaminate the drinking water, then tried to escape on a ticket in his own name?"

"Working assumption … yes, we're pursuing that."

"But speaking to a comrade-in-arms?"

Lehrer huffed. "Between us, it seemed unlikely at first, and more dubious now. He swears he didn't change his ticket, and there's no history of fanaticism or arrests. And the preliminary physical audit shows no uranium actually missing. If the NRC verifies *that*, Albright walks free with an apology, and we look for a computer hacker with the worst sense of humor."

Or the worst motive, Wilcox thought.

"But until then," the agent continued, "we're deploying all available resources to the water intakes for Philly, Camden, and Trenton, and you'll have to find your fugitive without sonar."

She forced a "thanks," hung up, and opened an online map. She grabbed another pen and mindlessly tapped a few measures before getting a final report from Conley. "We've moved everything around and checked a bit downriver. Still only eleven bodies. If there's another, it's not floating and it's not attached to the others. We also found a trove of equipment secured to the pier, a few feet underwater—thirteen scuba tanks, masks and pairs of fins, and thirteen underwater propulsion devices. But not ordinary ones—these are souped-up, with two extra motors mounted on. If the rest of this equipment is military grade, the sonofabitch could still be underwater, flying away from us at eight knots."

She looked at the map, frustrated by the possibilities—climbing from the river near Bethlehem or Frenchtown; ashore in Easton nearly an hour ago and now driving one of thousands of cars clogging the secondary roads around the river; or perhaps he lived in Phillipsburg and was changing in his own bedroom. The APB would be a joke: *One of twelve males, no evidence shorter than five-four nor taller than six-three, last seen in disguise now presumed discarded.*

One is on the loose.

* * * * *

After appealing to his sister, Ted Carson walked toward the cellblock door, stomach twisting; *he's left me no choice.* He pushed it open, and stepped out.

"He made it!" Bell called, leading a crush toward him. Ted saw his friend's smile flatten as he approached. "Aren't you happy to see us?"

"You'll see," Carson whispered, grabbing Bell's shoulder. Then he spoke up, emotions buried. "The bomb wasn't wired to blow. Gus, you double-check that, then catalogue the parts for evidence and haul them out. After that, medical and forensic teams only." Bell nodded, and Carson turned to Youngman. "Get two ambulances, patrol cars, and an investigative team to 92 Braeburn Way in South Orange—there are captives inside." Another nod, and Carson called to Rogers, "How about the truck?"

Rogers held up his finger, then put his cell phone down and yelled, "The last of the guards have just been rescued! And the scumbags are fish food!"

The collective cheers and smiling lasted close to a minute; Carson could only enjoy the news for half of that time. Then he hushed the crowd. "I know you guards had friends, maybe more like brothers, on that truck, in danger. And now there's relief for their families, and you. And me. But there's also bad news. The Panthera can't hurt anyone again, but they took risks. They were reckless. And the felons they wanted to free … and all the inmates in D block … they're … they've all perished." Carson paused; Minero alone shook his head. "Some things are beyond our control. All we can do is be thankful the guards are safe, and continue to live our lives tomorrow."

As the officers and guards dispersed, Carson opened the cellblock door and motioned Minero inside. "Autopsies sometimes get messy. Got any guys in here nobody gave a shit about?"

"Yeah—half of them. After five, ten years, they're lucky to get a birthday visit. Some of the old-timers list 'N/A' for next of kin, they won't be noticed at all." He rattled off five names.

While they watched the bomb squad work, Carson started worrying that his sister would change her mind. Then she arrived. *Don't say anything about your wrist.*

Harwood exchanged quick introductions with the warden, then turned to Ted. "You said there were eighty?"

"There were eighty-*eight* inmates in cellblock D," Minero interjected.

"County morgue can handle it, with our overflow site—we've drilled for a hundred bodies from the airport. Has your medical staff examined the victims?"

"No, nobody's been inside the cells."

"Bomb squad should be quick with this one," Carson added, "then you can get to the bodies. I'll start my team in the common area and control room, out of your way; that's probably where the intruders spent their time."

Harwood studied the room for a moment. "Warden, if the lieutenant's right, I'll need to borrow a nurse practitioner for an hour, pronouncing people dead. We'll need a route for wheeling out the bodies, and we'll need ventilation. This could take a while."

"I'll get the cells unlocked, then take care of the rest," he said. "I need to do that from there," he added, pointing to the control room.

Carson handed Minero a pair of latex gloves, then led his sister out of the cellblock. "Thanks, Beck. Truly. This is right."

"It's also *wrong*…. But the alternative seems worse."

Ted nodded. "These are the loners," he said, handing her a separate page from his notes, "so you can tell me what *really* happened."

"Not so fast. If your mastermind left any visible contraindications, everyone gets the same story—the truth."

"Of course. If you ever decide the lie won't be convincing, I'll jump to your side."

Rebecca nodded, then walked back into the cellblock. Bell came out shortly after, carrying a single block in a plastic wrapper. "I could do a lot of damage with this," he announced, "but only this one. The other four are inert, and the electronics were more threat than function. We diagrammed the wiring anyway, and labelled the parts, for evidence. The room's all yours."

Carson gathered his officers and re-entered D block, directing the fingerprint team to the control room and accompanying the photographer to the burned window. After a few minutes, Rebecca poked her head out of cell D2 and caught his eye, then nodded twice. He nodded back, and left for 92 Braeburn.

- 14 -

Jennifer Bolton rejoiced in the sunrise. In a few hours, the march on City Hall would begin without her, and her friends would worry; when it ended, they would find her—*free* her—at last.

* * * * *

She'd spent the first five minutes after they'd left her bound, spread-eagled, struggling against her ties, first trying to pull her wrists out from under the knots at full strength, then testing if less force might loosen their hold. When that failed, she made two fists and tugged, hoping to rip the terry cloth strips. On her last tug, she focused on the wooden bedposts, cursing the solid frame. Then she tensed her legs, hoping to flex inward, but just found herself arching her back against the secure bonds. The tape on her mouth held firmly as well. Finally, she lay still, catching her breath, pondering whether twisting the restraints would foil the knots. She resorted to force three more times before accepting the futility of struggling, her wrists chafed and sore but not bleeding.

After two hours, her suffering included thirst and a stiff neck. The afternoon brought shoulder pain, fist clenching to relieve numbness, and an anxiety attack the third time she dwelled on her helplessness. At three o'clock, she ended an hour of torment holding off the inevitable, soaking her panties, skirt, and mattress; her squirming leftward and down for the release and then rightward and up to avoid the mess proved barely worthwhile. It all became unbearable by nightfall, when any sleep was interrupted within an hour by jolting pain in her neck. Her only relief came from thinking about Phil, and all the time they'd spend together after their nightmare.

At 12:15, her countdown to freedom ended with flashing lights sparkling in her soundproofed window. After three raps on the front door, the police smashed it in and reached her room within seconds, followed by EMTs asking questions, taking vital signs, and directing her movements as they cut her loose. After a quick drink, she interrupted the ruckus. "My husband, Phil … he was in the basement … I need to—"

"Hold on," EMT Wende said, holding up his left hand. "We're looking out for him also. Besides, if you don't drink more and refresh your circulation, you'll cramp up on your first step."

"How did you know to come here? Did you catch those creeps?"

"We think there's a connection to another crime," Officer Leland answered. "That's what led us here. I can't say more than that."

Jen heard footsteps coming up the stairway, footsteps that weren't Phil's. The next three seconds burned into her mind in slow motion: she could see a hand sliding toward the top of the handrail, then a white cuff from an EMT uniform; next in view was a right shoe, black, and the bottom of a cuffed blue pant leg; and finally the rest, but she could only register his face, his young face, morose and drawn, eyes looking down, inches past his shoes. She started screaming "No!" before he could say anything, forcing hoarse cries from her parched throat. He wouldn't look at her, instead telling his colleagues that he suspected deep vein thrombosis from the confinement, throwing a clot that lodged in Phil's lungs, killing him just hours earlier. Everything she lived for was over. In her mind, it was a double murder.

* * * * *

Ted Carson sped to South Orange, siren blaring. The kidnapping of innocents doubled the unanswered questions, and learning Phil Bolton's fate stoked his fury. He was still fuming when he parked in front of the Boltons' house and returned Captain Wilcox's call. "One is at large?" he screamed at the faultless commander. "That scene is now part of *my* investigation! I get the evidence report from the bridge, and those bodies go to Newark for autopsy!"

He slammed the door of his Malibu. The last of the South Orange police cruisers was departing then, leaving an ambulance in the driveway and the familiar cars of his Newark colleagues lining the street. He met Detective Priestly in the entryway, and looked across the living room at a woman who was obviously Jennifer Bolton, sitting in a chair against the far wall, morbidly still, unmoved by the team examining her house. "She able to talk?" Carson asked.

"Just snippets. Four guys with guns, three of them masked. The leader was 'Alpha.' It started Thursday afternoon, they left her tied up yesterday morning. No other injuries, so they probably weren't planning a murder … but they sure didn't care about the risks and the sheer hell of it. First fingerprints are the Boltons', we're still checking for strays." Then, pointing to the covered windows behind the couch, "They planned this out all right, and wanted privacy, downstairs and up."

"Do you know why they picked the Boltons?"

"She bawled, 'They wanted me!' She teaches constitutional law at Seton Hall; no criminal record but dozens of permits to lead protests at City Hall—"

"Including one for today!" Carson closed his eyes. "Her editorial ran yesterday," he muttered, "but *they* had her on *Thursday*…." His jaw dropped, and he kept his next thoughts to himself. *They needed* me *at the prison to corrupt Rebecca, and they knew I'd be there if they drew Oppenheimer away! The Panthera hacked the police assignment hierarchy!* He opened his eyes. "I need to speak to her alone."

Priestly grimaced. "With all due respect, Lieutenant, shouldn't we be showing *our* respect to the new widow? Besides, she can barely sputter out the basics."

"*You* follow protocol, then: get family and friends over here, and plan to question her again in three hours. But I need to talk to her now. Stay on top of the rest while I'm doing that: prints and photos, and make sure a techie's on site before bagging the computer. Canvass the neighborhood; there's a lot of space here, but maybe someone spotted unusual traffic. Ask specifically about a paper supply truck."

Carson left to speak to EMT Wende in his ambulance, then returned, carrying a bottle of lemon-lime Gatorade. He knew it was right to leave the grief-stricken professor alone—she'd be dwelling on a future that would no longer be, or on shared moments that she could never share again. But this case was different. He *had to* approach her, *had to* make an impression, however heartless the conversation would seem.

He crossed the room, then bit his lip. She hadn't even tried to soothe the abrasions on her wrists or remove the remnants of adhesive around her lips. *But this case is different*, he told himself again.

"I'm Lieutenant Ted Carson. I'm in charge of the investigation. You and I are going to bond over the next few days, because we want the same things. First among them: getting you healthy," he said, holding out the medic's recommended drink.

Bolton stared past the bottle and sobbed. "You don't know what I want …"

"I *do* know. I'm sure you want to be left alone now. Right? And I'm sure I can't relate to what you're feeling. I'm sure because I've sat next to dozens of grieving relatives before, parents, and widows, too, like you."

She continued her distant gaze, and he pressed on. "The assholes who did this have a jump on us. The worst part of being a detective isn't sitting next to mourning families, the worst part comes months, years, later. It's when they cry to me to find the monsters who ruined their lives—the thing I'm supposed to do. But the links get too strained and the killers get away. They want answers. I lie and say they couldn't have done anything more to help. But that's a lie. Always."

She started trembling, and sobbing. He bit his lip again, then shook his head and leaned in. "I know this is hard now, but I need you to accept that you have a future, and that your future will be better if justice is served. There's a killer on the loose, and if I can get all the pieces—"

"Leave me alone, asshole!" the widow screamed, turning in her chair to face away from him and cry anew.

* * * * *

Carson put on latex gloves and descended the basement stairs. He inspected the electronics and furnishings, trying to ignore the professor's cries. He also made a cursory examination of the bedroom, giving leeway to the officers collecting evidence there. "They were careful," Priestly told him, "but I'm sure we'll find something." Carson nodded, then walked to his car and drove off.

Newark's block-long red-bricked police headquarters has a wide glass entryway in front and three mammoth glass atria in back, allowing sunlight to bisect the interior. Carson parked in back, took the stairs two-at-a-time to the second floor, and strode to his micro-office, turning sideways to squeeze around the desk to his creaky black vinyl chair.

He wasted his precious first minutes in the office instructing the press liaison—Righteous had left him no choice. He had to keep the reporters from uncovering the ruse. "Extol the guards' heroism, promise a thorough investigation, and vow that we'll capture any conspirators. End with condolences for the lost inmates from the governor's office."

After, he sidestepped from behind his desk and taped two rows of poster-sized sheets of ivory paper to his right side wall, one for each perp, creating a familiar canvas for clues and questions. Numbers one through eleven corresponded to the Panthera recovered from the river, a gory photo from the death scene taped onto each sheet. Number twelve stayed pictureless, titled "Escaped from truck," while thirteen was labeled "Boss? Restless and waiting." Fourteen through seventeen were for Phil Bolton's killers.

He returned to his desk. "Anything more from you, Bertha?" he asked his government-issued, slowed-by-the-security-software laptop. Reports from the interviewed guards had been posted to a secured folder, as had photos from the crime scenes. As the afternoon wore on, he printed pictures of the Panthera from the medical examiner's office, with any makeup not washed off by the river removed and injuries flagged, and added them to his wallpaper.

His sister was the first to call in. "The Staties couldn't get fingerprints from the bodies. You saw that?" she asked.

"They said some kind of covering."

"Yes, a latex derivative, which we've been removing and analyzing. Means you won't get prints from the crime scene, either. But as we've gone along, we've been sending the prints to the FBI. I'm guessing you also won't get any DNA, the guys were practically encased in a skin gel."

"Understood. Anything on the prisoners?"

"You know that on this call I'd be suggesting asphyxia resulting from inhalation of chlorine trifluoride as cause of death. But we still have more to examine, and then the tox screens."

"I'll leave you to it, then. Thanks, Beck."

Seconds later, Carson connected on his sister's personal cell phone. "The special convicts?"

"Yes, I managed to misguide my team and not lose my job, thanks for asking," she started. "Lung distress brought on pulmonary edema, which is fluid in the lungs, leading to asphyxia. The cause of death is consistent with inhaling chlorine trifluoride."

"So whatever he really used *would've* fooled your team?"

"Hardly! If he thinks that, he's certainly not a doctor. There was less-than-guideline burning and swelling of the eyes, and muted skin irritation."

"You can't let the other M.E.'s find that out—"

"Working on it, Ted. I've been the only one conducting full autopsies. With the large number of bodies, I invoked our pandemic protocols, so the other doctors are just evaluating the primary suspect cause of death—liver temperature establishing that they all died at the same time, pulmonary distress determined from examining the lungs, and tissue samples prepared for chemical analysis. It'll be my toxicology report on those samples that allays their doubts about the secondary symptoms."

"So *that* report will support the story?" he pressed.

"Only because we want it to, not because he'll trick the tests. The systemic damage makes me think it's a neurotoxin, not a caustic, and the symptoms suggest a carbamate or an organochlorine pesticide— not DDT, but maybe close. I'll only know once I run the labs."

"I'll leave the science to you." Carson paused. "How do the inmates get killed and everyone else walks away?"

"Maybe each cell gets gassed, the guards are kept away, and the killers have gas masks. Some poisons only linger for a few minutes. Ask me again after I run tox."

"Let me know as soon as you do. Restricted chemicals are high on the tracing lists, so I'll be able to track down the buyer."

"Sure. But you owe me a weekend for this," Rebecca closed.

Carson pocketed his cell phone. He was anxious for the FBI fingerprint analysis, putting names with the smashed faces, but knew that would run into the evening. Until then, he had an important trip to make—or perhaps he was going to waste an hour.

15

Carson rang the doorbell, and was confronted by a glaring, forty-something with blonde highlights. "I'm Lieutenant Carson, and this is Detective Priestly. We were here earlier."

"So you'd know my friend isn't up to another interrogation," she said. "It's 4:30, and the other detectives finished two hours ago."

"We need to speak with Professor Bolton again," Priestly insisted.

"Let's get this over with, Cassie!" Bolton called out. "I'll want to spend the night in peace."

Easing inside, Carson noticed more colors in the oriental rug with the windows uncovered. Jennifer Bolton sat on her living room couch, with a grape stem on the maple coffee table in front of her.

"Glad you consoled her enough to eat," Carson said to Bolton's friend.

"This is probably a good time to pick up dinner," Priestly added.

She looked at Jen, eliciting a nod, then waved her cell phone and said "anytime" before heading out the door. Priestly sat in the chair across from the victim, facing the window, while Carson stood off to the side of the couch, almost out of her view. The underling intoned a set of background questions: "Full name?" "Work location?" "Car you drove home?" The professor droned a response to each.

"Tell me everything you remember about their appearance," he said.

"Tripp had straight black hair, like the lieutenant, and you'd have his security camera picture," she said. Then she stayed silent.

"OK. But really, I want *everything* about physical appearance…. Try the other three now."

"Black mask, blue mask, green mask," she said, then looked down.

"I know this is hard," Priestly said, "but the more you can share now, the better. You told me more before—"

"About the workmen's uniforms," she said, looking back up. "But *now* you're asking things I don't know."

Carson nodded to his partner, and Priestly started acting annoyed. "And you couldn't tell *anything* about Alpha's face except that he's Caucasian?"

"Right. The mask. I'd told you."

"You never saw *any* of them pull up his mask, maybe to get a drink?"

"I was knocked out most of the time they were here.... I've explained that, too."

Priestly huffed, and scrolled on his phone. "You think it was the same four men both days but can't be sure, you only saw one face, you only heard two of them speak at length, and they never slipped and called the others anything but 'Beta' and 'Gamma'?"

"I don't care if those creeps left you a map or not! They were careful ... but they're also despicable! They killed my husband! They need to be caught ... and *you* don't have the passion to do it!" She started to sob, then held up her left index finger. Swallowing hard, she turned to Carson, looking him in the eye for the first time. "I'm ready to team up with *you. Alone.* And do whatever it takes."

Carson nodded to Priestly again, and took his chair when he left, suppressing his contentment at his two-act orchestration of the professor's decision.

"I'll answer your questions," she said, "but you'll have to answer mine after."

"At least most of them," Carson agreed, and she nodded back. "Did Alpha ever check in with a higher authority, maybe a phone call or looking for a text?"

"No," Bolton replied, "and he seemed very controlling. He also seemed to have his own sense of right and wrong, like he was playing God. Alpha was calling the shots."

Carson gulped. "*I* spent time with someone like that. Let me list a few words, and tell me what you think, focusing only on Alpha, not the others."

After the professor nodded, Carson began. "Controlling ..."

"Like I already said."

"Speech ..."

"Pretentious. No dialect or accent."

"Height and build?" he asked.

"He had at least three inches on me. Probably five-ten, give or take, and average-looking shape."

"Pistol grip?"

Bolton shook her head and waved him off.

"Don't worry about that one," he reassured her. "Vocal pitch?"

"High. Almost a squeak."

Carson sulked.

"Not what you wanted to hear? You lost your poker face."

"It's usually harder than we want, but we win in the end," Carson offered. "Besides, there's another possibility that fits just as well. Speech?" he asked again.

"Pretentious," she repeated.

"Unusual phrases or euphemisms?" he asked, hoping for "restless and waiting."

Bolton stared blankly for a full minute, occasionally moving her lips. "I'm going through every exchange … nothing unusual."

This time he worked harder to hide his disappointment. "We'll know a lot more tomorrow, and I'll have different questions then. You can have the night to yourself."

Bolton darted her eyes toward the kitchen, then toward the stairway, and bit her lip.

Carson said, "Some people feel safer with a patrol car outside the first few nights. None of that crew would return here, but it's whatever makes *you* feel better."

"It sounds silly—"

Carson held up his hand. "You'll have uniformed officers around the clock, and you can call me anytime, for anything," he said, sliding three business cards across the table.

He angled to leave, but her raised finger kept him seated. She stared at him, then started to cry. Her finger stayed up as she choked back the tears, gasping until the single word came out: "Why?"

He felt his face flush. It would shatter her to learn she'd been put through hell just to divert Oppenheimer to City Hall so he himself would be assigned to the jailbreak instead. And he could never, *ever,* expose his sister's forced role in the escape ruse. Risking the trust of his most important witness, Carson gambled on a lie: "We *will* figure that out, eventually."

* * * * *

Returning to headquarters, Carson gazed at the faces on his wall— *which one of you is Righteous?* Then he turned to Bertha, and found the server laden with information. He first opened the fingerprint runs. Seven of the assailants were identified—Calvin Denken from his Nuclear Regulatory Commission file, Nick Lorelz from his Cablevision arrest record, two others from the military, and three from job license inquiries. Carson printed their portraits and taped them below the morgue headshots, then spent an hour reviewing their government records and internet profiles. Lorelz's police record revealed his motive for that crime and the Panthera's, and Carson found that five of the others also had relatives victimized by D block inmates. The last one, Terry Rinecore, had formed the "NJ Right for a Reason" party to run for Senate on a platform denouncing criminal rights. Carson e-mailed his team: *Seven names, I want a complete timeline for the last two weeks—any shared unaccounted-for time blocks could be a meeting with the unnamed ones, or the one who got away. Particularly interested in Thursday PM/Friday AM. Canvass co-workers, acquaintances, and families, and get warrants for home and work e-mails, phone records, and hard drives.*

Carson's phone rang soon after. "Ted! It's been a whole year since you've ruined one of my weekends!" He immediately recognized the melodic voice of Darrell Goode, the longest-serving forensic analyst with the New Jersey State Police. "I didn't just want to post a report and have you call me at God-knows-what-hour with questions."

"You're onto me, Darrell! I timed the crime to ruin your Saturday, then would've called you tomorrow at six AM, report or no report."

"Well … your lab has the truck and everything from the prison. Maybe they'll grab prints or DNA, and maybe you can trace back and catch whoever bought the stuff. *I've* got really cool daredevil equipment, and now I know what they were thinking, at least about the escape."

"Do tell."

"The boring part was the underwater gear. With what they had in the river, anyone could've stayed under for about an hour. The propulsion system was a neat modification, but basically just three popular devices fused together and wired to start and stop in unison. I found videos for doing that on the internet, for anyone who can weld. The individual parachute was a popular variety and brand, so also boring; but not too many parachutists are BASE jumpers, so if your guy was dumb enough to brag about it, you could narrow your list to a few hundred prospects."

"I guess those are technically 'leads,' Darrell, but nothing you would've called about."

"Right … I just wanted to get those out of the way," Goode said. "The mutated roller coaster seats that the eleven men were strapped onto—the contraption was tethered to three large canvases. The theory seems to have been to create heat, inflating one canvas as a balloon for lift; the other two seem shaped for a parachuting effect at moderate velocity."

"But only in theory?"

"That's just it. Commercial balloons, for lifting a few thousand pounds, have to be huge. Theirs never had the capacity, even with the seats being hollow plastic. But I wanted to give them the benefit of the doubt—maybe they just wanted an initial buffer off the bridge, and then they'd rely on the drag from the other canopies. So they need to heat the air almost instantaneously. Remind you of anything?"

"It's been a long day, Darrell. Gasoline fire?"

"No, not a hazard! A life-saving device—airbags! They used a limited explosion to inflate the canvas, and probably secondary ones for the way down. I'm still analyzing the residue for a match."

"So if they'd had more explosives and a bigger balloon, or if the parachutes had worked better, eleven more men might've landed alive in the river?"

"Still, only in theory. Let's say all of that would've worked, and even that they had a successful trial run. Well, Ted, this morning they all would've died anyway. I found ten-foot-long splits in the seams of each of the canvases—not stress tears from the explosion, but identical cuts made ahead of time, no distress to the surrounding material. Dead men tell no tales, Ted. Someone wanted to escape alone."

Carson looked at the numbered pictures on his wall, then stared at the barren page for the escaped member of the Panthera. The Delaware River survivor was a murdering narcissist with enough control to sabotage his partners' getaway. Carson walked over to the blank sheet and wrote "Righteous?"

16

Carson returned to Bertha; the PENITENTIARY_CRIME_SCENE filename stood out like a stilt walker. He took three deep breaths before phoning Dr. Eduardo Quinones—the fate of the chemical accident ruse rested on Righteous's ability to deceive the head of the Newark crime lab.

"Glad the director called in our best for this one," Carson started.

"Must've been scary at the time," Quinones said. "My condolences to any families you'll have to deal with."

"Any highlights before I read the report?"

"Probably best if I just cover everything. We know what happened, and I can tell you about their equipment. But we can't help identify the fugitive: No stray fingerprints—they must've worn gloves. Only hairs belonging to the guards in the control room—they must've worn wigs. And too much traffic to try to isolate DNA."

"My sister warned me about all that, when she looked at the bodies."

"One of them is an electronics wiz, we recovered signal blockers and a camera array from the truck. The fired shot came from a twenty-two, but the recovered pistols had all been reported stolen over a year ago, so they won't be any help. They used paintball guns to disable the cellblock cameras—smarter than being in a cavern with bullets ricocheting around. But the projectiles weren't off-the-rack—what they shot was more like expanding foam than paint. No difference for the cameras, but it helped them partially block the canister vent tubes—you know, how guards can drop tear gas in from the rooftop during a riot. They started to secure a commercial winch to the floor, presumably to pry open as many doors as you'd let them, and they'd rigged it to run on a high-end battery if you'd cut the power. But they never finished that, obviously."

"Obviously," Carson agreed. *Sounds like he's buying in.*

"They also tried to burn out the heavy glass on cell door D23, probably to loop the winch cable through. But that was the dangerous part. Not sure they had much choice—if you only have what you can carry, it's explosives if you can move everyone far away, or chemicals. Have you checked whether any of them worked at a nuclear power plant?"

"Wow! How did you know *that*?"

"They knew to choose chlorine trifluoride. It's one of the most dangerous things there, besides the fuel rods. It literally burns anything you can think of—glass, sand, even firefighters' uniforms. We didn't find much, with the coroner's office tromping through, but I'm certain that's how they mangled the window. We also found an empty industrial cylinder with a defective valve outside of that cell. It's easy to speculate the canister was full enough to burn out a row of windows, then it malfunctions and someone knows to run at the distinctive nose burn, and you get this looming toxic cloud. Standard prison design is for control rooms to be air pressure-positive—more prep for teargassing the common room—and that's what must've saved the guards. But the cells aren't ... and the blocked vents wouldn't have helped any ... so ... better ask your sister the rest."

"Yeah, it sounds horrible."

"Gruesome." Quinones paused. "Then the rest. Bell was right about the explosive stack: five pounds of C4—the dogs would've gone crazy smelling that—and four inert replicas. But C4 doesn't prove a military connection, there's an active black market for the stuff. Most of the rest of that *bomb* was also fake—electronics that look imposing. One just turns driveway lights on when a car approaches. That leaves the message from the killers, the purple screen with the computer-generated text. You'd like an exact transcript of that, right?"

Carson stopped breathing, and felt a lump in his throat.

"Unfortunately," the scientist continued, "they went to great pains to destroy that computer code."

Carson slumped and exhaled through a grin, then straightened back up a moment later. "You mean you don't have it *now*, but you'll reconstruct it?"

"No. This time, it's gone for good."

"But, Ed ... you've testified that you could read *any* deleted file, with enough time."

"This one's different ... failure by design. An ordinary computer drive works like a strip of wax embedded with coins, one side reflecting and one side dull, rolled up into a disk. To write a message, a laser softens a bit of wax at a time, and a magnet flips the coins either shiny side up or down before the wax hardens. The sequence of reflecting and not-reflecting coins could be like dots and dashes in Morse code—it's actually binary code—conveying letters and then words. A thorough file erase reorients all of the coins up, so I have to use a microscope to see which coins were flipped during the most recent pass and reverse them. But your guys? They created a more heat-sensitive disk, and when the display was over, they melted it with a triple-strength writing laser. All that's left is a blob embedded with microscopic half-shiny specks facing whichever direction gravity dictated. The only record of that message is in your head, my friend."

"Dang! They went to a lot of trouble for that," Carson said, smiling again. "Is any of the other equipment trackable?"

"I made some suggestions in the report. Maybe the truck, even though they filed off the VINs and the plates are fake. The truck modifications required some industrial-grade supplies, and the drill is very high-end. Flash some pictures in the right places, and you might find where those were bought."

"As always, Ed, the facts are helpful, and the perspective, invaluable. One more nagging thing: you've seen the overview report—Panthera, the genus of roaring cats, and the feline nicknames. Just a name to you, right? Nothing about the equipment struck you as taunting or catlike in some perverse way?"

"The storied 'criminal who wants to get caught,' leaving the cleverest of clues? Unfortunately not. The genus name actually derives from Greek, 'all' and 'prey,' or 'predator of all animals.' Maybe they just feel above it all."

"My thanks again to the lab and its leader."

"You're welcome," Quinones replied. "And Ted ... be careful for yourself this time. The customized equipment, the ambitious scheme ... they won't be your typical shoot-and-run-away criminals."

"The predators won't know what hit them."

Hanging up, Carson opened Sergeant Fontana's forensics report on the Boltons' home. With a more contained crime scene, they analyzed every particle and smudge, including fifty-three fingerprints that weren't the Boltons'; but none were found on the window coverings, the restraints, or Jennifer's keyboard, so they were likely remnants from earlier interactions with deliverymen and friends. The team also vacuumed and identified six distinct hairs, besides the two over-whelming types presumed to be the couple's. Carson e-mailed Fontana: *Tripp roamed house unmasked, get DNA profile on any straight black hairs.*

The remainder of the physical evidence proved nondescript, the murderers stingy with errors. But the technology analysis was fruitful. Forensics matched the *Star-Ledger* phone call with Bolton's timeline, and discovered that her hijacked internet account had been used Thursday evening to post threats on jihadist websites, coded to seem sourced from overseas. He e-mailed Agent Lehrer: *Found out who re-booked the unfortunate Constantine Albright's plane tickets.* Then he walked over to the barren sheets for the Bolton murder and wrote "Computer expert—Nick Lorelz??" on the one next to Tripp. Carson stepped back and nodded. Then he closed his eyes. *Of course they'd use the same guys for both crimes ... the leaders would want* all *of their pawns dead!* He scribbled out the question marks and wrote "90%", then directed Fontana again: *Thinking the suspects overlap. Get hair samples from river dead, and compare to hairs from house.*

He broke for a late dinner, jaywalking across Clinton Avenue then striding three blocks past the cop hangouts to Claire's. He considered the trek worth every step, although he wasn't sure if it was the food or the walk itself that recharged him.

"Lieutenant's working another weekend!" Claire blared from the hostess station. "Should I send one of my pretty waitresses over to your corner palace, or just get Fred started on the chicken parm?"

"How much extra for the chicken parm *and* the pretty waitress?"

"Don't you go two-timing on me! One Detective Special!" she bellowed toward the kitchen, loud enough for all the cooks on the block to hear. "Susie, make sure our VIP is served right." Other than the overblown welcomes, Claire knew to leave Carson alone during his meals, and to never ask about his cases, even if he'd been on the news.

After dinner, he returned to his office, lined up three coffees on his desk, and opened the witness video folder. "Tell me something I didn't see for myself," he said. The guards' interviews were repetitive and sketchy, the murderers all disguised and the captives blindfolded and inundated with noise for most of the ordeal. Officer Breslin proved most descriptive of the lot, and Carson noted the timestamp of his account of the warning instructions; presuming Righteous had made personal work of that, he'd want to review that narrative again:

14:03: He made me repeat that poem. I'd recognize his voice, that low-pitched snobbish tone, threatening me and I couldn't do anything about it. Then the sucker punch, still hurts some, here on my left side, so the jerk's obviously a righty. I'm doubled over, which happened to me once during football practice, and I needed two minutes to recover then. But maybe twenty seconds later his guys are trying to yank me up, and I can't stand. One of them grunts "up, up" and it hurts but they pull me mostly upright, and I know I'm just to repeat that poem over and over and that's what I do.

He also gleaned a few impressions of Righteous from Reiley's interview, the two having shared the truck's front seat for over an hour. Then he lumbered, weary-eyed, past the third shift officers and headed home for bed.

17

Carson's last relationship had ended with the same rebuke as his prior two: "You're married to your job." The Saturday the investigation stole was his alone.

He woke for a repeat on Sunday, five hours after falling asleep; his first thought was, *I'm missing something*. He trudged across his sparse bedroom and pondered Breslin's interview while shaving, showering, and brushing his teeth on autopilot. He mulled over the timeline, then visualized the sequence of events. *Nothing.* But he'd learned to exploit seemingly useless interviews before: *when you hit a brick wall with the storyline, scrutinize the words people choose.*

He returned to his office to watch the video again. Soon, he was smiling, then calling Breslin. "I don't care if you're half asleep or look like shit, I'll be at your house in twenty minutes, with questions."

* * * * *

Breslin did look zombie-eyed when he opened his door. "You're crazy if you think you're going to hear more than what I said, over and over again, yesterday. And I only slept for *two hours* last night—that fuckin' poem, mostly, with *your* name in it."

"I didn't write it! And I'm not here for the whole story, just some particulars."

"Let's get it over with, then."

Breslin led Carson to his kitchen, past boxes of lighting fixtures stacked in the hall. Three sets of wires hung down from small holes in the ceiling. "Don't worry if your story changes from yesterday. I'm going to have you think about the events differently, and I want you to respond to my questions just the way I ask them."

"OK, but I don't expect anything to change."

"Of course," Carson said, nodding. "But for me, now, replay the events I'm asking about … actually picture them happening. Do it in slow motion, so everything you heard and felt, you hear and feel again. Even shut your eyes."

The guard closed his eyes. "OK."

"When they first sent you out of the control room, to tape you up, they weren't blasting the construction noise yet. How did you know what they wanted you to do?"

"This leader-type sends us out one at a time. It's the poem guy who hits me later, same voice. He has pale makeup with too-bright lips. He says, 'Cougar, the young one,' pointing at me. He'd been calling all of them wildcat names: 'Tiger,' 'Lynx,' and the like. So, two guys grab me, two hands on each of my arms. And they're pulling my arms back and one grunts 'wrists together, no fighting.' It doesn't take more than a few seconds after that, and they walk me farther into the common room—"

"Stop there," Carson interrupted. "That's what you said yesterday, about being grunted at; that's why I came over. Can you focus on that?"

"Like I'm hearing it now … 'wrists together, no fighting.'"

"Have I been grunting at you?"

"No. Just talking."

"Why did you refer to him as grunting?"

Breslin paused. "He had this really low pitch…. Yeah, deep."

"Thanks. Now I'm going to ask about a different event. Don't try to match what you've said if it isn't supposed to match, OK? Just tell me, slowly, what happened after you were punched."

Breslin squeezed his eyes tighter for a moment. "It surprised me and it hurt. I doubled over and collapsed, and I couldn't breathe. My hands were behind my back so I also hurt my knee, my left knee, when I fell. Maybe I forced three half-breaths and someone grabs my left arm and tries pulling me up. I squirm and stay curled up and another guy reaches under my right arm and they pull together. But I have to keep my legs bent to breathe, so I end up sliding out of the grip and fall back to the ground. Then the one on my right goes "up, up" and they both heave. This time they've each grabbed under my armpits so I'm lifted vertical, plus I've breathed a little more, so I can reach my legs down, and the poem guy starts talking to me again."

"Stop there. The ones who lifted you definitely didn't include the one who recited the poem?"

"Right. Separate guys, different positions."

"And the words were 'up, up'?"

"Just that."

"And …"

Breslin opened his eyes wide. "Low-pitched, just like the others!" Breslin shut his eyes again for a few seconds and bobbed his head. "It was just two words, but I don't think it was the same guy who taped my wrists. I'm not certain, but I don't think so."

"Nice work!" Carson said. "Coincidences are usually clues in disguise … and I know how to get to the bottom of this one."

"I hadn't focused on their voices yesterday."

"It's always a work in progress. Like my next question … The one who held up the sign, and then acted like the leader in the control room … can you picture him?"

"He was made-up, like I said, but sure."

"Great." Carson handed over driver's license photos of the identified killers and morgue photos of the others. "Some of them took a beating, but let me know if you see a match."

Breslin flipped through the pile quickly, pulling out three pictures. "Definitely not these." Then he looked again, made three stacks, and pointed to the short one. "The way these two got bashed, it'll be hard to say for them." He picked up the middle stack and fanned the three photos, looking back and forth across the faces. "He could be one of these, and if I had to pick one, I'd pick him," he said, pointing to the yet-unidentified number eight.

Carson thanked him again, and headed back to his car, more convinced that Righteous was alive. Number eight measured six-foot-two on the coroner's table.

* * * * *

Before starting his Malibu, Carson called his sister's cell phone. "Another day with you?" she answered after two rings.

"It's for catching the killers! Pretend you're a doctor beholden to me, or maybe scared, and I want you to disguise my voice for four hours without anyone knowing. What would you do?"

"You don't trust yourself to fake it, like actors do?"

"I'll be stressed, and don't want to have to think about it."

"Hmm. The cricothyroid muscle stretches the vocal cords; different paralytics depress muscle activity for different time periods, and their antidotes, depending on the effect you're going for, could increase contractions. But it's too dangerous to use them just to change someone's pitch."

"Even if the fate of the galaxy depends on it?"

"Well, if it's *really* no holds barred, a laryngologist probably could put your voice through puberty again, for a few hours. You liked it *so much* the first time."

"I think the Panthera did that. They were mostly silent, except Righteous, but it was an extra precaution against being identified. Would you find the paralytic in the blood tests?"

"No, Ted! A systemic dose would be fatal. It would be applied on site, probably a sedated injection in the larynx."

"What if I wanted to sound high-pitched one morning, normal during the afternoon, then deep the next morning? Multiple injections?"

"The drugs wear off, so returning to normal occurs on its own. Then since you're waiting most of a day, you should be able to switch from extra high to extra low. But again, the voice is tricky … you'd need trials to make sure the subjects don't go mute. Figure some malleable or fanatical volunteers for that, along with the pressured doctor."

"I need you to check for the injections, Beck."

"Serena's over there now. I'll ask her to look for the entry sites."

"I know you trust your team."

"Call you back in thirty minutes."

"Better if I call you then. One more trip to make."

* * * * *

A bulging inch-long section of vein seemed ready to erupt from the center of Reiley's forehead. "They gave me a stinkin' forty-eight hours off rotation! Two measly days! I was handcuffed and had a gun in my ear!"

"Newark PD does the same thing!" Carson said.

"Bastards!"

"If you're not the one who got shot, it's 'get back to work!'"

"Yeah!" Reiley bawled. Then he sat silent, and Carson watched the red and purple hues in his face fade. "But it could've ended worse, if that's your point. You said this would just take two minutes?"

"Or less," Carson replied, presenting the photos. "Find Righteous."

The guard spent a minute splitting the stack, fanning two pictures in his right hand. "Certainly none of these," he said, thrusting out his left hand, "and neither of these, either," he finished, putting the pair from his right hand on top of the others.

With neither Reiley nor Breslin singling out a viable candidate, Righteous surviving remained the best theory, however skeptical

Carson had become of witness identifications. He decided to return to headquarters before calling his sister.

* * * * *

"You should've called when you said," Rebecca scolded. "Hard work is OK, but people need discrete times for recharging. All of us. You should try it sometime."

"You're right," Carson admitted. "That was rude. I wanted to have access to the network."

"And around your admiring subordinates, it may be all about what *you* want. But the medical examiner's office doesn't report to you, and I'd mail out enough resumes to fill the National Archives if *that* were ever to change."

"I'll keep working on it, Beck. Can I ask about the injections now?"

"Yes. We actually have three things to discuss. I had Serena sample four bodies for the injections. Three showed signs of a single injection within ten hours before death. Rinecore showed signs of a recent injection and a trauma with more advanced healing, so a fake voice Saturday and maybe a different fake the days before that."

"That's exactly what I wanted to hear!"

"Well, you're the one who told me to look for it," she reminded him.

Another ploy foiled. Carson put the handset down and stepped to his wall, ripped down three of the Bolton sheets, and wrote "= Alpha" on Righteous's sheet and "Beta/Gamma" on Rinecore's and Lorelz's. He smiled at his handiwork for a moment, then picked the phone back up from the visitor's side of his desk. "Since I recorded Righteous's calls, sounding deep, could you measure what the drug did to the cadavers' throats and reconstruct his true voice?"

"Our voices are too complex for *that*! Your tech guy can alter the pitch and timbre with a computer, to get a more average-sounding voice. But that won't necessarily match his natural voice, and wouldn't be admissible in court."

Carson stood in thought, until Rebecca broke the silence. "Moving on … We identified another one, Oscar Domingo. He had a numbered surgical pin from a boating accident four years ago—actually one of those WaveRunners, not a boat. Didn't learn his lesson about water sports the first time, I guess. I posted the report."

"Thanks! I'll put his friends and family on the interview list," Carson said, circling the desk to open the report and type as he spoke.

"And that ends our business, by my count," Rebecca said.

He played along, hung up, and speed-dialed his sister's landline from his personal cell phone. "You promised a third something to discuss?" he asked.

"Yes, but not sure if you'd call it 'something.' No match on the toxicology last night."

"They weren't poisoned? You were wrong about the neurotoxin?"

"How often am I wrong about the cause of death?"

"Well … never … I thought never. I'm confused."

"Our standard toxicology screens for fifty chemicals—common and less-common poisons, and commonly abused drugs. That's worked 99 percent of the time when we suspected a poisoning, and over and over when we weren't looking for one. But whatever the Panthera used wasn't among those fifty, like I'd feared from the symptoms. My next step would be an occupational hazard analysis, but that ordinarily draws people into the loop—"

"You know we can't call anyone else in, Beck. But I need that analysis. Righteous is still a blank—no prints, no DNA, and disguised, with an altered voice."

"I figured you'd think it was all about you, again. From the tissue damage, I've narrowed it down to five possible chemicals, which I could test for myself if I had a lab assistant with police clearance …"

"Seriously? I wouldn't know the first thing about a modern lab."

"No time like the present. Our Sunday goes down together, or not at all. And you'd better bring us a good lunch."

"But …" he started, hoping a rebuttal would spring to mind. "Fine. Not that you've left me any choice." He hung up, then called in an order to Claire's, without a menu. "Two Coke Zeros, two waters, a Greek salad, and a turkey club."

"Hot date, Lieutenant?" Claire asked.

"Strictly business. Make it a drive-through?"

"Of course. Only for you."

He headed out, after writing Oscar Domingo's name over his morgue photo and scribbling "Underwater Gear?" below.

Claire's didn't have a parking lot, much less a drive-up window. Instead, he chirped his siren twice up the block, and the busboy came out between the cars parked outside the front door. The drive-through blocked traffic for only fifteen seconds, then Carson resumed his trip to the lab.

18

Rebecca was waiting for Ted outside the M.E.'s office in her Sunday attire, a Giants jersey and jeans. "Claire's! How original," she teased.

He started to smile, then stopped, registering that her mocking wasn't angry enough, then scowled. "You don't really need my help, do you?"

"Still the best detective in Newark," she said, initiating a hug he wouldn't reciprocate. "I knew if you were really swamped, you would've wiggled your way out of it. We'll be done by two, anyway. I did some prep yesterday."

Once inside the lab, he set the food down on the closest of the three desks, the one farthest from the four steel examination tables, farthest from the white wall stacked with refrigerated cadaver cubbyholes. "I'd never get used to working here."

"Imagine if there were no need for this place," she said.

"Or need for what I do …"

Rebecca nodded. "You'll want one of these," she said, grabbing two disposable uniforms from a metal cabinet and handing one to Ted. "Should I start by explaining what I already did?"

"Can I answer that truthfully?" he replied while starting to suit up.

"All right. As long as you don't presume it was easy."

"Never. I couldn't do half of this work in a hundred years."

"Suffice it to say, if you poison someone with mercury, we find the mercury; but some compounds react quickly in the body, and what we find is more like an ancient lakebed where water had once been."

"That's simple enough for me to understand."

"Good. Follow me," she said, pulling a plastic bin from a refrigerator and taking it to a table. After a few minutes of wielding her scalpel and filling vials, she carried a tray across the room. "Should I tell you what this machine does?"

"Only if it puts me in danger."

"Some help you're turning out to be! At least come over and turn the vent on, the switch says 'Vent'. It's just a precaution, anyway. We'll have some waiting time once the chromatograph gets going."

She went back and cleaned the lab table, then returned the bin to the refrigerator and placed a bag in the adjoining freezer. "Lunchtime!" she announced.

Ted grimaced under his mask, unable to continue pretending that his sister had been picking at something other than poisoned sections of human lungs. Rebecca proceeded unfazed, tossing out her gloves and mask and scrubbing her hands in the sink. "Don't wuss out on me now," she said. "Besides, we won't be eating here in the lab—that's for doctors only. And I didn't use a cadaver refrigerator for the drinks this time."

Carson took a deep breath and followed his sister's lead in throwing out his gloves and mask, then walked with her to her office.

"We have privacy here?" he asked. She nodded. "Do you think you know which poison they used?"

Rebecca chuckled. "You didn't bring me a bottle of the stuff! The chemicals interact at the cellular level; you only see the damage they do, and sometimes how the body defended against them. That's how I narrowed it down to five, once the regular tox screen candidates were ruled out. You'll have to wait another ten minutes, detective—or longer if this salad takes me longer."

"But he's out there now—"

"He's not a serial killer, Ted, torturing his victims as we speak."

"Who really knows what this nut is capable of? He filled the morgue four times over in one day."

"I know—I was just joking about the salad. When the machine finishes, we'll get our answer. Sometimes I just like pretending to have balance in my life; it helps me stay human. For example, you haven't asked about your nieces," she said, forcing him into a family conversation until her computer intoned a mechanized "Eu-re-ka."

"Come around here," she directed. "The results display as an image. You won't know what the lines and colors represent, but the software does most of the work, so even a layman can find a match."

Ted watched her open the file. Five chromatograms displayed on the right side, with two nearly identical ones labeled "Sample 1" and "Sample 2" on the left. His jawed dropped, and he looked over to see her mouth agape as well, a reaction to unexpected failure they'd either inherited or learned together.

"Some parts of ours match *some* parts of the known ones," he offered.

"No, we need exact matches on the reds and blues." She paused. "Both of my specimens look the same; that rules out contamination," she muttered, typing on the keyboard. "I shouldn't have narrowed it down to five." The screen soon flashed "Search in Progress."

"The poison could be more obscure than I thought," she said. "Now the server's looking for any rough match across the entire database. We'll get a bunch of possibilities, and then I'll have some work to do to narrow it back to one."

Instead of more chromatograms, Ted saw a growing list of long words ending in "ide" or "zene" with "<5%" next to each.

Rebecca's jaw dropped again. "Ted, every toxic chemical sold in the developed world is in that database, by law, and still no match." She turned toward him. "Your killer is a megalomaniac with a clandestine lab."

* * * * *

Ted staggered back to his seat. "His own lab?"

"Or worse," Rebecca replied. "The cover-up is over."

"No! We can't … we shouldn't …"

"We can't be complicit in some covert militia developing superweapons, killing a hundred people at a time!"

Ted closed his eyes for a moment. "This doesn't make us wrong about the cover-up, Beck. OK, they used a new poison—but different doesn't mean more dangerous."

"Then why did they bother?"

"Maybe it was just a tall order. They couldn't get into the cells, and the inmates wouldn't let themselves be injected or ingest whatever was handed to them."

"So it had to be a vapor. There are plenty of those around."

"Plus the attackers had to be safe. And the guards in the control room."

"Did the killers wear gas masks?" she asked.

"Not while the guards could witness them, and we didn't recover any."

"All right. So their poison neutralizes quickly, and if they didn't have masks, an antidote exists. I still don't think they had to go designer."

"But there's more to it than that. The delivery system had to be compact, and the small amount they lugged in had to be 100 percent fatal, or the ruse is over—no antitoxin effects from any drugs an inmate might be taking. Plus it needed to leave all the trappings of a chemical accident. And going designer makes it harder to track; recognized exotic poisons are some of the easiest weapons to trace back."

"You don't think they're too dangerous to be given the benefit of the doubt?"

"I found out last night that Righteous killed his eleven accomplices—deliberately sliced up the parachutes. He's not trying to build an army, he just wanted to get away with this one crime. This isn't bigger than us, Beck…. You're still on board, right?"

Rebecca rolled her eyes. "I'm still in," she said. "You say it's not bigger than us, but it's *certainly* bigger than *you* think. You'd better be careful on this one, Ted."

"You're the second doctor to tell me that," he said, standing up. He took five steps while mumbling, "Don't forget to say hi to—" Then he turned back to his sister. "You said the killers took an antidote?"

"You never know when to quit! Antitoxins usually aren't chemical mirrors that tell you the toxin's composition; they counteract effects at the cellular level. And finding some other unknown chemical wouldn't help either, especially with hazard response teams and the military being off-limits to us. I'll screen for the antidote myself to be sure—but just for you, and don't get your hopes up."

Ted fixated on one word of hers, muttered "Thanks, Beck," and walked to his car in a trance. *Military*.

* * * * *

Once Bertha connected to the network, Carson e-mailed his team: *Got a hunch. Alert me as soon as the service records of the two discharged army regulars are posted.* Then he checked his inbox; Darrell Goode asked for a call, and he obliged.

"Ted! Still ignoring that it's the weekend?"

"Neither rain, nor snow, nor day of week … something like that, right?"

"Something like that. This'll be quick. The sabotaged balloon had residue inside of it, like after a low-grade explosion—the airbag analogy I used yesterday. So I still believe an effort—a doomed effort—was made to inflate the fabric into a balloon." Goode cleared his throat. "Well, the canvas was in the river, but we salvaged a clean sample for the tests. But when we ran the chemical analysis, we couldn't find a match. I mean, I wasn't surprised that we didn't match weaponized explosives, but I thought industrial explosives, or propellants—somewhere we'd get a hit. But we didn't. There are a million chemicals we know about, and a billion we haven't made yet. Somehow, your guys were the first to have detonated this mix, and they knew what it would do. Sorry, Ted. I can't tell you which chemical to trace."

"So … you're telling me to search for a mad scientist running a lab?"

"In a sense, yes. Perhaps a problem child at a chemical company?"

"All right, Darrell. That's too bad, but I understand." He hung up and smiled. *Now I can investigate exotic chemicals without incriminating Rebecca*, he thought.

19

Jennifer Bolton's third day as a widow was becoming a wretched blur. Her friends tried to console her at the funeral, the eulogy was touching, and she and Phil's mother shared sentimental memories. But Phil was gone, and none of that helped—or maybe it had helped, and this incessant misery was as good as it was going to get.

When she cried, people would comfort her; when she stopped, they'd leave her alone. And everybody seemed to know not to ask about Phil's last hours. But—*damn it*—that was something she couldn't put out of her mind. Phil deserved a future, not death at the hands of a maniac. And she deserved three decades more with him.

Nothing was working right. Not the pre-funeral visits on Sunday. Not the post-funeral gathering today. Nothing, except those ten seconds, when the funeral home was silent and she closed her eyes and convinced herself this was a nightmare. Then she peeked at the cruel world and saw the fading abrasions on her wrists and remembered her lips sealed for an entire day. Nobody here could possibly fathom her anguish. Phil was everything, and he wasn't coming back. When she spoke to him now, she always said the same thing: "I'm going to make them pay, honey."

Jen sent everyone home before dinnertime, except the police, who obliged her request to search the house. But the brooding just got worse with the isolation. *Who cares about constitutional law? No parchment saved Phil, protected* his *rights. I dwell on nuances, while my husband is dead! And that nonsense about finding my own path without him, making a new life of it ... those scum wrenched* everything *away*.

At ten o'clock, she realized she'd been staring at the dim wall of her extra bedroom for an hour. *Phil would've wanted more from me— more* for *me—than stewing in misery*. She turned on the nightstand light and dialed out. "You're going to think I'm the most insensitive woman on Earth, aren't you?" she asked.

"There isn't a person in the world with the right to judge you," Lieutenant Carson replied.

"I keep thinking of Phil, but every now and then I want to think of something else, except what comes to mind are that creep's hand on my throat, and having to pee in front of him, and passing out from the injection. I'm sure this sadness is never going away, but maybe this rage ... if you catch them ..."

"I understand. My whole life is pursuing justice."

"Justice for *my* case, right? For Phil's murderers?"

"Yes, Professor Bolton. In fact, when you're up to it, I want to discuss the case. I didn't want to bother you at the funeral this morning, but we learned a lot over the weekend, and made some progress today."

"It comes in waves. Right now, I want to talk."

"I'll head over, but if you change your mind, I'll understand."

It was brief, but unmistakable—realizing that her thoughts about punishing Phil's killers weren't just wishful yearnings brought her first smile in four days.

While dressing for the lieutenant's arrival, she focused on Alpha, just as he'd had her do on Saturday. But she kept getting stuck on the highlight reel—the gun and the choking—again and again. *That's not where the clues are!* She went through each minute with Alpha instead, his every move, his every word. She'd be the perfect witness. *You played with fire, asshole.*

* * * * *

Professor Bolton greeted Carson, and led him into the living room. "This time, *you* take the couch."

He had just grabbed the armrest when she continued, "I have plenty of questions, but let's start with the update you promised."

He raised his eyebrows. She no longer seemed the broken woman he'd manipulated over the weekend. "I appreciate the zeal, professor; that'll help a lot. But to be clear, crime victims don't get to ask too many questions, or else—"

"—the jury could treat me as a tainted witness," she finished. "I know the rules. But to be clear back, you've stretched the rules for this case, when it suited you."

You don't know the half of it, he thought, blushing. "I *was* pushy the other day ..."

"It was important to be ... *then*. Let's move forward."

"OK. One of the intruders used your computer to hack overseas terminals and post terroristic threats. A suspect in another crime, Nick Lorelz, was a computer expert motivated to post terroristic threats. I'm confident it was the same guy, but that won't get adjudicated because he died attempting to escape."

"One of them is dead?" She kept silent for a few seconds, but Carson was familiar with that lawyers' trap and suffered the awkward void rather than reveal more. "The other crime was another kidnapping?" she finally asked.

"I can't discuss the other crime. Rest assured, it had nothing to do with you."

"Did it also involve a four-person gang, or was it this Lorelz alone?"

"There was another team, and it seems that the other quiet accomplice in your kidnapping was part of that with Lorelz, and he died as well."

"Other ... So Beta and Gamma are both dead already?"

He nodded. "Yes."

"What about the other two? Tripp was on the security cameras at Seton Hall."

"Unfortunately, when they told you he'd disappear, they probably meant it. If you're desperate enough, there are dozens of corrupt, lawless places where money brings protection. He'll be isolated and bored, but alive, and, technically, free."

"Can't you bring him back?"

"If I'm right about the Lagos shuffle, our window is already closed."

"Lagos shuffle?"

"That's just what I call it—he wouldn't be the first to pull it off," Carson explained. "From Newark Airport security videos, we confirmed him flying to Nigeria on Friday, still under the alias Tripp—Tripp Baxter. We examined the airline logs and found three passengers using the common surname 'Martin' starting complex itineraries from Lagos Saturday morning: one for Paris–Karachi–Frankfurt–Lagos, another for London–Manila–Frankfurt–Lagos, and the third for Istanbul–Karachi–Paris–Lagos. But most likely only two returned to Lagos; the third, Tripp, would've switched with an accomplice during one of the layovers, changed disguises, and flown to his final destination untracked. I'm afraid we don't catch him unless he resurfaces."

Bolton looked down. "I understand," she said. Then she raised her head. "So you're three-fourths done, after only a couple of days?"

"Well, I don't consider it three-fourths done; the ringleader counts for more than the others."

"Sure. How much have you learned about Alpha? He survived the other crime?"

"We've uncovered a lot about the other crime, and linked Alpha to it. But there's nothing more I can divulge to you."

"What? That's it?"

"I've revealed all I can. And now you have to focus on helping me—that's what's going to crack the case. Have you remembered anything new? Anything about Alpha?"

Bolton's eyes narrowed. "You police know how recollections work! The witness has to have context to process what's in memory! The brain has to find the information meaningful!" She paused, gaze locked. "You said you were driven to find him—tell me why I was kidnapped, and why he *killed* just to organize a march in my name! Don't make me Freedom of Information Saturday's crimes to track down what else they did!"

She was right—holding back was pointless. She'd readily discover that the only sophisticated crime Saturday morning was the prison assault. And he'd need her help, *all* of her help, to track down Righteous, regardless of protocol. "Before you were rescued, twelve men broke into Essex State Prison, led by a goon who self-identified as Righteous. We've reported that they were trying to free an unknown number of hard-core felons but accidently discharged a volatile caustic, leading to the deaths of eighty-eight prisoners."

Bolton nodded. "I saw the headlines—Cassie's been bringing my newspapers in."

"During their own attempted escape, eleven of the gang perished, but Righteous is still at large. He spoke in a deep pitch, but otherwise acted like Alpha. And there were other similarities, in the planning and attention to detail, and the way they used guns and technology. I now believe they'd altered their voices, medically, to sound high-pitched when they were here, and low-pitched on Saturday. I think Alpha is Righteous."

She nodded again, turned away, and stared for five seconds. Then she turned back, looking like a rabbi who'd been asked to bless a ham. "And *how* did my kidnapping help Righteous with his prison break?"

Carson paused, then put on his best poker face. "There's got to be more to it, but the protest march ... the march drew police resources away from Essex State. I'm sorry to say, that's my working assumption for his motive."

Bolton teared up, then started to cry. "He took Phil just to make his escape easier?"

Carson bit his lip and sat still as she wept, cursing that he'd be the only one sharing information that evening. But Bolton soon recovered. "I hate him even more," she said, wiping off the tears. "The police rescued me because you connected the crimes. But how did you even know about my abduction?"

"Righteous recorded a tirade for prisoners' rights. He left word to come here, saying you'd been kidnapped for—his words—a 'greater good.'"

Bolton stared off for another moment. "He used that same expression with me. But I'm not remembering anything else significant." She glanced away once more. "Wait ... The breakout was *Saturday*; on Friday morning, the way they acted seemed ... felt ... expeditious. And they took a risk leaving us alone all day. He must've had to be somewhere else on Friday! Maybe he would've been missed at work?"

Carson smiled. "Yes, that's a clue. Keep thinking of more. Someone who *wouldn't* have been missed on a Friday would've been even better."

"Well, then, tell me something else to think about. What's the most intriguing lead so far?" she pressed.

"It works better if I mix in some questions. Did Alpha say anything to make you think about chemistry or the military? They used an explosive propellant that had never been sold commercially, and his army vet accomplices hadn't had special weapons or demolitions assignments. And they used a special computer medium, perhaps developed just for him."

"You think he's a chemist? A true mad scientist?"

"At this point, yes ... or someone who helped him is."

"I told the detectives about the tracking device in my car, but I don't recall Alpha saying anything technical." Bolton turned away again, then back. "Sometimes Phil discussed scientific inventions with me. A new computer medium could take years or decades to develop; I'd guess likewise for a new propellant. You're looking for a couple of mad scientists, or maybe a team of them."

"But who would have access to a stable of mad scientists?"

Bolton stared, then started sobbing. "He said if I didn't drive as Tripp told me … his exact words … his exact words were … Phil's 'will goes to probate….' Alpha is a lawyer … a patent attorney."

Carson gaped at his witness, the only person who would have been able to answer his question in the heat of the moment. *Righteous played with fire*, he thought.

- 20 -

Ten cluttered detectives' desks, arranged in two rows, flanked the route to Carson's office. When he arrived on Tuesday morning, Kaleah Banks stood up from behind the second one and greeted him with a tired, dimpled smile, breaking his concentration on patent attorneys. "We finished and posted three dozen interview reports and two equipment reports overnight," she said, baggy brown eyes gleaming.

"Wonderful, Leah! Follow me in."

As they entered his office, he added, "Glad I got you as second-in-command on this one."

"You know I'm only on the force because of you." She closed the door behind them. "Well, because of your chemistry with Natalie Mays at the diversity recruitment fair, actually."

"And now I have the lieutenants' privilege of drawing from both the Major Crimes and Homicide Sections. You know we fight over you?"

Banks shook her head. "You train *all* of the detectives to be outstanding."

He sat down, facing her. His stomach had been knotting every time he'd deceived her about D block, with each omission about the Panthera's motives and each admonition to concentrate on the conspirators' schedules alone; now it was in full churn. "Anything on Righteous?"

"Nothing conclusive. The Panthera were careful, like you said. There were lots of times, mostly Sundays, when four or five of them were unaccounted for, but never the whole gang. So we can't be *sure* which of their meetings included Righteous. But you said he was controlling—"

"And then some. I'd bet he oversaw *every* meeting."

"Good … so he'd have holes in his schedule for each of those slots. They were also careful not to be seen with each other. We only found one exception—Domingo's sister thought she'd seen Rinecore and someone resembling morgue photo number ten at his apartment once, but didn't remember either's name."

"Almost lucky, then."

"Yeah. She also swore her brother *never* would've helped with a prison escape."

Carson took a deep breath. "And *her* explanation for what he was doing there?"

Banks shrugged. "She loves her brother, I guess."

"I suppose," he replied, nodding.

"There's one thing we are close on—we're down to four companies that might've supplied that beam that stabilized the escape truck."

"That's something."

"Sure. And you'll see in the reports, there are plenty of open leads. A little patience, and we'll figure out who Righteous is."

"Actually, Leah, I was pondering the physical evidence last night, and I think—" Carson stopped himself. Banks wasn't going to be the key to catching Righteous, not while he was keeping secrets from her. His hopes rested with Jennifer Bolton—she'd had the crucial insight, and knew about lawyers. He had to keep drawing Bolton in, even if that meant keeping Leah out. "I think we'll need *a lot* of patience."

"Whatever it takes."

When Banks left, Carson opened the reports; but for every minute he focused on them, he spent five dwelling on Bolton's epiphany. He returned to her house at noon.

"I know you've got to need time for yourself, and with your friends," he said, "but our conversation last night was a game changer. Are you up to talking again?"

"Honestly, Lieutenant, I'd love to talk about the case. Everyone else seems to think I should be bubble-wrapped, but that's not what's helping." He nodded, and they sat, together, on the couch. "Can I get *you* something to drink? Anything but Gatorade."

He smiled and shook his head. "Know any good patent lawyers?"

"As suspects, or as resources?"

"Both, eventually. But at this point, to help out. My lab has data on commercial and military explosives, but wouldn't know how to find a patented but unproduced one."

"There are plenty of patent attorneys in New Jersey, but I wouldn't want to find we've consulted the fox about guarding the henhouse.... I know some Three Ls—third year law students—who did patent work last summer who would kill to have independent research on their resumes. And I need an excuse to get back to Seton Hall anyway. Just get me the formula."

"This will stay secret? I shouldn't even be discussing it with you."

"I'm just helping another professor get a jump on her final exam, choosing a patented product at random. Expulsion if they leak it."

"Great. There might be a second chemical—I'll either send you one or two."

"The special computer disk?"

"Maybe," he bluffed, "or maybe an unrelated trace."

Bolton wrinkled her brow. "That's the third time you've evaded my questions. I'll let that one slide as well, because you're already breaking the police code of silence for me. But don't make it a habit."

I'm glad she's on my side, he thought. "And timing?"

"Law students are swamped with reading, usually five or six hours each day. But they're graded strictly on a final exam—no other tests or projects—so in the middle of the term, I can get them to do a lot for me quickly. They'll find out who filed the patent application by tomorrow morning."

"The bad guys won't know what hit them. I'll text you the analysis on the residue," he said, getting up to leave.

"Cassie said there were forty marchers and twenty police—not nearly the diversion he would've gotten if he'd called in a bomb threat for the train station or set off a smoke bomb in a hospital," Bolton challenged. "If you're concealing his motive, you'd better have a compelling reason."

"We'll learn more when we catch him; it's premature to share everything I suspect now."

She bit her lip, shook her head twice, then murmured, "OK."

* * * * *

Carson spent the ride to headquarters and his lunchtime considering how to approach his sister, then made the call. "You said the poison reacted with the cells. If you list out the specifics, Bolton's students can find the patent application that matches."

"Are you crazy?" Rebecca screamed before slamming her door. "Those searches are made by computer—permanent record! And it's the school's account—they scan the browsing history! Even worse, if this stuff *is* military and they've flagged it as high threat, who knows what *they'd* think, and how hard they'd come down on us! This is your dumbest request ever!" She paused her rant, then continued calmly. "Speaking of dumb, where do *you* draw the line between witness and collaborator? You know she can't be both."

"The more I tell her, the more she figures out. And the creep is a lawyer, too—a cunning one. I know I'm going to need her again. And … well … she's really smart.… She reminds me of you."

"*Very* dumb. Thanks for the compliment, I guess. But you can't bring her in on the case. You're already breaking the rules, and this just compounds the risk … *our* risk."

"A hundred people, Beck. He killed a hundred people. If he gets away … I can't have that hanging over my head. I've seen cops ruined over less."

"The way to catch him is to be thoughtful, like you usually are, and careful. Don't let on about the breakout ruse, don't share *anything* about the poison, and don't turn this victim relationship into anything more than that."

He tapped "End Call" on his personal phone, thought for a minute, then texted the lab analysis on the balloon explosive to Bolton. *I could end up in cellblock D for this.*

* * * * *

Carson was reading evidence reports when he received Fontana's e-mail: *Hair in Boltons' bathroom matched to Nick Lorelz. Prison killers were her attackers, 100%.*

Then Detective Youngman called. "Lieutenant, you'll want to hear this directly. None of the four distributors who might've supplied that beam they jerry-rigged for the truck would've sold a single unit, not to a new customer. So the Panthera buy ten beams, but know the police are going to end up looking for the nine extras. If I'm them, I think the choices are pretend they're hot and try to sell them cheap, or find a scrap recycler. I figure that novices would assume scrapping is safer, and overlook how odd it would be to get nine identical, flawless beams. And sure enough, I'm at Bi-County Recycling, with a story. I'm putting the supervisor, Shawn Holloway, on speakerphone."

"Shawn, I showed you eleven photos. What did you say about number ten?"

"This guy drives a truck in that says plumbing supplies—like Joe's Plumbing Supplies or Tom's Plumbing Supplies—but it just has construction beams in it. And I know that's not plumbing supplies, and I start making him nervous … that's why I remember all this. Then number ten comes over, talking about delivering bathroom piping for a new mall on Route 9, but some bankrupt hauler abandoned the wrong size beams, and they just got permission to get rid of them, so they paid the first guys with a truck. It still sounds fishy, but we keep a hot sheet here, and no one reported stolen beams. We can't stay in business if I turn away product that's not on the hot sheet, so I take them in."

Carson cut in, "Do you have records of the sale?"

"We log whenever we use the industrial scale, so when I find the date on the check, I can give you the exact time—his would've been the heaviest load of the day. And I just told your guy here, he'll stand out on my check register—the only one-and-done plumber who hasn't kept coming back with old pipes."

"And the part about writing the check …" Youngman prompted.

"So I'm making small talk when I fill out the check and I say 'Sam's Plumbing,' or 'Bob's Plumbing,' whatever, 'Are you Sam?' And he says, 'No, I'm Ty De … Tyler,' and he stops and he's turned red, and the driver kind of looks at him funny, too. So I remember 'Tyler De—' before he stopped himself."

"Thank you, Mr. Holloway," Carson said. "I need a minute with my detective; if you start tracking down that check, I'll be finished with him soon."

"Off speaker, Lieutenant," Youngman soon announced.

"Smart way to follow up on the beam! It should be a snap to cross-check all of the Tyler D. driver's license photos against our cadaver shot. And if they slipped up and deposited the check to Sam's or Bob's or Joe's Plumbing, you'll have another electronic trail to pursue."

He hung up, smiled, and wrote "Tyler D" on sheet ten, leaving three blank inches for the rest of his surname. Then he looked at Righteous's sheet and shook his head—*if only you'd been the one who revealed himself as "Tyler D., Esquire."*

✳ ✳ ✳ ✳ ✳

Carson had to waste late Tuesday afternoon managing up: a progress report for Captain Burgess, a conference call with Director Arden, and a press liaison update for a briefing that would make the evening news. He gave his team a rest for the night, except for the contingent investigating Tyler Decknor, the last-identified miscreant.

He worked in a three-mile run when he got home, then called Bolton. "Are we still on for ten tomorrow?"

"I'm meeting the students at 9:30 so they can make their ten o'clock classes."

"Great ... You're brave to push forward on this."

"It felt right for two-thirds of the day, and wrong for the other third."

"That's progress."

"I was actually going to call you, about my progress. I told the officer in my driveway that he could go fight real crime, but he said he had to hear it from you."

"Will get right on that."

* * * * *

"ID!" the Seton Hall Law School guard demanded.

"I'm scheduled to meet Professor Bolton at ten," Carson said, handing over his driver's license rather than draw attention with his badge.

The guard scanned a computer screen. "Carson ... OK. Sign in. Fourth floor."

Carson rode upstairs, then loitered in the hallway while textbook-toting professors strode past toward the elevators. He tempered his boredom by memorizing identifying traits for each passerby. A couple of twenty-somethings stirred a curious stoplight imagery, a towering crewcut redhead half a step behind a woman with a blond bob in a green sweatshirt. When the droopy-eyed duo passed, he assumed the coast was clear.

Bolton was flipping through papers when he arrived, a strained look on her face. "Did the kids screw up, or did we?" he asked.

"I think they did everything right; they even checked internationally. Nobody has secured commercial rights to your balloon inflator."

He sighed. "It could still be anyone, then."

"No ... no. We're not back to square one. This chemical, that disk ... they were developed by someone, and Alpha learned about them, like a lawyer would. He just didn't file a patent."

"Hiring an attorney, then not filing? Isn't that a stretch?"

"Maybe the explosive isn't suitable for commercial use yet, and they're keeping it secret while they perfect it."

"We're pursuing a *maybe?*"

"I can't *prove* anything. But a patent attorney is still the only fit. Think about it."

Bolton's speculation that the propellant wasn't commercially viable started to make sense, and applied doubly well to the hyper-toxic gas. "So if Righteous—I've got twenty officers calling him Righteous, can we just do that? If Righteous *is* a patent attorney, where do we start? New Jersey has three times more lawyers than plumbers, and they can conceal their records by attorney-client privilege."

"I know where I'd start," she offered. "Alpha—you stick with 'Righteous,' you're trying to stay in his head, but I cringe hearing Phil's murderer called 'righteous'—Alpha was so controlling and smug, he must consider himself top dog. And there's a nexus with New Jersey, maybe even Essex County. I thought about it last night, who would be on the patent application, and kept coming back to one firm. Plenty of lawyers claim to be the best in their fields, but for patent work in this state, there's one firm wealthy clients call first, one with the clout to write its own rules. Alpha must be a lawyer at Denton, Foster & Kahn."

- 21 -

Judy Novack, the human resources director at Denton, Foster & Kahn, had started cold-calling One Ls just before Labor Day, looking for students who'd filled their two- or three-year gaps between college and law school working as paralegals at the top firms. Gabe Jenkins had been a great find, and was one phone call away from a referral fee.

"I still feel guilty … like I'm poaching Sullivan & Cromwell," Jenkins said.

"Nonsense," Novack replied. "They made their offers to the summer associate class in August. If Doug Posey hasn't accepted yet, he's already weighing other options for after he graduates. My admin called the *Yale Law Journal* last week to get his cell number, and he was gone—three days in San Francisco. Sounds like Morrison & Foerster is wooing him as well."

"All right … if I won't get in trouble."

"No one else has…. Now, you've asked around, and you're *sure* Doug was the class standout, like a once-every-few-years star? If we wanted the whole top five percent, we could go through the law school placement offices."

"Everyone felt the same as me, and this was my third year there. They reassigned his mentorship to a partner—*a partner*—in Leveraged Finance, and he accompanied the firm's chairman to drum up business with the director who'd supervised his internship at Goldman Sachs."

"And the Facebook search?"

"I couldn't get his resume, but he definitely has a Master's in Engineering."

"A scientist, and a superstar at the law—just who we need, Gabe."

"Could I ask ..." Jenkins started. "The referral fee is generous ... so don't take this wrong ... and Doug is everything you asked for. But S&C and MoFo are considered top-of-the-top, and partners there earn nine figures before they retire.... How can you possibly lure him to do intellectual property work at a midsized firm like Denton Foster?"

"Distinguish yourself like he did, and maybe you'll find out." Novack hung up, turned to her computer, and highlighted Posey's name in yellow on a half-page list. *Five's always been enough*, she thought. *Time to make the pitches.*

* * * * *

First on Novack's call list was Ruth Gelfand; before excelling at Columbia Law School, she'd held an externship with the U.S. Patent and Trademark Office. "Ruth, we have a unique business model—we do things better, and charge accordingly. That presents a more lucrative opportunity for you—*substantially* more—than you'll get at any large firm. And you'll still work with the smartest attorneys. If that's piqued your interest, you should let me take you to lunch."

* * * * *

The pitch meetings required a week of travel, but Novack salvaged her weekend by conducting the last one in New York. She arrived at Delmonico's ten minutes early, and Gelfand, five. The recruit could have passed for her daughter—petite as well, with shoulder-length hair the same chestnut brown her stylist restored hers to. The hostess sat them at her reserved window table, and they engaged in small talk until the waiter arrived. "I always order the signature steak, even though I can't eat half of the slab they bring out," Novack said.

Gelfand closed her menu and nodded. "When in Rome ..."

When the server left, Novack slid a confidentiality agreement to the Three L. "My pitch wasn't just puffery—we consider our business model proprietary."

Gelfand underlined two sentences as she read the document, then turned back to them before signing. "If you're testing me, there are two provisions I'd advise a typical client to challenge."

"Oh, we'll test you; your interviews won't be a half-day of chitchat with junior associates. I become Mrs. Hyde, and the partners are even tougher. But today is for lunch."

Novack kept the conversation low-key until the waiter brought two seared Delmonicoes to the table. "I'm sure any firm you're considering has partners nationally recognized as experts in their fields. If you do your homework on intellectual property, you'll see that's also true of Lucian Denton, Mattias Foster, and Reuben Kahn."

"It certainly is true," the student said. "I *did* my homework, after our call."

"I should've expected that," Novack complimented. "And despite having only sixty attorneys, our client list includes every major innovator in the developed world."

"Yes, that was impressive, too…. You've alluded to the business model a few times …"

"Right. That's what make us different—better—for standouts like you. High-end lawyers sell time and expertise. The other top firms make your billable hours twice as important as proficiency. Denton Foster treats both equally. However simple that sounds, almost laughably simple, that's our edge."

Gelfand returned a slow, polite nod.

"There are three boring pieces to it. We build expertise with top-tier hires and low turnover, hence the grueling interviews and generous compensation. Then we tackle complex assignments with half the manpower of our competitors—you work hard, but you're getting more done. And we bill by the project rather than hourly, generating windfalls for the firm."

The recruit perked up at the mention of windfalls, then gave a poker-faced nod.

"And whether you'd think those things would make a difference, just hearing me drone on about it, money talks. If you join us, Ruth, your starting salary will be $400,000, twice what you'd get at Davis Polk."

Gelfand brought her hand to her face to conceal her grin, and Novack pounced. "Can you interview in Newark next Wednesday?"

"I'm sure I can," she replied, pulling out her phone.

Novack smiled. *Five for five*, she thought, *four years in a row*.

* * * * *

Novack had scheduled the candidates from Harvard, Emily Dao and Clayton Drummond, to interview last, during the final week of September; if they ended up among the top three, she didn't want to have to return to Cambridge to make their offers. Tuesday was Dao's turn. Novack grilled her first, then sent her for a grueling hour with Denton and another with Kahn before leading her to a small office in their library.

The name partners then gathered in Novack's office. "Impeccable resume," she began, "and she fared well on core competencies. Smart, articulate, highly motivated, mature, history of handling pressure and working well independently, and seems to understand what she's getting into. Maybe less of a track record on teamwork, could be the only shortcoming."

"Thanks, Judy," Denton said. She gave a slight smile; Denton's gratitude was usually sincere. The other two gave condescending nods, reminding her what they thought of non-lawyers. "I sent her my college thesis last night," Denton continued, "and tested her technical abilities. She would've made a great engineer. Perhaps she's not ready to go head-to-head with a PhD, but I think she'll master any science she's exposed to. Any job I'd give to a new hire, I'd entrust to her. She's definitely in my top three."

Kahn spoke next. "I covered whether she could apply what she's learned. She takes Copyright in the spring, so I tested her with a patent filing instead. She hit all three planted errors, and had a fourth challenge that was incorrect, ultimately, but that we would've wanted flagged. Knows the law, knows or figured out why it is the way it is, and figured out how to apply it. She responded well when I changed the facts, and well when I posited a change in the law. I'd also trust her with important work, and also think she's top three."

"So there's agreement," Foster said, drawing nods. "Time to test Ms. Dao outside of her element."

* * * * *

Emily Dao spent her time in the library replaying her interviews, feeling she'd done well overall. Novack's grin confirmed that before she spoke. "Congratulations! You passed round one."

She returned the smile. "Great!"

"You see what I meant about our interviews being trying?" Novack asked, still grinning, as she sat to her right.

"You must end up with a very select group. Glad I'm making the cut so far."

"Our recruiting *has been* very successful," Novack said. Then she dropped her smile. "Mr. Foster has been benchmarking prospects, using similar question sets for years. That works because, I'm sorry to say, we prohibit candidates from sharing the questions—not with Harvard's placement office, not with your friends on *Law Review*, probably not even with your husband, if you find time to meet a husband … or wife if that's your preference, we couldn't care less about that."

"Don't be sorry. You should protect your *own* intellectual property, after all."

"True. But, awkwardly, it's too early to rely only on judging your character, so you'll have to sign another confidentiality agreement." Novack handed her a four-page contract. "You'll notice the 'Damages' section is longer than in the first one, and almost too oppressive to be enforceable—*almost*."

Dao took the prompt to read and listen simultaneously. It *was* getting awkward.

"We call that the 'Kirke' provision," Novack continued, "after an unfortunate associate who'd divulged one of Foster's challenges to a law student. We not only fired Mr. Kirke, we fought to have him disbarred, and he no longer practices law."

Dao stared at the exacting paragraphs. *Disbarment? What an overreaction! And such high-handed leadership—the* Kirke *provision? But the other stories you've heard … all of these firms are oppressive in their own ways. And you can follow rules, and not get caught up in this. Twice the salary … it makes a lot of crap tolerable.* "I can keep secrets with the best of them," she said, penning her name. Onward to Mr. Foster.

* * * * *

Emily thought Mattias Foster looked thirty-five on the firm's home page, but in person, he showed each of his forty-six years and the signs of trading sleep for work—salt in his pepper-black hair, wrinkles where he furrowed his brow, and dark semicircles extending well below his eyelids, raccoon-like. "We have a very focused practice," he said. "You won't mind your friends being more impressed by the law firm names dropped by your lesser classmates?"

"Working where Fortune 500 companies turn to get the best, learning from experts—that's what's important to me," she replied. "I don't care what misperceptions others might have."

"Are you smarter than everyone else?"

Is he testing for arrogance? she thought. *Or confidence?* "It's too early to tell. I've impressed smart people at Harvard and Microsoft, and I think I could go toe-to-toe with anyone."

Foster nodded, and leaned back. "There's a word that starts with 'f' and ends with 'u-c-k.' Three-year-olds in the city say it more than three-year-olds in the country."

She felt her body tense, and wasn't sure if she was containing her blush. *Is he checking whether I can handle shocking material? Or express profanity? They've seemed too smart to think that's important…. F … u … c … k…. Damn, nothing's coming! I can't leave him in the lurch forever.* "I think you're driving at whether I can say 'fuck' at work."

"*That's* what you think of us?" the partner scolded. "Like we're a bunch of litigators, auditioning someone to perform in front of twelve ordinary people? Sure, *they* have to swear with a straight face—but that doesn't make them *exceptional. They* think lifelong coffee drinkers scalded from cups that say 'Coffee' should be judged differently than those whose cups say 'Hot Coffee.' Come on! *I'm* probing whether you'll be the smartest person in the room, that if you solve a problem in two hours that takes most people ten, you'll still have the right answer. That's who we need at Denton Foster."

The harangue blocked all creative thought. She decided to cut her losses and regain her composure for the next question. "I know it doesn't count for anything, but I'd hesitated because I'd thought you were looking for more. It simply isn't occurring to me in this short amount of time."

Foster raised his middle finger, made three circles in the air, and uttered "firetruck."

Emily tipped her head back, then forth, then repeated "firetruck" while nodding. Damn it, she *knew* he wasn't looking for profanity. She'd have to be prepared for anything.

Foster leaned back again. "I was at a water park years ago. Everyone wanted to go down the big slide—'Hangman's Drop,' I think. The line stretched all the way to the bottom, where you grabbed an inner tube to ride in. I trudge my way up, carrying the thing, and after forty minutes, I'm near the front. But this guy ahead, when it's his turn, he puts his tube in the water … and lets go. I mean, maybe it slipped, but the tube goes down the slide without him. Poor guy, right? Walk back for another tube, you think?"

Damn, this meandering story is an interview question—I hate when they do that. He's still trying to throw me off kilter. "That must happen a lot, especially with kids. They didn't have extra tubes at the top?"

"No tubes. Just a lifeguard."

Ahh … There's a fix! The lifeguard was there to tell them what to do. "Did the lifeguard have him slide down without a tube?"

"Not on Hangman's Drop! You needed a tube."

Emily kept thinking. *Shit* ... *Offer* your *tube, if you're so concerned! Wait ... that's it!* "You said the line stretched all the way down," she said. "Just have everyone pass their tube up to the next person, and at the bottom, someone fishes out two."

"You got it," Foster said, nodding. "I've always wondered if I would've thought of that if it had never happened before. Now I use it. I think puzzle questions weed out unqualified people who are good at preparing for standard interviews. We probably reject a few strong candidates, but we can't risk hiring a disaster."

"I've always liked logic puzzles, and it's encouraging that everyone working here can think well under pressure. But sometimes the answer just doesn't dawn on you, or the person is missing a helpful experience."

"I try to work with wrong answers. Some people push back on the water slide question: 'What if someone down the line won't give up his tube?' What do you think I say to that?"

Emily smiled. "My nephew is eight, and he'd do that—'my tube!' Simply bypass him, and everybody *else* pass their tubes up. It's basically the same solution."

"Exactly. I get to see how quickly they learn from their mistakes."

Emily started to feel like she was building rapport with Foster, but she could tell it was too early to relax.

"The next questions, I want you to answer fairly quickly. The twist is, I'm going to state a number after each one. If it's prime, you give me the opposite of the right answer. So if I say, 'Who's interviewing for a job? Five,' you'd say, 'You are.' And if it's a perfect square, give two answers, the first how you'd normally interpret the question, the second assuming I've snuck in a homonym. Understood?"

She did understand, but the interview had gone from strange to bizarre, and that was a lot to keep straight. *You can handle this, Emily.* "I *was* told to expect different ..."

"You do get the tools of our trade," Foster said, sliding a pen and blank legal pad toward her. "I prefer getting the answer, and a concise explanation. Understood, as well?"

She picked up the pen, and pulled the pad to the edge of his desk. "Understood."

"Tom won't take a walk with anyone who brings a dog. Whenever Amy's walking without her dog, Bud joins her with his terrier. Amy won't go for a walk without Bud. Would Tom ever walk with Bud? Fifteen."

Emily scribbled some notes, then looked up. "It *is* possible. Fifteen's a non-square composite, so you want the right answer, and Bud might take a walk without Amy, canine-free, even if she won't without him."

Foster continued without acknowledgment or pause. "A frazzled man runs into a room, yelling, 'Kate needs some air, now!' One-forty-four."

Twelve squared, word with a second meaning.... Damn, stuck! And he said "quickly." "Part one is the normal interpretation, so, 'I'll help you carry her outside.'" She paused to think some more, and felt herself sweating out of nervousness for the first time in a year. *Homonym.* She wrote out the sentence. *Can't be "Kate", could be "needs/kneads", with a ridiculous stretch, wouldn't be "some/sum"... ahhh! "Air/heir!" He didn't pick "Kate" at random.* "For the homonym, 'Which one, Prince William, or one of their children?' Your 'Kate' is Princess Kate Middleton."

This time, she noticed a slight nod from the partner. "If Tom is our judge, he'll follow the precedents from Canada. If this case were in Toronto, we'd lose. I think we'll win. Forty-seven."

"Prime, opposite." She thought for a moment. "Tom is your judge—the opposite."

"All top-tier lawyers want to work for me. Tom wants to work for me. Bud doesn't want to work for me. Rank them. Ninety-one."

"Inconclusive. Bud isn't top-tier, Tom might or might not be."

"Good so far. Great, actually. That brings you to the last one. I change the format, to make it the hardest. Forget speed and brevity: I want you to demonstrate that you can pull together *everything* we've discussed. Share your thinking as you go along. And ... I want you to get inside my head and tell *me* which number to append to the question. You should know enough of what I'm looking for to do that."

She started sweating again. *Tell him if he wants the opposite or not? Or if he wants me to read alternate meanings into his own words?*

He continued, "Amy lowered her gaze, then looked back up again, before telling Tom, 'You don't have any prospects here if I'm not pleased with what's in your briefs.'"

Vile! she thought as she wrote down the question. *Wait, out loud, he wants.* "The straightforward reaction is, 'blatant sexual harassment'... so I'd respond, 'hire us as your lawyers to protect your job.'" She closed her eyes for a moment. "But that's a lawyer answer, not a puzzle answer. A litigator, *any* litigator, could find that in ten seconds. You shared how you feel about *them*."

She looked at her pad again. "You made it crude to throw me off, like missing 'firetruck' by thinking 'fuck.' You watch for learning from mistakes.... Maybe the *opposite*, the opposite of harassment, so prime number: 'Tom smiled and replied, "All you Playgirl photographers say the same thing."' No ... that's the opposite, but it's stupid, and even more lewd.... Square number—homonym! That's got to be it."

She stared at the statement on the pad, sure she was onto something. "'Gaze' with your eyes/'gays' a group of people ..." She wiped her forehead, then thought about each word. After a few seconds, she grinned, circled 'briefs' three times, and fixed her eyes on Foster's. "The homophone from before was 'heir,' a legal term ... I should've caught this one sooner. One million, a thousand squared. Plain meaning answer: 'You've got a strong sexual harassment claim.' Homonym answer: 'You'll be pleased—the arguments are logical, well-written, and ready for filing with the court.' *Legal* briefs, a homograph."

Foster grinned. "You connected *all* of it." Then he extended his right hand. "Welcome to Denton, Foster & Kahn.... And I respect most litigators; the insults were solely for effect."

Emily leaned in to return the handshake. *Trial by fire.*

- 22 -

Carson shook his head at Bolton. "*Must be* at Denton, Foster & Kahn?"

"'Must be' is a little aggressive," she admitted.

"A little? You deduced Righteous is a patent lawyer from evidence—the expression he used, and the obscurity of their propellant. But you have *nothing* linking Denton Foster to that explosive. That's pure speculation."

"No. It's also a reasoned deduction."

Carson paused. "It would fit ... but it's still conjecture. So even if you're right about the firm, I wouldn't be able to get a warrant for the lawyers' schedules and phone records, and couldn't single out Righteous. I can't establish probable cause on a hunch."

"Lecturing *me* on the Constitution?" She scowled, and thought for a moment. "You're still holding back on me—would any of your secrets give us a stronger case?"

"No," Carson answered, "not yet. They were careful. The leads are all vague, especially any that might tie to Righteous. But we're still following up, and hopeful for a break. Maybe an accomplice's acquaintance saw him, or maybe he's remembered from a shopping run. That sort of investigating works most of the time."

"But this isn't a most-of-the-time crime."

"Well, if I had *some* evidence, I could convince my superiors to let me approach the firm informally."

"So you'd investigate them with just reasonable suspicion?"

"Sure ... informally ... seeing what they'd be willing to volunteer. I'd try to persuade the innocent lawyers to open their records, maybe piecemeal, and hope the murderer can't justify pushing back."

She thumbed the students' papers. "I can get you past your roadblock, to pursue my *hunch*." She paused, and folded her arms.

"But for that, you need to promise that once we identify Alpha, you'll tell me why he did this. The *whole* truth."

"Hold on!" Carson objected, waving his hands. "This isn't a negotiation. I'm already conflicted about having these sidebars with you. Besides, you wouldn't really hold out on me—we're after the same thing. So no more power plays ... or I'll have to cut you out completely, and go by the book."

"Now who's making idle threats!" She turned in indignation, rightward, and glimpsed the photo of Phil with the lemur. It drew her gaze, his smile so relaxed, sincere ... heartwarming. *I know, honey— save the fight for the enemy.* She looked at Carson and nodded. "Fine. I won't hold back, and no threats."

"Fine."

"And we'll keep focusing on Alpha."

"Yes."

"Just start calling me Jen, at least when it's just us."

"Then Ted for me."

"Figure I'll call you in a few hours. My students couldn't find a chemical replica. But Denton Foster would've filed dozens of explosives patents over the years; no doubt one functions close enough to an airbag propellant to cast reasonable suspicion on them."

"Hmm. I'd have to hide that we're picking out one of dozens," Carson said.

"Surely not the worst thing you'll have glossed over this week."

Carson stayed silent for a moment, his blush confirming the accusation. Then he spoke. "About you phoning me ... To keep our collaboration mostly secret, could you use my personal cell number? And memorize it instead of storing it as a speed dial, so it won't look like you're expecting to call me a lot? I've already memorized yours."

"Sure. I really don't want you to get in trouble over this."

"I know."

* * * * *

On Wednesday, after Clayton Drummond accepted Foster's offer, Judy Novack escorted him back to her office. "Not everyone leaves that interview happy," she commended. "You still have a lot to learn, and excruciating hours are the norm, as you'd expect. We aren't leveraged with associates like other firms, so most years we hire only three new graduates; but you'll make friends with the other junior attorneys."

"I look forward to that," Drummond said, nodding.

"Now, my favorite part of the job," Novack said, beaming. "A rare, positive surprise from the executive committee. You're to consider this as coming directly from each of Kahn, Denton, and Foster; I'm only speaking on their behalf to save them time. This stays within the firm," she emphasized before looking down at a blue sheet of paper:

> *We are sure that hard work and persistence have been core elements of your life, and that you will remain industrious at Denton, Foster & Kahn. In recognition of your accomplishments and your commitment to us, we are rewarding you with an eight-month vacation, of sorts. Our firm commits to honor your job offer regardless of your performance in law school from this point forward, with only the following stipulations: no issues of misconduct or impropriety, strong performance in any remaining intellectual property courses, and satisfaction of graduation requirements. Other than that, relax, and have fun, on us. This may be your last best chance.*

She filed the memo and looked up, finding Drummond suppressing his reaction, as others had done before him. "You aren't being tested anymore! Foster had his shot already. We *want* you. This is real!"

He nodded but remained stiff; Novack tried again. "Don't make me interrupt one of those pompous guys to convince you. Look, it's smart for the firm, taking credit for a break you get that's not on their time."

With that greedy explanation, the student relaxed and grinned.

"I've never heard of any other firm doing that," Novack said. "I know everyone catches a tinge of senioritis, but this is a green light for all-out indulgence." She withheld the rumor that Foster and Denton had conceived the offer based on their own experiences. "Now all that's left is this," she concluded, handing a three-page brochure to the new hire. "It's the history of the firm."

* * * * *

The official Denton, Foster & Kahn brag sheet was suitable for new hires and prospective clients, but a certain date-killer if shown to anyone else, listing firm milestones such as "first year with one thousand accepted patent applications," as well as achievements for the senior partners such as "Lou Denton becomes vice chairman of the NJ State Bar Association." The unofficial history, known completely only to Kahn, Denton, and Foster, was more engaging. The firm was Kahn's brainchild. He was two years ahead of Foster at Yale Law School, and the two standouts became friends through moot court competitions, any competitiveness tempered by the age difference, Kahn's brilliance offsetting his eccentricities. Kahn accepted a prestigious two-year clerkship after graduating, and then implemented his plan with Foster, who brought in his roommate and closest friend, Denton: the three would work at the same leading firm, advancing individually but always mindful of complementing one another's expertise, in a specialty with high turnover where they could depart with a bevy of clients and colleagues. When the time came, the trio left a skeleton of the intellectual property practice behind to avoid litigation.

* * * * *

Carson was at his desk, staring at Bertha, when Jen called. "I got one: ED-NHC45, rapidly expanding gas. And kudos to your lab—it was filed by Denton Foster for Expansion Dynamics, a joint venture of Chrysler and Erwith Chemicals formed to develop a new airbag inflator. They were tinkering with the chemicals because survivors were complaining about the numbing sensation from the byproducts after the bags go off."

"But the lab couldn't find it. Chrysler isn't using it yet?"

"The patent application just listed the good things about it: ignition certain when triggered, no false ignitions, the four-chemical mix is viable for ten years, and you get safe nitrogen and carbon dioxide gases upon combustion and an inert final-reaction solid. But that was in 2010. Expansion Dynamics dissolved in 2012, and Erwith was liquidated in bankruptcy shortly after. They listed the ED-NHC45 patent as their only asset, but attributed negligible value to it because cold temperature slowed the reaction, and inflation speed is crucial for an airbag. Maybe they patented it hoping to use it in the tropics?"

"So you'll send me a link for the filing?"

"Right. You can pretend to suspect the Panthera used ED-NHC45, but then your lab might prove they didn't, or you can surmise they used some unfiled variation."

"And with Expansion Dynamics and Erwith both gone, the only lead is the lawyer."

"*Lawyers*, actually. The filing was signed in the partnership's name. We can't narrow it down to one."

"Yet."

* * * * *

Carson had momentum with Captain Burgess and Director Arden, ten of the perpetrators identified within half a week and the press reporting favorably on police efforts to bring the "Essex State Bunglers" to justice. This and the ED-NHC45 patent report secured approval to tactfully approach Denton, Foster & Kahn.

The *Contact Us* tab on the firm's website directed inquiries to the Representative Partner, Stephanie Sulter. Carson was glad his initial contact would be a woman—an exceptionally short or tall or young or old man would have sufficed as well—anyone he could be sure wasn't Righteous.

"I'd be happy to meet about your police business at eleven tomorrow morning," she offered, the vestiges of an accent betraying her southern roots. "Technically, I'm also free at nine tonight."

"It *is* important. I'll come in tonight."

"Oh … I didn't think … Well, I guess you've uncovered my mistaken notion about police detectives. Nine it is, Lieutenant."

Before leaving headquarters, he reassigned half of his team to scour missing persons reports to match the eleventh corpse. The other half would continue pursuing leads, ignorant of his work with Jen and their suspicion of Denton, Foster & Kahn.

* * * * *

Carson fit in a jog and a grilled ham and cheese dinner before showering and driving to Newark's iconic Central Tower for his appointment. He met the tall brunette in the lobby, and noticed her simple engagement and wedding rings on their way to the elevators.

"I guess your badge would've trumped the guard's," Sulter remarked as they rode up. "Thank you for your discretion. You never know what people are going to think."

"You must escort a lot of visitors through security."

"Not really. Until eight, they just sign in and come to our reception area. And we don't get many later than that—our lawyers routinely work around the clock, but the clients rarely do."

"How long has Denton, Foster & Kahn been at the Central Tower?"

"Since the firm started. We've had half a floor since 2012, and starting last year, an entire floor." She led the lieutenant to her office, shutting the door behind them as he stared at the Passaic River. He glanced around before sitting down and noticed her penchant for forested hillsides, figuring that her office artwork cost more than all of the furnishings in his office.

"Congratulations on becoming the Representative Partner."

Sulter snickered. "You're not the first layman to say that. I'll let you in on a secret. At this firm, the title just means my client load is considered light, and the name partners think I'd be least inconvenienced spending a dozen hours weekly on business matters that are too trivial for them."

"That includes police requests?"

"Yours is my fourth one. I've been miffed that law enforcement is ignorant of the position we're in—no offense intended. Even though we don't conduct criminal defense work, anything we're told by clients, and any work product we produce for them, is shielded by attorney-client privilege. We don't even reveal the names of our clients. Any potential exception to the privilege involves a thorough legal analysis and a tailored request from the district attorney's office, or a limited order from a judge. And even then, we'd likely file challenges to protect the information. The only other exception is the client waiving the privilege, which is unheard-of for police investigations."

"What if some publicly available information could be construed as implicating an employee of the firm, rather than a client?" he asked, causing Sulter to raise her eyebrows. "That suspect would certainly have to meet with us ... and I think Denton Foster would want to be referred to as cooperating with the authorities."

Sulter gazed at him before responding. "You have a disarming demeanor, Lieutenant. You'd be great at taking depositions, if you'd consider law school."

"And they picked a very relatable individual to deal with outsiders."

She paused for another moment. "My assumption would be that your information was wrong or your inference was flawed."

"Learning that would be as helpful to me as learning that I'm right. But if not?"

"We wouldn't condone inappropriate behavior by our employees, much less *criminal* behavior. What exactly are you suggesting in terms of cooperation?"

"Right now, background information is important to us—Does Jane Doe's secretary have access to archived legal files? Does John Doe ever work on Sundays? It's really win-win—you end up either clearing the name of an innocent employee or helping me arrest someone who doesn't belong here, and I can dispel any suspicions that the firm itself was involved by characterizing you as cooperating fully."

"As a starting point, you'd have to provide enough information to assure us that this whole thing isn't a subterfuge to access our privileged communications. If you'll commit to that, I can discuss your request with the executive committee."

"No subterfuge. Who's on the executive committee?"

Sulter chuckled again. "For now, through history, and for the foreseeable future, the name partners: Reuben Kahn, Lou Denton, and Matt Foster."

"Of course. It's imperative that word of this request not spread further than absolutely necessary."

Sulter nodded. "Just those three and me. By the way, I hope your crime is weighty enough to warrant disrupting the legal hub of the intellectual property community."

Be careful what you wish for, he thought.

- 23 -

Owl ... rooster ... owl-owl-owl ... hmm? ... rooster.

The executive committee usually convened at nine, before most lawyers were in, those working past 2 AM permitted to arrive at ten; Kahn hosted on Thursdays. When Stephanie Sulter attended, she'd count lawyers *en route*—how many were still in the office from the previous day, and how many had arrived before her that morning. *All-nighters by a landslide. Again.*

Kahn looked up from his computer for a microsecond when she knocked, then turned back to his screen. She sat at his conference table and gazed at Manhattan, then became absorbed, as usual, by his bizarre decor. One wall seemed a tribute to Halloween: framed gory enlargements from anatomy textbooks, a collection of distorted masks, and a shelf of intricate replicas of ancient crypts and caskets. She knew the adjoining wall had displayed a large montage of indecent movie stills, most depicting topless women in front of mirrors, for the first hour Kahn occupied the office, until Foster and Denton nixed the affront. In its place were three Edgar Allan Poe first editions, with the illicit montage undoubtedly hanging prominently in his home since then. But Kahn's talents excused his faults; tempered by Foster and Denton to behave merely eccentrically, clients accepted his counsel, and she tolerated the discomforting aura.

When Denton and Foster arrived, Sulter gave her analysis. "If he's right and we've misjudged someone, we'd want the criminal caught ASAP. If he's mistaken, a discreet investigation would clear us quickly. And if he's trying to attack a client or pursue some political agenda, it still seems best to draw him in and pry out his true intentions, then retaliate."

"Any evidence he's right? That we have a criminal working here?" Kahn asked.

"He used the right buzzwords—'suspect' and 'arrest'—but didn't provide any proof," Sulter responded. "I don't think police usually disclose their evidence before an arrest, but there's likely not enough for probable cause because—"

"You said," Foster interrupted, "he referenced publicly available information implicating the firm. So regardless of what they *usually* divulge, we have a right to know what's aroused his suspicions. I have a newsfeed and still read the newspapers, and haven't seen a thing related to us."

"Yes, yes," she said, "I intended to push back. I'd strictly condition our cooperation on the strength of the evidence he's willing to share."

"It's also too vague on where his suspicions lie," Denton added. "We can't have sixty lawyers on eggs if he just suspects one."

"Yes, we get the best of both worlds on that," Foster said. "The whole firm gets cleared if it's nothing, or the individual alone gets disgraced if there's wrongdoing."

"So if he meets the conditions, we give him a couple of hours, and either he names a name or backs off?" she summarized.

"Agreed," said Kahn while the other two nodded. She left for her office, closing the door behind her.

* * * * *

"I didn't want to sound alarms in front of Stephanie," Kahn said, "but police don't usually target intellectual property firms. Or clients."

"Relax," Foster said. "If he were *confident* about anything, he'd be *telling* us to talk instead of *asking*."

"Can we really vouch for *every* employee?" Denton asked. "If one bad apple is using our computers to traffic credit cards or our messengers to deliver drugs, it would make the firm look bad. I'd want the police to provide the name, so we can isolate the jerk and keep the firm from getting a black eye."

"You're presuming the police would act with integrity and restraint," Kahn responded. "We have competitors, our clients have competitors, and of course we have our own secret to keep buried. He can't snoop around unfettered."

"He's asking for background information," Foster said, "and stonewalling might increase his scrutiny. Judy Novack doesn't know anything about the clients or the legal work, and Lenox Evans has only been here a couple of years. Let's give him an hour split between those two, and only if he convinces Stephanie he'll play by the rules."

"That should limit our downside," Kahn replied, nodding, "and the sooner he gets this over with, the better."

Denton nodded as well. "Let's also agree that if this escalates to us, we don't share anything that only we three know. Especially the Kahn Registry."

Kahn blushed. "You didn't even need to say that, Lou. Besides, that would be an investigation by the FBI, not local police."

There was a sullen lull, then Denton broke the silence. "Ten bucks says it's a secretary, and it's just a misdemeanor!"

Foster rolled his eyes. "Don't act like we're still in law school—I drop ten bucks for a shoeshine. A thousand says it's a client, but he doesn't know which one."

"Whoever it is, he must think he's doing *something* worthwhile," Kahn said. "He probably stayed up past his bedtime to meet with Stephanie."

* * * * *

Carson sought to improve his odds at Denton Foster by calling Dr. Arthur Burnham, the department's consulting forensic psychologist. "I'm focusing on the guy who landed safely in the Delaware. Leah's kept you up-to-date?"

"Chatted yesterday," Burnham replied, "but since you haven't turned up any new information on him, we could've discussed it earlier in the week, to the same effect."

"Yes, I know this is all preliminary … he's done a good job covering his tracks."

"So I'm relying on the reports, particularly yours, and also the professor's, despite the duress she was under, because both are consistent with a single psychological profile. Righteous is obviously controlling—"

"Obviously."

"—and he would have acted accordingly. They would've rehearsed time and again, and he would've been there, correcting the others, changing course if things weren't happening as he envisioned. He would've picked every member of the team, so this has been in the works for a year—or years—and maybe the idea has been on his mind since adolescence, 'rescuing the unjustly convicted,' let's say."

Let's say the opposite, Carson thought, shaking his head and allowing the misinformed doctor to continue being 90 percent helpful.

"The team picking also means he was recruiting the accomplices while he knew he was going to kill them. Eleven men fooled into following him for months—years—without discerning his true intentions. But then he doesn't really injure the professor, doesn't intentionally kill her husband, and was fairly restrained with the guards under the circumstances. So he's not a sociopath and I believe not a true psychopath. I think he has innate capacity for emotions and connects with people to some degree. The lives of others are simply subordinate to his aspirations; only if you might interfere with his crimes or his getaway are you marked for death."

"So you'd hate him as much as I do?"

"Violent … egocentric … duplicitous. He deserves what's coming to him."

"Is he wearing a psychological scarlet A? I need to *find* him."

"No beacon. But some clues. He must live alone—there aren't enough excuses to sneak away for all those rehearsals. He'd want to be controlling at work—whatever sacrifices he needed to make, whomever he had to hurt, he's a boss by now, or an unhappy, reluctant follower. He wouldn't necessarily seem mean-spirited; he might be charitable and have friends. Probably a deep thinker, solving complicated problems behind a desk rather than, say, making quick trades for an investment bank. I'd lean toward him having money, funding the operation on his own."

"Very helpful, Art … I think. But there's a spoiler: suspect thirteen. Officer Reiley heard Righteous call someone just before 11:30, someone he called Chief. That was right about when they decided their escape was far enough along for me to enter the cellblock, and *another* male made that call. Isn't there anyone else he could've been partnering with, maybe otherwise keeping control, but answering to that one person at the end?"

Burnham paused. "That wouldn't fit the profile, Ted. Righteous wouldn't have risked being forced into anything he didn't want to do…. The only exception might be if his biological father were calling the shots—they develop a shared obsession, and dad being in charge is so ingrained it overrides the other impulses. But short of that, no. From my perspective, Righteous would've initiated that call to you, whatever it sounded like, and whatever Reiley thought he was hearing."

"It was a trick! The voice, Art! Like at Jen's house! He recorded the code phrase ahead of time, before the injections, so I'd add a phantom to the suspect list. And his indiscreet call in front of Reiley was just part of the show."

Carson hung up, grinning, tore down the "Restless and waiting" sheet from his wall, and rewrote the quote under Righteous's name, with "Already Boss at Work."

Only one left to pursue.

* * * * *

Stephanie Sulter spent the rest of Thursday morning on client work, then contacted Novack, first, and Evans. "I just busted my ass on recruiting, and obviously I'm not gunning for partner," the HR director objected before agreeing to a five o'clock meeting; "I'll be swamped with Boeing tonight, but can squeeze in whatever you need," the associate replied.

Sulter deduced those two were chosen for being the credible informants least exposed to sensitive activities, and called them to her office to make sure that wouldn't become obvious to Carson. "If you don't know something that you should, imply secretiveness rather than ignorance. And remember as many of his questions as you can, particularly any inquiring about someone by name." After outlining acceptable and prohibited topics, she ended the meeting. Then she called Carson with the executive committee's meeting prerequisites.

* * * * *

Carson hung up with Sulter and stared into space. *Might as well stop pretending I'm following the rules on this one*, he thought, pulling out his cell phone. "They're objecting that I haven't presented any specifics, that I'm just casting a wide net to snare privileged client information," he told Jen. "My rebuttals don't seem persuasive; I need something that sounds … lawyerly."

"Have you narrowed down which attorneys it could be?" she asked.

"Some. Behavior points to a partner, and we both saw his size. I ID'd the white male partners from the firm's website this morning, then got vital statistics from their driver's licenses. That cut it down to six suspects, the three senior partners and three of the junior partners. If five have alibis or don't fit the psych profile, then I'm down to one. But I won't know that until I get my foot in the door."

"Why not turn their concern for protecting clients against them? Offer that newly patented products have been linked to a criminal ring. Tell them the only commonality is Denton Foster as patent counsel, so you suspect someone there is sharing trade secrets, or unwittingly exposing them."

"Devious! And not entirely untrue … But if that's my cover story, it sets me back for singling out the final suspect later—they won't believe a *partner* is leaking files."

"Nor that a partner is a murderer. Each request is going to be based on a lie, Ted; we'll just have to change the story to fit whatever evidence you dig up."

"Agreed," he said. "Thanks. Now I'm ready to confront Sulter."

"No you're not! Lawyers are trained to cut through bullshit like this. You need a good answer for any question she might ask, and there better not be any inconsistencies with what you've already told her."

"You think I can't …" Carson stopped and glared at the phone, then brought it back after a few seconds. "How do I keep her from outlawyering me?"

"Let's start with everything you told her last night."

He related the details of his encounter, and Jen honed in on his assertion that published information implicated the firm. They wove together an explanation that some of the robberies were making the news, as were suspicions that they were linked.

"You present that," she said, "and worst case, she'll think you were exaggerating, not fabricating an accusation. *Now* you're ready."

* * * * *

Jen's number displayed on Carson's phone five minutes before he needed to leave to meet Sulter. He recognized the ploy, a time squeeze to induce agreement, grimaced, then answered. "Last-minute advice?" he preempted.

"No, a request … but no threat, and I know your dark secret is off the table. I've been considering the times you should've called someone else instead of me, and the secrets, and that you rarely mention hearing anything from a colleague. I think you're isolating yourself in some extreme way. And I don't think that's going to work unless *our* relationship changes—you can't feel conflicted about keeping me in the loop. Sure, you've needed me and known it plenty of times, but you've probably also needed me and not known it other times, and that's hurting the case. You've got to treat me like a deputy—like a *partner*—putting our minds together to catch this jerk, this lawyer; me helping you think about everything, not just legal issues."

"If you're interviewed by the DA for the trial—"

"Stop, Ted! I can tell you've already crossed that line, and tainted any prospects for a fair trial. I'm convinced you already have something else planned."

He *had* made his decision, and kept it to himself: *after interrogating Righteous, when he was sure he had the right man, while transferring him to the feds for nuclear terrorism charges, he would have to use lethal force against the fleeing killer.* Jen declaring it aloud was a jolt. He pulled out his badge, rubbed it, and scoffed. Victims often felt enough rage to cast off a lifetime of scruples, but he was supposed to be better ... he was trained to be better.

Then he gazed at his wall, eyes darting across the grisly photos. This was his once-in-a-lifetime case—he *had* to catch Righteous, *had* to see him brought to justice, *had* to protect the sister he was forced to draw into the charade. He was doing it for her and a hundred murdered strangers; and he understood Jen doing it for Phil alone. He should've seen this moment coming. "Whatever implicates me in wrongdoing is just your opinion," he felt better saying. "I intend to remain in good standing while I pursue this case, and to have a life in the police force when it's over. So long as you understand that, you may consider our relationship changed."

"Ted, I'd assumed all that without you spelling it out. Trust me, I'm a good friend to have."

"This isn't who I am, Jen ... who I've been." He needed her, especially her, to understand. "There's just ..."

"Same for me, Ted. Doing what has to be done doesn't change who we are."

24

Sulter met Carson in the firm's reception area as he finished admiring the decor—iconic photos of inventors from Thomas Edison through Steve Jobs, and renowned gadgets with their numbered patent drawings in three display cases under a placard reading *There Are No Boundaries to Human Imagination.* "We like being seen in good company," she told him.

"No weapons?"

"Our clients tend to be the peaceful, law-abiding type. This way," she said, nodding toward the entryway. "We'll use the back door again; it's closer to my office."

After reaching Sulter's office, Carson offered the more nuanced accusations he'd prepared with Jen, spinning the firm more as a victim than a knowing participant. Sulter predictably disparaged his earlier references to public information, announcing he had "one strike" for being somewhat misleading. After a further fifteen strikeless minutes of vague but consistent answers to her questions, she called Judy Novack, allowing him another tap against the wall of secrecy protecting Denton, Foster & Kahn.

* * * * *

The scent of Novack's mint tea permeated her windowless office. Carson walked past locking file cabinets labeled *Personnel — A&B* through *Personnel — U–Z* to reach her desk, which was graced with a hand-decorated *Best Mom* pencil holder. "So, Lieutenant. Stephanie probably told you that I'm the head of Human Resources. The employees view me as their resource manager—retirement accounts, health insurance, disability benefits. So I know a lot about their personal lives—pregnancies, deaths in the family, and so on. That's information I don't share with anybody, including you. That's clear enough to understand?"

He attributed the condescending tone to Novack knowing she earned at least twice his government salary, and concluding that her job was more important than his, her confidences tighter. "I'm not here to gull you into betraying any trusts," he played along, "and I'll even assume lawyers are a particularly sensitive bunch about that. This is strictly for background. You can speak in broad generalities and it would still help me a lot."

"Well, then, I've explained my role here. Now's your chance to ask about it."

"I understand lawyers bill by the hour. Do you keep track of the hours everyone works, lawyers and others?"

"Your understanding's incomplete—remuneration is determined in various ways. To answer your question, though, lawyers are responsible for their own hours. They know when they're expected in the office and when exceptions are called for, how to get their work done, and how to track time when the work is billed hourly. The non-lawyer employees all have supervisors to keep track of attendance: a paralegal supervisor, a supervisor of admins—or do you still call them 'secretaries' on the police force?—and so on."

"Thanks. That sounds very professional … and I might need to speak to those supervisors one day. But let's say something urgent comes up, maybe a judge comes charging in looking for a particular lawyer, and the lawyer's away."

"We *have* calendar software, don't you? The lawyer's admin could access the calendar, and interrupt any meeting here, or send a text."

"So a hacker could target the calendar software to find out who was meeting with the lawyer, and which client files the lawyer might've downloaded?"

"When I see the calendars, it's obvious most client and product names are in code. Do you have a warrant for someone's calendar?"

Carson paused. "I'll answer that one—no. But really I have to be the one asking the questions." He paused again before shifting topics. "Tell me, briefly, how the firm is managed. I understand there are thirty partners, so is it sixteen makes a majority?"

Novack smirked. "Not all partners are equal. The name partners, Kahn, Denton, and Foster, form an executive committee, so any two of them together can make decisions for the firm. The other partners, collectively, make decisions only on designated matters. All the partners have a say on the compensation and promotion of the associates, otherwise the associates might not listen to them. Besides that, it's mostly the things that aren't terribly important to the firm, like expenditures for office furnishings. We try to get lawyers drawn by the outsized compensation and top-notch reputation in intellectual property, not aspirations to rule over others. Unless you're Kahn, Denton, or Foster—you create the firm, you run it." Novack glanced at her closed office door before continuing. "You didn't hear it from me, but each of those three should get two offices—one for the lawyer, and a bigger one for the ego."

"I know the type. You're drawing me off track with these tidbits," he feigned, "but now I'm curious how many partners end up unhappy with their restricted authority?"

"That's hard to say, because nobody wants to be seen as a complainer." Novack closed her eyes for a moment. "Once the executive committee and I had to pick some partners for fake interviewing, and the only people we felt sure were implicitly happy were Harold Garfield and Lori Witherspoon."

One down! Harold Garfield's happiness as a junior partner disqualified the six-footer, per Dr. Burnham. The other question had been begged, "Fake interviewing?"

The director blushed and took a deep breath. "Please don't make a big deal of that. It's nothing particularly wrong, but I don't want it shared. OK?"

Carson held up his hands. "Definitely not a police matter. Your secret is safe." Novack continued to force her breathing; their rapport was probably blown for the afternoon. At least he'd learned about Garfield. "Scout's honor."

She took a sip from her mug. "We don't recruit the usual way. We're looking to hire the two or three very top people. The law school placement offices never send us who we want, so we have no *reason* to conduct full-day interview sessions. But once we contemplated getting our name on the interviewer lists to raise the firm's profile, to help attract the few we do want. And because most of our hires come from Harvard, Yale, and Columbia, we sent the junior partners we thought were happiest to interview there—just to spread the good word. So I called it 'fake interviewing.' After two years without extending any callback offers, the schools banned us from on-site interviewing."

Novack took another deep breath after the long explanation. Carson focused on restoring her confidence to speak freely should he need her later on. He led her to feel she'd regained control of the session by asking questions about salaries and client relationships that he knew she'd refuse to answer. Then he asked questions that she wouldn't be able to answer but Evans would. She eventually suggested moving him along, with a relaxed smile, probably believing she hadn't divulged sensitive information regarding any individual at the firm.

* * * * *

Lenox Evans had a window office, smaller than Novack's but with a larger desk. Top-tier credentials graced the wall behind him, his JD from Harvard and BA from Brown overscoring a framed photo from the Harvard Law Review and a mounted letter of gratitude from his clerkship for Justice Ginsburg. After introducing himself, Carson broke eye contact to glimpse his watch, even though he knew it was approaching six. "I'd sound ignorant if I thanked you for staying past five to meet with me, right?"

"Maybe not if I'd been here since Tuesday morning," the associate replied. "But if I'd had to pull a double-all-nighter, I'd surely be too busy for this meeting."

Carson shuddered. "You say that so casually; I felt like crap the one time I went three days straight without a free hour to catnap. I guess it's Rank Has Its Privileges here, only partners can schedule free evenings?"

"You wouldn't make partner if you thought a full workday meant leaving before nine. You're a detective, you must've noticed the lawyers' offices mostly occupied when you walked through with Stephanie Sulter last night."

"True. What made you choose Denton, Foster & Kahn? Well, I'm presuming you had many options."

Evans huffed. "More small talk? I had options, including with the large firms. Denton Foster impressed me as a place where I could work with the best, including at the top of the firm. And patent lawyers get to see the future, and, sometimes, shape it."

"But the lifestyle ..."

"Everything in life is a trade-off. I partied less than my friends, and now I make more in a day than they make in a week."

Compensation! He's finally opening up. "You were right before— there were a lot of people here last night. I wouldn't know if that's typical, though; what if I were here a week ago, or a month ago?"

"Every weeknight's busy, and plenty of weekends, too. Although a week ago was technically our biennial hooky night."

Carson suppressed his smile. "What happened last Thursday?"

"It's interesting," Evans said, tipping back slightly. "Very interesting."

The gesture and prologue were familiar to Carson from his years of conducting interrogations: the lawyer believed he'd been presented an opportunity to burn time on an innocuous subject.

"Lou Denton's project for the Bar Association," Evans continued. "He's the vice chairman. They wanted to recognize state judges, but there are strict rules against judges and lawyers interacting. His idea was to throw an annual brunch honoring *retiring* judges, to avoid any appearance of seeking influence. Even though Denton conceived it, the Bar Association is mostly run by litigators—who all hate him, between you and me—and they wanted turns to run the event, so every other year the chairman takes charge. But this year was one of Denton's; when it's his year, each of our three name partners prepares and delivers a big speech—one gets the opening, one the keynote, and the other closes—so none of them are available after lunch the day before, or morning of. It's not really a hooky night, though; the other partners man the fort. It's just a joke that everyone *could* get away with leaving early."

Poker face ... poker face. "But you don't think anyone actually did?"

"Play hooky? No. There's the rare evening when a lawyer isn't working, maybe sneaking in a play or anniversary dinner, but you couldn't pull that off more than a few times a year, and you'd face a lifetime of mockery if you scheduled your excursion for that particular night."

Carson dared not ask about the junior partners under suspicion, nor express any higher level of interest in hooky night that might get reported back to Sulter. Instead, he shifted to his diversion question, starting a line of inquiry matching the fairy tale he'd sold her: "How do the firm's lawyers retrieve archived privileged communications, and what steps are taken to keep non-lawyers and outsiders from accessing them?"

"Is someone stealing confidential information from us?"

"You shouldn't infer that; best to rule it out, though. I assume the lawyers would know better than to abuse confidentiality, that's why I'm asking about others."

"Well, who specifically? The mailroom? An admin?"

"Even if I knew that, I couldn't say now. If someone is in the wrong, we'll catch them, and your partners will find out soon enough."

"Then I'm going to have to answer very generally." Evans proceeded to describe the firm's protocols for protecting paper and computer records. Carson interrupted with questions, reinforcing the fiction that he was after a layman, then brought the meeting to a close when Evans finished, offering a joke about a lawyer entering heaven.

The associate waved him off. "Heard at least twenty of those."

"World's oldest man ..."

"Based on his billable hours."

* * * * *

Carson returned to his car and dialed Bolton on his cell phone. "Have you had dinner yet, partner?"

"Not yet." Her voice cracked when she answered. "You should come over.... I'm trying to add an hour of normalcy to my life each day, and that'll put me up to five."

"Have you been crying?"

"Don't worry about that—I don't want consoling from you. It's just hard to come back to an empty house."

"Well, whatever ingredients you have there, you don't want me to try to cook."

"Sumo's Choice has great sushi. I'll call if you pick up."

"Um ... I haven't been the most adventurous eater; could you get me the sushi for beginners dinner?"

"A sushi virgin? I'll make sure the combo includes crab rolls—the shellfish is cooked."

* * * * *

Carson held his own over dinner, enjoying the crab and shrimp and tolerating the salmon.

"It *does* taste better if you use chopsticks," Bolton teased.

He relayed details of his meetings at Denton Foster, mocking the arrogant tones of Novack and Evans in turn. "The workload knocks out a couple of the junior partners, plus the pearl of ruling out too-happy Harold Garfield. Picking the one time in two years that all three name partners would be unaccounted for fits Alpha, spreading suspicion away from himself if we get this far. It means I'll have to dig deeper than last week's calendars."

"I'm going to call a lawyer friend, and get a schedule for the judges' brunch. If Alpha needed his fake voice here until eight, he probably didn't want to be on the lectern before ten."

"That could help. But I'll still probably need to question those three myself, and Righteous won't just roll over for that."

"And the ED-NHC45 isn't evidence enough to force it."

"Right, that's spent.... I'm glad the case is heavy on logic, but wish it weren't so light on proof."

"You'll find something. We're connecting the dots, and keep finding a next dot to connect."

25

Orange and red swirls crept across the horizon as Carson started his jog. He'd run at sunset often over the past months, but couldn't remember the last time he woke to exercise at daybreak. Sunrises always felt more serene, before he dealt with other people, before his thoughts turned to work. But his thoughts always turned to work—today, to three accomplished men, upstanding by all public measures, one a loathsome killer.

* * * * *

Kaleah Banks thrust a vaguely familiar photo at Carson when he arrived at headquarters. "Recognize this excuse for a human?" she asked.

He stared at the picture, then mentally blocked the nose and left eye. "You've restored cadaver eleven!"

"Credit the Motor Vehicle Commission. Todd Sapphire drives—drove—a bus for Rutgers, and missed his shift Monday after taking a week off. His coworkers tracked down his neighborhood friends, the local police got involved Wednesday, and we made the match staying late last night. I've divided up the canvassing, so you'll get a report on him over the weekend."

"You've made my day, Leah, and the day hasn't even started."

"Any luck on the scum who didn't smash his head jumping into the river?"

"Suspicions, yes; proof, no. We'll still be employed next week."

"I'll prep the team to shift gears after reporting on Sapphire. Everyone'll be ready to help you catch that worm."

"More like a snake, I'm afraid. Or a sorcerer."

"I'm sure he's no match for you."

Carson still relished compliments from his underlings, but hid his reaction. He continued to his office, taped Sapphire's license photo below the morgue headshot, and penned his name. He started Bertha, and sent a *Sapphire Questions* e-mail: *Drove Woodman's truck? Photo to gate guards. Truck with recycling beams? Photo to Shawn Holloway.* Then he gazed at Righteous's sheet, thinking, *Time to learn about Kahn, Denton, and Foster.*

Carson spent two hours examining the overachievers' internet footprints, stifling a dozen yawns, then a more important two looking for gossip. After lunch, he received an e-mail from Stephanie Sulter:

> *We trust the record to show that Denton, Foster & Kahn cooperated fully in your inquiry, and having promptly made our associates available per your request, we trust our involvement in your inquiry is complete. If there is a material change in facts that you wish to bring to the firm's attention, please continue to use me as your primary contact.*

He called Jen to share the message.

"Sounds like Alpha's concerned, but not panicking," she said.

"Evans must've had the good sense not to mention elaborating on hooky night."

"Speaking of that … I found out about the brunch. They honored Judges Frenzel and Hay. Foster opened at eleven, Denton followed him, and Kahn closed with a slide show an hour after that. If Alpha were playing it safe on the voice trick, he'd be Kahn."

"OK … although that's not a big time difference. Hmm … Since you're tapping the lawyer grapevine, I should text you the time slots when some Panthera may have been preparing with Alpha. If you hear that one of the partners missed an appointment then—"

"I'll let you know."

"Great. I've also done some research, trying to single one out, and hit a dead end. Heck, they could be triplets—same law school, started at the same firm on the same day, then left together to found Denton, Foster & Kahn. Denton majored in engineering, the others had science minors. They've all lived in New Jersey for fifteen years. None of them are married now, but Foster was once, for four years. And they haven't made the news except for law firm matters; no officerships at charities, no politics, nothing requiring a license except driving. No arrests, no legal proceedings except Foster's divorce, and Kahn was co-executor when his father died. So single-minded, and dull—makes me want to cry."

"You thought he'd have revealed himself a miscreant?"

"I wasn't expecting wrongdoing, but maybe some interest that would tip his hand—*pro bono* work on prison reform, skydiving as a publicity stunt, part-time firearms safety instructor. Any proof of life."

"The culture at those firms just feeds on itself," she said. "The lawyers are loathe to publicize spending time on anything but work."

Carson paused. "So much for ending the week on a hopeful note."

* * * * *

Saturday brought clear skies and another run—thirty paced minutes for self-reflection. Carson decided that "hypocrisy" would be his word for the morning. He'd mocked the partners' monotone biographies while disregarding his own obsession with work, the long days at headquarters then dwelling on theories at home, the fifty straight hours he worked hoping to find Kitty Ranchada alive. And his best friend off the force was probably the sarcastic manager of a humdrum diner who didn't even know his address. *Maybe Righteous exasperates me because he's like me? Maybe that's why Jen thinks I can catch him?*

Returning home, he stripped for his shave and shower, resolving to straighten up his apartment before the day was through and spend a few evening hours slimming his backlog of recorded movies. He made it as far as washing dishes when he received a frantic call from the youngest member of his team, Ryan Munsen. Munsen had a flair for science. Although he suffered from test anxiety, eking by at Rutgers and getting a form letter rejection from Newark's own Forensics Department, Carson had sensed his potential.

"I have to show you something, Lieutenant," the officer spouted. "The phone companies finally shared what I needed, and it's not something we usually do so I'm not sure, but this could be important. I mean, if you're OK coming in on Saturday."

"Easy, Ryan. You'll get a chance to talk to me. This has to do with the case?"

"It has to do with Righteous. I found him, sort of; well, if what I did was OK, then I've sort of found him."

"What you did was legal, right?"

"I think so … nobody ever told me it wasn't, and I didn't lie to anyone. But it's technical, and I don't think it's been done before, so nobody told me it *was* legal, either."

"I'll be right in. Practice explaining the technical part so I don't have to be Einstein to understand it."

* * * * *

Carson brought Munsen into his office, and tried to put his excited subordinate at ease. "I knew if anyone could come up with something, it would be you."

"I started on this when we'd identified ten of them, the Panthera," Munsen said, pushing too-long blond hair off of his forehead. "I checked their phone records, to see when they called each other, and whether they shared anyone else as a contact, meaning, hopefully, the other accomplices. But there was nothing—they never called each other's home numbers, work numbers, or cells, and no e-mails or texts or private group posts. Really, nothing."

"But Leah says, 'There can't be *nothing*, they had to communicate.' So I consider other criminals who try to talk without leaving a trail, like drug dealers, and I think of burner phones— prepaid cell phones with each guy using a fake corporate identity. That's who we're looking for."

"Good start, Ryan," Carson said. "But that just narrows it down to a million phones."

"Yeah … not a million, but lots. But we also know these guys were super careful, maybe rigid with their precautions. That would set up a pattern. I think, 'What's the safest protocol?' And I come up with using these phones only to call the other burner phones—no landlines, no registered cell phones, nothing that would leave any connection to an address for us to track. So I want to filter call records for prepaid phones that have only called other prepaid phones in New Jersey, with no activity after last Saturday morning but active during the month before that. And I assume they didn't use all of the time they paid for, unlike most people, in case they needed to be reached at the last minute. And I'm just looking for patterns and not capturing any caller names or content, so it's cleaner than the stuff that the lawyers have been challenging. The phone companies agree and spend a night filtering that out. Only about five thousand prepaid cells with minutes left have been used that way."

"So we can scrutinize the records on the five thousand phones?"

"Actually, I asked the assistant district attorney a hypothetical, without explaining how I'd narrowed it down, and he said we couldn't invade the privacy of five thousand phone customers just because a dozen are criminals. I don't have actual phone records."

"But there's more?" Carson prodded.

"Oh, yeah … lots. It's down to five thousand phones, and I put myself in their shoes again, and I think one person probably initiates most of the talking. Maybe it's the leader, or the number-two guy, or someone's the messenger. Whoever it is—and this part I'm guessing again, but it's what I'd do—there'll be a pattern of this hub guy calling one of the spoke guys, finishing that call, calling another spoke guy, finishing that, and calling another. Maybe three, maybe four … maybe all eleven. Some pattern like that."

Carson held up his hands. "OK, you've thought through a pattern they might have fallen into. Can you keep it simple like that when you explain it?"

"I'll try," the technophile promised. "The last thing I assume is he—the caller—calls when they're home sometimes, maybe for privacy, or just it's late. Now, each of the criminals lives closest to a particular cell tower—really we all live closest to one tower or another. That's important because the phone companies know which towers are used for every call, incoming and outgoing. So yesterday I compile a list of the eleven towers in each phone network closest to where each of the dead Panthera lived, including the one we just ID'd, and have the phone company computers search for my pattern over the last two months. Namely, one of those five thousand prepaid phones is used to call another of the five thousand phones, at one of those towers—and there'd be plenty of just those calls—but then that call ends and the caller dials another of those prepaid cells at another of those towers, and then a third call to yet another of the criminal's towers. I'm sure I miss a bunch, right—someone's not at home when they're called and it breaks the pattern. But I'll get some."

"So, Ryan, you're saying because you'd narrowed the search to calls using these five thousand burner phones and only when they were received at the towers where the Panthera lived, sometimes you'd find a specific caller who fit your pattern?"

"Exactly. And I did find one. Their computers identified the pattern seven times over the last two months, sometimes three calls in a row, usually more. Five of the seven clusters, the calls originated from one phone at the same cell tower—I figure the other two clusters just follow the pattern coincidentally. And best part, those calls didn't source from the towers near the Panthera we've identified, so we luck out and the missing leader is the hub calling everyone else, and I don't have to spend another day backtracking his cell tower from individual call records." Munsen unfolded a map of Newark with a deep red boundary drawn in marker. "I believe Righteous was in or close to the Central Tower on at least five occasions when he called his colleagues. He works there, he eats near there, he parks there, something."

"You got all this without having any of the phone numbers?" Carson asked.

"Well, I had to make those assumptions, but yes. I mean, maybe there's another group, maybe it's just a football team. But all using prepaid cells, living near those very same towers? I could figure the statistics for you—the fact that there were only two coincidental cases of the same calling pattern, that's compelling."

"Convincing indeed."

"All we need now is a warrant and we can get the number of that phone Righteous used—we might even be able to tell exactly which building he was in and which floor he was on, once we get the warrant."

Carson smiled. Munsen uncovering that Righteous had called from the twentieth floor of the Central Tower would bring the investigation of Denton, Foster & Kahn out of the shadows and give him leverage to force interviews with the executive committee; better still, if Righteous had ever used that phone from his home, or from the office while his cohorts were gone, the pursuit would be over. "Ryan, you've certainly earned us that warrant. I'll make sure Ed Quinones and the other lab big shots hear about your work," he added, eliciting a grin from the officer.

Up went the map with Munsen's heavy red outline.

- 26 -

When Munsen left, Carson checked his notes and made a research call. "This is Bruce," came the response.

Wrong person on a cell phone? "I'm calling for Daniel, please."

"This is Daniel Bruce. Who's calling?" he fumed.

"Oh … of course … I apologize. This is Lieutenant Ted Carson from the Newark Police Department. I'm calling about a police matter—one you'll be happy about."

"I've had enough bullshit in my life, and haven't been to Newark in years. This call is over—"

"Wait! I'm telling the truth! Sorry I was flippant—I can't say much now. I *can* say that the enemy of my enemy in Newark is my friend."

It took Bruce a moment to reply. "How can I help, and can I take pictures?"

"If I'm right, there'll be pictures in the newspapers. Can we meet tomorrow morning, maybe at ten?"

"Do you know Long Beach Island?"

"We used to go to the beach in Harvey Cedars."

"I'm a realtor in Harvey Cedars. But I live one town up, in Loveladies … which you probably already learned, when you pulled my phone number."

"I've gleaned a few tidbits…. I'll meet you there tomorrow." Carson hung up, then plotted trying his luck at blackjack in Atlantic City after the meeting, since he'd already be at Parkway Exit 63. He also decided to return to his other plans for the day, chores and then a movie in his den.

* * * * *

Carson slapped his alarm, groaned, then registered the Sunday appointment. He dressed casually, but hung his blue sports jacket in the back of his Malibu for the Tropicana. He drove five minutes to the

Garden State Parkway, then settled in for eighty miles of monotony, pleased that he wouldn't have to fight the summer traffic jams.

Route 72 was uncrowded as well. Reaching the crest of the causeway to Long Beach Island, over the boats in Manahawkin Bay, stirred fond memories. In addition to playing in the surf as kids, he and Rebecca had climbed to the top of Barnegat Lighthouse, and watched fudge being made. He turned left onto the island's backbone, Long Beach Boulevard, and enjoyed the sea air for the short travel north, stopping like a local for each of the families crossing to the ocean side.

Bruce greeted him with "How did you find me?"

Carson held out his hand for a shake, but held his tongue until the door closed behind them. "Before that, I need to trust that you'll keep this confidential … although if I'm right, I'll need an affidavit later."

"Notwithstanding what you might hear, your confidence in me is well-placed."

"To answer your question, then, I simply looked for you. I need information on the founders of Denton, Foster & Kahn, from someone who won't just repeat the party line. Law enforcement can access the internet archives of the *Martindale-Hubbell Law Directory*, and I saw Daniel B. Kirke as an associate in 2010, but I didn't see that name at Denton Foster in 2013. Then I search for *all* attorneys in good standing with the Bar, and figure out what happened. There's no record of *why* it happened, what you were accused of, but I assume by the way you answered my call that you were faultless."

"Exactly … I learned from a new hire that Foster had changed one of his interview questions, and then someone I know who'd be a great fit got scheduled to interview and I shared the *old* question. But the bastards are paranoid about their *secret* business model and *secret* governance arrangement and *secret* recruiting process. They apparently wanted to make an example of someone, and boom! The executive committee deemed me expendable, and they beat me to leather."

"So now it's 'Bruce'?"

He nodded. "Since then, D. Bruce has had more opportunities than Daniel B. I hear they *still* warn people they could turn out like me if they don't toe the line…. No crying, though. I'd earned enough to pay off my student loans and buy this house for cash. And selling beach real estate is as good a job as any."

"'Bruce Kirke' has a nicer ring to it, no offense to your parents."

"I've settled into it, thanks. Do you want something to drink?"

"Iced tea or water would be great."

"The extra bedroom on the second floor has a few chairs, if you don't think the view will be too distracting."

"I can't decline a change of scenery," Carson replied.

* * * * *

The bedroom windows faced the ocean. Although three houses blocked his direct view of the beach, Carson had the pleasant choice of gazing straight out, the homes framed by a wide grassy dune and the waves beyond, or looking up the island, catching strips of sand and water toward Barnegat.

"I have two rules," Kirke said. "Anything related to client work is protected by privilege, even now. And I don't know of any criminal behavior, although I wish I did, so that idea of an affidavit is off the table—whatever I discuss is just for you. However distant you think my life is from them, they get no more ammunition against me…. Can I still be helpful?"

"I take it you're mad at all of them, not just the one with the interview question?"

Kirke nodded. "Absolutely."

"Then you'll be quite helpful. I just need to understand the firm's politics, and what makes each of them tick. Then one-third of your dreams can come true."

"Oh, you're only getting one of them? Make sure you consider drawing the others in on conspiracy; they run the firm together."

Carson pulled a notepad out of his laptop bag. "Just for jotting some memory prompts," he assured his host.

Kirke nodded again. "Because you'll want the full story quickly, I'm going to tell you things I've heard myself, things I've heard secondhand, and things that are common knowledge at the firm. So you might later find one or two details to be wrong, but nothing major. OK?"

"Hearsay is fine, for background."

"Associates spend the first two years working under partners on almost everything. Half of your time is with a single, mentor partner, the other half you get tapped by the others. Every six months, you rotate to another mentor partner. Those four—well, the ones who like you—become your sources for the scuttlebutt about the firm. Now, you've said only one of the leaders is in trouble. I'm going to start with Loon; if you hear what you want, it can be an early day."

"'Loon'?"

Kirke stared at him. "You haven't even heard the nicknames yet? OK, square one. Reuben Kahn goes beyond eccentric. His behavior wouldn't be tolerated at the firm—at *any* firm—except for three things: He embodies every lawyer skillset—memory, presentation, insight, you name it. He'll take on any assignment, no matter how distasteful. And he's attuned to his social failings, and follows prompts from Denton and Foster without question, like cutting off a tasteless joke or ending a come-on to a receptionist. Not only that, he's credited with most of the firm's business innovations."

"So the guy's a genius, an awkward genius?" Carson summarized.

"I *would* say 'genius,' and I don't use the term lightly; but 'awkward' is an understatement. They've settled, records sealed, at least three complaints from women working there. Never any physical contact or coercion—he just finds the strangest things interesting, sometimes offensive things, and presses on. I've seen mental illness in my family; the guy doesn't have a diagnosis or need treatment. Something, maybe his intellect, just got in the way of him learning social behavior. I heard this partner, Eden Gurley, discussing patenting a special clamp for laparoscopic surgeries, and Kahn asks whether there'd be more breast enlargements if the incisions were smaller, and how much time women spent deciding whether to get one or not."

"He just starts talking about breasts ... in the office?"

"Just like that ... creepy. Gurley cut him off, of course, and left before he could get personal about it."

Carson shuddered. "That was one of the settlements?"

Kirke shook his head. "Not even close. The firm's solution, if you call it that, is to empower the female attorneys, and desensitize them to Kahn. Their first year, Denton or Foster has to be there when they're with him, and they're shown they can walk away without recrimination, like Gurley did. In return, they accept having to work with him on rare occasion."

"Why don't they solve this by fixing *him*?"

"Beats me.... I think the pressure wanes because he's not a constant menace—he's usually fine around women, and he's restrained around clients, too. But then a caucus on a medical clamp brings out Bacchus."

"Isn't there gender relationship training for executives? So he learns to control it consistently?"

"The settlements have been gender-related, but it goes beyond that. He's talked my ear off about the layers of human skin and how many capillaries would be severed with an inch-long cut, and so on. And the other guys have heard the same."

"Jeez ... *How* is his work so important that they tolerate him?"

"Like I said, he's one of the best lawyers around, taking away the personality, and we consult him on anything really tricky. And even though Loon relishes science like the other partners, he lets them hog the patent work, and concentrates on copyright and trademark; those clients are loyal to him. There's another benefit, in an odd way; sometimes we'd get disturbing works—an old cannibalism photo collection, or the biography of a sadistic killer. Well, none of us worried about getting stuck with that—'another job for Loon,' we'd say. We deal with the creepy partner, we don't have to deal with the creepy projects."

"And you said he's deferential to Denton and Foster?"

"Not across the board. He is when they're checking his personality, but they've compartmentalized that part of the relationship, and the other two don't use it against him to win partnership disputes, as far as the rest of us can tell. But remind me later, there's a point about voting I want to make after I've discussed the other two. Anything else about Kahn?"

Carson flipped to a blank sheet of paper and readied his pen. "This is for Kahn, and Denton and Foster when you get to them. Is anyone close enough to him that they'd lie to the police about his whereabouts if he asked them to?"

"Hmm ... I'm not sure. That goes for all three. I guess they'd lie for each other ... maybe their admins would, out of job loyalty, and maybe even Judy Novack for the same reason. But they don't speak of other friends, they don't have group pictures in their offices, and they don't bring guests to the firm's holiday dinner. I assume they each have a mother, but you mean someone credible, right, not family?"

"Yes, that's what I wanted to know." He put down his pen. "Could we take a break?"

"Sure. I should've offered, with your long drive and the iced tea."

- 27 -

"Denton next?" Carson asked.

"Sure," Kirke replied. "We'd call Denton 'John' behind his back. He works absurd hours to free up time to vacation where prostitution is legal—that's his pastime. He'll also try to add an evening or weekend when he travels to one of those places for business. He's never spoken about soliciting a local hooker, but he's recited volumes about his escapades in Amsterdam, Nye County, and so on. Of course, he's more discreet than Loon—there's no hint to clients, and he lays off associates if you ask him once."

"Hmm … Could he hold a grudge against people who mistreat prostitutes? It's an ugly business: trafficking, drug addiction, violence. He'd still see that, just less, where it's sanctioned."

"He brags about being a good customer, like paying for a full day even if he's only with them a few hours. So I guess the abusers would piss him off. But he never sounded attached to any particular one, scheming a vendetta in her honor; nothing *Man of La Mancha* like *that*."

"But you said he recited volumes. If there's not a passion for someone, what? Locker room banter about how good he is?"

"No, no … think quirkier, even though he's more balanced than Loon. Denton's a stellar lawyer, and he fancies himself that same way as a scientist, from dealing with all those inventors. Think about it: they approach the firm with cutting-edge discoveries months—years—before publicizing them, so he knows things about chemistry that other chemists don't, things about medicines doctors don't. They even discuss near misses—drug variations that are too potent, fuels that are too volatile. It can go to your head. Denton takes that, and applies it to his hobby—real romantic, huh? The imagery is still etched in my mind, him overanalyzing it and oversharing:

When you get there, all the women line up, and you pick one. Like an ice cream flavor, but no tasting ... until later. The other guys are dopes, they look for the firmest chest, or the youngest, or some such thing. What I do is ask a question, usually math, like "What's eighty-eight times eight?" About half sneer, or joke, like "eight hundred eighty-eight." Those are the rejects who teased us brainiacs in school. The other half understand it's about what pleases me, not them. And those other half, they won't get the answer, but they pretend to try and keep smiling. Then the silence gets awkward, and ... Voilà! They start glancing at the smartest one, looking out for the competition, and that's my Venus. They're all pretty, after all, but if I'm paying four figures, I'm getting a ninety-five-percenter.

And then I asked what he meant by that, although I debated just nodding to end the conversation. He explained:

Most sexual partners care about each other, so the sex is half what you want and half what she wants. If you both want the same thing, that's even better. But let's say you want each hump to be your fantasy lay. Well, even if she agrees to that, you'd still care about her and the relationship, so you'd self-compromise to make her happy. You end up with, say, 70 percent of what you want. At a whorehouse, the stupid ones don't keep track of your entire fantasy, so they'd get some of it right, but mostly default to whatever gets most guys done the quickest. You end up with 70 percent again, just for a different reason. You pick a fairly smart one, she actually remembers what you ask for. You get 100 percent, and it's great ... predictably what you imagined. But the smartest one remembers what you want and *gets inside your head. She'll throw in a few improvements, some moves or toys you never thought of. So instead of another rerun of your favorite movie, it's a new sequel to your favorite movie. You get 95 percent of your original fantasy, plus whatever the virtuosa thinks will rock your boat. It's the one time 95 is better than 100.*

That's how John practices his hobby."

"So Denton's quite an outlier as well," Carson said. "And his ideal is a surprise each time, so he wouldn't have grown attached to anyone in particular," he added, crossing out "knight-in-shining-armor complex" on his pad. "Could you cover what he does at work?"

"Denton focuses on patents. He likes the scientific ones, but he's fairly democratic about it, and collaborates with each of the partners at least once over the course of a year. He also works directly with associates sometimes, rather than using junior partners as intermediaries. That makes him the most liked of the name partners. As far as clients go, he's responsible for more business than anyone, with Foster close behind, and new clients seek him out."

Kirke sipped his tea, and Carson stared at the waves until his informant continued. "John also has lawyer responsibilities outside the firm. Most practicing attorneys are members of the State Bar Association, and by far the biggest block are litigators and others who appear in court—divorce lawyers and the like. So the governance of the association tilts heavily toward litigation. But that's only 10 percent of what Denton Foster does; some firms don't do any at all. So he starts networking, cutting his firm hours in half for a year to schmooze the patent attorneys and corporate attorneys and real estate attorneys, and gets nominated for the chairmanship, with enough backing that he might win it.... *That* would've been a coup for the firm."

"And bad for everyone else?"

"Exactly. The Bar Association drives changes to the ethics rules, and the rules suit the litigators as they are. They allow—actually, *require*—the attorneys on both sides of a case to put in a zealous effort on behalf of their clients, leading to tons of billable hours. And they've also had the effect of fixing high contingency fees for all types of cases, regardless of the work required. So the large litigation firms cut a deal: they agree to support him for *vice* chairman, forever, provided he won't propose any rule changes without the chairman's assent. In terms of power, John's both a name partner at Denton, Foster & Kahn *and* the long-standing vice chair of our State Bar Association."

"Quite the feat," Carson said. "How about Foster? Is he quirky, too?"

"You could say that. To make partner, you have to either believe or pretend that work supplants every other priority in your life. Most important is putting in the hours to prove that; but there should also be personal sacrifice, shortchanging *something* in deference to work—an interest, or a relationship. It's just weird, even there, to have *only* work in your life. But that's Foster—he has no outside interests, no apparent vice. So the associates refer to him as 'Loser.' Childish, like the other names; but it makes the point."

"So Loon obsesses over inappropriate things, and John visits brothels and does Bar Association work. Does Loser simply work more hours still than those two?"

Kirke shook his head. "Not necessarily. If Foster goes home at midnight and Denton stays until one thirty finishing Bar Association papers, maybe Foster squeezes in time at home to draft another patent application, but probably he just sleeps, and Denton's just more tired."

"You seem to have less disdain for Foster, even though it was *his* interview question ..."

Kirke nodded. "Loser was the most normal of the three. His wife came to the office, maybe weekly, to have dinner with him, and she was friendly and funny. He told me about weekends with her on this very island. Maybe she approved in concept of his long hours, or maybe he'd promised a change. But the reality ends up being too hard on any relationship. The only thing he says if you ask about her is, 'I'm happy being free to choose my own pursuits.' But if he's done anything besides work since divorcing, it's nothing he talks about. It sounds like sour grapes to me."

"Did anybody else drive the divorce? Did his wife end up with someone else, anyone Foster would hold a grudge against?"

"He blames the work, and as a name partner, that means he blames himself."

"How about his ex-wife—if I approach her, would she reveal any dirt?"

"She got a plum divorce settlement—a huge payment to keep the firm's financials from going public, plus alimony. I'm sure she wants the firm to do well."

Carson glanced out the window for a moment, then pressed on. "How about his skills?"

"I think they're all brilliant. Loon's credited with the best business ideas, and John's the best scientist, but Loser is the most clever. I'd bet on him to win a survive-on-the-island show, and he'd be the one they send to give a toast honoring the governor. It's just incremental, though."

Kirke paused, then his eyes widened. "There's something else I wanted to cover, and maybe it's related. I've heard that when the executive committee makes a tough decision, Kahn and Denton often split, so Foster usually gets his way. Maybe the other two just have different business leanings and he's the natural tie-breaker; but maybe it's more, maybe he steers the agenda somehow to get one of the others agreeing with him on the items that get voted on. That's just how it seems from Denton and Kahn complaining sometimes; we don't hear much about the workings of the executive committee."

Carson jotted down "Loser—Vote power?" before speaking. "Specialties?"

"Foster's like Denton—mostly patents, and he likes the scientific ones. When he does copyright, it's always for movies. Plenty of established clients, and plenty of new business from client referrals." Kirke paused. "And that's Foster."

"I'm extremely grateful. Now I have some big-picture questions—you can think about all three partners for these. If one of them wanted to sneak away, let's say for a picnic lunch, could he, without anyone knowing?"

"Well, as an associate, I could never guarantee being free for lunch. Some mornings I'd know that I'd be working during lunch hours, and others I'd come in with lunchtime free but then get tapped to work. I think partners are in the same boat, except if work can be done later in the day, they might be able to keep lunchtime open. But the executive committee, if their calendars say 'meeting potential client at noon,' only the other two would dare ask about it. So for those three, yes, they could lie about having work without getting challenged or being pulled away for something else. But not often; then the other two would get suspicious."

"OK. How about whether those three could make personal calls, doors closed, during the day?"

"They wouldn't miss a client meeting for that, and they wouldn't miss a partner's meeting. But they could put 'hold for XYZ call' on the calendar, and make personal calls instead. And after about seven, you'll see some open slots, but they're still in the office working; they could fit in calls then."

Carson nodded. "Anything incriminating you haven't mentioned?"

"Make sure when you talk to Loon, it's in his office; if it still looks the same ... well, it leaves an impression. You'll let me know when you nail them?"

"If it doesn't make the news, I'll let you know."

Carson left Kirke's house with three suspects still on his list, but with perspectives he couldn't have pried from anyone still employed at Denton Foster. He glanced at his blue blazer as he approached the driver's door, but shook his head; he'd gambled enough for the week. Before driving off, he thumbed a text: *Beck, on LBI. Sunny, wish you were here. Lunching with twelve pearl makers. Taffy and fudge coming for nieces.*

28

Carson reached Jen's house just before five on Sunday, his clothes no longer scented with sea breeze but the Chevrolet still filmed with salt. "I'm going to disparage two innocent individuals, along with the killer," he said as he sat on the couch, "and I hope you'll—"

"I'll keep everything just between us until I'm un-deputized, and won't ever cast aspersions on the ones who aren't Alpha," she promised.

He relayed what he'd learned about the three partners. "The nicknames do sum it up, except Foster probably wasn't always Loser, while Kahn and Denton have likely been budding Loon and budding John for life. Unfortunately, each would've had access to whatever patent files he wanted, and could've put fake entries on his calendar for planning the crimes."

Jen sighed. "You said there was also a breakthrough?"

"Yes. Someone with peculiar cell phone habits was calling eleven other people with secretive cell phone habits and suspicious addresses. From near the Central Tower."

"And you're not telling me who that is because …"

"Because we just made the statistical connection. We're hoping your Constitution won't keep us from getting the phone records."

"Hey! Don't kill the messenger! A woman wouldn't have exactly held sway in drafting the Bill of Rights. Besides, in this case the Fourth Amendment just tells you to check with a judge … you should be acting like you're a search warrant away from our biggest break so far."

"We're a search warrant away from getting the phone numbers and call records—so yes, it's big. But these are prepaid phones, since destroyed, I'm sure. And the Panthera wouldn't have used credit cards or real IDs for the paperwork."

"Oh … Now every clue has a 'but.'"

"It's still progress. The Central Tower part is a good opening. And maybe Righteous made a call from somewhere we can place him without the others."

"You don't really think he … well, let's hope for that."

"And even if we don't get *that*, if the judge rules for us, my tech guy can narrow down the caller locations, probably tightly enough for me to compel meetings with Kahn, Denton, and Foster on my own terms."

"That's promising."

Carson nodded. "Actually, I've thought of a way to force those meetings. But I'm not sure it'll work…. Could you pretend to be an important law firm partner?"

"Do I have to be one of those creeps I heard about at Denton Foster?"

"This won't involve the creepy parts. I got my interviews last week by making vague threats against the firm's reputation. If we get that warrant tomorrow, we'll gather compelling evidence of felonious activity. That should push the innocent two past stonewalling me. But Alpha will still want to stop my interrogations, without appearing guilty to his colleagues. All I can imagine is he strikes fear that I'll uncover the firm's worst secrets—any skeletons from their climb to power. And I just don't know whether a law firm's transgressions would be grave enough for Alpha's argument to prevail."

Jen shook her head. "He'd lose. Very few lawyers actually break the law, and when they do, it's almost always white-collar, like overbilling or lying on affidavits. Bad enough to get the attorney disbarred, but not enough to sully an entire firm. But involvement in a felony, they'd get scared about the firm collapsing. They won't consider their secrets so important if you threaten to taint them with a major crime."

He nodded and smiled. "First things first, then—on to the warrants. Would you like some fudge? Fresh from Long Beach Island …"

"No, thanks," Jen replied, standing. She escorted him to the door, and he took a couple of steps outside.

"Ted!" she called, turning him around. "I guess in my life … I guess I'd gotten used to being around someone … we'd go to each other with questions and problems, Phil and I. And not the way my students do. So you should know this is working out for me. I realize that's not why you're doing it, but you should know how I feel."

"I'm glad, Jen. I think you deserve for some things to work out for you." He averted his eyes, and felt himself blush. "I mean, I'm just glad." He turned back to walk to his car, shaking his head. *Stupefied by her mentioning how she feels?* he thought. *Any rejected greeting card would've sounded better! Got to work on that.*

* * * * *

Bertha had just whirred to life on Monday when Banks knocked and entered, sulking. "Work problem?" Carson asked. "Or just too much of it?"

"Munsen and I worked pretty hard this weekend, on the hearing for the warrant."

"I feel confident about that. It's a novel approach, but statistical at its core—nothing infringing on privacy."

"It ought to go well. I think it will. But ..."

"But what? Did the DA's office say otherwise?"

Banks bit her lip. "No ... but ..."

Carson squinted at her for three seconds, then his eyes popped wide open. "Timid Tepstra? Lloyd Tepstra is our ADA for the warrant request?"

"I didn't get to choose! He's better than when he started, Lieutenant. He's taken borderline cases to the bench ... recently. And he's gotten cell phone warrants before."

Carson flushed. "You go with him to the hearing!" he ordered, pointing. "Offer to take Munsen ... and his map. Push him to find a judge born after the Korean War, who might understand prepaid cell phones, and tell him to stress that a killer is loose."

"Got it."

* * * * *

Banks called at noon. "We got the warrant! Judge DeBello approved it as drafted."

"That's great!" Carson said.

"The phone records will keep Munsen busy awhile. We'll keep you posted."

Carson hung up, then dialed out. He'd planned his next step: preparing to interview someone nicknamed "Loon." "Art, I need you again—"

"It's nice to be needed," Dr. Burnham replied.

"—but we have to discuss Ranchada first."

"You're back to being mad at me over that?"

"I told you I *never* blamed you for that. Being honest and having a razor-sharp memory are *assets* in my book. I mean the outcome."

* * * * *

Before his promotion to lieutenant, Carson's most notorious case was the murder of seven-year-old Kitty Ranchada. Kitty was an aspiring gymnast and singer and mommy and sometimes artist who had the misfortune of overturning her mother's coffee cup one Saturday and scalding her hand. She went to school on Monday, showing off her bandages to all of her friends. At eleven sharp, the nurse called her down for Advil and to check the dressing, and the second-grader dutifully took a hall pass and marched to the front of the school. Kitty was confident and probably became confused when she opened the door adjoining the nurse's office and found her gym teacher, Adolf Vertsen, sucking powder off a stack of paper cases in the supplies closet. Whatever questions she had she must've decided would wait until she was home with her parents, and she proceeded with her day, talking to the nurse only about her bandages.

Vertsen would've figured every minute of freedom was a lucky one, but that the luck wouldn't last forever unless he made his own. He would have had no trouble abducting and strangling a second-grader, and his claims of regular student-to-gym-teacher contact were unconvincing in light of the quantities of clothing fibers, hairs, and gauze strands recovered from his car.

The only trouble at trial came during Burnham's cross-examination. "You were convinced that someone who knew the victim had killed her?" the defense attorney asked.

"Yes. That was my opinion."

"An opinion you now want the jury to accept as gospel …"

"My professional opinion, based on the autopsy report and the police reports. The girl went missing from a crowded location, and there were no injuries other than those from the murder. So I deduced that the killer probably wasn't a stranger, nor a sadist choosing a victim at random," Burnham responded.

"And how many professionals reached the opposite conclusion?"

Burnham paused. "I don't recall anyone challenging that conclusion."

"Well, to that effect at least," the lawyer said, stepping closer. "Didn't Detective Carson ask you to profile a *stranger* who would've targeted this girl for murder?"

"Carson had interviewed the family, and cleared them. I think he just—"

"Please, doctor!" the attorney interrupted. "You're a witness now. The jury just wants you to answer *my* question. Didn't the *lead* detective ask for the profile of a *stranger* who would've targeted this girl for murder—yes or no?"

Burnham looked to the prosecutor, who sat stone-faced. "Yes, he asked for that."

"You said you'd worked with Detective Carson on several occasions. Would you characterize him as a good detective?"

"Yes."

"And characterize his requests to you as reasonable?"

"I would say so, yes."

"So this expert reasonably doubted your conclusion that Kitty's killer knew her?"

The prosecutor jumped to her feet. "Objection! Calls for speculation on the detective's state of mind. And leading."

"Withdrawn, your honor," defense counsel said, adding a glance at the jury.

The prosecution explained away Carson leaving no stone unturned, and Vertsen was convicted. But since then, Newark detectives who asked any forensic expert to speculate on secondary theories had to detail their rationale first; they nicknamed the process "printing a Ranchada."

* * * * *

"What I need," Carson said, "is for you to put on your Ranchada hat, but keep it between us. I'm just calling about the weather. No printing required for that, right?"

"Relax, Ted," the doctor replied. "Everybody does fake Ranchadas. I just have two rules. You can't tell anyone else what I say about *the weather*—this is just to satisfy your own curiosity; and if anything comes of it, you thought of it on your own."

"Yes, of course."

"Then tell me how I can help."

"I'm looking at suspects who fit your profile of Righteous— power, free time, and money. One of them has no idea what offends others, and has to take social cues from his colleagues. Possibly he views people as biology projects. That detachment makes him more likely to be the backstabber, right?"

"Hmm … I'm seeing it the other way, Ted. It's not likely that the person you've described could form a team of strangers, keep them loyal to him, and bend their perceptions of right and wrong. Besides, Righteous was driven by a passion, maybe an obsession, however misguided. Look at the painstaking planning, then putting his life on the line to rescue prisoners. Your disconnected sinner wouldn't have the empathy for that. Your guy may get in trouble someday, but not from committing this crime."

Empathy toward prisoners, Carson processed, shaking his head. He leaned back and stared at the ceiling, and reached into his pocket to rub his badge. Then he tipped forward. "Art," he said, "that wasn't the Ranchada part."

"Oh?"

"What if … what if I consider the unlikely possibility … between us … that the convicts were murdered, that Righteous wanted them dead instead of freed? *Then* would the distant suspect stay on the list, or even top it?"

"Wow! Taking all that risk, to kill?" The doctor stayed silent for a minute before continuing. "I still don't think so. The body count is disturbing, but looking beyond the carnage, to his thinking, the executions were targeted … precise. Some of the guards must've slowed him down, but he didn't kill them; and there were other prisoners on the dock. He knows murder is wrong, and has the capacity to appreciate the human condition. Just these particular killings made sense to him—seemed righteous—in whatever misguided way. It wouldn't be the detached one."

The doctor paused, uttered, "Hang on a minute," then paused again. "There's another possibility. Someone lacking an innate ability to fit in, who's just faking connecting with people, is prone to mimic behaviors—sometimes inappropriately, and sometimes, obsessively. Especially if he's overwhelmed with life at the time—he just latches on. It's conceivable that's what happened here. That socially flawed suspect could be Righteous, preoccupied with a movie he's seen or a book he's read, following it as the impetus for the crime. If you find that source, the interrogation is easy; he'll be able to recite it verbatim, and won't tolerate errors if you deviate from it in the slightest detail."

"So I search for a fictional account of a prison break-in with one guard shot, eighty-eight inmates slaughtered, and eleven accomplices thrown into the Delaware River?"

"No, no. To him, the story *is* perfection, and he'd *want* to copy it literally. But after years of obsessing over it, he realizes that his re-creation—his tribute—must be unfaithful in some regards. If it were set in 1950, he knows he can't go back in time; if his hero were seven-foot-two, he couldn't replicate that. Listen, you get me the story and twenty minutes to interrogate him, and I'll let you know."

29

All roads lead to Jen, Carson thought, picking up his cell phone. "Kahn may be fixated on a book. Kirke said the firm's disturbing projects were sent to him, so his obsession probably came from work. Is there a way to review a lawyer's copyright work and determine if a story captivated him?"

"Filing the original copyright isn't terribly complicated, so his effort for each book would be the same.... But an obsession *would* show in how often he challenges other stories for infringement."

"Would the original copyright lawyer also be involved in that?"

"For experts like the name partners at Denton Foster, yes."

"Great. Should I just check for infringement claims with the copyright office?"

"No, not there ... Damn, most copyright disputes are resolved lawyer-to-lawyer, without *any* public filing."

"So I'd need the firm's own records?" he asked.

"Unfortunately, yes.... Wait ... No, we don't! An *infatuated* attorney might overplay his hand, and that would force the disputes into court."

"Got it."

"Do you need me to—"

"I've imposed on you enough, and you've hoodwinked enough students. Bertha and I can handle this."

Carson started with records from the federal courts in New Jersey and New York City, and soon realized what a dominant player Denton Foster had become. Bolton's counsel that court was a last resort held sway, with few works litigated more than once, putting the outlier in the limelight: Reuben Kahn had filed six infringement lawsuits on behalf of Kateri Runyons for her short story, *Bullets for My Cause*.

* * * * *

Carson was in his office at four o'clock when Munsen and Banks entered. "You got the data?" he asked.

"And analyzed it," Munsen replied. "We found plenty more calls from the source phone to the prepaid cells near the criminals' homes, beyond the five clusters that had fit my filter pattern. That got us the other eleven numbers, and Judge DeBello authorized access to the records for those phones as well. Unfortunately, they were really careful—that's why the analysis went so quickly. Their first precaution was to use these phones only to call each other's burner phones—well, each other's, and one more burner besides."

"OK. You probably found Tripp's phone. More important, could you track down Righteous's house from his calls when he wasn't at the Central Tower?"

Munsen looked down. "No." He looked back up. "Their other precaution was keeping the phones stationary until they were destroyed. There's no hint as to where they traveled. Any calls from the escape truck must've been made from a different burner phone. The log gives us one clue, though: Righteous usually called between eight and ten on weeknights, so you can look for anyone who stayed late all of those nights."

"Good," Carson said, pretending that would matter at the sweatshop. "Did you pinpoint Righteous's location within the red zone?" he asked, pointing to the posted map.

"Depends how you define that," Banks interjected.

"From the signal records and hardware configuration, I could tell that his calls came from between the fifteenth and twentieth floors of the Central Tower, from several different locations," Munsen said. He handed Carson a two-page spreadsheet. "Lots of professions are represented in the rent rolls. One tenant is an engineering company, and another does security consulting; that's where we'd start, right?"

Carson pretended to focus on the highlighted lines of the printout, then shook his head. "You're considering capacity and motive, but you've ignored your own deduction—that the calls came from different places. He wouldn't have plotted the crime from the open hallways. Are those two tenants large enough?"

Munsen looked at Banks, who was shaking her head, then took back his papers. "Thinking of it that way, I'd say the only tenant that leases enough space to account for the signal variations is this law firm—Denton, Foster & Kahn."

"A law firm?" Carson responded, feigning as much surprise as he could.

* * * * *

"Arden!" Captain Burgess grumbled to Carson. "No escalating with that law firm without the director's approval."

"Sure. Should we call now?"

Burgess shook his head. "Face-to-face. This is our top case—he'll see us. But lay low on the psych profiling; he won't risk political backlash over speculation."

* * * * *

Carson presented Munsen's work at the meeting, then concluded with a practiced understatement. "I can't rule out the firm's leadership as suspects."

Arden stared at Burgess. "You agree with this?"

The captain nodded. "It's solid … as to *someone* at that firm."

"I'll agree, too," the director said to Carson. "But tread lightly. Those guys would know how to push back, and it's easier for them to muck up the gears than for you to keep them greased."

"I'm still playing their friend—I identify one bad apple, and save the entire firm from getting smeared," Carson said.

"Don't just *say* you'll be sensitive to my concerns," Arden warned. "I know diplomacy isn't your strength, Lieutenant. If you cross the line, I'll be quick to change my mind."

"I'll be around if he has any questions," the captain offered, "or if he starts to rub people the wrong way." A few seconds lapsed, and Burgess motioned Carson to leave the office with him.

* * * * *

Sulter had recognized Carson's number and let the call go to voice mail. She listened to it right away, then listened a second time: *This is Lieutenant Carson. I have new evidence that Police Director Arden feels is most sensitive in nature. I need to meet with whichever senior parties there can squeeze me in during business hours tomorrow, with the morning being best. I'll be checking for messages for the next few hours, at least.*

She forwarded the message to Kahn, Denton, and Foster: *Attached just came in. Sounds like more than a rehashing of last week's threats.* She then checked the electronic calendar, saw that the three partners were not booked at seven o'clock, and posted the usual discreet invitation: *Meet re: Representative Partner recent issue.*

* * * * *

On Mondays, the executive committee met in Foster's corner office. Kahn once—only once—called it "the catty corner," successful women plying over the years for partners' offices farthest from his affronts and Denton's lewd conversations. There was no direct evidence of Foster's short-lived marriage inside, although his etching of *The Judgment of Solomon* had been a birthday gift from his ex-wife, and his photograph with Steven Spielberg occupied a silver frame once graced by a wedding portrait. Sulter had arrived first. "I assume you three will decide, then tell me what to do?" she asked Foster. He nodded immediately and she left, with Denton and Kahn walking in soon after and closing the door behind them.

"*Sensitive evidence* again!" Foster started. "Could he be more opaque? Our client, Danbury Fullman, produced local ads for the governor, and *ran* the ad campaign for Mayor Wyeth. It would take just a few phone calls to keep the police in check."

"Let's not go outside the firm yet," Kahn said. "He keeps coming back for more information, right? So he doesn't have all the pieces. Maybe if we stonewall, he'll be forced to wither away."

"Or maybe we actually talk to the dolt, without saying anything," Denton countered. "We convince him he's barking up the wrong tree, then we report back through the mayor that the guy is harassing us and he gets put in his place."

"I know he didn't do it last time," Foster said, "but what if he pushes for confidential information? If we agree to talk, then can't give him answers, he might try to make good on his threat—"

"No, no," Kahn interrupted. "If he crosses a legal line, that works in *our* favor. We go straight to a judge and shut him down, and get a gag order so he can't threaten us with bad publicity."

"Right," Denton said. "I think the three of us can handle him. We protect our clients' confidences, take him to task for any mistakes, and find out what he thinks he has on us."

"The things we *need* to keep private," Kahn said, "what if he uncovers those and then the media publishes an exposé, citing 'unnamed sources'?"

"You think he's a shill for the newspapers?" Denton responded. "We're a boutique firm doing obscure work, as far as the mass media is concerned. Investigative reporters aren't chomping at the bit to bring us down. And the police director wouldn't be involved if this was just to snoop out if one of my girlfriends takes money or if your photo montages constitute child pornography."

"There aren't any kids!" Kahn bellowed. "Those are from R-rated movies!"

"Missing the point, Reuben," Denton said. "The police director and the media aren't teaming up to unearth our indiscretions. We're not rock stars."

"I agree with that," Foster said. "And if he veers that way, we revoke the invitation. But shouldn't we at least make it hard for him?"

"Absolutely. I'm just saying engage, *then* obstruct," Denton said. "This is our chance to find out what he has, because if it's enough for a warrant and we *don't* cooperate, he looks everywhere except the client files, on his own, and keeps us in the dark. Think of who we are—we'll get more out of these meetings than he will."

"I'm curious, too," Kahn said, "but not enough to trade information back and forth."

"I'm with Lou on that—none of *us* would reveal any of the things that would hurt the firm," Foster said. "We give him the minimum, appear to cooperate but starve his investigation, and have him wither away, like you said before. And if we get him to divulge his concerns, so much the better." He paused, and the others nodded. "I guess we have to schedule some meetings," he said, swiveling his chair toward his keyboard, and turning the screen for his colleagues to see. With a few clicks, he pulled up their calendars for Tuesday, the familiar color-coded slots lining up side by side.

"Our civil servant can't *really* think we keep open blocks of time during government hours," Denton snarled. "I'm booked all day."

"I'd blocked out until eleven for a meeting with the brass at Merck, but they've scaled back the agenda, so I should be back by 10:30. I can give him a half-hour then," Foster offered.

"I'm open right at 9," Kahn said. "Lenox Evans will be researching past midnight, and he's reporting back at 9:30. I'll see what I can squeeze out of the prick, and let him see what the executive committee is made of."

Foster shot Denton a wide-eyed stare.

"I ... I wanted to confront him, too," Denton said. "How about we make him bend from the get-go? I come in at 8:30, and he can take it or leave it."

"I'll have Stephanie send him the schedule," Foster said, turning his screen back. He started typing, and Kahn and Denton left.

30

Denton walked Carson to his corner office on Tuesday. Ted saw the floor as lifeless for the first time, until he passed Conference Room C, where a handful of attorneys in disheveled clothes gathered over breakfast sandwiches and coffee. Denton's spacious office exemplified Novack's remark about inequality among the partners—Sulter's impressive furnishings would themselves have cost less than Denton's oak desk and matching glass-doored bookcases, while the four-chaired square table still left room for a motorcycle-sized Rube Goldberg machine.

"You're gazing at my stapler," Denton said, "the one I use when I have downtime, so, maybe once a year. I won the 1998 Sibley Undergraduate Engineering Contest with it, at Cornell. Actually, with the original. I found a brass sculptor to make an artistic version for the office, on the condition that it work."

Carson didn't want to waste any of his meeting time and soon quit tracing the pulleys and pendulums that dominated the work. "You must have quite a passion for engineering."

"*Had*, Lieutenant Carson. If you want to refer to anything now in my life as a passion, that would be the eighty hours I work each week, and the twenty additional ones I'm thinking about the practice."

"Oh, that's why someone else sculpted your project—too busy with the law?"

"Honestly, I wouldn't know the first thing about welding—it would've looked like maggots feasting on a carcass, and wouldn't have been functional, so what would've been the point?"

Carson assumed Righteous would downplay his technical skills, but he couldn't read whether Denton was doing that, or merely thought his questions annoying. "Thank you for fitting me in so early," he said once they sat down across from each other at the table.

"My first police interrogation," Denton responded.

"Before I begin, I understand that your executive committee would've reached agreement on scheduling these meetings. Is that right, that all three of you were on board with this?"

"Before I begin to answer," Denton mimicked, "please don't waste any more time with interview tricks, like saying your first question is 'before you're beginning,' or perhaps planning your last question to be 'now that we're done, could you tell me X.' The answer to your question, though, is that you certainly wouldn't be here if we weren't in agreement on it."

"Sure. But there must've been a debate."

"It was discussed, and agreed to, like I said when you asked the first time. No offense, Lieutenant, but instead of repeating your questions, why don't you explain why you're here, and we can use our time constructively? Maybe I'll even get all of your issues resolved, and free my colleagues for real work."

Carson strained to match his counterpart's appearance to the disguised figure from Essex State, to link his arrogant banter with Righteous's smug demands; but he was stuck in limbo. "It doesn't *usually* work that way," he said, "but this case probably requires some give-and-take.... We believe that someone used information—sensitive information—from one of your client dealings to perpetuate several crimes. And if there's exculpatory evidence for the firm, you're in a Catch-22, because it would be protected by attorney-client."

"There *are* exceptions to the privilege. If a minor revelation would put an important matter to rest, I could ask the client for a limited waiver, for instance. Just tell me whom you suspect and what information was misused."

"I can't reveal that now, but of course we'll make an arrest at the appropriate time."

"Can you narrow it down? Should we be encrypting files? Oracle's contracted for a year-end network security audit, should we move that up?"

"It never hurts to overprotect your computers.... What would be most helpful in moving this along, while keeping the investigation under the radar, is to get exonerating records for all of your lawyers—"

Denton raised his hands. "Hold on! Our lawyers—"

"I know it seems out of character for lawyers—*your* lawyers—to break the law; but the evidence pushes me beyond relying on character."

"There wouldn't be enough evidence in the world to persuade me that any of our lawyers are capable of misconduct, much less a crime, and less still an offense worthy of the police director's attention! Frankly, the only cooperation I'm now inclined to give is helping you sort out the flaws in your *evidence*, so you can clear our firm."

"Presidents, senators, judges, lawyers ... detectives—lawbreakers hold every title. People you wouldn't expect."

Denton took a deep breath. "You seem professional enough to back down if we prove you wrong. What exactly were you hoping to get from me?"

"One of the things I have is a timeline of events; the attorney calendars could exculpate the periphery suspects."

Denton paused. "I might be convinced to advocate sharing the calendars; the meeting descriptions would have to be heavily redacted, of course, to protect our clients."

An innocent man accepting a reasonable request? Carson thought. *Or Righteous impersonating one?* "I just need to know when the lawyers were in the office meeting other people, when they were in the office working alone, and when they were away from the office. I don't need to know which legal matters they were working on, yet."

Denton shook his head. "You're hoping for too much. Meetings run over or end early, and lawyers don't usually block time to work in their own offices. I wouldn't consider the calendars persuasive if I were a juror."

"We'll just treat them as a starting point. The police *are* good at verifying alibis."

"Well, we don't have time for a fishing expedition, nor for each lawyer to catalogue witnesses and alibis for entire days or weeks."

"It should boil down to a handful of people fairly quickly," Carson said.

"I think we have the right to know if any of our clients have been victimized by this criminal activity," Denton demanded.

If he's feigning ignorance of the nature of the crime, he's doing a convincing job, Carson thought. "That's also too early for me to share. *You* haven't heard anything from your clients about misappropriation, have you?"

"I probably can't say, directly. But we would've told them to contact you."

"That's perfect," Carson said, trying to loosen Denton with a compliment, intent on gauging the lawyer's reaction to his next question. "Could you vouch for the whereabouts of any of your lawyers after noon on Thursday, the twenty-first?"

"You're going to be out of luck. That was the day before the judges' brunch. Reuben, Matt, and I all made speeches on Friday, and we block off the day before for prep. I didn't even call to check in, Stephanie Sulter held down the fort.... I guess I can vouch *she* was probably in the office that day."

Fifteen minutes in, Denton's words and body language had revealed nothing implicating himself, a vindicating performance that most criminals couldn't have faked ... but Righteous wasn't like most. *He* could've pulled this off ... he was smart enough, and calculating, like Denton seemed to be. Carson shifted to asking about other lawyers—family problems, erratic attendance, and unlikely acquaintances—partly to reinforce the pretense that the executive committee wasn't his focus, but also to concentrate on matching Denton's voice to the induced bass Righteous had used for hours, or the rasped "restless and waiting," and to picture the makeup job that could've transformed this attorney into the pale, rose-lipped caricature that had presented himself as Righteous.

They continued until just before nine. It could have been Denton. It could have been someone else. The interview had changed nothing—Kahn was still his primary suspect.

31

Kahn was plain-looking like Denton, with smaller but darker bags under his eyes. Carson feared failing to react to the macabre decor would arouse suspicion. "The dark side strikes a special chord with people, doesn't it?"

"Yes!" Kahn replied, grinning. "The songwriters focus on love, but the authors have it right—fear stirs the imagination most."

He returned a nod, then proceeded with questions, reversing the order he'd used with Denton and inquiring first about other lawyers' concerning behaviors. Kahn acknowledged only a few, possibly being more defensive than his colleague, or perhaps less attuned to others around him, so he moved on shortly. "Regardless of who's raised any red flags, the easiest way to clear the lawyers is to compare their calendars against my timeline for the crimes."

"Lou must've pushed back on that. You're burdening us without sharing any proof of wrongdoing, and seeking constitutionally protected client information."

"He objected, but we reached a compromise that protects what's privileged."

"Well, I won't make you rehash that now. *You* couldn't convince me to back down, anyway. But perhaps Lou will."

Carson studied the speech patterns, the voice, the look. This partner as well could've transformed himself into Righteous. "Could you vouch for anyone being in the office the Thursday before last, in the afternoon?"

"Unbelievable!" Kahn accused, red-faced. "Picking the one day we were all out to hold against us!"

"If anyone orchestrated a crime spree around your calendar, it certainly wasn't *me*! Take my questions at face value, or I can come back, with a warrant!"

Kahn returned to a calm voice. "I'm sure Lou told you about the preparations for the judges' brunch."

"Yes. I know you weren't here. But maybe you called in, or received a call?"

Kahn turned red again, but it was different: he darted his eyes toward his right, and the blush faded in a second. The lawyer was about to lie. "I worked on my presentation, and had no need to contact anyone. And nobody called me."

Carson wanted to savor the guilty tidbit, but quickly played to put Loon back at ease. "Your firm has an impeccable reputation for client service."

Kahn gave a relaxed nod. "Every client gets a smart, highly capable attorney—we're very selective—and there's never a surprise when the bill comes."

"You three in particular are sought after."

"We pull our share."

"But there must be some projects the senior partners relish, and some you throw to the junior people?"

"Everyone has their favorite clients, and favorite type of work: Lou likes patenting gizmos, and I'm all for a good read. But every client gets our best effort."

"Do you ever get the best of both worlds, a good client and a great story?"

"More than you can imagine."

"Meaning ... your favorite client writes the best books?"

Kahn grinned as Carson said "favorite client." "Actually, it's a short story ... not *my* story's short, but my favorite client published a short story.... Self-published it."

Carson nodded encouragement to his stumbling counterpart.

"Kateri Runyons—yes, the actress's granddaughter, gorgeous like the rest of them—graduated from NYU, then lived on family money while she wrote a novel." Kahn paused for a second, and Carson added a smile to his prodding nods. "Her story was a masterpiece, set amid the tension in New York after the September 11 attacks. But the publishers must've had a moratorium on novels on the subject, so she condensed the first chapters into a short story, *Bullets for My Cause*. Six thousand three hundred eighteen words ... brilliantly captured it all. I walked her through registering with the Library of Congress and did the rest of the copyright work on it, and it sold a million copies." Another pause from Kahn, another set of disarming nods from

Carson. "Well, only technically. The publishers reject her again, and she's denied the credit she's due. But then they copy her work over and over—the plot even ends up in a movie. I mean, not in every detail, they aren't stupid. But neither am I! And I've been fighting for her rights to this day."

Burnham couldn't have painted a clearer picture of what to expect, Carson thought. *Sixty percent chance I'm staring at Righteous? Sixty-five? Keep nodding ...*

"It wasn't just *Bullets* that made her my favorite client. Most women don't seem to like me for who I am. Kat was different ... we got along, and she gave me the ride of my life—" Kahn bit his lip, and glanced to his left, perhaps wondering why Denton or Foster hadn't interrupted his ramblings. Then he focused an angry, narrow-eyed stare at Carson. "But regardless of these tangents, we're done here. And you'd be well-advised to limit your reports to what's relevant to the investigation," he warned, fully composed as if a switch had been flipped.

Back to the threats, Righteous? Carson thought, narrowing his eyes as well. *Handcuffs now? Or wait until Burnham reviews* Bullets? He took a deep breath. *Damned Arden, "tread lightly." But he's the director.* "Done?" he challenged. "So you want me to leave knowing you lied about the afternoon before the judges' brunch?"

Kahn blushed again and looked away for a moment. "It's become a habit to hide my weakness from outsiders; I don't want to lose clients.... But I guess I'm already at the mercy of your discretion."

"I'm just looking for the truth."

"Well, Lieutenant, the best copyright lawyer in the country can't always do his job alone, and only three other people know it: Lou, Matt, and the world's most loyal paralegal, Trevor Boyle. And now you're four. I suffer from protanopia—severe colorblindness. It has no effect most days, but for some trademarks, some illustrations, and yes, when I put together a slideshow for the judges' brunch, I need a double check on the colors. I can't err on the legal work, and I can't give myself away. I met Trevor around five thirty at the Starbucks in Millburn to go over my slides. I can vouch for seeing him then, and calling him at the office about forty minutes before that."

Carson's thoughts started swirling. The alibi left open a world of possibilities, better considered at headquarters than in Kahn's office. "If you have no other fictions to correct, I guess I'm done."

Kahn glanced away once more, then escorted him out through the reception area. *There Are No Boundaries to Human Imagination, indeed*, he thought.

* * * * *

Carson thumped closed the passenger door of his Malibu, then called Munsen. "Get immediate surveillance of the Central Tower. Have them trail Reuben Kahn if he leaves the building, and arrest him if he goes to an airport. Then, track down the short story *Bullets for My Cause* and gets copies to Dr. Burnham and me."

Following that, Carson updated Burnham on Kahn's meltdown and confirmed that the doctor would evaluate *Bullets* as inspirational material for the crimes.

Next was sharing the interview details with Banks, and brainstorming. "Pull up the reports," he instructed. "We'd pegged Righteous as being with Bolton until five thirty or six; it would be just his kind of deception to muddle her sense of time, then establish an alibi with his loyalty award winner from the firm."

"I'm opening them now. It seems odd, Lieutenant … if the crime imitated that short story, wouldn't he have been more careful, and not raved about it to you?"

"Burnham said the obsession would throw Righteous off. Kahn seemed to realize he'd made a mistake after he finished."

"Well, you've had more time to process that. Let's see … the phone records show the call to the *Star-Ledger* ending at 5:21. That started the threat to kill them, and the gun in the professor's face. She thinks that ran five minutes, then five more minutes until the blindfold and headphones. I guess he could've left then, but I think he would've waited until the editorial was accepted. *That* e-mail wasn't received until 5:40."

"He *wouldn't* have waited if he was establishing an alibi. And I've driven through Millburn from South Orange; I think he still could've gotten there early enough.'"

"So I'll follow up with the professor on the timing, and then send Priestly to check the coffee shop records?" Banks asked.

"Reverse that … start with the questions we haven't already asked. Send Priestly to Starbucks first. If Kahn *was* there, find out when he arrived and how long the trip would've taken. Meanwhile, I've got to refocus … you sound like *you* still think it could be Foster."

- 32 -

Carson thought Foster's office bespoke his profession tastefully. The wall behind his desk displayed four lawyer-themed prints, and the longer, adjoining wall was a walk of fame, Foster giving the same stiff half-smile in twenty autographed star photos, except for the one with Tom Hanks, where the two seem pictured mid-laugh, and the older stock photo with just Ed Harris and Scott Glenn signed "To The Kid With The Right Stuff." He followed the pattern he'd used with Denton. "It seems the three of you would've been top-notch scientists if you hadn't gone to law school."

"I want the clients to think that, but I only minored in Chemistry," Foster said. "I've learned what questions to ask when I'm drafting patent applications, though."

"You must be tempted to try your own hand at inventing, with the bird's-eye view you get from this job."

"Sometimes I think I have an original idea, then realize it's derivative of something I've heard at work, so I pass my thoughts back to the *real* scientists. Getting to your case … I'd like to hear whatever you've told my partners about this evidence you have."

"I told them a police investigation isn't an open forum. But I did share that sensitive information from one of your client dealings was used for perpetrating crimes, and that we don't hold your lawyers above suspicion."

"Well, you should! Our lawyers lead very successful and complete lives without resorting to crime. If you tell me which one you suspect and when the crime occurred, I can clear the firm, and you can look for the real culprit."

"Our protocol for singling out criminals doesn't include getting civilians involved." *Other than exploiting Jen*, he chastised himself, taking an extra breath before continuing. "But the timeline *is* somewhere you can help. Lou Denton offered access to redacted electronic calendars."

"Surely you don't need *every* lawyer's calendar! If you have convincing evidence, it must point to *someone* in particular."

"Like I said, when it's time to treat one of your attorneys as a criminal, I'll tell you. You know I can't circumvent the presumption of innocence."

"It's not just a presumption! I work with these lawyers every day. You won't find any criminal links with this firm." Foster leaned away slightly and stared with lips pursed, then leaned right back in. "Look. Lou must have reasons to consider sharing the calendars; we can certainly get back to you on that."

"Would that be up in the air? Weren't all three of you in agreement about cooperating?" he asked, baiting for an overreaction.

"We discussed it, and the executive committee decided to schedule the meetings, so you've gotten the help from us you asked for," Foster responded.

Calm, not defensive, Carson thought. *Innocent? Or calculating?* "I'm still surprised how hard the upper echelon works here. You've seen the movie portrayals—or maybe worked on them—the partners have dramatic, affair-filled lives and fancy dinners, and the associates toil like slaves."

"The best people wouldn't really follow a bunch of sluggards. And there's reward for committing to your career: you get to do the best work, and get respect from the smartest people."

"I'd ask about it being hard on a marriage, but I haven't seen family photos on the desks today."

"Aah … detective vision. I'm the only one of the executive committee to have been married, but in hindsight, it was destined to fail. I never had time to be a good husband, and nobody should want less than that. We also had some disagreements, and she wanted me to be a nicer person. I have no regrets; I gave her free rein over our limited time together—a consolation of sorts—and I had some crazy experiences."

"Crazy, huh? Mattias Foster, the bungee jumper?"

"Not that," the lawyer corrected, "not crazy compared to what a police detective must've seen. Just adventurous for a lawyer and violist couple—like climbing the Sydney Harbour Bridge. But enough about my personal life, OK? The marriage ended seven years ago, and now what you see is what you get."

"Fair enough ... back to the calendars. I've been asking about the Thursday before last."

Foster paused briefly. "The others told you about the judges' brunch, then?"

"Yes. Did you ever call in ... any interaction that would place another lawyer here after three?"

"No. The event's a big deal for Lou, and the firm benefits from the exposure we each get. It's worth my single-minded attention."

Carson opted to finish as he had with Denton, asking questions to suggest he was still casting a wide net at the firm, imagining Righteous undisguised as Foster. Open-minded until he left the Central Tower, he banked Foster's interview and resumed focusing on Kahn during his drive back to headquarters.

33

Carson arrived at headquarters with a drive-through lunch from Claire's. Bag in hand, he diverted to Banks's desk. "Has Priestly debunked Kahn's alibi yet?"

"He's at Starbucks now, but hasn't reported back."

"How about Munsen? Any luck with the Library of Congress?"

"No. *Bullets for My Cause* isn't part of the permanent collection, so it's taking longer."

Carson nodded, then held up the bag. "Share a turkey club?"

Banks shook her head and smiled. "We'll start talking, then Munsen or Priestly will call about the case and you'll treat me like I'm invisible."

"I wouldn't do that to you, Leah."

She held up three fingers. "I've been counting. I'll eat with Youngman if I want a lunch buddy."

He flashed an inkling of a smile, then muttered "maybe next time" as he walked to his office.

Opening the overwrapped sandwich brought the smell of turkey and toast to his office, and masked the sound of Bertha wheezing to life. After scanning for pressing e-mails, he turned to documenting the interviews, starting with Kahn's.

Banks's knocking pulled his attention from the screen. "You're too late for the sandwich," he said, pointing to the aluminum ball in his trash can. "I guess breaking the prime suspect makes me hungry."

Banks shook her head slightly as she stepped into the office, and sat across from him. "You're wrong about Kahn terrorizing the Boltons. Priestly cross-checked the old payment records. His credit card was used for twelve dollars at 5:32; sounds like he was buying for two, like he told you."

Carson shook his head. "Don't forget how scrupulous he was with the crime; of course he laid *some* alibi. But you should've heard him today. I almost arrested him."

"I've thought about that too, Lieutenant, but I think the interview *clears* him. Righteous wouldn't harp on an obscure short story that's a blueprint for the crime. Plus Kahn said he called his paralegal earlier; Righteous wouldn't lie about something we could check."

Banks sounded right, but that *couldn't* make him wrong; he'd just reduced Kahn to a rambling mess. "Righteous was clever enough to escape at the bridge; we're just missing something, maybe something brilliant. Or maybe he just practiced the route. Couldn't he have left at 5:21, and bought coffee in Millburn ten minutes later?"

"I already ruled that out. They hung up at 5:21, and even if the professor's too scared to track it precisely, those threats afterward had to have taken a few minutes. And the internet says the drive takes thirteen minutes, without rush hour traffic, plus parking and ordering."

Carson closed his eyes to concentrate, then looked at Banks. "Maybe Kahn's given his card to loyal Trevor, under instruction to get to the meetings first, and have the coffee waiting?"

Banks sat silent for a moment. "That's conceivable in isolation, but it's not like him to leave an accomplice alive, remember? Especially one who'd notice the voice change." Banks crossed her arms. "Why are you *straining* to shoot down his alibi, with two other viable suspects on the list?"

"I distrust the alibi because first he lied—he said he'd been alone. He only came up with that story after slipping up about *Bullets*."

"Privileged white men worry about their privileged problems. Colorblindness *could* seem a big issue to an innocent, ambitious lawyer—menacing enough to lie about. But Righteous ... if *he* laid an alibi, he wouldn't have raised doubts by lying about it."

Carson looked down at his desk silently for a full minute, mouthing his favorite expletive four times. "The student becomes the teacher," he complimented, looking up, "and I succumb to tunnel vision. I went in looking for Kahn to crack over his obsession, and he did, and we always hope to catch them in a lie, and I did that, too. But everything you said seems right."

"Should I make sure by interviewing the legal assistant?"

"No. Arden's only going to give me one chance to single out a partner, so I have to save it for the guilty one." He huffed. "And I guess that's not Kahn."

"An optimist would say you've narrowed it down to two today. Anything from the Denton and Foster interviews worth sharing?"

Carson shook his head. "Nothing stood out ... but I was preoccupied with Kahn." He looked at his notes, then shook his head again. "I'm on the fence. It was as if Righteous responded like he thought his partner would've: same answers to my questions, same objections. Smart."

"I'm sure once you think it over, you'll figure out how to move us forward."

It won't be me alone, he thought.

* * * * *

Jen's friends had warned her not to only shuttle from home to school and back, but to expose herself to her shared environs with Phil. She drove to the Big 12 Movie Theater after class on Tuesday, and expectedly Phil loomed large. They'd shared innumerable laughs together, discussed some dramas together ... she'd even cried on his shoulder once, although more typically they'd both be holding back tears in front of the crowds. He'd been her soulmate. Within a few minutes she was weeping, without a shoulder to lean on. She stayed composed enough to be left alone by the other patrons milling about, and after a week of practice, knew how to move past the sadness. *I guess I needed that,* she thought, returning to her car. She drove home, preparing for a letdown after Carson's flat message: *We need to talk today. Nothing urgent.*

* * * * *

Carson perked up when he saw Jen's number as the incoming call. "I just got home," she started. "Do you want to meet in person, or chat over the phone?"

"This one needs to be at your house." He tried to keep his disappointment from his voice. "I'll pick up dinner again. How about Italian?"

"You've had enough raw fish for a while?"

"It was a good experience, but let's leave it at that."

"Fair enough. I'll take a tricolored tortellini from Taste of Venice, and surprise me picking a salad. Could you get here at a normal dinner time?"

"I can leave now, this is business. Well, it's the between-you-and-me business, but that's still business. Do I have to look up the number, or do you know it?"

"You're in luck. They have my home number, except their last two digits are five-zero."

"Figure forty minutes," he said. He called the restaurant without downloading a menu, certain of finding chicken parmesan at any Italian restaurant in New Jersey, and arrived when promised.

"Beware of policemen bearing gifts," he tried to joke, carrying the bag into the kitchen.

"Your message sounded like you'd sparred with Mike Tyson. I would've sounded worse, if I'd called back right away; I'd been getting over a long cry about Phil."

"Oh, I'm sorry."

"No need; it's normal, and I'm past it."

They brought their plates and glasses into the living room; Jen moved two pictures of Phil she'd put on the coffee table. Carson did most of the talking, staying vague when discussing the psych profiling, frustrated that his confidantes were each working with different facts. "Kahn's belated alibi holding up was the dark cloud, but the silver lining is we're down to two, and the promised calendars *should* clear one," he said, raising his pitch as he overemphasized "should."

"You sound as doubtful about that as I feel."

He nodded. "Yeah, I should've only said *might* clear one. Alpha was here the one day he thought all three partners would be unaccounted for, and he probably tried to take the same precaution for Saturday at the prison and the rehearsals. If he also made the phone calls only when all three were in the office, then we hit a dead end on that."

"But that wouldn't stop everything, right?"

"The rest of the investigation continues, and something'll turn up," he said. "It's just annoying that right now it's a toss-up. What I want to do next ..." Carson trailed off. He glanced at the larger picture of Phil, then looked at Jen, who returned a puzzled look.

"What you want to do next ..." she prompted.

No, he thought, *don't push her again. She's still dealing with the sadness, still crying. Don't be a bastard when the calendars might work, painlessly.* "The next step is to see what the schedules show," he declared, poking the remnants of his meal.

Jen left a few seconds of awkward silence. "You're going to pretend you came here to say *that*?"

"That's what I want to say *now*," he said, looking up. "It's the best thing for you."

"For *me*? Are you trying to protect me from something?"

"I meant for *us*, for the investigation," he lied. Then he took a deep breath. "Ninety-nine detectives out of a hundred would be at home, waiting for the calendars and celebrating their progress." He paused momentarily, but was unable to discern a reaction. "That's how I should be handling this case. I almost made a big mistake."

Jen looked down at her plate, and started halving the leftover tortellini with her fork. "Well, Ted," she snarled, clunking her utensil down, "I've been helping you a lot, and Thursday we agreed about being open with each other. Yet now, suddenly, you don't want my opinion, and you aren't even being truthful. Of course the calendars won't be conclusive, he's devious and meticulous. You're just wasting time hoping otherwise."

"I've gotten pretty close to him so far. The calendars may very well—"

"*We've* gotten close to him," she corrected. Then she shook her head. "If you decide some police secret needs to stay under wraps, fine; but if you decide you can't share what you're thinking, honestly, then you've been misleading me about our partnership, and that's unacceptable. I need you to leave."

He'd had the best of motives, protecting this woman he was growing to care about, but she was right; he'd crossed the line. He walked to the door, then finally decided he couldn't make things worse by sharing his regrets. "I screwed up, but I'm sincerely, truly on your side." He headed home, determined to ring-fence his awful encounter with Jen and focus on Denton versus Foster.

* * * * *

Ted's headlights lit the living room wall as he backed down the driveway. Jen sat still, gazing at the wall, more angry than perplexed. *Damn, I shouldn't have put all my eggs in one basket.* Then her mangled pasta caught her eye, and she chuckled. *Yeah, I can get past this.* She hadn't read Ted perfectly, but never expected to, and knew he'd have his flaws, like everyone else. At first he hadn't seemed quite discerning enough; now he didn't seem honest enough, either. *And did he really shift to patronizing me?* But he'd seemed shrewder than the other detectives, and still did. And he'd been aggressive in pursuing hunches, and usually forthcoming. *Maybe I threw him with the distraught widow remark; maybe I should credit him for the lame apology. He must feel frustrated searching for Alpha—a killer too careful to be implicated by the calendars, by the phone calls, by Ted's interrogation.*

She leaned back on the couch and closed her eyes. This wasn't the time to dwell on Ted's mistakes; it was time to focus on two men, two law partners, one of whom was a monster. *And you know the monster. The monster outlived the eleven men who'd risked everything for him; the monster snapped his hand around your neck when you said "Mags." You know his instincts; you know his thinking.* She opened her eyes and gasped, then smiled. They *were* on the right track. All she had to do was help Ted while he chased the monster—and keep a secret of her own.

34

Righteous locked the office door. He'd been distracted from work, seething: *Carson's chitchat wasn't idle at all—it was directed, and personal. He knows it's one of us! Thank goodness for Plan B, or I'd be in jail!*

"You're worried someone would interrupt Matt Foster and Lou Denton?" his partner challenged.

"That was overkill," Righteous admitted before sitting down. "I'm worried about Lieutenant Carson, though … he asked some broad questions, but inquired about the executive committee a lot."

"We haven't violated New Jersey law—the Kahn Registry would be a federal matter, and the cronyism is unseemly, but not illegal."

"Maybe he's going after *our* old secret," Righteous said.

"That was so long ago. A few people probably witnessed it, but only one person has been milking it, and I can't imagine the police getting involved then or now."

"So if not the executive committee, who?" Righteous asked.

"*I* sense he's investigating something recent, probably involving a junior lawyer."

"You believe one of our associates is a criminal?"

"Of course not! And I told him that during our meeting."

"Same here. I don't want him executing a hatchet job, and don't want him stumbling upon any embarrassing files, or making an arrest that sullies the firm. We gave him the benefit of the doubt, and tried to learn what's concerning him. Now, we should end our cooperation."

"I don't think we have to cut him off to protect ourselves. He's implying we've made a mistake, misjudged someone; we'd want to know if we have."

"He's given us nothing but words," Righteous objected, "no evidence whatsoever, after *seven* separate meetings! If someone's making a mistake, it's him, not us! You *have to* agree that we play hardball from now on—he approaches us again, we pretend he's working for the *Times* and keep quiet."

"Why can't this wait until the morning, when Reuben can join in?"

"Because I'm sure about this. I'm *insisting* you agree with me, which you know I only do in private. Remember the last time I insisted you change your mind? That turned out fine."

"It might've turned out better, but we'll never know. You're going to go too far with that one day," Righteous's colleague warned.

"This will turn out fine as well," Righteous replied. "Care to grab a coffee?"

"You don't realize I hate you right now? Maybe I'll go chat with someone normal, to restore my faith in humanity."

"On this floor, it'll be easier to find a coffee."

* * * * *

Ordinarily, Righteous would work all night to make up for being distracted during the day; he'd have to. But tonight, that wasn't an option; the police were getting too close. Someone had to be helping Edward Carson—someone motivated, someone familiar with lawyers, someone now indispensable to him. When he was sure he was the last member of the executive committee in the office, he packed some homework and headed for his BMW coupe. He had the route memorized. *No tolls, no tickets, no accidents*, he thought; any mistake could get him caught.

His heart raced as he approached Bolton's house and pressed the garage-door opener on his visor. Lynx and Leopard's handiwork, which the Panthera had secured in her ductwork, was engineered to accept the signal from his transmitter, turn the valves on the canisters two hours later, and reprogram itself so investigators couldn't track the signaling device or determine when he'd been there. The simple, nerve-racking task completed, he continued down Braeburn Way, then toward the highway, and home.

* * * * *

Jen was back to sleeping through the night, and dreaming. She was a child sitting at a long table in a sunny yellow kitchen, and everywhere she looked, a new treat would appear—jelly doughnuts, then muffins, then chocolate cupcakes. The aroma was wonderful, and she just sat smelling the food instead of eating it. Then the kitchen grew dark, and the sweet odors transformed into a foul stench. She looked to her right, and, horrified, saw a werewolf reaching for her throat, its breath suffocating. The creature grabbed her neck, and she gasped and coughed, fighting for air.

She woke with a fearful start, and felt she'd been coughing in her sleep, the smell of gas very real and very strong. She held her breath and reached for Phil, slamming the empty mattress three times. Then she dashed out of bed toward the hallway, and then the stairs. She had to take another noxious breath, unsure if it would prove fatal, and kept running until she reached the front door. As soon as she cracked it open, she inhaled again, the fresh smell flushing her body with relief. She cleared her head, realized she needed distance between herself and the explosive, and ran to the Lowerys to call 9-1-1.

The emergency dispatcher was insistent about two things: the police, firefighters and gas company were on their way, and the house should not be approached, not for the most important papers nor the most sentimental memento. She hung up and called Ted, shaking. "He's trying to kill me!" she sobbed. "He knows I'm still involved, and now he's trying to kill me, too."

"Where are you?"

"Next door, at Erin Lowery's house. I called 9-1-1."

"So you're safe now, Jen."

"No, I'm not."

"Yes, you are. And I'm coming right over. The other police will get there first. You tell them I'm coming over to talk to you, OK? I need to hang up to get over there, though. Is that OK?"

"Yes. I want you here."

* * * * *

Carson's blue strobe illuminated the PSE&G truck as he pulled alongside the South Orange police cruisers. He ran to the policeman nearest the utility workers. "Has the danger passed, Officer … Wilson?"

"They're turning the gas off at the street, but the foreman … name's Rheingold … said the house needs time to air out."

"The owner, Jennifer Bolton … any injuries?"

"Mostly scared. She'd coughed up a few lungfuls, but didn't want the paramedics, and I agreed." Wilson nodded over Carson's shoulder. "You can check yourself, she's been in my car waiting for you."

He turned toward the car, only to turn back, drawn by the foreman's resonant announcement. "We tooled the curb valve to cut off the gas. But only luck's kept it from blowing yet; a smell that bad, it's been leaking awhile."

"When can we go in?" Carson asked.

"*In?* You should move farther away! And you won't be part of the *we*, Miller and I go in first … unless you have one of these," Rheingold said, holding up a mango-sized device with a bright yellow surface, black trim, and a long silver tube. "It's a CGI—combustible gas indicator. Can I talk to the homeowner about the appliances?"

Carson cast an angry stare at Wilson while responding to Rheingold. "You *should* have been warned this is a crime scene. You're not looking for an oven knob turned halfway on; I'd suspect a punctured supply line."

"Crap! That means we're here the rest of the night, not just an hour. Well, either way, the explosion risk passes when the gas dissipates. Then my partner turns the gas back on for ten seconds at a time, and I find the leak."

"Can't we do something to make sure it doesn't explode while we're waiting?"

"If you want to risk going in and opening some windows, go ahead. But if your timing's bad, there won't be enough of you left to fill a shot glass."

"Ted?" a familiar voice called from behind him.

He turned to see Jen approaching, wearing dancing sheep pajamas and a borrowed jacket and sneakers. He stepped toward her and apologized. "They never get vicious like this … they try to keep a distance—"

"I was more scared than the first time…. What if I'd suffocated? What if the house had blown up? What … what if I hadn't woken up?"

"That part's over. You're here and we're here, and now we'll make watching out for you our first priority. We'll keep you safe until I nail him."

Jen shook her head. "You don't understand—it's not going to end. Promises don't change reality. I'm not safe here."

"I don't *want* you staying here now. I want to make sure *everything's* clear before you come back. And then you get around-the-clock protection." He held her shoulders and stared into her eyes. "You will be safe."

She stared back, then nodded. "Erin said I could sleep at her house; there's no chance I'll actually be sleeping, though ... not after that."

"I'll post an officer with your neighbor, then, for as long as you'd like."

"We're going in!" the foreman bellowed to Wilson, loud enough to turn Carson and Bolton as well. Carson watched the helmeted workers approach her open front door, then race back. When they reached the street, Rheingold waved the officers forward. "The smell's as bad as when we started; there's still gas pouring out of the place!" He shook his head. "Normally you can feel if there's a problem with the curb valve."

"Could it have been sabotaged?" Carson asked.

"Hmm ... You'd have to access it with the gas cut off. That means blocking traffic and leaving a dozen houses without gas for an hour, without anyone complaining to us about it. So I'd say 'no.'"

And I'd say you haven't met the predator of predators, Carson thought.

Rheingold turned to Miller. "How high did the gauge register?"

"Piece of crap is busted," he replied, tapping the CGI. "The display was showing nothing, and the history reads zero-point-zero."

"Let's open and reclose the valve, make sure it isn't that," Rheingold grumbled before leading Miller away. They soon returned, and the foreman yelled past the officers to Jen. "You pay for your gas, a few hundred a month in the winter and a twenty or two in the summer, right? There's not some illegal hookup I wouldn't know about?" Her scowl rushed his apology before she could speak. "I just had to rule that out, lady; no offense." Then he lowered his voice for the first time that evening. "Smells like enough gas to demolish the home if it blows, but fifteen years tells me it's not coming from us. For some reason, there's a pressurized tanker feeding that house, and it's unleashed."

"Like someone opened a tank from a barbecue grill, or like someone pumped a truckload of methane down the chimney?" Carson asked.

"An odor that intense for half an hour ... I'd say closer to a truckload. I'd be more sure if the CGI hadn't failed; that was a first for me."

"There's another possibility. Can you test it on the neighbor's oven?"

The workers left, then returned. "It sprang back to life!" Rheingold reported. "What made you think of that?"

"More of a *who* than a *what*. What's that chemical they add to make the natural gas stink?"

"The full name's 't-butyl mercaptan;' I call it 'merc.' You're dealing with a twisted SOB."

Righteous had apparently schemed to terrify the Boltons again; Jen's face attested to his success. Ted walked over to her, and placed his hands back on her shoulders. "It just *smelled* like gas. He could only frighten you, not hurt you, not blow up your house. Everything I said before about protecting you, that's still true. And you're *still* not staying here for a few days."

Jen gave a strained nod, and staggered across the yard to her new haven. Carson knew she wanted out—out of the danger, out of the investigation. And with Righteous's new show of force, who wouldn't?

35

Trust the indicator, Carson kept telling himself as he trudged up the walkway against the stifling *eau d'merc*; but he couldn't remove the last trace of doubt. "Methane doesn't kill your cells," Rheingold had explained, "it just displaces oxygen, which of course you need. But none of that even matters if you make a spark." Tact would have to be a later lesson for the foreman.

He crossed into the foyer, sweating, rechecked for the double zero on the gauge, and knelt down. He counted each time he inhaled the irritating vapor, envisioning Jen's horror when she woke up choking. After ten breaths, he stood up, inhaled again, and knelt back down. No dizziness in either direction, and no change on the CGI display. He was right again—Righteous was up to his old tricks.

He rose, walked toward his car, and pulled out his cell phone. "Wake up, Sergeant Fontana! Your team's back on duty."

"It's three in the morning, Lieutenant! You're at another crime scene?"

"Same scene, new crime—faked a gas leak. Righteous wouldn't have broken in again for a scare; they hid a container of t-butyl mercaptan during the kidnapping. I want you to find that, and leave no stone unturned to clear out any remaining threats. Every place your team skipped, for whatever reason, you check now."

"Sure, Lieutenant."

"I need thirty minutes alone in the house, so don't break any speed records. Oh … Also make a second sweep for transmitters," Carson added before disconnecting. *Awfully prescient that Righteous linked Jen to my progress*, he thought. But the killer had. And he was to blame—his reckless partnering with Jen had put her in peril. *Idiot!*

He pulled an evidence kit from his trunk, and fumed as he walked to the house. He'd wronged her. And then—just when he needed to treat her as a witness again—he'd let his rare concern for someone else's feelings get in the way. He should've reexamined the house right after dinner, with Jen by his side, narrating everything she could remember as his detective's eyes scrutinized the scenes. Now he had to do it himself. *Stupid!*

He reached the doorway, mumbled "doing the rest by the book," and crossed back in, notepad in hand.

Step by step. Phil left work at his usual three o'clock, wearing a button-down and khakis; he'd been home long enough to change before the killers confronted him. Carson walked to the threshold between the kitchen and the den and visualized the attackers restraining Phil, shading the windows before Jen arrived, and confronting her, compelling surrender. The show of force, the scripted directives—is that more like John or Loser? Still a toss-up. He continued to the basement—regardless of what might have been disturbed since, it was still worth a look. He stood at the foot of the stairs, taking in a wide view of the desks, picturing the control, the success with the *Star-Ledger*, the violence—nothing pointing more to one suspect than the other. Then knocking Jen out for the night, smart but risky—unless they knew her medical history. He scribbled "Check if any Panthera could be linked to a medical records theft."

Now Jen is unconscious, and Righteous is brimming with success. A control freak in a stranger's basement—he's going to look around. Carson scanned the room, trying to see everything fresh as Righteous would have. *Phil's gadgets! If it's Denton, he's getting a hard-on.* Righteous would know not to break or take anything; but if he's John, he might be touching the toys, moving them out of place. Carson checked for any telltale signs, and found none—possibly it wasn't Denton, possibly it was him, being careful. Likewise for the bookshelves—no signs a dormant text was handled by a gloved intruder. Then he checked the back wall, mostly pictures and a few awards ... and a name that caught Carson's eye: *Sibley!* Phil Bolton had been the 1996 Sibley Undergraduate Engineering Contest runner-up, a kindred spirit with Denton. His plaque would've been irresistible! Carson bagged it for personal delivery to the lab.

He moved up to the bedroom, and opened the windows to clear the fetid air before reenacting Friday morning. The outfit, and the makeup and hair basics—someone knew just a little about women, more than you'd learn from a hooker, but exactly what you'd glean from a wife.

If Righteous wrote that part of the plan, he was more likely Foster than Denton.

Carson headed downstairs, still undecided between the two partners. *Walking a circle is not the same as standing still*, he encouraged himself, glancing at the Sibley and his notes.

* * * * *

Fontana had only been inside for thirty minutes before he emerged, presenting Carson a contraption that resembled two Thermoses lodged in a garage-door-opener. "Do you want the good news or the really bad news?" he asked.

"I'm on an awful news streak, how about breaking the monotony?"

"The good news is your victim didn't die from exposure to poison gas."

Carson returned a confused stare. "That's *good*, but it isn't really *news*."

"Actually, it is," Fontana replied, pointing to the tanks. "This smaller canister was opened recently, releasing a t-butyl mercaptan blend. You see why they use it, just a little makes that alarming stench. The motor opened it, but the valve is connected to a clutch, so if the motor had run again, the force would've reversed and the small canister would've closed back up. The large canister wasn't opened enough for the contents to seep out, but the valve was worked partly up the neck. If the motor had been signaled to run twice instead of once, the contents of this second canister would've filled the house instead. Quinones will have to open it in the lab for a full ID, but these high pressure, temperature-resistant seals are only used for hazardous materials. Whoever stunk up the house could've turned it into an execution chamber instead."

Carson felt his face go pale. But for Righteous being content to scare Jen into helplessness, she would be dead ... *because of him*.

"You OK, Lieutenant?" Fontana eventually asked.

"With this job?" Carson said.

"I know what you mean. But she's safe now."

"You think so? They had an entire night to rig the house."

"Give us through lunchtime. We'll find anything bigger than a deck of cards, anything drawing electricity, anything behind a switch plate or hinge, and anything down the drains or up the chimney. They might've scribbled 'Boo' inside the walls, but if they've planted anything dangerous, we'll find it."

* * * * *

Carson debriefed Fontana on his progress at dawn, then drove to headquarters. He left the Sibley award, in its bag inside a box, for Quinones. At nine, he updated Banks and shared the scant new leads. Then he called his sister.

"Using my work number? What's up, Lieutenant?"

"The nutjob's trying to intimidate us."

"Like which relative predicted ..."

"You *did* call that early on. Beck ... I don't think he has any limits." Carson proceeded to detail the evening. "I initiated phase three security for you last night," he concluded. "Maybe you noticed the extra patrols on your street?"

"Thanks for thinking of me, but you should be thinking of *yourself*. My work on the case is done, but yours isn't, and I guess for some reason he thought hers wasn't—"

"Witnesses often prove more helpful as the investigation develops," he interrupted quickly ... too quickly.

Rebecca raised her voice to drill sergeant. "Didn't I call you an idiot the last time you spoke to me about Jennifer Bolton? *Please* tell me you stopped involving her in the case!"

"He couldn't have known, Beck. I was really careful, just a little help here and there. Righteous wasn't sure himself—he could've killed her if he wanted, if he *knew* she was helping ..." Carson reached into his pocket and made circles on his badge, and continued only slightly louder than a whisper. "He could've killed her, because of me. I was zealous to nail the creep, and I almost got her killed. I'm in over my head, Beck."

"Look, Ted. I was right to be angry, but that doesn't mean Righteous is getting the better of you. He's after her because you're making real progress and flustering him. He'd planned on getting away with this, and you figured him out in a couple of weeks. You're still the best detective there."

"So my sister supports me ... I'm *really* grasping at straws."

"I'm a scientist first, Ted. Doctor's honor—people with big responsibilities make weightier mistakes than this."

"Don't forget the part about being careful," he diverted. "The police won't be more than three minutes away if you call."

"I love you, too," Rebecca closed.

After seven early hours of work, Carson's to-do list consisted of waiting—waiting for the lab to check the second gas canister and the Sibley plaque, waiting for his team to follow up on his insights, and waiting for Denton Foster to make good on the calendar delivery. But waiting meant thinking—dwelling on putting Jen in danger. He opted for a field trip, casing Bertha and driving to the mansions Mattias Foster and Lucian Denton called home. Without a warrant, he'd have to settle for a couple of driveway views.

Denton's homestead was sized for a family of six. Martinsville had its share of hill-set chateaus, gaining extravagance with the altitude, and Denton's sat at the pinnacle. The lavish stonework housed elaborate stained-glass windows on a first-floor great room, and the yard, the bushes, and even the flowers in the second-floor window boxes seemed freshly manicured. Carson could readily picture Denton's pavered arc crammed with the other partners' Cadillacs for a steak-filled Fourth of July. And despite bragging about legal entertainment, he couldn't help but assume that John would be regularly cavorting with the priciest of Newark's one-night beauties in those moonlit bedrooms, that he probably played by his own rules. Perhaps his subconscious was signaling a stronger match between Denton's voice and the too quick "restless and waiting" than he was willing to process as fact. But he couldn't base an accusation on that whim, or worse, risk accusing an innocent man of one hundred murders.

Foster had kept his married residence in Morristown after his wife returned to Arlington. The sandstone wall separating the width of his property from the street was an elegant privacy measure, as were the burning bush hedges along the property lines and the six spruces scattered across the front yard. Carson figured the contemporary mansion had replaced a once-endearing colonial or Victorian befitting the ritzy neighborhood. The exterior featured a façade of dark wood beams laid diagonally, punctuated with bay windows, and a roof built in five distinct sections. *Why would anyone who could come home to this shatter the social contract?*

Although the case remained on his mind, the tour hadn't been for naught; by the afternoon, he only replayed the terrified call from Jen in his thoughts every few minutes instead of every one.

* * * * *

Righteous awoke Wednesday and perked up quickly, gleaming at his foresight to booby-trap the Boltons' ductwork while the crime was afoot. *Pity the wannabes who try to undertake endeavors as great as mine but don't ponder the contingencies!*

Then he gave more somber consideration to Carson's progress. The detective had revealed nothing about why he suspected the firm, but Plan B seemed to be holding: avoiding being singled out, and thwarting the investigation. In fact, the stage was set to cut off the lieutenant entirely: Kahn had confided his inexplicable soul-bearing, and wanted nothing more to do with the police, and his other partner was, reluctantly, in his pocket. *Better advance Plan C anyway, with its shitty ending, in case Plan B collapses. I'm not spending my life in jail!*

* * * * *

Absent dissent, the name partners made quick work of stifling Carson, refusing to identify who attended any meeting or which client was being serviced when, and adopting an extended timeline for defending their interpretation of attorney-client privilege: Sulter would draft a memo to the district attorney over the weekend, then the three of them would take through Wednesday to finalize it. Meanwhile, Novack would target that following Thursday for delivering redacted attorney calendars categorizing each hour only as "Scheduled for billable work," "Scheduled for non-billable work," or "Unscheduled time." Righteous couldn't help his grin being the widest.

Then Kahn dropped his bombshell. "Thirty million dollars is enough for me."

Denton and Foster looked at each other, with Foster speaking first. "What do you mean, Reuben?"

"The Kahn Registry. It's been up for six years now, and we've made a hundred million off of it. That's more than anyone can spend, and none of us are popping out heirs, so there's no reason to keep exposing ourselves."

"Exposure?" Denton challenged. "Carson's local, the Registry's federal; he's not looking for that. I think you were the one who made that point. I like the income."

"He's not looking for it, but he's made me realize someone could find it. We have a hundred people working here, too; one of them could figure it out someday."

"Shutting it down before we have to will upset a lot of clients," Denton said.

"Well, Lou, don't forget our arrangement. We knew the drug companies patented new meds long before they were ready for sale, to claim prior rights against any competitors, and that half-year deferrals would translate into billions for them. I found the loophole so nobody could prove an illegal delay, and proposed the Registry. Since then, the pharma executives have sent us all of their patent work, at our special premium, and the three of us drag out the process so the first-to-invent gets all of a much larger pie. But we agreed—I made you two agree—that any one of us could pull the plug. And I'm doing that now. No more special arrangements, no more extra payments, and no more records."

"Reuben, you're overreacting," Foster said.

"No, you're being piggish. I don't need more money out of that, and there's no other reason to do it.... It's done."

The three conspirators sat in silence. There was still enough money to buy a city to squeeze out of the scheme, but it couldn't continue with a schism.

There was that much less to fear from the persistent detective.

36

Carson arrived in a hopeful mood on Thursday—nobody had been gassed overnight, and his colleagues had been pursuing leads. "Full inbox!" he beseeched Bertha as she stirred awake. He shot his screen with his index finger and thumb when he saw only spam for *Cheap V1agrrrrah* and *Sea-aliss*.

Guess I have to work.

He first called Stephanie Sulter, or, more precisely, her voice mail. "Please call. I'm sure your partners told you Tuesday that they agreed to share some readily available electronic records, and I'm sure everyone innocent is anxious to be cleared." Then an e-mail to his detectives, his favorite kind, provoking yet short enough to fit in a fortune cookie: *Information has no value unless shared.* He was likewise concise with Quinones: *You must know those canisters didn't come from Walmart by now,* to which the doctor replied: *You know where to find me.*

Carson presented Dr. Quinones with a latte. "For the man who knows his priorities."

"Another detective who thinks his cases are the only important ones. Let me take that before you add the arsenic."

"Arsenic? You've known how to trace heavy metals since puberty. On you, I'd use an organic compound. But it's not going to come to that, is it?"

"It's not. We've been working on the plaque, since it got here first. But it's tricky. We roamed the building for dusty frames as benchmarks, and found all sorts of variations in dust accumulation. If a small picture hangs over a larger one, the lower one gets dustier on the corners than in the middle, for example. And then you get the occasional cursory cleaning, the rag wipes only half the frame. Plus there's no device to measure the thickness of dust. I'd proposed using transparent tape to clear the edges, then measuring the tape's opacity—how much light it blocked—along its length. But that removes all the dust, so you can only do it once. After getting no better ideas for the rest of the day, we decided to do that to your Sibley. I doubt this would be admissible in court."

"Don't worry; I won't need to use that if we go to trial. Did you find anything?"

"You heard me just say that a dozen other things could've affected the dust pattern, right? Including you bagging it, however careful you tried to be?"

Carson smiled. "That means you found something! Spill it, Ed."

Quinones huffed. "Fine. There was a fifteen millimeter length of lighter dust partway up the side from the lower right corner."

"In English?"

The scientist stood and stepped to his framed doctorate hanging on the wall behind his desk. "There was missing dust consistent with a forefinger tilting the plaque upwards, an inch from the bottom on the right side, like this," he said, sliding his index finger behind the right corner of the frame from the side and his middle finger along the bottom.

"The bastard wanted a closer look at the Sibley award!"

"Hold on, Ted. There wasn't enough dust on the bottom to check for the second finger, that's speculation. And there's no way to tell how slowly dust accumulated there, so we can't estimate how long ago the contact was made. I can only say that someone touched your plaque there after it was last cleaned."

"How often do you visit someone's house and they bring you to their basement office? Never! And I'd bet a *year* of lattes that if we hang a Sibley in every precinct house in Newark, nobody would be intrigued enough to tilt it out for a better view."

"Phil Bolton might've straightened it out himself at some point. And the people who went by to remember him, to console his wife— don't pretend you're going to harass every mourner to see if they recall *not* touching the thing."

Quinones was right—the dust analysis was a mere crumb; but a crumb with Denton's name on it nonetheless.

* * * * *

Carson's Thursday continued at a dull grind until two words sent him trudging to Captain Burgess's office: *Let's chat.*

Burgess had the only comfortable chair at headquarters, brown leather with thick armrests, passed down from Lieutenant Arias when he took early retirement for his bad back. Carson sat in the stiff guest chair across from him. "I feel bad for your witness," the captain droned with no sign of sympathy. "You no doubt realize that such a blatant attack puts pressure on us."

"No doubt," Carson played along.

"So the director backed you up on the law firm meetings, and you had the gas threat. I should expect a nice report about how much closer we are to catching this jerk than we were at the beginning of the week, right?"

"Look, Captain … I feel I've narrowed it down to Denton and Foster, but there's no smoking gun. Righteous was disguised, and his voice was altered. And he's slippery."

"So it might be either of those two, or someone else, and there's no hard evidence even though we've analyzed all the crime scenes and you've interrogated both men?"

"Well, no … not that last part. What I did wasn't a formal interrogation, more of an interview on their terms. Remember? 'Tread lightly'? If I could arrest and *freely* interrogate either of them, I'd know which one—"

"You can't work backwards, arrest maybe the wrong guy and shut down a hundred-million-a-year law firm; Arden would have a seizure. Your *interviews* must've pointed you to one more than the other."

"It's the lawyering. They're trained to make people sound innocent, to prepare them for police interrogations. And they get to cite attorney-client privilege. I had to settle for a promise to get redacted calendars delivered, and so far, nothing."

"Aah, the lawyer angle," Burgess said, leaning back snug against his chair. "You can't do what you normally do. That doesn't leave you helpless, Ted. Let your team handle the leads, and you think big picture and figure out a different way to push these guys. They're not the usual punks, but they haven't lived in a bubble, either. They'll have weaknesses and fears to play on. And you probably know them better than you think."

Carson relaxed at Burgess's rare display of encouragement. The advice seemed reasonable, even sage.

He returned to the creaky vinyl chair in his narrow office, and thought, first about Denton. And thought. Desperately. *Grasping at straws …*

He tracked down Nye County Deputy Sheriff Kyle Ellison. "You're going to fly out to Nevada to interview prostitutes ... *smart* prostitutes?" the deputy asked.

"Maybe he said something suspicious, while he was ... occupied."

"Wouldn't that kind of guy have *occupied* himself with your local girls, between trips out here?"

"I considered that. But the hookers here lawyer up, because it's illegal. I was hoping the prostitutes *there*—"

"An indiscreet working girl? Might as well be an abstinent one! There wouldn't be a brothel in the Silver State that would hire her, either. Unless you don't pay, or you damage the merchandise—*then* they threaten you with publicity."

"No other exceptions?"

"Even under oath they follow the script, 'I've had so many customers, I simply don't recall.'"

Carson's next unconventional idea was approaching Denton's clients. Although the attorney-client privilege bound the lawyers to secrecy, an angry client was free to complain about how much he charged and whether he seemed obsessed with failed poisons and explosives. But Kirke said the clients flocked to him; they probably loved his work, and he would've taken care to impress them as level-headed and honorable.

What else did Kirke say? Denton's enemy! The chairman of the Bar Association, his equal! But their détente had been stable for years; if he had any dirt on Denton, he would've used it against him by now.

Carson needed something more imaginative. He tried re-booting by clicking on the Yahoo story with the trashiest headline: *Honeymoon Bride Discovers Mummified Limb*. "I saw the shoe, and the rest was so shriveled, it had to be a leg sticking out of it."

He might've wasted a minute of his life on the article, or the distraction might've opened his mind for his next idea. It was unorthodox, but the more he pondered it, the more enticing it became, until finally he decided to seek the captain's support.

"You'll need a lot of manpower," Burgess grumbled. Then he stared at Carson, silently, until he blinked. "I'll agree to it, but if you don't make any headway from that, the blame falls on you."

* * * * *

At five, Carson was at the lectern in the roll call room, drawing the attention of his team and the vice squad to John's headshot on the 36-inch touch screen display. "Lou Denton is not a formal suspect in any crime. But he *is* a person of interest—great interest—to me. The weekend's coming up, and he's known to pay, generously, for … companionship."

The room resonated with howls from the vice officers.

"Tomorrow," he continued, "I want his prowl to end with us. We get the edge by scaring away the competition. Leak word to the streetwalkers that we're borrowing white middle-aged undercovers from Woodbridge to drive fancy cars for a sting operation, and they won't give this guy the time of day. Then, tell the usual concierges and bartenders that some new girls from Miami are offering a high-roller chocolate-and-vanilla special; Banks, you OK teaming with Rodriguez on that, and Donley and Carrasco, doing the same with the internet trolls?"

The room erupted in catcalls.

"Keep a lid on it!" Carson demanded. "It's a one-night special operation, all talk, no action. I don't even need the charges to stick. I just want some quality time with him." He looked at Banks and nodded reassurance, and she nodded back.

Rodriguez called out. "Hey Lieutenant! Maybe Carrasco passes for vanilla; I tempt johns as silky caramel …"

She drew some more whistles, and Carson realized he'd have to play along. "Fair enough, how about chocolate and sugar? You can be the brown sugar team?"

His reply earned some hoots, and Rodriguez shouted, "Lieutenant's one of *us* today!"

Carrasco challenged next. "I'm OK being bait, but if you don't care about the charges sticking, why not just tail this one guy, and arrest him whomever he approaches?"

"Great idea, but I need enough of a case to force him to talk his way out of it. If the girl he solicits isn't a cop, they both claim it was a misunderstanding and keep quiet, and he walks within the hour."

Carrasco nodded, and Carson continued. "Denton has no police record—he must've developed a technique for avoiding arrest. He also might wear a disguise, or solicit through a surrogate. Anyone with a big bankroll who's as interested in your mind as your body gets brought in for interrogation." He glimpsed a few more nods. "This means a change in schedule for my team—your Friday starts at 8 PM. Vice is going to take the lead on logistics; you probably have to start the rumor mill tonight. Any questions?" He scanned the silent room, mouthing "thank you" to Banks when his eyes caught hers. Operation Skewer-the-Pig was under way.

* * * * *

Jen had prepared a classroom contingency plan one week after Phil died. On Wednesday morning, after the gas scare, she called Dean Marshall from the Lowerys' den and warned that she'd be out for between two weeks and forever. At lunchtime, an understanding Officer Vellis accompanied her home to pack. She felt uncomfortable about backing her car out of the garage, and the patrolman served as valet. Then she drove to Edison to stay with her mother.

In a once unlikely scene for the two strong women, they greeted each other by embracing and shedding tears. Jen steadied first. "He only scared me, Mom," she whispered, before trembling again. "But it was such a scare. I'd just started feeling normal … thinking of normal things."

"You being safe is the most important thing."

Jen let go and stepped back. "I don't know why he went after me the first time, or now. *I* want to see *him* dead, but I don't deserve this."

"No, dear, you don't deserve this at all. He's just sick. They'll catch him soon, and you'll be done with him."

Even though she knew it wouldn't be that easy, her mother's words were still comforting. Returning to the landscaped colonial where she'd spent her high school years, being out of the crosshairs, also offered solace. "Can I just go collapse in the den? All I want to do is rest, maybe even fall asleep."

"Of course, Jen. Watch TV, sleep, whatever you want. I was going grocery shopping today anyway; I can stock up for us both."

Jen nodded and headed for the familiar velour couch, thinking back to when her biggest worry was whether her parents would be proud of her academic successes. She spent the afternoon much as she would've spent a sick day in high school: watching syndicated TV shows, dozing off for a couple of twenty-minute stints, eating a tuna sandwich, and drinking hot chocolate. She chatted with her mom about relatives over a chicken dinner, likely hearing repeats of stories that hadn't sunk in during her bereavement. The catnaps hadn't made up for her lost sleep, and after clearing the dishes, she retired to what was now the extra bedroom.

Thursday started low-key as well—breakfast and television—but the sleep and passing of a day had lifted Jen's mood. She prepared a chef's salad for their lunch, and shared all the details of Tuesday night's scare without re-experiencing the fear herself, eventually realizing that this trauma would also pass.

Her mother must have sensed her rally. "You make it sound like the shock was the worst part," she said. "Now he can't surprise you about being after you anymore."

"I don't want to find out if he's prepared other surprises."

"Nobody would! But at least you're past that."

* * * * *

The conversations with her mother turned in her head through another night. The reflecting transformed her fear into relief, then resolve. "It's different when you're on notice," Jen announced over Friday's breakfast. "All I have to do now is stay a step ahead of him."

"That's right. Be cautious, and stay clear until he's caught, and you'll be fine."

Jen nodded to comfort her mother. But she wasn't one to hide— she was a fighter. *Round Three, asshole!* she thought. *Let's see how you fare when we're on equal footing.*

- 37 -

Carson arrived at headquarters at nine on Friday, after a morning jog, despite the sting schedule. He read a spate of e-mails on Skewer-the-Pig, and sent one to Lieutenant Schilling, head of the Vice Section: *Thanks for arranging this on such short notice.* He then turned to the rest of the investigation, first leaving another message for Sulter, insisting on a status report for the calendars before business hours on Monday, then calling Quinones in response to his e-mail: *Call me about the canister. Boring.*

"Ted, he went old-school for this one. Chlorine gas, like trench warfare. In this quantity, you can see it coming, and a wet rag to breathe through can usually save you. But if you're sleeping and it vents into your room, then we're probably talking mortality. He didn't have to be an innovator for this."

Carson hung up, and thought about Jen. He didn't want to re-involve her—if the calendars panned out or if John got skewered in the sting, the case would be closed, shortly, without her. So he shouldn't call … he knew he shouldn't. But he *had* to.

"It's Ted. We're all concerned. *I'm* concerned."

"I'm feeling less scared today. I was going to call you if you hadn't called me."

"I'm *so* sorry. He could've … I put you in danger. That's the last thing I wanted."

"Listen, Ted. I realize … this'll sound stupid … well, maybe not to a cop … Being on a flight when an engine blows is scarier than being on street patrol during a riot, right, even though you're more at risk in the riot? It's when the danger's outside of your control, unforeseen … Well, police aren't the only tough ones, willing to stick their necks out to mete out justice. I needed a few days, but I still crave vengeance on this creep, and I'm ready to rejoin the case."

"I'm supposed to say, 'You're a civilian, and this isn't your case to join.'"

"I'm not asking for anything more than we had; I'm not expecting you to hand me a gun and a badge. But he hasn't scared me from consulting with you, and he only would've come after me if he thought I had more to offer. So you should drop whatever dead-end leads you're pursuing and pretend we're back to Tuesday ... early Tuesday, before you decided to coddle me."

"You'll let me protect you, though? No questions asked?"

"I insist on it. I'm not trying to take a bare-handed stand against an armed maniac. But I'm willing to stay on his enemies list. It's my fight as much as yours."

"We should meet, then. Where do you feel safe?"

* * * * *

Jen reserved a reading room in the Short Hills library whenever she wanted writing time out of the house and away from her students and colleagues. "Hi, Ted," she greeted with a slight smile.

"Great you bounced back so quickly." They walked to the glass-doored Room A, Ted carrying a laptop bag with a stuffed folder hanging out, her just a brown purse.

"Is this private enough?" she asked as she sat next to him at the six-chaired conference table.

"Perfect. The last place we'd run into a Newark police squad." Ted stared at her for a few seconds.

"What?"

"I have some disturbing news. You seem ready to take it in stride, but we could take care of business first, to play it safe."

"If it's about me, I'm truly ready to fight," she said. "Go ahead and share."

"I told you that the merc odor wasn't signaling methane, that you couldn't have suffocated and it wouldn't have exploded."

She nodded. "You did, when the utility workers were running back and forth."

"Well, the device they hid also had a tank of chlorine gas. Alpha did have your life in his hands, and we were lucky he decided just to scare you."

"Oh ..." Jen looked down. She *had* been within a hair's breadth of dying, sleeping on a powder keg after provoking a psychopath holding a match. "You're sure he *decided* just to scare me? It wasn't a tank malfunction ... he *chose* not to kill me?"

Ted huffed. "This makes it more disturbing ... he was outside your house, and triggered the motor. Probably he, but maybe someone else, signaled the device with a garage-door opener. There were two possible signals, and he chose the one that released only the odor.... He probably doesn't know just how helpful you've been."

Jen took a long, deliberate breath. "Then good thing for me he doesn't."

"Amen."

"What about my house? Will it ever be safe?"

"My lab team spent half a day there with spy equipment and contractor tools, looking everywhere—down the drains, up the chimney. They said there's nothing else dangerous, and nothing bigger than a deck of cards."

"That sounds safe, right?" she asked softly. "But he's been ..." She paused for another deep breath. "I think I'll sleep at my mom's until you catch him."

"Smart. And brave. We'll nab him soon, and you'll have no need to worry."

She thought for another moment. "You know what—screw him! I wake up thinking he's trying to kill me, then you say he wasn't and couldn't have, and now it turns out he wasn't but could have. He wants me scared off? He gets the opposite! Which of the partners does that gassing device point to?"

Ted's eyes widened. "Wow ... he's messed with the wrong woman!" He updated her on the investigation, the apparent stalling on the calendars, and the evening's trap for Denton. "It's been slow without you."

"You think Denton will confess to Alpha's crimes if you bring him in for solicitation?"

"Not spontaneously. But he'll want to talk his way out of the charges, to avoid an arrest record and a court date, and that opens the door for lots of questions: him ever using disguises, alibis during the prison break and when the calls were placed, and large bank withdrawals. Sometimes a suspect's reaction when you ask direct questions, like about parachuting or firing a gun, is all you need. When the dust settles, either he's snared or we conclude it's Foster."

"We hope ... There's no guarantee, same as with the calendars."

"I'm not saying it's a sure thing. Actually, that's why I brought this," he said, pulling the folder from his case.

"I figured that was for me."

"Just pretend you haven't been my detective partner; be an ordinary witness."

"All right."

"Think carefully about Phil's desk, the last times you saw it before any of this happened. Be as particular as you can about what's there and where everything is. But don't get stressed out, most people can't recreate an exact picture of things they've seen, even things they see every day; just do your best and let ideas come to you as they may."

Jen nodded and closed her eyes. She could picture the rectangular desktop, and, bit by bit, his electronics: the ergonomic wireless mouse, the silver-rimmed flat-screen monitor, the external hard drive, the photo scanner, and the micro speakers he used only when he was alone in the basement. She saw a pile of papers on the left, and, thinking carefully, pegged it at slightly shorter than a ream. She knew he had a framed photo of the two of them at Busch Gardens, and remembered it being offset behind one of the speakers. Then she smiled—those geeky contraptions, so … Phil: the NASA slide rule he bragged about to their friends; the nutcracker with all those gears that could split a pebble; and the rock that had something to do with the Brooklyn Bridge. "Ready," she declared. "But I'm a terrible artist."

"No drawing required," he said. "Usually, I'd bring you to the scene, to see if anything is out of place. But maybe the mourners, and definitely my lab team … let's just say there was a lot of traffic, making sure your house was safe."

"Is that what you were going to have me do before our fight Tuesday?"

Ted's jaw dropped. "Even during a thought exercise, you pick up everything! I worried about bringing you back to the basement, and it didn't seem like a priority, but yes, I'd planned this for Tuesday. So now we'll do it this way." He opened the folder and laid out eight photos of Phil's desk. "Tell me if anything's been added or removed first, that's the easy part. Then tell me if anything's been moved or disturbed."

Jen first studied a wide-angle picture. "I missed a few," she said.

"That's typical," he encouraged.

She had correctly remembered the larger items, the stack of papers, and the technology components. The photos jarred her memory of the metallic pencil holder and pencil sharpener, plus Phil's newest addition, a dark blue stress ball with letters spelling "SPHERE" that morphed into reading "SPHEROID" when squeezed from the top, which amused only him. Everything she'd remembered was still there when the pictures were taken, and everything in the photos belonged on his desk. She scanned two close-ups to make sure the pencil holder was appropriately full and the paper stack was the correct height before speaking. "Nothing added or removed."

"Hmm … Try scanning across the desk. Focus on each item in turn, and think if it's in its usual place, and if what's usually next to it still is."

She gazed at the pictures once more, occasionally closing her eyes and bobbing her head before staring again. "I've got an inkling something's wrong, but I can't point to anything specific. The big items look right to me, our picture looks right, and the pencil holder and slide rule I can't even say belong in a particular place, so I wouldn't know if they've been moved. And everything seems next to its proper companion."

Ted's lips turned down. "Oh."

"You thought something had been moved?" she asked.

"It's not that."

"You think something's missing?"

"Only if you do."

She scanned the pictures again. "Sorry, Ted …"

"Fine. Phil has a typical Generation X office setup, new mixed with old—the latest electronics, but also papers and a pencil holder. He's missing something only the kids go without, something you have on your desk—a paper calendar."

Jen grabbed one of the close-ups, and grinned.

"I'm right!" Ted exclaimed. "The calendar's gone! I don't know why he took it—"

"The slide rule! You're right for the wrong reason. Phil's calendar wasn't paper—he'd keep the slide rule open to whatever day Sunday was. If I asked him for the date, he'd do the math and say, 'it's Friday, so it's the ninth.' Whenever he finished showing it off, he'd open it back to the right place. Look, Ted! The slide rule shouldn't have been closed like that in the middle of the month."

"The bastard couldn't keep his hands to himself! Just like with the Sibley! Don't you see: only an engineer would be intrigued by the slide rule, an engineer like Denton. It's not proof, but it's not a toss-up anymore, not to me."

He gathered up the photos, smiling, and Jen kept smiling, too, glad to be back in the thick of pursuing Alpha.

- 38 -

"Here's how your sting's going to play out," Lieutenant Schilling said as Carson crammed next to him in the surveillance van. "The girls get approached by four types of johns. You got 'in over their heads and they know it,' they bring enough money for a toothless meth head but go after the prime meat first, like a hot warm-up before the skanky main course. Our ladies weed them out quickly on price. Then you got 'in over their heads but they don't know it,' usually newbies, they start at twenty bucks and our girls say three hundred and they think they're special and the ladies will meet in the middle at thirty."

Carson shuddered when he realized Schilling would keep referring to the vice officers and Banks as "girls" and "ladies," as if *he* were also undercover, trying to build credibility as a pimp.

"They eat up time," Schilling continued, "but then they go away. The third group is the 'wait and sees,' they swear if the girl drives off with them, they'll pay a good price after. The real hookers say, 'Then fifty for the car ride,' but things can get messy if the john says 'OK' then won't pay once the girl's in the car. You mentioned your guy might use a go-between, so I told our girls to say, 'Two hundred, up front, for the car ride only.' I'm thinking that keeps your guy in the hopper while scaring away the other 'wait and sees.' Then the fourth type are high-roller regulars. They're pretty forthright with anyone they've picked up before, and careful but decisive on new ones—our girls will be zeroing in on them, and we bag the ones looking for smarts."

"You've got it down to a science."

"World's oldest profession. After all these years, I know what to expect. Actually, Ted," Schilling lamented, "it *is* wearing me down, especially seeing how many of the girls are forced into this. I lie in bed thinking our arrests keep some damper on it, but there's no end in sight."

"You can only do what you can do."

Schilling looked down and nodded. "Right ..." Then he resumed looking at Ted. "Getting back to tonight ... I'm worried we're so focused on the one guy, the girls might overreach. They normally wait for the perp to offer money and let the backup team make the collar, but if they think they're losing Denton, they might try for the arrest before support moves in; it could get dangerous."

"That's why I wanted Banks in the miniskirt; there isn't a situation I wouldn't trust her to handle."

"Well," Schilling said, pointing to a monitor, "her first prospect is pulling over now." Then he pressed an orange button, numbered "3." "We can hear them, but she won't hear us."

Carson turned to the screen as Leah's voice, seductive as he'd never heard before, came over the speaker. "*I'm sure a classy guy like you would pay extra for the consummate courtesan.*"

"*I don't know anything about that, but you sure are sexy,*" the driver replied, drawing a thumbs-down and head shake from Schilling.

As Schilling foretold, most of the drivers balked when price talk stayed above a hundred dollars. The undeterred ones were apprehended, as were the internet customers filtered by Carrasco and Donley. Predictably, almost every arrestee was seeking a prostitute for himself, had a prior record for solicitation, and wasn't Denton. But into the late hours, Detective Priestly called Carson. "We had Carrasco and Donley hit the street, and they snagged a kid that could be Denton's errand boy."

Carson left Schilling and drove to headquarters, listening to the conversation replayed over his speakerphone as he traversed the quiet streets.

"*Hey, classy!*" Carrasco quipped. "*My friend and I can show you more than Masters and Johnson.*"

"*That might be just what I'm looking for,*" the driver replied, apparently vaguely recognizing the names of the famous sex research team that predated his parents' puberty.

"*Might be? I'm also* magna cum laude *in dexterity.*"

Carson smiled, imagining the delivery boy's excitement at the intellectual display.

"*What I want is different ... it'll involve a drive,*" the john replied.

"I love special orders—but they're extra. You'll be paying in hundreds."

"I expected that."

"It basically ends there," Priestly said. "He was smiling while Carrasco played up her act, and after she mentioned money, he flashed five C-notes. We arrested him on the spot, and all he's been saying since is that he needs to make a phone call. All the other johns knew this was entrapment, with the undercovers bringing up payment, and they spilled their guts to get out quickly. This kid's definitely hiding something, or he's scared of someone. He also probably gave us a fake name, 'Robert Ball;' claims not to have his driver's license with him."

"And the car?" Carson asked.

"Registered to Alfred Burch, 815 Ardsley Road, in Clifton. But this isn't him—Alfred's fifty-three."

* * * * *

As Carson strode toward Interrogation Room 4, Priestly kept pace and relayed an update. "Still running his fingerprints, no match yet; no criminal record for Robert Ball; Burch's Acura not reported stolen. And before you go in, here's his phone—password-protected, of course."

"Of course," Carson repeated, dropping the silver iPhone into his pocket.

Carson grabbed the doorknob, pulled, and froze as he caught sight of the suspect, his fingers tightening into a clench. He didn't know the john's real name, but recognized the cropped redhead from the week before, plodding toward the law school elevators from Jen's office.

This explained everything: how Denton kept tabs on Jen before the kidnapping; how he knew she'd gotten involved in the investigation; and why he chose such an elaborate scheme to divert Lieutenant Oppenheimer from the prison break. How easy for Denton to win Ball's allegiance—what law student wouldn't be awed by a name partner at Denton, Foster & Kahn, the vice chairman of the Bar Association! Ball had probably abetted a dozen crimes by now, and likely sat stunned that his idol's instructions hadn't kept him from trouble.

"I want to make my phone call now," insisted the shackled Ball, snapping Carson from his thoughts.

"We're going to chat first," Carson said, walking into the gray room. "You must know it works that way. Or are you ignorant of the law?" he baited, sitting down at the middle of the long table, across from Ball.

"I don't *know* the law; the movies say I get a phone call."

"Tell me who you want to call—maybe I'll make an exception."

The suspect shook his head. "It's private. Maybe it's my lawyer."

"Your lawyer will insist that I file charges or let you go, in which case I'd have to file. I'm thinking you don't want that."

Ball simply stared at Carson.

"The funny thing, Mr. *Ball*," Carson scoffed, "is that lying to the police, like giving a fake name, *is* a crime we could prosecute, even though the solicitation charge *wouldn't* have stuck. Was that your idea with the large bills, or did someone coach you?"

"If I didn't do anything criminal to begin with, you shouldn't be holding me."

"Does Alfred Burch know what you were doing with his car tonight?" Carson asked, crimsoning Ball's cheeks. "We can always ask him while we're checking that he let you drive it—you have his permission, right?"

"He has nothing to do with this, it's *my* car!" Ball protested.

Carson shook his head. "I just explained about lying—"

"Hold on!" Ball stared at the table and bobbed his head, as if counting his lies. "Al's my dad. He gave me the car, but sure, we kept it registered to him."

"So you're actually Robert *Burch*? Or is 'Robert' fake as well?"

"It's real. I'm Rob Burch."

"So besides deceiving us about your surname, you misled me about who legally owns the car—"

"*I'm* the one who drives it."

"—and you told me you *didn't* know the law! That'll go over *real* well at Seton Hall!"

Burch went pale. "How did you—"

"Uh-uh. *You're* not asking questions. Your job—your *only* hope of salvation after all those falsehoods—is to start being truthful and help *me*." Carson rested his hands on the table and stared, then forced a slight smile. "Here's an example of a truth, Rob: I'm not interested in jailing you. I'm a *lieutenant*, and a lieutenant wouldn't conduct an interrogation for a solicitation charge; maybe you sensed that. I just want to know what your plans were for tonight. That's all."

"I just wanted to hire two prostitutes," he blurted out. "We weren't even going to touch them—just watch and do the rest ourselves."

"Ah, yes, you're not alone in this. Don't think I believe the hands-off part—not for five hundred dollars—but I'm focused on your wealthy acquaintance. Do you just show up with the hookers, or do you call him first?"

"It's not like *that*, it's not a *him*."

Carson shook his head. "Truth involves openness ... details ... *names*. There's no deal if I have to pry the story out."

"But she *can't* get involved! That would be the worst thing you could do, and you promised I'd catch a break if I shared my plans."

Carson shook his head again, and pulled out the silver phone. "I bet you've called your confidante a lot. Since you've confessed to conspiracy, I can get a court order for the password, and interview each of your contacts until I find *her*, and—"

"No!" Burch objected, arms surging toward the phone, pulling the chains taut. "I'll tell you the rest! You don't have to hassle anyone!" He took a deep breath and sat back straight. "I worked before law school, so I'm twenty-six, and this Contracts professor is thirty-one, and we hit it off two years ago; but Seton Hall has a fraternization policy, so we've kept everything secret. The sex has been great, as is, but we tried watching porn last month, and it really turned Erica on, as much as me. So, I hatch this plan to get some upscale prostitutes for a live porn show. And we research that if *they* ask for money first, I can't get arrested. But you dragged me in anyway. I know I can beat the charge, but if the school finds out about *us*, she's toast. I just wanted to call and warn her away from my apartment—that's all. I was just lying so nobody would go there and connect her to me."

Carson's stomach dropped, the confession ringing true—plenty of details he could check, and a compelling explanation for the deceit. But protocol ... he'd resolved to go by the book. However much the story didn't *feel* like a tale scripted by Righteous, he knew he was supposed to bring the professor in for proof. *And end her career and Burch's in the process.* No, he couldn't destroy two innocents for his overzealous pursuit of Righteous. He scribbled a story of his own, and slid it across the table. "I need to verify your statement quickly. If it pans out, there won't be any publicity or charges."

Burch read the script and nodded, then opened the contact for E.S. on his phone.

"'S?'" Carson asked.

"Sorvic."

He left to get an identification match from Verizon and instruct Banks, then returned, the call going through on speakerphone.

"What's taking so long?" she asked.

"It's harder than we thought," Burch ad-libbed before following the notes, "but I found the perfect pair. They've done this before; they said a fake camera makes it feel more natural for us to direct them around. I'm getting one from their friend, so their cab should get there a little before me. Set them up however you want."

"I was getting distracted, you being gone so long. But *that* puts me back in the mood."

Carson slumped. Banks's visit to the professor with Rodriguez would be the final check, but Sorvic's response left little doubt that his evening had been a bust. Denton was not to be caught cruising Newark's streets this weekend.

- 39 -

Carson reached his bed an hour after releasing Burch, then tossed for another hour, and woke up anxious a few hours after that. He cursed his naiveté—*John must have a more discreet system for arranging outcalls*—and scribed "Interrogate Elliot Spitzer's madam" on an imaginary to-do list.

After downing jellied toast and a peach, he faced up to calling Jen. She spoke before he did. "I assume if it were good news, you would've left word last night?"

"I was hopeful about a hopeless plan. I'm back to sifting through crumbs, and meditating for inspiration."

"Can I help?"

He would be getting help, but from a partner who knew him better. "I'll need you, but not today," he spun. "Can I check in tomorrow?"

"Sunday's fine," she replied before hanging up.

When the line was cleared, he speed-dialed number four.

"Hello?"

"Beck, it's me. I need you for an hour today—nothing doctorly, I just keep hitting dead ends, and then I got a jolt yesterday and I want to make sure I'm not overlooking anything obvious."

"You *are* overlooking something obvious—today is *Saturday*, which is part of the *weekend*, and not every bit of detective work is an *emergency*."

"Come on, sis! I've been making my whole team spin their wheels."

"Is that because you decided to play Pinocchio to forestall Newark's apocalypse?"

"No ... honestly, no. I'd be no further along if my team knew the truth about the prison murders."

"I'm taking Felicity to her soccer game right after lunch. If you'll watch her play and compliment her afterward, you can come over beforehand and discuss your case."

"Deal!" he replied, tapping the phone off.

* * * * *

Carson rang the bell and heard his sister yell, "Kids, Uncle Ted's here!" before she opened the door. Eight-year-old Mary-Kay reached him first, waving a drawing of herself surrounded by horses. "Look, Uncle Ted! I'm gonna be a sheriff, just like you!"

He knelt down and squinted, and saw a splotch of silver crayon where a frontier lawman might display a badge. "It's important for sheriffs to treat their horses well. You're kind to animals, aren't you?"

"I love animals, Uncle Ted."

"Well, then, you deserve to be an honorary sheriff!" He unpinned his badge from his wallet and handed it to his smiling niece. "Only report back when you've caught all the bad guys."

As the youngster ran off, he looked up at Rebecca and shrugged. "Your badge is boring already." Then he turned to hug ten-year-old Felicity, who was already wearing her uniform and shin guards. "I can't wait to see you play. Who's your opponent?"

"We're playing the Coyotes. We already beat them three weeks ago, but I didn't score any goals then."

"Well, Felicity, having the team win is the most important thing. But if you score today, your mom and I will certainly be watching."

"When do I get a turn being sheriff?"

"Well, some towns are so gnarly, they have a second sheriff sneaking around to stop crimes before they happen. You have to be extra smart to be a sheriff without a badge. Are you as good at multiplication as your mom says?"

"I know all of my times tables, and can multiply long numbers."

Ted rubbed his chin, then grinned. "Then you can be the secret sheriff!"

"Yay!" she yelled, running off to join her sister.

"They sure have a spot for you, Ted," Rebecca said.

"Three years of elementary school safety presentations," he said as he stood up.

"You made quick enough work of them, though," she scolded. "But a deal's a deal." She led him upstairs to the spare room furnished with a guest bed and a cluttered desk, and sprawled on the quilt as

Ted swiveled the chair to face her. "You think you've overlooked something?" she asked.

"There was this odd coincidence last night. It made me realize I could be missing something big, that there were other ways all the pieces could fit, maybe involving someone not on my radar. And the captain's losing patience, and you're the only person who knows the whole truth.... Maybe playing Pinocchio *is* making the problem worse."

"Then this counts as your birthday gift, too."

He shrugged. "I constructed narratives implicating three people I haven't been investigating. First is Craig Benson, chairman of the State Bar Association, Lou Denton's enemy. Motive would be throwing Denton into disrepute, even if the charges don't stick. Has tremendous influence in the legal community, opening doors to all sorts of patented devices and to skilled accomplices beset by legal troubles. Would've known to plan the crimes around Denton's schedule at the judges' brunch. Could've tricked other lawyers meeting at Denton Foster's offices into placing calls with the burner phone. Might also have disdain for convicts, depending on his criminal defense work—so could be two birds with one stone."

Rebecca shook her head. "Relies too heavily on others. Using lawyers to find good patents and desperate accomplices leaves a huge web for the police to stumble upon. Plus, it's too elaborate: you frame someone for a simple crime, with overwhelming evidence, not one where a SWAT team's pointing rifles at you. And why would he gas Jen Bolton when you were making progress against Denton? Good try, but you're right to be ignoring him."

Carson sat silent in thought, then nodded. "Next is Daniel Bruce Kirke, an enemy most particularly of Matt Foster. I also thought about Foster's ex-wife, but she's moved on, and not just physically. Kirke has a good life, but Foster kept him from doing what he wanted. He had access to the patent files while he worked there, and likely has some disgruntled buddies at the firm who could've helped with the cell phone."

Rebecca sat up before raising her objections. "Same issue with scaring the professor—why? And his beef with Foster is more personal—he would've murdered *him*, not a hundred other guys. Plus he wouldn't get inside help—who'd put his own firm on a suicide path? Don't spend any time on Kirke."

Again Carson took a minute to think, and again he nodded. He turned to look out the window, and admired the leafy oaks and sweet gums, then lowered his gaze to a portrait of Felicity and Mary-Kay. He could change his focus to stare at his sister's partial reflection in the glass. He'd loved growing up with Rebecca.

"What are you doing now?" she asked. "Are you stalling, or are we done?"

He swiveled back to face her. "Who's always on the short list when a married man gets murdered?"

"The wife. And the husband when it's a woman, and the parents when it's a child. Plain, awful statistics."

"This stays strictly between us, OK? Forever."

Rebecca furrowed her brow. "You weren't so wary for the other two long shots! I'm tired of warning you to keep your distance from her!"

"I'm keeping plenty of distance, Beck! Detectives just call this 'foresight.' There might come a day—later—when these suspicions could be embarrassing."

"Yeah, *later* … Go ahead, then. Tell me how your goddess did it."

"There's an accomplice she trusts, to play Righteous, the right size for framing Denton or Foster. The crew arrives home with her, or she lets them in herself, and she lies about the timeline. Either they stress Phil enough to kill him, or they were going to gas the house while I was in D block so the police would arrive only in time to save her, but he dies on his own so they don't have to. She fakes the suffering, sadness, and fear, and even wets herself. She makes the other crime monumental so I'd gloss over Phil, and compromises me with the prison escape ruse so I'd shun my inner circle, who might point me to her. She knows lawyers who could infiltrate Denton Foster's offices, and steers the chemical search to implicate them. Topping it off, she picks the crime an activist constitutional law professor is the least likely person in the world to commit—murdering convicts. And me believing they victimized her because they wanted you and me running the investigation! I miss that her help is just to play me for information, and her insights just lead me to someone else. The gassing draws me back to her after our fight, and raises the heat on Foster and Denton, with her endgame being me making a false accusation—setting the case back to zero, with me off of it."

He stopped talking, and stared in vain for a rebuttal. Finally, he broke the silence. "If you look at her … talk to her … what I laid out is nonsense. It's *not* her."

Rebecca shifted on the bed, and closed her eyes for a full minute before looking at her brother. "She doesn't sound like she hated her husband, or that she would've murdered him if she had. But is it conceivable? With trustworthy accomplices to pull off the prison job and plant the phone signals, a diabolical genius could've— would've—done it like you described, and you don't have an inkling of a case against her. And after two weeks without a single slip, you probably never will."

* * * * *

Uncle Ted attended the soccer game in a trance, struggling to remove Jen from his suspect list. Her face, when she was talking about Phil— it wasn't easy to fake. And she was successful, strong; she would've ended her marriage with divorce, not mass murder. Plus the huge risk—Righteous slips up once, and Jack's fall leads to Jill's tumbling after. However clever this crime would've been for Jen to mastermind, it didn't fit her.

He tapped his sister's shoulder ten minutes into the second half. She kept her eyes on Felicity and leaned over casually, as if expecting a compliment on her daughter's passing. "There's no way to be sure that you're giving someone a thrombosis that'll become a lung embolism, right?" he asked, delighted at having the medical examiner on hand to ponder his question at inception. Rebecca flushed and grimaced, then straightened up and angled her shoulders away from him. His delight turned to impatience after a couple of silent minutes, then frustration, and finally rage when he realized she was ignoring him, silence having long been her weapon of choice against his impositions. He'd been wrong when he glanced at her reflection that morning—he'd *hated* growing up with Rebecca. "I know you heard me!" he blurted out.

"Think about why we're here," she responded with well-practiced serenity, "and maybe I'll speak to you after the game."

He took some deep breaths. Then he stood and yelled, "Go Roadsters!"

"Road*runners*, Uncle Ted!" Mary-Kay corrected, drawing a smile from Rebecca.

The rest of the game proved uneventful, as far as the case was concerned. Ted became a model uncle, treating his nieces to an ice cream celebration and commending Felicity's perfect attendance at the practice sessions.

When the kids got in her car, Rebecca spent a minute with Ted. "Still wondering about blood clots?" she asked.

"Some of what I theorized seems far-fetched."

"Including the embolism. They're not medically predictable—she would've planned to kill him another way."

"But you'd seemed convinced about the rest ..."

"I only said it was conceivable, because I don't know her. But she'd have been leaving success to her accomplices—*conceivable*, but risky, probably too risky. And where's this mystery man who's willing to stare down a gun for her?"

"Glad we talked," he said, giving his sister a hug, "and glad to see the girls." He drove home liking Rebecca again, thinking he could probably take Jen at face value, and wishing he had a job where "probably" was good enough.

* * * * *

Carson trudged into headquarters on Sunday morning. *You aren't here investigating Jen*, he told himself. *You're looking into the weather ... again.*

Priestly had downloaded the Boltons' phone records, hoping the kidnappers might have carelessly called out, besides contacting the *Star-Ledger*. Carson could identify everyone they spoke to over the previous three months: there were no calls with any of the Panthera. Likewise, the standard six-month data dump from her bank and her broker, ordered to search for tampering during the three-day ordeal, showed nothing to indicate Jen was funding an elaborate crime, and nothing to suggest divisive money issues with her husband. He then reread the victim's file, this time with detached skepticism, and found nothing out of place: *abrasions and tenderness consistent with extended restraint; moderate dehydration consistent with duration of captivity; furniture placement consistent with narrative.*

In the end, the only things implicating Jen were the glut of wives convicted of murdering their husbands, and the Catch-22 of presuming that evidence pointing to others would be part of the setup from a devious killer. It wasn't in his nature to hold anyone above suspicion, but he went for an afternoon jog no longer thinking Jen in the same league as John and Loser.

- 40 -

Carson arrived Monday with low expectations. He'd squandered any goodwill with Captain Burgess on Skewer-the-Nobody, and was left hoping for a break where none had been found before.

When Bertha sputtered on, he found that Sulter had indulged his deadline stingily, sending from her phone at eight fifty that morning a memo on Denton Foster electronic letterhead that she'd probably composed much earlier:

> *Lieutenant Carson:*
>
> *The greater the scrutiny we apply to the current rules of professional conduct, the more constrained we find ourselves in meeting your broad request for protected client information. As these rules are ultimately grounded in protections afforded the citizenry in the U.S. Constitution, they are inviolate regardless of the importance you otherwise place on this aspect of your investigation. I have drafted a preliminary memorandum on how the law applies to your request, which my firm will finalize and provide to the District Attorney this week, barring unforeseen delays.*
>
> *Meanwhile, Denton, Foster & Kahn is making great effort in cooperating with you by preparing schedule information that is within our purview to provide. This endeavor should also be completed this week, barring unforeseen delays.*
>
> *Yours,*
> *Stephanie Sulter*
> *Representative Partner*

As little as possible, as late as possible, Carson thought. He looked at the ceiling, shook his head, and looked back at the screen. *"Barring unforeseen delays"* ... *Damn! Righteous has won over the executive committee! Nothing they agree to share is going to help.* He shook his head again. *Might as well speed this along, and hope they slip up*:

> *Ms. Sulter—Thanks, will await DA review of memo. Please limit firm's efforts to male attorneys at the firm—should cut the work in half, so calendar information likely close of business Tuesday? Would be a great help.—Ted*

Carson closed Sulter's message, closed his e-mail, and turned off his computer. Righteous was getting the better of him; maybe he'd been bested altogether. His wallpaper typically resembled a royal's family tree, leads begetting other leads, the occasional intermarriage connecting separate branches in new ways. But Righteous had prevented that, ruthlessly terminating eleven lines of inquiry. The meager connections from the nuclear scare and industrial beams implicated his accomplices but not himself. Everything that usually came together, wasn't.

He spent an hour dwelling on the failures. Then the realization hit him—he'd been milking the bulls instead of the cows! Ryan Munsen had pointed to Denton, Foster & Kahn; maybe he had more to offer. Bruce Kirke had revealed the firm's inner workings; maybe he'd know how to split the executive committee. Edward Carson was back in business.

* * * * *

"You told me Righteous's calls came from different places in the building. What made you think that?" Carson asked Munsen.

"The call records show signal strength. There'd normally be disparities for different phones, location, and even if the phone is on low battery mode. But with one prepaid phone rarely left on, I figured it was just different calling locations."

"Can you use those variances to pinpoint which office was used for each call?"

"Maybe I could narrow it down to clusters of offices. But I'd need records of sample calls on that phone from different sites."

Carson thought for a moment. "Is that because you can't tell which locations would register the stronger signals?"

"Not with enough detail. I need a granular sense of how the calls are picked up from different places."

Carson paused again. "I can't get that same phone for you. What if I take another cell phone and make calls from different parts of the floor?"

Munsen nodded. "If we get the phone company data on each of those calls, I can establish baseline differentials for the various locations, and judge Righteous's relative position when he called out."

"Meaning, you could determine locations from the old phone records?"

"From the old and new records together … I'll draw you tight arcs where the signal strength indicates the phone could've been."

Carson smiled at Munsen. "You help me with a fib, and I'll get you all the pocket-dials your heart desires." Munsen returned the smile, and nodded.

Carson sketched out a floor plan from memory. "I'll try to do this early, before John and Loser get to the office. But let's avoid stops in their corners, just in case."

The pair spent an hour plotting to map the signal signatures of Denton Foster's floor. When they finished, Munsen said, "I can probably set up the electronics by late tomorrow, including getting the phone company on board."

"Then I predict a successful ruse for Wednesday," Carson said, grinning.

* * * * *

Righteous had spent most of Sunday in his den, reviewing patent challenges in the morning, working on Plan C in the afternoon, and reminiscing about law school, over a decanted Merlot, in the evening. His opus should have made him happy for years … for life. *Damned Carson!* Now he had to look back decades for joy.

The old adage about law school had proven too true for his classmates—scared to death the first year, worked to death the second year, and bored to death the third year—but Mattias and Lucian were too astute to suffer a year of slavery and another in the doldrums. After mastering the secrets of good grades, the bright classmates studied law on their own terms, slacking off on class assignments to focus on independent research and a game they invented called "Screwtops," short for "Screw the cops."

Screwtops involved scheming to elude punishment for crimes, budding from a lunchtime conversation about soliciting prostitutes under the pretense of casting for a nude documentary to avoid falling victim to the well-publicized police stings. Between the two of them, they planned their way out of a dozen murders, in excruciating detail, including one by exploiting a jurisdictional loophole under the decade-old Interstate 78 Toll Bridge on the New Jersey-Pennsylvania border. A recurring theme was means of avoiding self-incrimination during police interrogations, repudiating established beliefs that the authorities held an advantage. He missed those times, when he didn't have to take real risks to get a thrill, when he could share anything with his best friend.

He was helpless when Sulter interrupted Monday's executive committee meeting.

"Carson's revealed that the suspect is male," she reported, "halving the calendar request. It would be disingenuous to argue that doesn't cut our delivery time."

"You two are flying to Copenhagen Wednesday morning," Kahn said, looking at Denton, then Foster. "I'll put the DA on notice that any objection to our memo or the redacted schedules has to wait until next week. They still receive very little and they still can't steamroll through any unsubstantiated accusations."

Righteous, trapped, nodded with the others.

* * * * *

"You can still make an open-faced sandwich with rare roast beef, right, Claire?"

"Going off your diet again, Lieutenant?"

"Haven't had much of an appetite the past few days, until now."

"Too much gore, not enough sex?"

"Nah, that's my captain's marriage. Just had to work through a few things."

Carson used his lunch break to eradicate the remnants of his suspicions about Jen, then returned to his office and called her.

"I was expecting to hear from you yesterday," she answered.

"Nothing panned out until today. You're still up to chatting? Nothing's changed?"

"I'm *more* ready than before, and getting restless staying at my mom's. I'm going to spend my days—at least my mornings—at Seton Hall."

"I thought you were taking a break?"

"Sure, I can't keep disappearing from class and reappearing. But I have a research backlog, and the Constitution isn't sitting still, so to speak. But helping you is still my priority. Any news?"

"From Denton Foster? Just some pushback on the calendars. But we've developed a plan to locate where Alpha was when he called the Panthera. I just need to circle their floor with some of Munsen's electronics."

"How are you going to manage that?"

"Denton mentioned a network security audit they've scheduled; those are usually kept secret from the employees. I'll tell Sulter that one of my suspects discussed it on a line we're tapping, implying the criminals are eavesdropping on the firm. If I prove they're being bugged, that clears the lawyers."

"You're giving her a chance to single-handedly end the whole investigation?"

"She'll think that. When she lets me sweep the hallways, I surreptitiously redial Munsen every few yards."

"She might ask why you aren't finding the bug as you move along."

"Um ... Modern bugs make low-energy transmissions—the computer at headquarters separates them from the signals of legitimate wireless devices?" he tried.

"I think that's persuasive." Jen paused for a moment. "Now, from a legal perspective, evidence acquired under that sort of pretense—"

"This part isn't for court, either. I just need to be sure which partner to pit against the other. That's all."

"And locating where the calls originated is going to help?"

"Denton and Foster are diagonally across from each other, so yes ... or at least possibly. It depends if he tried to scatter the calls around the office, and how diligent he was about it. But if I keep doing possibles, I'll eventually get my arrest warrant, or build a story that turns the other partners against him."

"That sounds worthwhile, then."

Carson ended the call, then clicked open a message from Denton Foster:

> *Lieutenant Carson: Very busy ahead of partner travel later this week. Your request for "end of business Tuesday" instead will be taken care of before I leave tomorrow, well after business hours.—S. Sulter*

He jumped on his first lucky break in two weeks:

> *Ms. Sulter: Understandable. But timing is important. Must insist on stopping by 8:30 AM Wednesday to pick up the delayed work.—Ted*

41

Carson greeted Munsen at eight on Wednesday. "You were my busiest investigator yesterday."

"I had to explain to the phone company techies how *their own system* works. But we're set now. Here's the fake bug sweeper," Munsen said, handing over a milk carton-sized device. "I put dummy dials and lights over here, and this green button makes the cell phone electronics silently dial my number then disconnect for the next call. I tested it and the sensitivity of the signal measurements by self-dialing throughout the Central Tower's lower lobby. You try it."

Carson poked the green button, and a small yellow light glowed green while Munsen's ringtone played from his pocket.

"See? The action takes ten seconds, or less, then the light goes back to yellow. Try to stand still during that." Then Munsen pointed to a thumb drive in a USB port. "This isn't connected, but you wanted the appearance of storing data."

Carson tucked it into his empty laptop bag and left for the Central Tower.

* * * * *

Sulter arrived at the lobby just as Carson did, and gave a polite smile. He led the small talk with the bleary-eyed partner. "You haven't been to a movie theater in two years?"

"We're free so rarely, and then exhausted when we are—I kept falling asleep in the middle. Now I watch movies at home, sometimes."

"Back entrance, same route?" he asked as they exited the elevator.

She nodded. "You could probably find your way without me, by now."

As they traversed the halls, Carson remarked, "Lots of people today, for 8:30."

"Lou Denton and Matt Foster are flying to Copenhagen this morning; there's plenty to delegate ahead of that," she explained.

Of all the days for them to be here early! he thought.

They reached her office, and she handed over two reams of paper. "If you have any questions about the redacting, the district attorney's office will be able to explain the limits of what we can provide, later in the week."

Carson parsed the scant pages with sweeping blocks of gray shading. "Please thank whoever helped pulled this together."

"I already have."

He turned around, as if making sure the door was closed, then drew closer. "I received some disturbing information late yesterday, from a wiretap. Who here knows about Oracle's security audit?"

"Just the executive committee and me. We keep it secret from the tech department until the morning of—that's the point of an outside audit."

"Damn," he muttered, "I figured that. I'm afraid the criminals I've been after may be eavesdropping on the firm, particularly on the executive committee." He feigned a concerned look, and waited for Sulter's expression of dismay before continuing. "It explains a lot, and could clear your lawyers of wrongdoing altogether."

"Are you saying our office is bugged?"

"I'm concerned it might be."

"I knew we wouldn't have hired a criminal! Do you know what information they stole?"

"This is really breaking news, I don't have any details yet. But since there's no innocent explanation for the information leaking out, I want to run a signal test." Carson reached into his bag and pulled out Munsen's apparatus. "I wouldn't have to remove any ceiling tiles, and this receiver's small enough that your coworkers shouldn't give me a second thought."

Only Righteous himself would know to doubt Carson's story. "Where do you need to go with that?" Sulter asked.

"Tech told me to circle the floor. I can start outside your office." She nodded and accompanied him out.

Carson began the drudgery of taking five or six steps to prearranged stops, raising the device to eye level, and making push-button speed dials. Some of the passing lawyers cast curious stares, but none challenged him with the Representative Partner at his side.

After ten minutes, Sulter caught his gaze and signaled "Well?" with her palms and shoulders.

He looked around and whispered, "Some bugs, we find on site. The more sophisticated ones, the tech team finds by analyzing data on this drive and filtering out the interference. That involves testing the whole floor."

Carson continued his trek, most stops silent, some filled by a lawyer's half of a phone call or a frazzled attorney spewing expletives at an e-mail. Just past the two-thirds point, he would stop outside Conference Room D for another important speed dial, Righteous possibly having called from the common areas to lay a false trail. As he made the last stop approaching it, he judged from the occasionally uplifted voices that three or four people were inside. Continuing to feign concentration on his device, he took six more steps to stand aside the conference room door; he could hear the phone ring, though the occupants remained out of view.

Carson pressed his green button, and heard Denton's voice boom over the conference room speakerphone. "Harold, did Matt swing by there looking for me? I thought he'd have reached the limo first; maybe I got the signals crossed."

A male, presumably Harold Garfield, answered. "No, still just the Pfizer team here, drafting that request for reexamination. Mind if we run some wording by you?"

"As Professor Wiltmore would say"—Denton replied before clearing his throat and continuing in a rasp—"restless and waiting!"

Carson turned toward the room, then turned back, fighting to contain his excitement. His struggle to match the voice he'd heard briefly outside of cellblock D ended with Denton's throaty rendition of the same three words, an expression he'd apparently been mimicking for some time. The case had finally come to a close.

"You found something?" Sulter whispered.

"I can't *officially* say," he replied, nodding conspicuously to the dupe, "but I should get this back to headquarters right away. Please, not a word to anyone yet, in case I'm mistaken."

"Understood." She led him to her office to get his bag, and then to the elevators.

* * * * *

Carson started jockeying against the rush hour inflow, and called Munsen. "What happened?" the young officer asked. "I stopped getting your calls—"

"Breaking development. Send two uniform cars and everyone else on the team to meet me at the airport, but you stay there for support. You have five minutes to tell me which flight Lucian Denton is taking to Copenhagen, and the departure terminal—international is usually B, or C if it's United. Then notify the TSA and airport police that we're making an arrest, intended before the security check. OK? Three important things."

"Send team to meet you, find the flight, notify airport. Got it, Lieutenant."

Carson's siren-blaring Malibu zipped past the congestion on the McCarter Highway, and he figured he'd leapfrogged several minutes ahead of his foe. When he reached Route 1, he called Captain Burgess. "Don't forget we still have a judge and jury to convince," Burgess said. "Concentrate on getting a confession, an *admissible* confession. Then I'll give you time to celebrate."

Next was answering a callback request from Munsen. "Lieutenant, Denton has a first-class ticket on United's 10:30 flight to Copenhagen, Terminal C. Uniforms and detective teams should be there in four minutes."

"Well done, Ryan."

After parking, he made his last call. It went straight to Jen's voice mail—her phone was off. "Jen, I'm calling from Terminal C. I heard Denton repeat the code phrase—it matched exactly. He's arriving here soon, thinking he's flying to Copenhagen with Foster. I've got the bastard nailed."

* * * * *

Carson positioned his team near United's first-class check-in counter. Shortly after, the lawyers trudged in, wheeling oversized carry-ons. Foster seemed to spot Carson first, with Denton stopping alongside his partner as the squad closed in.

"Lucian Denton," Carson said, "you're under arrest for a long list of crimes which will be made available to you." Then he nodded to Banks.

The partners shot each other surprised looks as Banks handcuffed Denton, then stepped back around to face him. "You have the right to remain silent, and if you waive that right, we may use anything you say against you, including in court. You also have the right to a lawyer, at the state's expense if you can't afford one. Do you understand these rights as I've stated them, Mr. Attorney?"

Denton glanced at Foster again, then turned back to Banks. "I do *not* completely understand my rights," he said. "I'm sure you couldn't use what I say if a policeman held a gun to my head. But what if I confess to something because sirens traumatize me? Or handcuffs? What you said raises more questions than answers."

Foster simultaneously shook his head and bit his lip.

"Lieutenant?" Banks called, eyes fixed on Denton.

"Mr. Denton," Carson said, "do you have adequate hearing and command of the English language to have understood the individual words spoken by my colleague?"

"I do," the suspect responded.

"Good enough for me."

* * * * *

Denton continued feeling defiant. He watched a policeman grab his luggage, then turned to Foster. "Sergeant Schultz!" he declared, harkening back a couple of decades to the Screwtops scenario of the police being unsure of themselves and unable to make progress if the arrestee denies knowing anything, so the partner just waits.

Foster's jaw dropped, and Denton could tell that though he'd surprised his partner, their youthful analyses had burned a lasting impression on him as well. "Inspector Clouseau!" Foster responded in kind. The Inspector Clouseau variation also implied that the police were unsure of themselves, but that their muddled efforts could unearth incriminating material, requiring the arrestee to draw out his interrogation while the partner cleaned house. The more Denton considered it, the more he felt Foster was right: the police would learn less questioning him than they would combing through his life's records. The patent icon was ready for another round with Carson.

42

Carson and his team watched the shackled suspect survey his barren gray surroundings through the two-way mirror. "He seems more bored than scared," Banks remarked.

"He'd know to try to look untroubled," Carson said. "Let's see what we can do."

He picked up a large carton and led Banks into Interrogation Room 3. He laid the box under the mirror, then sat with her across from Denton, backs toward the glass. Carson poked his police cell phone. "If you clear yourself in the next ten minutes, you can still make your flight," he taunted.

"Lieutenant, surely they taught you that the burden's on *you* to make your case, not on *me* to clear myself," the lawyer replied.

"I wasn't suggesting otherwise. Some people have important things to say; they'd rather explain the greater good of their actions than make me stick to protocol."

Denton sat emotionless, then lifted his wrists off the table. "I assume *protocol* usually ends with the person wearing these hiring a lawyer and getting out of here?"

"Nobody's ever *proved* that's best for the accused, but you technically have the right to do that."

"Careful about downplaying the value of my rights, Lieutenant; that's a thorny area of law, and I don't think *you* are qualified to improvise. At least your helper here knows to stick to the script," Denton added, nodding toward Banks.

Carson watched Banks's eyes narrow; she'd upbraided suspects for lesser slights. But he held up his hand, opting for diplomacy. "I apologize for failing to introduce the officer who frisked and handcuffed you. Lucian Denton, this is my colleague, Detective Kaleah Banks."

Denton smirked at Carson. "Apology accepted." Then he turned to Banks. "May I address you as 'Detective'?"

"'Detective' is fine," she replied.

"I probably won't be addressing you much, though, since this three-way will be over in a minute or two."

"So you *are* ready to confess ..." Carson prompted.

Denton looked at him, confused for a moment—head tipped sideways, left eye squinted. "Oh, I didn't mean what *you* and I are doing will be over soon, unless you want to leave with nothing happening. I meant that I have conditions for talking to the police, because *I* only talk when the odds aren't unfairly stacked against me."

"Well, before we get to your new rules, why don't you share what you're already comfortable discussing? We can continue from where we left off in your office—"

"Pass," he declared, turning his gaze toward a corner of the ceiling. "Let me know when you'd rather hear my terms than silence."

Carson looked at Banks, then at Denton. "No need for the display ... that was just a suggestion. You can recite your conditions, and we'll go from there."

"I didn't intend that as a tantrum—you'd limited my options for nonvocal cues," Denton said, jangling the handcuffs. "My stipulation is that I'll only speak with you as an equal: you're not chained down, I'm not chained down; I'm in this room alone, you're here alone; I don't have a cell phone, you don't either; I can't leave and talk to my colleagues, neither can you."

Banks scrunched her face. But Carson wasn't outraged; though he couldn't figure out why, Denton's demands intrigued him. Then it struck him—*they were familiar*. Righteous had wanted him alone before, to set up the chlorine trifluoride lie! *He's withholding his confession to see which story I want pitched—whether the official account matches the news reports.* He picked up his police phone and turned it off, pulled out his personal cell phone and turned it off, then slid the devices to his second. "Make sure we aren't interrupted."

Banks shot him an incredulous glare, then huffed, grabbed the phones, and left.

"There," Carson said. "When there's a proposal I can live with, I will steadfastly abide by my end," he offered, the secondary connotation transparent to Righteous alone. He raised his eyebrows and gave three slight nods, inviting a furtive acknowledgment that Denton understood he'd concealed the poisonings; but it never came, or it was too subtle to be noticed. The only thing coming from Denton was silence, frustrating silence, for forty seconds that seemed like forty minutes, until Carson challenged him. "We're alone; you wanted to speak to me *alone*."

"Oh. Since you didn't comply with my conditions, I assumed you didn't want me to talk."

Carson clenched his fists and narrowed his eyes; Denton stayed still, watching. Then Carson shook his head, stood up, and walked around the table next to his enemy. "You could've been more specific," he scolded as he unfastened Denton's wrists.

"I don't like repeating myself."

"Do people tell you how arrogant you are, or just say it behind your back?"

"It's not something I don't already know, so I suppose they mostly just think it."

Carson sat back down. He'd seen enough to know that trying to burden Denton with regret, harping on how badly the victims' families were suffering and how good it felt to confess when your guilt was obvious, wouldn't move the smug killer. Instead, he would let Denton hang himself. He hadn't even asked for the charges, so any utterance about the Boltons, Essex State Prison, or any of a dozen implements would reveal the demon as Righteous.

"I didn't get to ask about the most interesting patents you've worked on," Carson prodded.

"You know I can't—"

"Just what's in the public filings, of course. Nothing privileged."

Denton's response wasn't incriminating, nor were those to the questions after that, but Carson continued probing topics tangentially related to the crimes, hoping an extended conversation would trip up the attorney. He was surprised by the length of Denton's answers, as if the suspect felt time was on *his* side. Denton discussed a wide range of chemical discoveries, none lethal or explosive, described a slew of engineering achievements, devoid of any about unfolding trucks or cargo balloons, and denied ever vacationing on the nearby Delaware River. The lawyer managed to be talkative yet evasive, seeming worried by some questions but never divulging a detail that implicated himself.

After two hours, Carson had to respond to biology. "Any interest in exploring the city's plumbing? We can also plan ahead for lunch."

"It feels like time for that. Nothing straight from a vending machine for lunch, though. I'll pay for mine if I have to."

"Even convicts don't have to buy their own lunches. Haven't you ever talked to one?" Carson asked, reaching the twentieth question— twentieth so far—laying varyingly subtle and not-so-subtle traps for Denton.

"Not every lawyer is a TV lawyer."

"I guess not." Carson rose to lead Denton to the bathroom.

"Same conditions," Denton said, standing up as well. "I can't call my colleagues, you don't check with yours. And no handcuffs."

Carson nodded.

"I don't think *they* saw that nod," Denton said, pointing to the mirror.

Carson turned, facing his reflection. "Unless the world's about to end, nobody is to violate the understanding I've reached with Mr. Denton." He turned back, and the lawyer nodded.

43

Jen planned Wednesday as a return to normalcy: breakfast with Cassandra Vier, a phones-off meeting with Dean Marshall, and research in her office. She also expected to feign excitement about Carson's phone test, which she assumed he'd eventually discover Alpha had nullified.

She turned on her phone when the meeting ended, and heard Carson's message as she stepped into her office. "Shit!" she yelled, slamming the door and pressing "Call Back." "Shit!" again when she got dumped into his voice mail. "You have to call me, Ted. If you've been pointed to John, that's a setup and the real killer is Loser!" Although Carson seemed an exceptional detective, Alpha seemed smarter still, and had had years to plot his misdirection, casting heavier suspicion onto his innocent partner. She'd intended to make her case once Ted got close to singling one out—she hadn't planned on a sudden breakthrough. "Giving the code phrase in a voice you might hear again … he was too careful for that to be an accident. It's a phrase he could have—must have—recorded some other time, a last diversion so he'd know you were closing in. And he'll have an escape plan, like that Nigerian shuffle. You've got to head back to the airport!" Another "shit" when she saw the hour-old timestamp on Carson's call.

There wasn't time to wait for Ted to check his messages. *He said who he'd be dialing ... think ... Munsen!* She called the Detective Bureau, and was on hold for a long minute before he picked up.

"Officer, this is Professor Jennifer Bolton. Lieutenant Carson is investigating my husband's murder, and I must speak to him right away."

"Professor Bolton, I was just observing the lieutenant. He's working on your case now, but he can't be interrupted."

"No, he *must* be interrupted. I made a crucial omission earlier," she lied, "and I'm *sure* it's leading him to the wrong person."

"I'm certain we'd discover if we were pursuing someone innocent. But I'll tell him to get back to you, if you want to explain your mistake to him. Or you can explain it to me."

Sure, she thought, *your boss and I have been running a shadow investigation ...*

"Yes, thank you, Officer Munsen," she surrendered. "Please have him call me."

Jen hung up and called for Captain Burgess, getting connected to his assistant instead. "I'm involved in a high-profile case, and have news the captain would want to speak to me about, for a few minutes," she implored after identifying herself.

The push seemed to work. "Professor Bolton, I'm sorry I haven't been able to personally express my condolences to you until now," Burgess said.

Helpful witness, not needy victim. "Thank you, but I'm calling for something more urgent. I've got to speak to Lieutenant Carson right away. I just remembered something important." *Amp up the lie!* "When I was tied up, they were speaking to each other, and the leader's voice was changing, and for a short while I heard what he really sounds like. I could positively identify him if you let me listen to the suspects. It would make whatever else Lieutenant Carson is doing moot."

"I appreciate your offer, but we're beyond that—I have a voice identification from a trained officer, who wasn't under duress like you were."

"With all due respect, I just need fifteen seconds from Carson. You can see he'd do his job better with the right information than the wrong information."

"I can't share details with you, Ms. Bolton, but what Lieutenant Carson is doing requires his uninterrupted focus. You've got to trust us to do our jobs."

Jen threw her head back, then forward. She was powerless to move the police force, her convictions holding sway only with Ted. Denton *had* to be innocent, so he'd reveal nothing; and Ted was persistent, and stubborn. They'd be locked in a standstill for hours—hundreds of flights for Foster to board in the meantime.

He was going to get away with it, just like Tripp.

She'd never learn why they killed Phil. Ever.

Unless …

Jen picked up Phil's photo with the lemur, and took a deep breath. "Please tell Lieutenant Carson to call me. If he can't get through, I'll be at the airport."

"The airport?" Burgess paused, but whatever he thought about the coincidence passed quickly. "I'll tell him."

* * * * *

Jen bolted diagonally across Raymond Boulevard. She'd called Fleet Transport, which always had at least one cab in the taxi line at nearby Penn Station, and arranged to meet the car on the southbound side of the McCarter Highway, shaving two traffic lights from the drive. "Terminal C," she barked at Chris Jarecki's badge when she got in. She peeled forty dollars from her wallet and shoved it through the partition. "Payment in advance, Chris. The extra twenty's so you don't hit the brakes after we reach Route 1."

"Thanks!" Jarecki smiled, nodded, and leaned on his horn to force his way into the crowded left lane.

Jen leaned back and dialed a contact on her phone. "Mom, I've got something really important to do, and I need your help. It's going to sound odd, and I'm too rushed to explain it. You'll have to trust me."

"I've always trusted you, dear. But should you make important decisions now, with all you've been through?"

"This is OK, Mom. If Phil were here, I'd be asking him instead of you."

"Go ahead, then."

"Are you online? I need you to buy me a plane ticket, for today. United flies out of the right terminal."

"Well, where are you flying?"

"Just read me the flight schedules. I'll be there in fifteen minutes … If it's an international flight that leaves a half hour after that, I'll get priority through security. But nowhere that needs a visa—"

"Stop! That's too much! There's an 11:15 to Lisbon and an 11:25 nonstop to Paris, then they list 11:25 departures to everywhere else like Lagos and Tel Aviv, but those seem to be connections off the Paris flight. Then a bunch more between eleven thirty and noon. But why don't you just tell me where you're going—"

"I will, Mom. But for right now, book me on that Paris flight, round trip so I have some chance of clearing security—Whoa!" Jen was jolted as Jarecki swerved back from the left-turn-only lane after leapfrogging four cars. "I'm OK, Mom. Make it first class, I need quick check-in and maybe access to the Club Room."

"Since when have you been flying first class?"

"You're typing while you're challenging me, right? I'll be refunding the tickets, to answer your question. There's just someone I have to approach quickly."

"I assume you don't care about the return date, then?"

"Right," Jen responded. "No, wait … I don't have luggage, so I need to say it's for a one-day business trip—two days tops if there's nothing tomorrow."

"Seven thousand dollars! I don't even know if my credit cards go that high!"

"Try the one you've had the longest, they used to raise everyone's limit each year or so."

"Fine. It's processing. Now we get to wait."

"The other thing's a little harder," Jen whimpered.

"Other thing! This better not be one of those radio pranks, 'Would you send your daughter to God-knows-where?'"

"I don't have my passport with me; this just came up."

"I can tell."

"Cassie lost hers once. They can accept a faxed copy under extenuating circumstances, and I'll have a few minutes to make up a story."

Jen noticed Jarecki shooting her nervous looks, and pulled the phone away from her mouth. "I'm a law professor, Chris. I need to reach a client. What I'm doing has been approved by the courts, except I don't usually pull it together at the last minute."

Confident she'd forestalled his instincts to call the TSA, she returned to the phone. "Mom, as soon as you're sure the ticket has gone through, look up first-class customer service, and find out where to fax my passport page. But don't say you have my passport, my story is it got lost; pretend you're faxing a photocopy you've kept for emergencies. Then make a copy to send—my passport is in that reddish folder I brought from my house."

"I hope you're wearing clean underwear—you know this scramble will get you strip-searched."

Jen recognized her mother's coping mechanism. "One step ahead of you—I'm not wearing *any* underwear," she joked back, drawing another unsafe glance from her speeding driver. "You're the best, Mom."

"Could you at least tell me that you're sure about whatever is going on?"

Jen paused. She couldn't prove beyond a reasonable doubt that Foster was Alpha; she didn't really have proof at all. She simply knew that Alpha was smart and meticulous, and that setting up a colleague was smart. Ted would say she only had a hunch—but it was a hunch she couldn't shake. "I'm sure," she said—*that it's the right thing for you to do for me*, she thought.

* * * * *

The early stalemate frustrated Carson: the evasive lawyer seemed unlikely to blunder while in his comfort zone. Returning to Interrogation Room 3, he decided to take a more forceful approach. "Why don't you tell me why you think we brought you in?"

Denton paused before responding, possibly containing a blush. "I don't know; nobody's ever accused me of a crime before, and I didn't like being arrested in public. Maybe I'll file a lawsuit when this is over." He paused again. "Now that that's off my chest, if you're asking me to speculate, I'd guess some lawyer I squashed is a sore loser and has been crying to the right politician."

Carson leaned in with a scowl. "We both know that's not what's happening here."

"Why don't *you* explain it to *me*, then?"

"No. It's still my turn to ask questions. I get a really long turn because you made me kick Leah out." He leaned back. "You must understand that someone in your position can be a dangerous person."

"Because I'm a lawyer?"

"You know things other people don't. You probably hear about next-generation weapons and top-secret poisons."

"I guess that's empowering, theoretically. But all of our lawyers take their jobs seriously. Revealing secrets is anathema to us."

"I'm sure you take your job *very* seriously. What mistake would you say is the one that's bothered you the most?"

Denton paused again before answering, and seemed to start forcing deep, controlled breaths. "I consider the top one, actually the top few, to be personal in nature; but since none involve criminal activity, you're not going to hear about them."

"How about sharing something you worked hard to cover up?"

The deep breathing continued. "No crimes, so no criminal cover-up. I don't even recall anything improper that I've worked to hide. You don't count citing attorney-client privilege as a cover-up, right?"

These blanket denials are lies! Just look at him! Push! "So you're saying someone in your position would never be forced to use an alias or a prepaid cell phone?"

"Sometimes we use codenames for clients—that's actually considered prudent."

"You were very busy the afternoon before the judges' brunch, right?"

"I spent a fair amount of time on my speech, and had some client paperwork of a privileged nature. Not much busier than other days, though."

"How do you feel about heights?"

"Airplanes are fine … I like scenic views … I'm OK with ladders."

Carson stared at his adversary. Three disjointed questions, three spontaneous answers, and nothing to suggest that what he was hiding was the Essex State massacre. At this pace, the subtleties stacking against Denton would build to a solid case in thirty years—or until he slipped up, whichever came first.

44

"I'll have you curbside in a minute," Jarecki said as he navigated the airport.

Jen looked at her phone. "That was fast."

"You get what you pay for," he said, glancing in the mirror. "Hey, are you OK?"

"Just nervous, maybe. It could be worse." *It could be worse,* she thought, *I could've had to confront Foster somewhere else. Here, he's been screened for weapons, and the edgy travelers are itching to report any commotion. And I won't have to fight him here—just find him and tell Burgess he's ticketed another flight.*

The cab stopped, and she ran into the terminal, ran past a serpentine maze of coach ticketholders, and cut, apologetically, to the front of the first-class line. A United attendant beckoned her forward, then muttered to her coworker, eliciting a scoff. "Welcome, Ms. Bolton," Carolien van der Laan announced with her work-practiced smile when Jen reached the counter. "We've done everything possible to get you on your Paris flight. I have the fax of your passport—do you have any ID? That goes quicker than the photo and signature match."

Jen handed over her driver's license, then began her search, noting the gate numbers of the next-departing flights and scanning the crowd in case Foster was still in the pre-security section of the terminal.

"Any checked bags?" van der Laan asked.

"No," Jen replied, turning back to face her.

"You've probably heard these *yes-yes-no* questions before," van der Laan said, nullifying the security questions before blistering through the verbiage of whether Jen had packed and possessed her presumed carry-on bag, pausing only briefly enough for Jen to say "yes" when she nodded, then "no" when she shook her head. The agent then gave another frozen smile while handing over the license, the fax, and a boarding pass. "Pat will escort you to the front of the security line," she said, pointing to a young man in a United uniform, "and we have a cart on the other side to drive you to Gate C84. Thank you for flying United," she added before turning again to her colleague. "Hope the rush job enjoys her pat-down," she said ten decibels too loud, adding sincerity to her smile at last.

The faxed passport and last-minute ticket had marked Jen with a TSA bullseye, but that humiliation was a small price to pay. After retrieving her purse and hurriedly re-shoeing, she hopped on the cart. "You depart in twelve minutes—I can make it in three," the driver assured her. "You didn't leave a carry-on at security, did you?"

"No. Business trip. I'll be lucky to have time to eat, much less change clothes."

The driver sped them along, routing around texting zombies and blaring her mechanized horn, while Jen looked for Foster. She paid extra attention as they passed Gate C74, where the 12:20 flight to London was about to pre-board, and grew frustrated that, with only a passing glimpse, two men might have been her assailant, disguised.

Jen got off the cart at C84 and hustled past the waiting gate attendant. "I have the quickest message for my colleague in coach," she warned the flight attendant as she marched past her empty first-class seat, making eye contact with each of the male passengers. When she reached the back of the plane, she turned around and pulled her phone to her cheek, drawing exaggerated watch-pointing from the uniformed Frenchwoman. "What do you mean she's stuck in traffic?" Jen barked at the device, raising a finger to hold off the tenacious worker. "It's pointless for me to go there alone! If Jackie doesn't fire her this time, I'm quitting!" She dropped the phone into her purse. "I can't believe this!" she said. "I need to get on a later flight, after all that! Do you think they can rebook me in the United Club?" The flight attendant shrugged, and led her off the plane.

After Jen disembarked, she rechecked the departure board. Foster's escape plan would include hidden funds and an alias—smarter still, a second identity change at a connecting airport. She'd have to check passengers on the puddle jumps as well. *Damn!*

The first fifteen minutes of traversing the structure felt overwhelming—gates 70 through 140 were in Terminal C, which branched into what would be three separate terminals at most airports, thousands of faces every hour. But as she grew familiar with the layout and developed an intuition for the travel time from one gate to another, she felt less frazzled, and found herself absorbing more information about her surroundings. She recognized the sweet scent from Cinnabon when she was forty feet away, and knew she was passing Exotic Gourmet for the third time, the line of customers still winding into the corridor. The only shelf seemingly ignored blared CONSIGNMENT SALE – XXOTIC ELIXXIRS; she presumed the juice salesman was paying handsomely to showcase his bottles in the busy shop and store his supply cases in back.

After passing a few more empty gates, a restroom, and a bookstore, Jen arrived to scan the passengers gathered for the flight to Istanbul. Still no luck. On to Miami.

She doubled back onto the other side of the rolling walkway, then grew concerned that her to and fro searching could get *her* removed from the airport. *More thinking, less wandering*, she chastised herself; *and don't just think, think like a criminal.*

Foster would worry about Carson realizing his mistake; he'd fear being stuck—trapped—on a plane if the police grounded the flights. So he'd to wait to board until the last minute, saving a final chance to flee a manhunt. And he wouldn't be at the gate, mingling with other passengers. *The bastard's probably hiding in a stall!*

Jen double-checked the departure screen and grimaced: *Miami, C82, 12:01 ... Dulles, C107, 12:05. I can't be two places at once.* She swallowed hard. *It's intermission at* Phantom of the Opera *again.*

Gate C82 was directly across from a men's bathroom. Jen marched in, head down and with her hands over the sides of her eyes except when she was sneaking glances at faces. "I'm sorry!" she announced with a sheepish inflection. "I'm just checking the floor. My husband lost his keys, and he can't walk back through the terminal with his bad knee." Most of the men were standing; the only stall occupant didn't seem to have a carry-on, and she was sure Foster would have some papers and supplies for his journey, if not whatever luggage he'd brought for his business trip. "Sorry again! I didn't see anything," she declared as she headed out.

Suddenly, as she passed the sinks, a strong hand grabbed her right shoulder from the blind spot she'd created. "You don't care about your life?" a stilted voice demanded.

She trembled, then pivoted, simultaneously twisting out of the aggressive man's grip and turning to view him head-on. He was tall, but obviously younger than Foster. "I said I was sorry. This is urgent, and I covered my eyes as well as I could."

"You get people here not from America, who could get offended by that. You should befriend a gentleman to find your keys for you."

"I'll try that if it happens again," she said, regaining her composure and exiting into the corridor. From her direction, the men's room nearest Gate C107 was slightly before it, to the left of a women's room. The entryways to each were goofenecked, and the men's was blocked by a small "Do Not Enter" sawhorse. *Probably being cleaned; he could still be hunkering down in there.* She flouted the sign and hooked down the hallway, catching sight of a translucent plastic tarp sealing off the entrance, the far end secured from the outside with blue tape. Edging farther along, she could read the bold multilingual stickers: "Keep Out—Disinfectant in Use—World Health Organization." She reflexively held her breath as she backtracked. *Just breathe! You won't die from this!*

The second-nearest men's room was beyond C107. Jen stayed there until she could rule out each of the stall occupants, then headed back, toward London.

Nearing the sawhorse again induced a shudder. *Scary.* Then she stopped. *Scary ... compelling ... clever ... Alpha!* She looked around for someone to tell, then started toward the screeners. *Wait! The warnings could be real. Cry wolf, and you're banished—he gets away. Make sure.* She returned and skirted the sawhorse, turned left at the entrance, then hung right to follow the bend. Then her legs stopped moving. And her heart started pounding. She forced three deep breaths. *He couldn't be armed in the airport; just see if he's here, then run.*

She plodded on, finger hovering over the flashlight icon on her phone. Four more steps would take her to the end of the wall, where the tarp began; three thereafter to the taped end, where she could peel back the cloak to the dim room. Except the sixth step was her last. Crinkling plastic gave a flash of warning before the back of her left thigh seared. And her body failed. She heard her phone smash on the ground just before the sheeting swirled counterclockwise past her eyes and the floor rose to slam her shoulder, first, then her head. She couldn't even turn to see who'd lunged at her from behind the wall— but she knew. The paralytic had left her conscious but immobile, breathing but mute. She was once again at Foster's mercy.

45

Foster grabbed Jen's ankles and dragged her through the gap in the enclosure, next to a Juice Concentrates box with protruding sheets of WHO stickers. He stayed behind her, out of view, and she heard him repositioning the tarp and smashing her phone. "I thought that might've been you before, alone," he said in his unfamiliar natural voice, "and I figured you'd come back." She felt his clammy hand on her temple, tunneling her vision, and glimpsed his other hand removing a roll of dark tape from the carton. "Can't let you see my disguise; I might've overestimated the stalling powers of my partner, Lou." Then he callously taped over her eyes.

She felt on the verge of shock—the blindfolding and the paralysis were each disorienting alone, and she was suffering both, fearing worse to come. Foster flopped her onto her back, grabbed her ankles again, and dragged her across the length of the bathroom floor, her hands and bare elbows occasionally braking on the cold tiles until her arms stretched wide and then rose above her head. Eventually, he banged open a door, turned her sharply, and pulled her into a stall, feet first against the toilet.

She heard footsteps, getting close to her head, then his voice from directly above. "I was keying a confession that would reach Lieutenant Carson tonight, so my friend wouldn't suffer for my crimes. I could finish that, and turn you to drown in that toilet ... or I could confess to you. Your cognition is *supposed to be* fine at this dosage. But it's crucial that you remember what I say. You're comprehending this, right?"

Jen had been unable to resist the madman; how could she prove she could understand him? She tried to nod, then wiggle her fingers ... nothing! Moan? Hold her breath? Impossible! *How am I even breathing?*

"Well, I know you can't answer. You're not turning blue, and you've survived a longer hell before.... I'll take my chances."

She felt a tinge of relief through her flood of distress.

"The crime was nearly perfect," Foster bragged. "I did start to like Lynx Lorelz, so I'm sorry about him, and about your husband. But not about anything else." A trace of excitement rose in his voice. "You know the problem with society? It's our eye-for-an-eye approach to crime. If I steal a hundred dollars every day, and one day you catch me, should the punishment be returning the hundred dollars? Of course not—you don't catch me every time, I'd end up way ahead and keep on stealing. So you make the punishment worse than the crime—you have to."

Jen was revolted by the technician's ignorance of centuries of research discrediting punishment for imputed crimes and debunking support for excessive sentences, but remained a silent captive audience of one.

"And we do that for lesser crimes—a year in jail for stealing a used car, a five-hundred-dollar jump in insurance premiums for speeding. But for harsh crimes, we do the opposite. Just twenty years for a multiple homicide? A few years for a sexual assault that scars a woman for life? Ridiculous! I out-argue anyone who will listen, and still the worst scum aren't being punished enough."

The deluded lawyer seemed passionate enough to orchestrate the crimes, but what grudge against leniency would he satisfy with a prison break?

"Even in *my* life," he said, "my allies fought meting out conse-quences harsher than the misdeeds. This twit at the firm violated a pledge, but maybe there was some ambiguity, so everyone else wanted to give him a slap on the wrist. But I knew we had to make an example of him! I even threatened Lou Denton; he's my best friend, but this was crucial ... *crucial*. We eviscerated the guy, and it was the best I'd felt in years. Oh ... Even my wife tried to talk me out of it; she tried to make *me* feel bad—*me*, not the rule breaker. That's what started our divorce—taking his side, on something so important. Imagine!"

Jen was repulsed by the depths of Foster's fanaticism—*how about accepting punishment for what you did to Phil, jerk!* But now, something good was happening as well: she'd started acclimating to her body defying her impulses to move and speak, and her panic was abating.

"So it made me feel wonderful, and it was the right thing to do. And I realized, however brilliant my acquaintances might be, they weren't in my league. The world needed me to act, alone, as *I* saw fit. I had to apply my insights on a *grander* scale, for the greater good. Those convicts deserved to die, every last one of them!"

What! He faked the prison break! It was really a mass execution! How could he have pulled that over on the police? Who's going to believe me?

Wait ... Better, foil the egomaniac with silence! Don't establish Mattias Foster as a vigilantism messiah ... let the world believe he bungled an escape.

"Which brings me to clearing my friend."

No! she wanted to scream. *What about me? Why did you attack me? Why did you kill Phil?* The fire inside did nothing to rouse her numbed shell; the rage and adrenaline yet left her motionless. But couldn't she now sense her ribs? Yes, the silent outburst *was* tensing her abdomen. It felt like she could force her breaths, ever so slightly—the prelude to speaking, screaming, thwarting her tormentor.

"Lou Denton had nothing to do with it. I am Alpha, and I am Righteous, leader of the Panthera. I led the crimes alone, and planted evidence implicating him. I pretended to call a chief during the escape, and I recorded his annoying impersonation for a passcode. BPT was developed by one of *his* clients. None of that should be considered to incriminate him. Understood?"

As Foster paused, Jen lay still and muted on the chilly floor, and continued testing her muscles, unable to produce movement but sensing the control to clench her stomach.

"Speaking of punishing the wrong man—don't think Edward Carson is faultless. He would've known of the wildcat alias we used for Lorelz at the prison, and then at the office I told him, 'You won't find any criminal links with this firm,' and I practically choked on the homophone; but he didn't even blink. Five more of his synapses fire, and I would've been on death row myself."

More flexing—just don't let him see. She kept working her diaphragm, and grew sure she was budging her tongue from side to side.

"Now for my last problem with you, *ever*," Foster snarled. "The paralytic should wear off soon, and I need you to keep my story secret for a while longer, even if airport security finds you early."

Jen heard Foster walk away, fifteen echoing footsteps. *That box!*
What's he going to do to me now? She continued straining to get
control of her lungs and ready her throat—every second was
helping—and rued his quick return.

She heard him open a zipper; he was so close, maybe leaning over
her. "It's empowering to blackmail a perjured anesthesiologist," he
said, "especially one who'd also studied laryngology. Hmm … I
shouldn't risk a sedative on top of the paralytic. I'll make them think
they've found a careless heroin addict! You shouldn't be at risk if they
find you before nightfall."

As she felt Foster grab her right forearm, she took her chance,
mustering her strength for the scream of her life.

But the lingering drug remained too potent, her struggled moan too
faint to alert anyone but her abuser, who continued with his painful
stab, pushing her toward oblivion.

He spent the next minute setting the scene for her rescuers,
needling both of her arms in an addict's pattern, tearing her skirt, and
popping two buttons off of her blouse. He walked away to clang her
shoes and purse into the trash, then returned, turned her head away,
and yanked the tape from her eyes. By that time, she was losing her
sense of the present, and of why she was being manipulated like a
doll.

* * * * *

If anyone puts out a "Do Not Enter" sign in Terminal C during the
day shift, it's Dusty Blodgent. Pushing a cart as tall as he and twice
as long, Dusty collects garbage, mops floors, and, as best he can in
ten minutes, scrubs porcelain. When he saw the older sawhorse
marking off the corridor to the men's room between Gates 105 and
107, he left his cart to investigate. *My boss never tells me anything*,
he thought. Making the necessary turns, he balked at the hazy plastic
sheeting with the bold warnings. *I was just in there four hours ago. If
I get a sick day from that, I'm going fishing.*

At the three o'clock shift change, he brought his supervisor, Cecil
Rawlings, to investigate.

"Management never tells me anything," Rawlings grumbled.

* * * * *

Most of Jen's hallucinations in the dark bathroom were triggered by
sound. The drips from a faucet started a waterfall, pretty at first, then
cloaked by too many birds with too many teeth, then serene again
after an orange rain. The beeping carts introduced Beethoven's Fifth

Symphony at times, and at others, more cawing toothed ravens. Time passed haphazardly, and though she was no longer medically paralyzed, the opioid proved long-lasting, and the confusion and lack of coordination bound her in place for what had to be hours.

Eventually she registered bouts of pain in her head and shoulders from lying still on the cold floor, but it seemed to take an hour more to roll onto her side, ending the pain and adding a rush to her continuing high, with rainbow-striped puppies licking her neck. Then a dreadful thirst signaled through the haze, as real as her dizziness when she tried to raise her head. She prodded herself to crawl in search of water; that was the one resolution she could remember and act upon—even so long after the injection, any notions of approaching the dim tarp or calling out were fleeting at best.

46

"Six o'clock," Carson announced. "I guess we should discuss dinner."

"Sorry, Lieutenant," Denton replied. "We're actually wrapping up here. I presume from how vague you've been that you don't have a case without a confession, and we've seen that you aren't going to get one from an innocent lawyer today."

"Not so. I *have* a case, and controlling your breathing during the tough questions doesn't mean you've been passing for guiltless this whole time."

"Oh, you've *divined* my guilt—"

"I'm as professional as you are, Denton! Besides, we can't end without discussing the props." Carson walked to the paper case under the mirror and took out a folder, a large envelope, a small object wrapped in brown paper, and a pair of leather gloves. He placed them on the table, then pulled Phil Bolton's Sibley award from the carton and hung it on a hook on the door.

"Good of you to recycle your boxes," Denton remarked.

Carson ignored the comment, sat back down across from Denton, and resumed his questioning. "Tell me where you were the day before the judges' brunch."

"You covered that a while ago—the day before, the day of, and the day after. Once again, I left work early, would've taken my usual route home, and worked on my speech. Then I did some other work— legal work—which is confidential."

"Put these on for me," Carson directed, sliding the gloves.

Denton paused for a moment, then announced to the mirror while putting them on, "Any fingerprints on these are from today. I've never seen these gloves before."

"Do you know Phil Bolton?"

"It doesn't sound like an uncommon name, but it doesn't ring a bell."

"Can you explain *that* to me?" Carson asked, pointing to the plaque.

The lawyer walked over to the award, then tilted it outward with his right middle finger along the bottom and index finger an inch up along the side. Carson's eyes widened—the grip exactly matched Quinones's demonstration from analyzing the dust pattern! He watched for a blush, a twitch, any tell that Denton had examined that same plaque while the Boltons were his captives.

"This says Phil Bolton won a Sibley, just like me," Denton answered dryly, turning to face the detective.

Still hiding it ... keep pushing. "A Cornell engineering major, too. Here are two pictures," Carson said, shoving the envelope across the table, "college-aged and recent. You *can* tell me if you know him."

"I *know* I can tell the truth," the lawyer said before ambling to his seat; Carson registered his indignation as neither contrived nor overly defensive. "I think I knew every engineering major who graduated with me at Cornell," Denton said while inspecting the photos, "but not all the ones from the years before. Phil Bolton isn't one I recognize."

Carson continued processing Denton's expressions and inflections, and didn't pick up any telltale sign of recognition while his suspect was looking at the pictures. But by discussing Phil, he'd taken away Denton's easy route of making blanket denials. *He'll have to trip up now—have to.* "You've never met Phil Bolton?" he pressed.

"I don't *remember* meeting him; I suppose I could have, decades ago, on campus."

"What color is his hair?"

"Black, from these photos."

"Where was he during the judges' brunch?"

"I have no idea."

"At work?"

"I wouldn't know."

"But you know his job ..."

Denton paused. "I could *guess* he's an engineer, because you said he studied that, but I'm certainly not the only engineering major not to become one."

Damn! So careful! Righteous would've read about Phil's death, and should've reflexively answered in past tense, "guess he *was* an engineer." *So vigilant. That has to be it. Pressure him!* "We both know that wouldn't be guessing; you know him, and you've already revealed it."

Denton seemed to resort again to deep, slow breathing. "No, Lieutenant. I knew nothing about him until minutes ago."

Carson leaned in; Denton was locked into a lie he couldn't conceal with relaxation techniques. "Then how did you know he graduated before you?"

Denton remained poised, his breathing steady. "The date on the Sibley."

Carson shook his head. "I *know* that's not how you know about him! You were sure when you said it: the award's ambiguous—he could've won it as a freshman and graduated after you."

Denton paused, but retained his composure. "Fine, I made one mistake the entire day. Him graduating earlier than me was a deduction, not something I knew as fact, taking it as self-evident that upperclassmen are better engineers than underclassmen. Anybody would've concluded the same." Denton looked at his watch. "Are you done with the props? It's late."

Now it was Carson's turn for deep breathing. He'd overplayed the graduation angle; anybody *would have* reached the same conclusion Denton had. The unflappable suspect hadn't revealed himself a liar. But there was still the code phrase, and the way he grabbed the Sibley. *Push again!* "You might be a careful talker, Lucian Denton, but murderers don't walk so easily."

At last, a blush Denton couldn't stifle. "You think I *killed* someone? You're way out of line, Lieutenant!"

"Oh … You think I haven't seen these phone records?" he asked, pushing papers at Denton. "Or couldn't trace where the calls originated?"

"This … this isn't my phone number," Denton objected. "I don't recognize it."

"You must remember working on patents for propellants like ED-NHC45?"

"I won't rule it out, but not recently enough to remember that name. I've … I've filed over a thousand patents in my career."

"Misdirect all you'd like—you're not going home. The phone records point irrefutably to your firm, so I can hold you for obstruction of a murder investigation. Denton, Foster & Kahn will start collapsing, and the loyalty of everyone who helped you will follow. How hard will it be then to learn about your parachuting? Or discover your connection to *this*," he finished, unwrapping Phil's slide rule and pushing it forward.

The lawyer's face changed from flushed to pale. "I don't want to be charged with obstruction," he said. "And it's not really me you're after."

"I overheard your call today! You *are* the one I've been after! And if you're just going to keep lying, I'll jail you now."

"You don't have to threaten me anymore, Lieutenant. I see what's going on—no more dodging. Just promise that if I haven't committed a crime, you'll be professional about the bygones in my life."

"As unlikely as it is that I can't tell one voice from another, if I'm wrong, I'll admit it—provided that's your last condition."

"You're sure it was someone at my firm?"

"Those calls came from your offices!" Carson said, pointing to the papers.

Denton shook his head. "But *not* from me. Is that why you wanted the calendars?"

"The calendars your underlings have now made worthless ..."

"I didn't know you needed them for *that*. Matt was forceful about pushing back, and he was at the judges' brunch, too, and out the afternoon before. I can't imagine him ever resorting to violence, but if you're so sure of yourself, you'd best go after him."

"You think you're free just because you can name someone else?"

"Parachuting was him also. He's made tandem jumps at Sussex County Airport ... probably too long ago for them to remember, but he did."

"You didn't appreciate me handing you the slide rule ..."

"Because that points to Matt, too. It's why I believe you now. He owns an exact replica of it—all the kids in the movie cast for *The Right Stuff* got NASA props and signed actor photos. He was going to be an extra until they scaled back the barbecue scene. That's why he insists on doing all of our movie work."

Shit! The out of place photo on Foster's wall wasn't a tribute to his copyright skill—it harkened back to 1983 and a boy getting exposed to actors' makeup and the space program and slide rules. *What else did I miss? Has it been Loser all along?* "I heard your voice on the phone during the crime," he tried.

"I hadn't spoken to you before that interview in my office." Carson just stared back. "I swear ... Was someone impersonating me?"

"You tried to throw me off by recording the code words before getting the throat injections—'restless and waiting.'"

"Throat injections? Code words? I've used that expression forever, especially around Matt and Harold! We had a Torts professor who sounded like Bruce Springsteen—he said it to intimidate students.... Maybe Matt *recorded* me, for the code.... I don't know why he'd set *me* up, but I'll stick around until you get this settled. Just question him before you charge me. You'll see I'm telling the truth."

"You're weaving quite the web around Foster now. Why were you so opaque before?"

The lawyer took a deep breath. "The Bar Association is very political; for some of the votes I got, I had to give a little back. Nothing unlawful, just embarrassing—job assignments and the like. I figured Chairman Benson caught wind of that and set you to root it out. Matt signaled me at the airport, and I stalled today believing he'd delete *those* records, not that he needed to cover his own tracks. You were asking such open-ended questions, I kept thinking you were fishing for any excuse to search our files."

Carson shook his head. "If that's all you've been worried about, you would've just destroyed the Bar Association documents yourself, when I first called."

"I'd thought about doing that. But the way we run system backups and the like, it didn't seem easy to get everything expunged. And if anyone found out we purged files in the midst of an investigation—"

"I know there's more! Even if your Bar Association sins explain why you stalled today, they don't explain you going along with rebuffing me on the calendars!"

The lawyer looked down. "I went along on that because Matt forced me to." He paused and looked up, and Carson just glared back. "He has leverage—it'll sound like nothing to you, dealing with murders and such, but it's everything to me." He paused once more.

"Either you want me to believe you, or you don't."

Denton swallowed hard, then continued. "I have a theory that everyone's made at least three cheats in their lives that should send them to hell; my first is from my last semester at Yale Law. The jobs we were all facing—cafeterias open for breakfast, lunch and dinner, seven days a week; pasty-faced drones taking gym memberships just so they could shower during all-nighters—it seems normal now, but I grew up thinking adults had fun, too. So Matt and I devised these last flings at the end of law school. We now encourage our new hires to do the same, but back then we were left to our own devices."

"The rub was each state required us to pass Professional Responsibility, the only class with a mandatory attendance policy. Can you imagine, the brightest law students being told not only to master this basic course, but that they'd be taking attendance as if we were convicts? So Matt signed me in to the last four classes while I was in Florida. I passed the test, easily, yet technically I hadn't satisfied the course requirements. It's not a crime, but my Bar Association chairmanship is over if my secret's exposed. Being vice chairman sets me apart from Matt and Reuben, you see; we all lead the firm, but I'm heeded by every lawyer in the state. And that cheat lets Matt get the last word, still. He made us overreact against Daniel Kirke, and forced our pushback on your investigation."

Damn, Carson thought, *thrown by another privilege problem.*
Perp on the loose, again.

47

Carson burst into the observation room barking orders. "Munsen, in the unlikely event Foster boarded his flight to Copenhagen, I want him arrested at passport control. If he's on another flight, nab him when *that* plane lands. If you can't find him, check for him flying under an alias—coordinate uniform teams to show his picture to everyone who worked a counter or gate at the airport, and get a list of same-day tickets purchased after Denton was in handcuffs." Munsen bolted off.

"Priestly, you have to rule out him returning to his office—if he's hanging around, Denton is lying."

Carson then turned to Youngman. "Kennedy, LaGuardia, and Philadelphia Airports are all less than ninety-minute drives from here. I want Foster's picture in front of everyone there who dealt with a same-day ticket buyer. Then make sure we have an APB on his car; if he's escaping that way, we want our bases covered."

"And me?" Banks asked.

"Go challenge Denton; make sure he's telling the truth. If he is, find out more about Foster—where he likes to travel, for starters, and whether he has acquaintances overseas. If anyone can teach us about Loser, it'll be him."

She started out, then turned around. "Almost forgot to give you these," she said, handing Carson his cell phones.

Captain Burgess entered after Banks left. "It's worse than 'I couldn't get a confession'?"

"He confessed, all right—to an honor code violation, back when you were in a uniform ticketing jaywalkers." Carson shook his head. "That's probably what Arden will have me doing before long."

"And all this commotion?"

"It was Foster. I'd encircled the most prolific killer in New Jersey history, and left him free in an airport for nine hours while I played footsy with his friend."

"Damn! I guess it's also my fault, then—for trusting you. That professor, Bolton, wanted to talk to you this morning, something about changing her story and identifying the right guy, but I assumed your voice ID trumped whatever memory was troubling her."

Carson felt his face flush. "She was here?"

"No, she called. Wanted you to call her back, and said if you couldn't reach her, she'd be at the airport."

"I need everyone there, Henry! Trust me."

As Carson turned to run to his car, Munsen hurtled into the doorway. "Lieutenant! The same-day ticket list is coming in. Nothing for Foster yet, but one of the first ones after Denton's arrest—and she also called for you this morning—was for Jennifer Bolton. She booked a flight to Paris, got a boarding pass at the counter, then disappeared."

"I'm taking the first squad car I can reach and calling you in five minutes," Carson told Munsen. "I want the gate number for her flight, and the gates for anyone else who booked a same-day flight who could possibly be Foster. Plus any unusual happenings at the airport, any altercations or arrests … or anyone injured." He dashed past Munsen and passed the detective desks. "Priestly, drop that and come with me!"

He had to be there for her.

He could hear the captain's booming order from behind as he ran to the cruisers. "Put out an APB to all airport agencies for Jennifer Bolton, my authority."

* * * * *

Carson and Priestly met TSA Director Sanders inside Terminal C just as the displays flashed *DELAYED* next to all of the departure times and collective groans filled the building. "I'm now public enemy number one," Sanders introduced, "and that makes you public enemies two and three." He walked them toward the gates as he spoke. "We've trained for fixed target search, like locating a bomb, sweeping the terminal all at once; and evasive target search, sweeping individual sections then closing them off, which takes twice as long. I don't think your victim's being moved around, so I picked fixed target—making sure one team started at Gate C84, her last known location."

"Good, the Paris flight," Carson said. "I don't know how she might've deduced … Anyway, the gendarmes are going to scrutinize the arriving passengers, and if Foster is on that plane, they'll tell us what he's done to her."

"Since my teams are spread out, I thought we'd wait just past security."

"No. My guy called. Someone going by 'Sam Smith' bought a last-minute ticket to Boston, departed 12:30 from gate C135. I want to head there."

Sanders nodded. "That works, too." He marched the trio past the stalled security line toward the shift supervisor. "She just needs a gun count—anything that passes this point has to be accounted for before we start letting passengers back later."

"One each," Carson declared, Priestly nodding agreement.

"The search includes boarding areas, maintenance areas, restrooms, and stores," the director said, striding toward C135. "I hate to throw my teams off their rehearsed protocols, but we can cut the search time in half if I'm right and we focus on the supply closets and dumpsters—"

"You don't know that he's …" Carson snapped at Sanders before turning to face forward and quickening the trio's pace. Then his phone chimed. He turned back to Sanders. "Just make sure you consider that Foster always plays it smart." He pulled out his phone. "E-mail from Munsen," he said to Priestly. "Make sure I don't run over anyone while I'm reading."

> *Can't single Foster out as passenger without another lead. Over 100,000 people on flights landing tonight that departed from Newark or could've been connected onto from Newark. Motor Vehicles photo database rules out all last-minute ticket purchasers—guessing Foster pre-purchased tix using aliases to make provision for escape without raising alarms.*

As they passed Gate C132, the director's radio crackled. "Officers investigating suspicious partition, men's room between 105 and 107." Seconds later, it crackled again. "Officers need medical assistance, men's room adjoining 107. Victim found."

Carson sprinted down the wide corridors toward Jen, "need medical assistance" repeating in his head. He'd run thousands of times before, but it never mattered like this.

He reached the flashlight-illuminated bathroom, panting, and saw Jen speaking to a kneeling officer who was holding her hand. "Have the medics responded?"

"On their way!" an agent yelled out.

Carson took a step toward his troubled friend. "You're a cop, too!" Jen screamed, raising her arm in an awkward attempt to point. "You can't fool me with that outfit! I know my rights!" After an extended moment, she said in a calmer voice, "Hey, I *do* know my rights. All of you better treat me well, I'm some important lawyer or something. And you!" she blurted, waving her finger at him again, "I know you. You're that good-looking lieutenant, right?"

Carson walked over to her and knelt down. "Jen, we're here to take care of you."

Jen seemed to struggle to focus her eyes on him. "Ted? I don't remember why I'm here, Ted. There are things I should know but I don't, and all of today seems lost."

"Jen, the medics are on their way." He turned her arms over. "Look, you were drugged. Someone wanted you out of commission, but just awhile."

"Did I do something wrong?"

"No, not at all. The hospital will fix you up, and you'll understand everything by tomorrow, maybe even tonight."

She nodded, then whimpered, "OK."

"Do you remember anything about Paris, Jen?"

She closed her eyes, then reopened them. "Only things from books, and a couple of movies."

The medics arrived and helped Jen onto a gurney, covered her with a blanket, and checked her vital signs and pupils. She was partially successful with the coordination tests, named her high school mascot, and repeated back a short list of common furnishings. "I think she's just coming down off a high," the older medic told Carson. "Unlikely there'll be any long-term effects after treatment, except the hours since she's been injected might stay lost." He turned to Jen and continued, "Did you understand that, ma'am? I think you're going to be fine—we'll just need you to spend a night with our doctors until you're 100 percent."

Jen nodded and smiled. "Thank you!"

Carson smiled as well—Jen was improving before his eyes as reality was being thrust back upon her. If Foster considered an anonymous life on the run to be success, then successful he was, and for these ten minutes, Carson didn't care. This smart, brave woman he admired so much was going to have a life. And she thought he was good-looking.

The medics maneuvered the stretcher out the slalomed entryway, bringing Jen into full light at last. The bed detached and locked securely onto the airport cart.

As the younger EMT repacked the last of their equipment and strode toward the driver's seat, Jen turned to Ted, who was smiling encouragingly. "I have something to tell you. I can't remember it now, but it's important. He said it was important. I'll be better soon, and I'll tell you."

Ted nodded. "And you've been asking me something that's important to you, Jen. You'll be better soon, and this time I'll tell you. I promise."

Author's Note

The publication of *Righteous Judgment* is only possible because of you, the reader, and the Internet.

If you had a good read, please leave an honest review online.